Of Magpies and Men

By **Ode Ray**

Of Magpies and Men

Love and thanks to :

My magnifique petite sister Pauline McBride
The awesome Candy Watts
The eagle-eyed Erin Dowd
The inspiringly artistic Helen Wu
The witty Richard Edwards
All the erudite ladies of letters @AquintillionReads
And the incredibly supportive Jamie Dury

For : My eco-warrior parents

Prologue

Manarola, Cinque Terre, Italy
Now, July 2017

'*The world is waiting to meet you*' reads a travel brochure's headline held by the woman manoeuvring knuckled fingers around her mouth. 'Waiting to meet me', she muses coquettishly, eyes perusing the photo of a half-naked Californian surfer.

Her hollow-cheeked husband sits across from her, hunched over his copy of *Le Monde*. *'I speak Spanish to God, Italian to women, French to men and German to my horse (Charles V, King of Spain, 1531)'* quotes the article holding his attention. This draws a philosophical 'hmmm' out of him before he launches into battle with the newspaper. Alas, *Le Monde* is in no way inclined to let itself be folded. So, the middle-aged man capitulates, scrunches up the rebellious paper, and slams it petulantly on the metallic table, rattling the breakfast set in its wake. This briefly interrupts his spouse's tooth picking, arousing in her a silent mixture of condemnation and battlement.

"Do you think Italian men are sexier than French?" he asks seemingly out of the blue whilst dipping a buttered slice of baguette into his mug of caffè latte.

Paying him no mind, the woman gazes back at stunning photographs of idyllic beaches.

"Dearest? So, sexier or not?" He insists, trying to gain her attention. Drips of coffee dribble onto *Le Monde.*

"Wha'? I can't hear you." She cups her ear.

"Do. You. Think. Italian men. Are. Sexier. Than. French men?" He yells over the background racket.

"Not at all." She dismisses his nonsense. Her distracted, hooded eyes drift to the rocky shore. "No pain-au-raisin for breakfast. And now, this..." She points towards the commotion and tuts. The scene unfolding beneath their hotel room is now finally drawing their blasé interest.

"Have a romantic break in Italy, they said," the man grunts in agreement.

"Wha'?"

1

"Have. A. Romantic… Nothing, dear." He waves it off and turns his attention back to his stubbornly scrunched up, and now coffee-stained, newspaper.

Amidst the small boats berthed on Manarola's main street, groups of tourists are consoling one another. Flashing lights reflect against the town's medieval watchtowers. Reporters hurry down a warren of narrow alleys, like a murder of vultures sensing a rotting carcass. Some have already set-up their top of the range cameras to capture the grisly scene in all its glorious technicolour detail. Others were being pushed back by the police. All of them covered their noses from the pervasive stench of rotting flesh.

Crouched down at the scene, an Italian police officer lifts his head. His shaded eyes take a comprehensive look at the tumble of brightly coloured, quaint buildings facing the shore.

The scrawny man who is having breakfast on the geranium-hung balcony, has the distinct impression that the officer is pointing in his direction. He swallows his mouthful of soggy bread in one noisy gulp. Their hotel phone rings and the couple exchange a silent look. Someone on the other end of the line summons them down in Italian.

"Detective Paoli." Giandomenico extends his right hand whilst removing his branded sunglasses. The woman automatically readjusts her bouffant hair in response, while staring at Giandomenico a little longer than necessary. Giandomenico does not notice. Or, more accurately, he does not register it as an unusual reaction. This is not due to any arrogance on his part, it is what it is. Like a double espresso, everything suddenly becomes sharper for women in Giandomenico's presence.

The detective switches on a recording app on his phone. The couple shakes hands with him whilst nodding sternly. Giandomenico waits for them to introduce themselves. But nothing is said.

"My colleague tells me you are French, is this correct?" Giandomenico interrupts the impromptu staring contest.

The man wedges his hands under his armpits and parts his legs a little wider in response. "We're Corsican," he defies, lifting his chin.

A faint smile sweeps across Giandomenico's lips. Okay, so they are, indeed, French. To gather himself, the detective takes a fleeting glimpse at the locals being questioned on either side of him. His guess is they are local fishermen. The type that mainly fish on tourists during the high season. They look alike, the two Corsicans in front of him; flag-wavers, with the sort of calm composure that seeps hot blood.

"How long have you been staying at this hotel?" Giandomenico nods to the stunning building in full sight of the usually picturesque coastal inlet.

"A few days."

"Did you notice anything unusual last night?"

In unison, the couple press their lips downward, before shaking their hair-sprayed heads, not one hair steps out of line as they do.

"Did you hear or see something out of the ordinary this morning?"

They shrug, their faces wear the same expression as before, Don Corleone-esque.

A few paces away, an Italian reporter shoves a fluffy microphone in front of an African-American man bursting out of an XL 'keep-fit' polo shirt. "We heard a crash in the middle of the night. But not like cars crashing. More like crrr-raaash. Like a tree splitting, ya know?" His baritone Southern American drawl speaks of charming steamboats and jazz and cuts through the background noise. "It felt to me, 'hmmm this is odd.' But personally, I thought that one of the boats fell off and crashed onto the rocks. Though when I opened our shutters this morning, hmmm, so, ah, I saw them…" He stops to wipe his eyes with the back of his meaty hand. The petite African-American woman next to him buries her head against his shuddering shoulders.

The camera moves away from the American tourists. The boat wreckage and the two bodies on the rocky inlet come into shot. The grey-skinned corpses are lying face down.

"The identity of the two deceased has yet to be established," the feral Italian reporter starts to prate on. "But, it is no secret that Italy's long coastline makes it one of the EU's main targets for migrants. One government official recently warned of a new influx hitting Italy this summer, forecasting figures north of four thousand." She pauses to let the dust of her indignation settle. "Only yesterday, diligent Italian coastguards are believed to have reported seeing men and women dangling infants over the side of rusting ships, threatening to throw their babies into the sea if they were turned back." She turned her head towards the two dead bodies. Her brown ponytail enclaved within the gap in her cap flicks, bringing to mind the image of a cow shooing flies with her tail.

Giandomenico rolls his eyes at the reporter's vacuous extrapolation, before turning his attention back to the uncooperative Corsican couple. "Your hotel room is directly above the scene. A boat smashed into the shore last night, but you heard and saw nothing of what that gentleman just described?"

The Corsican man tilts his head upward. "I'm sorry, detective, my wife and I didn't understand this gentleman... We don't speak Mac-uh-Dough-nald's."

Giandomenico chews the inside of his mouth.

HERE'S WHAT HAPPENED...

Chapter 1

"Pippa"

London, United Kingdom
Seven years ago, December 2009

Through the glass partition wall, Benedict Grant could tell that the fidgety analyst loitering by Laure's desk was getting on his leggy secretary's nerves. The analyst had arrived five minutes early for their meeting, which was now overdue by ten minutes.

But Benedict was going to let him simmer for a bit longer. It was not a power-play. Well, maybe it was a bit of a power-play. This meeting was not exactly necessary - Benedict was not executing deals with clients anymore. He had people under him to do that for him, like this guy, Frank, Mister I've-Got-One-Over-On-You. Always bragging on about his perfect little family, rubbing it in everyone's face. *"Hi, I'm a high-flyer with a beautiful wife, a little champion, and another one on the way, but I still make time to volunteer as a reserve fireman. And you, what have you done with your life?"* And it was late. Way past the religiously observed 3 pm Friday after-work drinks.

Benedict's personal phone pinged.

Dear Benedict – My apologies for having been so evasive earlier. The subject matter isn't fit for conversations over the phone. And I must admit, I'm terribly apprehensive about sharing this information with you. But I want to, I have to, you have a right to know. I will, soon. I promise. See you tonight. Mummy.

Benedict could not recall ever receiving a text message from his seventy-something mother before. It must have taken her about half a day to craft this letter-cum-text message. A smile of endearment flitted across his groomed face. But it also worried him. His mother could be secretive, but it was unlike her to be so melodramatic. Then again, she had not been acting herself lately. Oddly distracted, when she was usually so focused.

His stomach tightened. Whatever it was she wanted to discuss, it could not be good. Even the devastating news of her cancer relapse had not unnerved her. Nor the loss of her husband, her partner of thirty-eight years. No vacant looks. No wallowing in self-pity. No endless embraces with her then fourteen-year-old son. She mourned through her work. Winning case after case, battling in court as if her life depended on it while she inflated her many bank accounts.

Laure opened the glass door of his office and peeped in. "Are you ready for your next appointment?"

"Sure, send him in," Benedict replied without lifting his mocha eyes from his phone. He took his time responding to his mother. Eventually, he looked up from the tiny screen in time to see his appointment standing before him.

"Take a seat." Benedict offered, before standing up and gesturing for the analyst to sit on one of the sofas lost in his conference room-sized corner office.

Now perched on the edge of his glass desk, Benedict peered down at him. There was something frail about this well-built, if sweaty, man. A moment passed in silence. Benedict drummed his fingers to indicate that he was waiting, rather impatiently.

"Shall I take you through the deck?" Frank spluttered, flicking open his laptop. A photo of the happy family popped up as his screensaver. A vision of Frank teaching Clark Jr. to ride a bike flashed before Benedict's eyes. A pang of green-eyed jealousy pursed his thin lips in a smirk.

"It won't be necessary. I've already read it."

"Oh. Ah, great." Frank's tone was an octave or two too high. Good.

"It's all good."

An involuntary sigh escaped the analyst.

"Although," Benedict stood and put his hands in the pockets of his tailored suit trousers. "Your benchmark against CGP's merger is a bit light. Why didn't you use the audit number?" Benedict knew the reason why. The audit report had not been widely circulated.

"I... Ah... Didn't know there was one," Frank stuttered, red-faced.

"Well, get your hands on it." Thrown out with an unnecessarily harsh, if somewhat affected, undertone.

As if not knowing what was expected of him, Frank still sat on Benedict's sofa when his boss was back at his laptop. Benedict's eyes met the analyst's. And just like pressing reset on a fuse box after a power cut, the young man fizzed back into motion, burdened by Benedict's appraising gaze.

∞

Time to go home. Christmas lights reflected on an array of skyscrapers. Their flickering of red, gold, and green rendered Benedict's office block less intimidating. Though, deprived of its usual buzzing activity, the area also looked more sinister, much like a set for a dystopian movie.

The banker gazed at his reflection in the darkened glass walls. Average height and weight, there was nothing about his appearance that made him stand out. And yet, he did. He had this rare *je ne sais quoi*, this indefinable appeal, this transcript of a charismatic personality onto his ordinary physique. It attracted the eye, the way the quiet strength of an Apex predator mesmerizes TV audiences.

Thirty today, he thought. Ancient in some ways, still young in comparison to others, such as his mother… His darling mother. If she were to pass, that would be it. He would have no family left.

It occurred to him that perhaps what his mother has been so secretive about may not be about him after all. Was it her cancer? Had it taken a turn for the worse? He put on his helmet and switched the engine on. The roaring sound reverberated against every corner of the surrounding glass-jungle.

Benedict had limited memories of his grandparents. They were all dead by the time he turned seven. And his short-haired, trouser-wearing aunt never had children. Though, as his aunt cut ties with the family, Benedict would not have known any cousins anyway. So, there you go, it was just him and his ageing mother now… He really ought to find himself a girlfriend and have a child. Pronto.

As Benedict cut through London's traffic, his leathers his only protection, the idea of having his own child whirled around his mind. Benedict picked up a faster pace. He felt the raw power of the machine between his legs, the intense pull of the tarmac with every turn, and the cars like currents of water around him. The rain was now racing against him. Benedict usually lost himself to the layers of exhilaration and adrenaline that riding such a powerful machine through the London bustle afforded him.

But today, his ride did not offer the usual respite from his overactive mind. It could all end now, he thought, looking at the perilous junction ahead, and to what end? If there's no one to remember me? Three decades have passed, and he knew what he wanted out of the next thirty years. But, unlike his achievements to date, he could not make the next one happen on his own. To himself, he would admit he did not understand women well but given the intricacy of their ever-changing code of conduct, who did? They probably struggled themselves. What women want or meant or expected always seemed unnecessarily complicated. But, on reflection, inevitably, they all wanted children. Maybe not all, but most of them, right? And if not out of intrinsic urge, the strategists would view him as a good bet. A proverbial provider to an indulgent life… So, he really ought to get his act together.

His right hand and foot were on the brakes and the gate of his five-story Kensington house opened automatically. Everything was quiet, every light switched off bar those activated by the outdoor sensors.

Yet, he braced himself for the heave of activity that his entrance would produce. Diane, his old school friend who was more like a sister to him, had to tell him about his 'surprise' party. Otherwise, he would have been mid-air. It was just as well because surprises were not his thing. His life was too much of a smoke and mirrors exercise to allow for surprises. It was first-rate smoke, the Havana cigars of metaphorical smoke if you will, and exquisite mirrors, but still a lonely façade all the same.

As he opened his front door his public persona switched on. A chorus of loud cheers and a shower of champagne welcomed him. He laughed and shouted insults in good humour. Diane pranced around his vast hallway in his general direction, glasses in hand.

"Happy birthday, darling," she breathed.

She brushed her designer lips against his cheek and gestured at one of the stewards employed for the event to bring Benedict a towel. Benedict craned his neck.

"Where's my mother?"

"She said she was coming down with something. She sent her apologies and said not to worry." That was disappointing. He would have found a quiet room to get her to reveal what was on her mind. Never mind.

A staccato of stilettos against marble approached them.

"Oh my god, Sarah! Look at you. You look divine," Diane professed, flicking her bouncy chestnut hair tensely.

"You look gorgeous."

"Don't be silly," Diane protested waving the compliment away, "but you do."

"Oh, stop it."

"I swear to God, if I hadn't seen the proof, there is no way I would have believed you had a baby only three months ago."

"Actually, we ordered Archie off Amazon," Sarah's husband quipped.

A chorus of overly raucous laughter of the kind you only encounter at these types of events echoed around the group.

Sarah finally mouthed an affected happy birthday to Benedict in acknowledgement of his noticeable achievement of another year around the earth. She was still smarting from his rejection several years ago.

Benedict looked at his watch. God, only five minutes had passed?

Two more people appeared by his side. Arms locked with a man, Petunia, a fashionista with a teeny forehead, flashed an ice-skating ring on her left hand at Diane and Sarah. It triggered shrieks of high-pitch delight. Still, Benedict felt Diane's hand tensing around his arm, another couple beating her to the engagement-curb.

"Congratulations! We're *SOOO* happy for you. You guys are perfect for each other," Diane exclaimed with fierce intensity

And they were. All glossy hair, both dressed immaculately in the latest fashions. During a skiing trip in Switzerland, Benedict once overheard Petunia asking the receptionist at the Spa if her head was small enough to qualify for a mini-facial. While Petunia's fiancé was caught scribbling on the cleaning rota in the gents, thinking it was a consumer feedback form. As Diane pointed out, 'they were perfect for each other,' soon to become Mr. & Mrs. Vague n' Vogue.

"Thanks, Diane. Now, y'all," Petunia, a Brit, had lived in America for two months, so 'y'all' was happening, "save the third of Jan."

"Wow, you've already found a venue?" Diane asked, genuinely surprised, her accent revealing a tiny bit of her native Scouse.

"Not just yet. It's for our engage' party, hun. We'll have it on the *playa* where we met." Petunia turned her pouting lips to her fiancé.

"How romantic," Sarah swooned, a slight edge to her voice.

With the stealth of a hungry cat, Benedict discreetly lifted his sleeve and took another peek. *Are we there yet?* Benedict's eyes asked... *We've only just left!* Replied an exasperated watch, by snappily phasing its digital clock back to a black screen.

"Oh. My. God. You're not engaged, are you?" Somebody else shrieked.

'Engaged' is a funny word, thought Benedict. Either used to declare one's rights to somebody else's genitals until they kick the bucket or to advertise that one is busy defecating in a public toilet. A crude word, really, but packaged primly.

Half an hour later, a band started to play. Trim, modish, young men who had a recent hit, which Benedict would have heard if he listened to anything other than Radio 5 Live. The evening was a whirlwind of laughter - some fake, some genuine, some chemically induced - peppered with discussions about people at the party, the banking crisis (they knew nothing), brands of dogs' collar (Benedict knew nothing), etc... The guests were mostly family friends, sons and daughters of entrepreneurs, media people, bankers, consultants (the Sultans of cons), with their off-the-scale attractive plus ones. Some of whom you would recognise off the screen and a scattering of trendy aristocrats. Benedict had been comparing dick-size with this crowd since his elite pre-school days. He had found that his achievements had been instrumental in staying socially afloat and key to gaining the Grant family's love and respect, or so he had always presumed.

"What are your vegan options?" was asked, with uncompromising gravity, of a stewardess carrying sushi. The enquirer's accent had been bred somewhere between Singapore, Shoreditch and New York's Upper East Side. She was all cheekbones, hipbones, and collarbones with a December tan tempered only by thin white specks under her nostrils. You have probably heard of champagne-socialist, or if you are highfalutin; the caviar-left or BoBos (Bourgeois-Bohemians). Well, Benedict liked to refer to some of his lot as cocaine-healthist. They voiced their concern about the world's poverty and climate doom. They were pro passport for pets, edits on vegetable provenance, and very insistent that anyone feeding chocolate to children before the age of three-hundred months was utterly irresponsible. Then, they gorged themselves on Molotov cocktails of alcohol and pills... *They might have a point about the sugar though,* thought Benedict.

Anyhow, Benedict skilfully limited his intake of alcohol and avoided other things on offer. Ever in control. Three hours into the party and the birthday boy headed out onto his colonnade porch to

catch his breath. It was not as peaceful as he had h̶̶
had opened the window of the drawing room a̶
overheard a guy asking another what he would do if h̶
kind of money, implying Benedict's. 'I'd pay to watch ce̶
have sex on this couch.' Benedict's eyes turned upwards a̶
leaned his head back against the white brick wall and sigh̶
Seconds later, he found himself cornered by a Jessica Rabbit
lookalike red-haired beauty in a low-cut green dress.

"What a beautiful house you have," she observed wolfishly.

When Diane eventually spotted him, Jessica Rabbit had her
head thrown back in laughter, one arm tightly locked with
Benedict's and her surgically augmented bust pressed against his
side – for warmth one could only assume.

"Hey," Diane stretched her red wine tinted lips to Jessica
Rabbit into a crisp smile, before turning her tipsy gaze to Benedict.
"I want to film you cutting your cake," Diane slurred, before
performing a territorial tug-of-war with Benedict's arm against
Jessica Rabbit. Diane won pulling him back inside. Her ingenuous
request was endearing, if a little incongruous, but he found it hard
to refuse Diane. So he indulged her then resumed his carousel of
conversations.

"How's everything, mate?" Benedict shouted to his right… He
checked the time… "Why's your glass empty?" He winked to his
left… "It's been ages! How've you been?" Benedict boomed with
outstretched arms… A surreptitious look at his watch… "How's
business?" and so on.

Parties served a few purposes, he thought whilst disengaging
from conversations happening around him. 'Catching up' was the
main one, as if people were balls to be caught. Right then,
Benedict himself had been well and truly clutched. He felt like a
lonesome ping-pong ball at the bottom of a barrel squashed by
bowling balls. The need to 'fulfil a cyclical urge to cluster and
move in unison' like a family of sardines, was another purpose of
parties, he mused. Our birthday boy had become acutely aware of
this, years earlier, at a drum and bass gig. Hundreds of people
jiggling their bodies and sweating randomly on strangers, and yet
under the crisscrossing of laser lights they formed a uniform
swarm of darting silver. But for others, 'copping off' was the main
hope. They were the fragrant ones, spending the evening sniffing
each other's behind. And then, some needed, 'something to say on
Monday'.

ıests had left, Benedict put a stewed Diane
flat, whilst he joined the last of his friends
pt, Benedict stole away from the group to
:. He had promised himself he would not
frustrated and disappointed with himself

one for more news from his mother.
/s of hers, this secret or confidence, had
...............g to do with money. It very often was about money with
his mother. His parents had set-up an inheritance scheme from the
day Benedict was born. Its Byzantium mechanics were brought up
regularly in painstaking detail. Which Benedict always interpreted
as one of his mother's ways of saying "I love you."

Benedict wondered if his mother's secretive behaviour had
anything to do with the chatterbox of a nurse who took his blood
a few days ago. Amongst the plethora of idle chattering which,
under different circumstances would have made him believe he
was at the hairdresser, the nurse informed him of his blood type.
Was it AB+ or AB-? He could not remember now. Anyway, the
nurse had blathered on, about Benedict's 'useless' donor status.
Recovering from her indelicate comment, she went on to explain
that his blood type was hereditary – maybe because his mother
was there with him. And she was only there because they were
going to some French restaurant straight after, not because this
grown man's hand required to be held by his mummy at the sight
of a needle. Of course not, that would be preposterous… All the
same, Benedict lost interest in the nurse's incessant words but
became acutely aware and confused by his mother's expression,
which was growing more pallid by the second. She looked contrite
and vulnerable. And his mother never looked contrite or
vulnerable. She was more often described as strident with a side
serving of stern, to be honest. Did her secret have something to do
with that? Now that he thought about it, his mother had been
acting strangely ever since... And then the cryptic text message…
His mother had never been the type to beat around the bush, so
why now? Benedict vividly remembered the collected ferocity of
her words when something negative was touched upon by his
teachers. Or the family legend of her taking him on a campus tour
of both Oxford and Cambridge at age five, already seeking out
information about admission requirements. Tiger-mothers had
nothing on her. Yet, he adored her. Being overbearing came from
a place of love, he thought, his own child would see that one day.

House music seeped out through the building's walls before Benedict pushed open the door. The floor was covered with cloggy spilt liquids. A thumping bass pulsated inside of him like a bouncing ball trapped within his ribcage. It smelled of sweat, feet and bad breath, yet Benedict could finally breathe. He had fantasised about it all week. Fantasised about sex. Good sex. He wished he had not, but he did.

The throbbing lights and hazy cloud of smoke made it hard to see. However, it did not take him long to spot a pretty, little thing by the bar; doe eyes, skinny and shy. Probably dragged here by extrovert friends, before being left to fight for a quiet corner. Exactly his type. He quickly noticed the shirt, three buttons undone. So, one did not want to go totally unnoticed tonight then?

Benedict approached. He took position. He liked the game. His taut body was nothing particularly impressive to look at and his features were pleasant but nondescript, so he had to work for it. Yet, he was rarely sent off the field. 'There's something about you,' Diane had once pointed out to him. And he was set to make full use of whatever that was tonight.

At that exact moment, a fragrant man swooned in, right between Benedict and his ambition for the night. Flexing his grotesquely large biceps over the counter, he ordered two drinks. A vodka and lemonade was placed next to the other guest's empty glass. The two of them made eye contact. Of course, it was the right order. Fragrant-man moved even closer, clinked glasses, and was rewarded with a bashful smile.

Never mind, plenty of fish and all that, Benedict thought, already losing interest. Benedict tried to get the barman's attention whilst Fragrant-man leaned across the bar, whispering something into the other guest's ear.

"Oh, get a room already," Benedict muttered to himself, his words lost to the squall of the throbbing soundtrack. He lowered his eyes to a tatty beer mat in front of him and smiled when noticing it missed the crucial first two letters of its presumed name 'Dynasty IPA'.

Seconds later, Benedict overheard Fragrant-man declare, "your loss, Princess," and clink glasses again, before plodding back onto the crowded dancefloor.

Benedict smiled from across the empty stool and slid on to it.

"Let me guess. He offered flute practise on his instrument?"

He was rewarded with a smile. "You've nailed it," asserted their appealing voice, soft in tone and silvery.

"What's your name?" Benedict leaned back and beamed at his new friend, giving them the full power of his compelling charm.

A fleeting frown of recognition ran across their face. "Ryan. My name's Ryan, but are you…" He pointed gingerly at Benedict. "Benedict? Benedict Grant?"

Benedict's eyes widened, then hardened slightly. He had never run into someone who knew or recognized him as 'Benedict' in this sort of premises. Within a split second, Benedict's mask was firmly back in place.

"You must have me confused with somebody else. I'm Mike. Is that an American accent that I'm detecting?" The lies came easily. Benedict extended his hand as if to put an end to the matter of his identity.

They shook hands, but Ryan's eyes remained intently on Benedict.

"Yep. New York." He kept Benedict's hand in his. "But the photo… You were in Forbes, a few weeks ago. I read the article this morning. You had an interesting take on the collapse of the Lehman Brothers..."

The barman returned with Benedict's neat whiskey.

"Not me. Sorry." Benedict downed his drink and started to stand ready to leave. But Ryan put his hand on Benedict's lap.

"Look, I get it."

Benedict laughed a humourless laugh, dripping in rancour. *Oh, you get it? You think I'm from an old-fashioned family. You think I had to perfect a straight man act to make it to the top of the food chain in a ruthless, intolerant industry. You think I had to quietly accept the gradual damage of pretence and the loneliness it induces… Well, you're wrong. I'm not. I'm straight. Gender curious, okay, but straight. Like everybody else, right? Everybody is 'curious.' Anyway, I don't have to explain myself to you…*

But Benedict voiced none of this, instead, he slipped down from his stool taken aback by the virulence of his thoughts. He could feel an all-consuming rage creeping up inside him, working against him. A rage he had to contain so as not to let it turn into a physical outburst. But Ryan grabbed him by the elbow.

"Look, I only came here to have fun… Not to discuss the Lehman Brothers. I'm flying back home tomorrow… And, I, ah, wouldn't out you anyway. Hell, I'm not fully out myself."

Benedict clasped his hands in front of him to stop them from shaking and slowed his breathing. "To have fun, eh? Well, I'm flattered that you'd think I'd be more fun than the stud-beast over there."

"Do you mean the STD-beast?"

Benedict chuckled and perched himself back up onto his stool. "Didn't enjoy being called a princess?"

"Not so much… It gave me the Disney heebie-jeebies." Ryan ironically bumped his chest at this point.

"How so?"

"I feel like some love stories are under-represented by the Disney's of this world."

"Militant?"

"Nope. But a Cinderello film would've been nice."

"Then again… A prince looking for a dude who could fit into a tiny glass condom, would have been a harder sell as a U-rated movie?"

"Haha. Granted." Ryan shrugged. "Yet, it's weird to think that I'll have watched more people being murdered on TV in a week than I'll see men kissing on screen in a lifetime."

Benedict lowered his gaze, feeling uncomfortable and restless with this topic of conversation. He started to rotate his empty glass on itself with the tip of his fingers.

"… Or maybe, STD-man mistook me for a member of the Royal family," Ryan continued, maybe fearing that he was losing his audience.

"I have to say. There's an air of resemblance to the Middleton's."

"Kate at the front and Pippa from behind, right?" Ryan raised his eyebrows in put-on emphasis.

"Pippa. From behind. My favourite words in one sentence."

Ryan smiled but frowned at the same time. "I'm not following."

"'Pippa' is how you say 'blow-job' in French. In Southern French, to be precise. Parisians would say 'pip.' I'll let you figure out the rest."

"Interesting. And how would you say, *voulez vous coucher avec moi ce soir?* In Southern French?" Ryan sang in tune to the famous song, looking at Benedict seductively.

How refreshing it was to be in the seat of the one being charmed for once, Benedict thought. He had to admit if only to himself that this man had surprised him. Benedict usually read people and situations well, but Ryan was more assured of himself than Benedict had anticipated. Yet, something in the back of Benedict's head told him that it seemed too easy. He chose to ignore the nagging thought. "They would say: shall we take the party elsewhere?" This was uttered with a put-on French accent but the message could not be any clearer.

They went back to Ryan's hotel room. It was not the Savoy, but its blandness made it fit for purpose. Ryan's boldness faded as they got out of the taxi. The timidity that attracted Benedict to him in the first place made a comeback. Their elevator ride was carried out in absolute silence. Ryan's hand shook as he slotted his room's key card into the opening. It took him three attempts before the security light turned green.

Benedict gently took the card off him as they stepped in. Ryan's hand felt icy cold. They stood so close that Benedict could feel Ryan's muscles trembling across the small gap between their bodies. Trying to set him at ease, he ran a hand down Ryan's slender back. Benedict's fingers wavered across the sharp ridges of the man's protruding shoulder blades and dainty ribcage. His whole body was quivering.

"Are you alright?" Benedict probed, lifting Ryan's chin to meet his gaze. He held Benedict's stare for the briefest of moments.

Ryan responded with a nod. Talking still seemed outside his remit. His skin looked several shades paler than before.

Suddenly, Ryan pushed him aside and rushed to the bathroom. Benedict pivoted. The veil of confusion on his face ebbed away when the sound of convulsed sickness coming from the bathroom reached his ears. Ryan seemed sober when they'd left the club.

"Do you want a glass of water?" Benedict's offered uncertainly. No answer. The flushing sound of running water broke through. And nothing.

"Would you like me to leave?" Benedict continued.

There was another lull. Benedict took a couple of slow steps towards the door.

"No. Please stay." Ryan's voice sounded tight and raspy.

"Is there something I could get you from the pharmacy?" Peering out of the bathroom door's archway, Benedict saw Ryan hunched over the bathroom sink, head down, supporting his upper body on stretched arms. His fine-boned, slim back looked child-like in this position.

16

"I'm not ill... I'm… a mess."

"First time?"

"No." It was barely audible.

"First time with a man?"

"Yes."

Benedict was touched by Ryan's candour and tumultuous state of mind. Conversely, his own first time had been spoiled by a lack of anticipation. He was sixteen, wearing enough wax to turn him into a functioning candle if a wick were wedged on the top of his head. His friend's older brother was sat next to him at the cinema. As Nicolas Cage became John Travolta in Face/Off and everyone's eyes were glued to the screen, Benedict felt a hand on his knee. Fingertips skimmed the bare patch of skin poking through his ripped jeans. Benedict's eyes fleeted to the twenty-one-year-old, six-foot-three frame next to him. And that was all it took. Their own face-off occurred in the disabled bathroom.

The pleasure that came from it was mechanical yet out of this world, then marred by Benedict's resentment to what it meant. 'Gay', this ubiquitous slur of a word, this go-to insult, began to roam through his mind. Growing up, only negative things seemed to be said about homosexuality. Suddenly, the sting of mockery and society's disapproval felt directed at his young self, oppressively so. His mother called as he left the cinema and he started crying, but he could never tell her why.

At that point, Ryan had become irresistibly attractive. Benedict put his arms around the man's rounded shoulders. "It's all right. You don't have to do anything you don't want to." Benedict cajoled.

He poured Ryan a glass of water. Ryan accepted it and touched his glass self-consciously before taking a long sip from it. A moment passed in silence as Ryan's eyes remained on the glass.

"Have you changed your mind?" queried Benedict.

Ryan shook his head and Benedict took the glass from his new friend's hand and put it down. He took Ryan's hands in both of his. They were still freezing. Yet, Benedict was more vividly aware of their soft daintiness, a similitude to Diane's hands. The parallel stopped there and he pushed away the thought of Diane with a shudder. As he guided Ryan's hands on his body, there was nothing forced about his enthusiasm. The thrill of genuine physical attraction was intoxicating. Ryan said something, but Benedict didn't remember what it was. He did not hear it. Ryan's voice became background noise. His tumescent appetite for Ryan, harrying and burning for the past couple of hours, had quickened in pace. It was all over soon after. Too soon. Nonetheless, the sensation was exquisite.

Benedict did not linger afterwards. Ryan asked if he would stay the night. There was time for them to brunch before his flight... They could keep in touch... Work would lead him back to London again soon. Ryan was hooked. And Benedict was tempted. There had been a connection beyond the physical one. Then there was Ryan's puppy eyes, the golden sincerity in his voice, Benedict was beginning to waver. But he had to go. He could not fall for him. He was not part of 'The Grand Plan'.

As Benedict collapsed onto his plush bed at home, he did not notice the blinking blue light of his cellphone. He had not listened to the voicemail left by the hospital. He fell asleep. The thought of what his mother had to say to him did not keep him up. Although truth be told, he may not have been in a hurry to be taken into her confidence. Whatever it was, it would become an inconvenience. He was sure of it. It would be something he would have rather never known about. Little did he know...

Chapter 2

"The phone call"

Marseille, France
Seven years ago, December 2009

That Tuesday started quite ordinarily, up until the phone call.

A young man from the mental health facility was brought into the general ward where Marie Boulanger worked. One of his eyes was fully closed, an oil spill shade of bluish-black glossed his puffed-up eyelid. As it turned out, this psychiatric patient was a newbie who became a bypassing casualty to a daily fight between two patients, Moïse and another nicknamed 'Jeanus Christ.' To prove his superior Messiah status, Jeanus Christ professed to Moïse that he was going to heal a blind man. The only problem with this intended miraculous act was the lack of blind men available and willing to be healed. Hence, the need to create one with a borrowed needle from another patient known as Knitting Earl for obvious reasons and the latest patient on the ward. In the grand scheme of things, this was your average Tuesday morning.

Marie instantly felt motherly towards the unshaved, droopy-faced newbie. He was a chronically depressed man with bags under his eyes who took himself in and made no fuss about his lot. "*C'est la vie*" (that's life), he'd remarked about the event, combined with a defeated shrug. His depression set over him like a cloud of indifference. Marie was determined to cheer him up. How could he be so accepting of his lot in life being poked in the eyes with a knitting needle? Not on her watch! Marie always felt this way around depression, with physical ailments she could help treat patients in ways that would see them getting better. But when it came to depression, she had to stop herself taking every patient for a home-cooked meal and a good chat.

Marie loved Tuesdays. Well, she enjoyed most days, but Tuesdays were the only workday she shared with Médélice. Ah, Médélice was a poem, a patch of soft turf and daisies in a field of thistles. However, the phone call had severely dampened Marie's enjoyment on this particular Tuesday.

On their way to the staff room, Médélice and Marie stopped by the nurses' board. Marie remained silent as they took in their rota for December pinned behind the fingerprint-smeared glass in front of them. Metaphorically, she could feel the steam starting to whistle out of her ears like a children's cartoon from years gone by.

As they stepped into the neon-lit room, their crocs squeaking against the resin flooring, Marie opened her mouth. Médélice flung an assertive hand up. It was rude of her but also a testament to their close friendship as Marie, or most people for that matter, would only tolerate this sort of familiarity from a handful of people.

"It's no bother," Médélice declared in her sunny accent that swallowed every 'r.'

"It's taking the piss, that's what. You always work late to fit in with the others' childcare and now, this! It's like you're being punished for not having children." Actually, more than being punished, she was singled out. Her childless status separated her from the herd, turning her into an easy prey on the savannah plains of the working world. Hence, Médélice's 22nd-28th December would be spent at the hospital. As always. Despite Médélice's extended family flying from the Caribbean to spend Christmas in Marseille and her supervisors having known this for months.

The forty-something Guadeloupean lifted her broad shoulders into a shrug. Clearly it bothered Marie more than it did Médélice which... well, bothered Marie even more.

"So, my dear..." Médélice began, changing the subject whilst stuffing something down her ample bra. It could have been anything, pens, tissues, forms, money, anything. Marie would only be mildly surprised to discover her storing a roasted chicken down there one day. "...How was yesterday evening?" Médélice's eyebrows bounced twice.

Marie blushed, even though it was only the two of them in the windowless, tired room. After much hype and schoolgirl encouragement on Médélice's part, Marie had gone on a date with a tempting surgeon, a single, polite, and accessible man. They deduced the former in the way his voice lowered in volume every time he spoke to female colleagues within his age bracket.

"Good. Fun," Marie replied, feeling lucky for all the lovely dates she had been on over the years. Well, not that she'd had that many. And some had been better than others. But overall, there had always been something worth her while in all of them. Take

20

the surgeon last night, sure he smelt his hands between each course, and he made her take off her shoes as they climbed into his car – there was a plastic shoe rack in the back of his car for this purpose. But his vehicle was immaculate as a result. So, she got this – cities were dirty, and Marseille more than most. But the thing she struggled to get her head around was that he had sniffed his bedsheet after they had sex, this she thought most peculiar indeed. Anyway, she still felt very flattered that a well-to-do doctor would want to go on a date with a commoner like her.

"What was he like?" Médélice grabbed two sachets of instant coffee from a screechy cupboard and poured boiling water into their thermos. The hospital used to have a machine dispensing free hot drinks for staff, but budget cuts decided saving lives was reward enough for a vastly overworked, underpaid, and frequently insulted, if not threatened, staff.

"Kind, polite and…" on the spectrum, but who wasn't on the spectrum, quite frankly? So no, she would never say that. "…Obviously, very clever."

A small group of senior doctors entered the staff room, bringing with them an eruption of unintelligible chatter. The muscles of Marie's face tensed with nerves. She mustered a timid 'hello' which they all acknowledged with a perfunctory nod.

Médélice handed the pink thermos decorated with penguin and star stickers to Marie.

"Clever, how? Snarky-clever or clever-clever?" A protective undertone brushed Médélice's question. Marie cast an eye towards the intimidating group, no one was paying attention to her, yet she remained silent as she shadowed Médélice towards the sitting area of the room.

The plastic armchairs let out a crisp sigh as they sat down, in a way that suggested a telling off for idling. Marie hated the noise. To her, it sounded like a reminder of the extra weight she ought to lose, rather than a telling off for idling.

"Well. You know. Clever. As in, he used words like 'milieu' and 'cognizant'..." Marie imparted quietly.

Médélice pulled a face. "Cogni-what?"

"Cognizant… I had to look it up. It just means 'awareness.'"

"Galling?"

"I can't recall."

"Not the word, you nini. Did he get up your nose?" Médélice muttered with a smile.

"No. No, no. He was lovely. It was a, ah, good date." Marie nodded a little too enthusiastically. This sensible man was too good for her, if anything. He would be a great addition to her son's life and hopefully bring Marie one step closer to her H&H goal - otherwise known as the 'Husband and House' plan.

Médélice looked unconvinced. "Uh-huh. What did you talk about?"

"This and that. He knew a surprising amount about the mating rituals of jellyfish."

Taking a sip of her coffee, Médélice stifled a giggle. "And, did you get back to his 'milieu' for a formal introduction to his little surgeon?"

The group of doctors burst out laughing. Marie's eyes darted in their direction but no one was watching. Their laughter was totally unrelated. As they left, she could finally feel her body relax.

Marie first met Médélice in the hospital's cafeteria seven years ago. Marie had been sitting by herself, trying to engage with a group of senior medics sitting on the other end of the table who were paying her very little attention. It wasn't out of meanness or disrespect on their part, Marie was very junior and did not belong, hence was invisible to her colleagues, a proverbial wallflower. So, when Médélice, an established nurse, sat next to her and engaged in chit-chats, Marie felt so indebted to her she offered to pay for her coffee even though she was beyond skint.

"Médélice!" For a devout Christian, Médélice was anything but a prude. And despite Marie's put-on shock, Marie loved her all the more for it.

"What? C'mon girl, indulge good ol' Médélice." She nudged Marie and winked.

Marie blushed again. She remembered Médélice bragging about her second husband's manhood being so big that he could wrap it around his neck to keep himself warm on a cold day. A little crude and graphic, yet, it made Marie very much doubt that her anecdotes were Médélice's only source of indulgence.

"We did. But that's all I'm gonna say on the matter." It had been a quick and polite affair, immediately followed by, well, a sniff of the bedsheet for him, and a shower for her. As she switched on the light of his spare bathroom, a symphony of singing birds filled the room. It was pleasant but curious. Did he want to cover the sound of his guests going about their little business? Or was it to help them with going? Anyway, in the shower, the water flowed with the speed of entitled freedom, eliminating any worries of being intermittently scolded or frozen as she did at home. Stepping out, her eyes fell on a fresh towel folded on a chair, sitting atop it, a small lavender pull string bag. Before wrapping herself with it, she nuzzled the fragrant, plush fabric. It transported her to idyllic summer days. Was it left especially for her or was it always there she wondered? Either way, she found it a nice touch. And the thought of a spare bathroom alone, hmmm. What. A. Dream. Actually, the idea of a bathroom larger than a portaloo, was enough to make her go a little weak at the knees.

Once dressed and proper again, he could not stop thanking her. It had been the best evening of his entire life, he claimed, which was delightful to hear. But she suspected this was his grateful hormones talking as she had accidentally been made aware that he had only ever been on two dates in his life and both had concluded he would make a nice friend only. She wanted him to mean it though. She had liked his responsible, thoughtful personality. He struck her as a great guy, even allowing for his *quirks*. He had her at the mention of being bullied as an overweight teen. From chubby-probably Asperger's-bullied-kid to doctor, he was not one to let adversity defeat him. Just like her, and she respected him for it, making her want him even more.

"Party pooper." Médélice stuck her bottom lip out.

It was at this point that the phone rang. The call that would sour her mood that Tuesday morning. Médélice picked it up.

"Marie? Marie Boulanger?" Médélice glanced at Marie while listening to whatever was being said on the other end of the line. She eventually covered the speaker-end with her hand and theatrically mouthed. "The police want to talk to you."

"Romain?!" Marie queried in fear. Médélice shrugged, whoever was on the other end of the line had not detailed what they were calling about.

Two sentences into the conversation, Marie had to lower herself into one of the sticky Formica chairs near the phone.

It had nothing to do with her six-year-old, Romain. That, at least, was a relief. Yet, Marie was conflicted about what she was hearing and what she would do about it. It distracted her for the remainder of her day. She did not feel angry, *per se*, although she would have had every reason to be. However, she foresaw her eczema flaring-up again. She had finally been able to get her life back on track. She even allowed herself to dream again and have goals – the H&H plan. But, in all likeliness, the news was going to rock her rickety boat once more.

On her way home, Marie stopped to look at the properties in estate agents' window displays. She liked to visualise the owners and the lives they lived. She knew some people would mentally undress others as an automatic reflex. Well, Marie had a reflex that when she saw a house made her automatically picture the happy owners. They were always happy of course, in their lovely spacious abodes. To tell the truth, when Dr. Edgy-Shoes made the offer to go back to his place, the prospect of seeing his house and the motive for his invitation got her heartbeat going in equal measure. His house was how she had envisioned a bachelor, medic by profession, to live. It was in a row of clones, painted in a medic's white throughout. In his kitchen stood a clock with working cogs and a moving pendulum on show, as if in a permanent state of open-heart surgery. All other bits and bobs were in zany colours, like you would expect from a guy wearing edgy shoes.

Once confined at home in her nest-like bed, Marie struggled to fall asleep, mulling over what lay ahead. She would turn thirty in a few days. But that was neither here nor there in her list of worries. In fact, she had long suspected that she was born forty or fifty. Even as a toddler, Marie would be found in the playground warning other children of the danger of swings. Or as a teenager, whilst her friends baked themselves to a unique tinge of Côte d'Azur mahogany orange, she would be avoiding direct exposure to the sun for fear of the wrinkles it would give her in her seventies.

Therefore, birthdays were simply a signifier of time catching up with reality. No, what worried Marie was the vow she made to herself that she would get her son into a proper home – like Dr. Edgy-Shoes' house, safe and healthy – before she turned thirty. She was failing Romain. And anyone who had ever told Marie that all that a kid needs is 'love', had a) never been dirt poor and, b) not raised a child like hers. She had paid off nearly all her debts. Things were finally looking up, she thought. And then that phone call happened. She shook her head at the thought and shuddered.

Chapter 3

"Mother's letter"

London, United Kingdom
Seven years ago, December 2009

Sundays were for eating roast dinners with his mother, nursing hangovers, and driving fast cars, not necessarily in that order. However, that Sunday had to accommodate the latter two simultaneously. Benedict did not listen to the voicemail in its entirety. He didn't have to. The sombre tone of voice alone was enough.

"Mr. Grant. This is Barbara Leigh speaking. I'm an administrator of St. Mary's Hospital. I'm sorry to inform you that your mother has been admitted to our intensive care unit this evening. We'd..."

As efficient as a bucket of cold water, Benedict had bolted out of bed. He was in his car before his hazy brain cells had worked out a route to the hospital.

The sky was a dirty grey. The same colour as the Victorian building welcoming him with all the warmth of a stony-faced butler of that era. As he stepped inside, the brightness of the white fluorescent strip lights felt like an assault on his senses. There was a queue at reception. Benedict tapped the tip of his foot against the grey lino floor, in tune with the jackhammer drilling happening in his brain. He was about to lose his patience with the dawdling at the front of the queue when the procrastinators finally moved on.

"How may I help you?" offered the aggressively jovial receptionist.

"I'm here to see my mother, Rochele Grant. Where will I be able to find her?"

The plump receptionist turned her attention to her computer screen. The unforgiving light gleamed on the exposed skin revealed by her thinning blonde hair. Her cheerful expression sobered as her eyes rested on a specific line. She picked up her phone and with a hand blocking the speaker, she mouthed, "someone will be with you shortly, take a seat."

Benedict could not sit, but he stepped aside. He was dimly aware that some people looked vaguely awake on their seats.

Others were hurrying by or slowly pacing. Toddlers were fidgeting, and their parents fussing about them or the noise they made. No-one was paying attention to him. His disarray was confined to the merciless space between his ears until a petite figure in blue scrubs holding a clipboard locked eyes with him and then his heart started to race. He had to fight an urge to bolt.

"Are you Benedict Grant?" Her dark eyes were unreadable, her tone patient yet authoritative. She looked unwell herself, gaunt, her black hair was thinning like the receptionist. Yet, her intelligence transpired through every little detail of her facial expression, a professorial intellect that we have come to expect of our doctors.

"Ahem…" He rearranged the phlegm in his throat. "I am," he croaked. It was highly unusual for Benedict not to be holding all the strings. His bearings were confused. Yet, he was undeniably aware that this petite woman in front of him was his lifeline to his mother. His dear mother. He would do anything it took to keep this lifeline on his side. Charm, bribe, cheat or threat were all in his remit and his bow was drawn, ready to shoot the required arrow.

"I'm Dr. Acharya. Please follow me." A slight Indian inflexion ringed her final sentence. They shook hands and Benedict flashed a toothy smile. She nodded once and immediately started back down the corridor. His mother, the last member of his small family, was only another patient to her. The staccato of their pace against the hard flooring was echoing in the charged silence of the wide empty corridor.

The hushed, impersonal environment of the small white-walled room they entered, with the same sinister white brightness, made him feel uncomfortably hemmed-in.

Dr. Acharya gestured for him to sit as she shut the door. He wanted to stop her, inexplicably hankering for the door to remain open. When Benedict was a little boy, he always asked his parents to leave his bedroom door open. The comforting noise of their evenings lulled him to sleep. He would scream in terror if he woke up in the night to find his door shut. This occurred until he turned fifteen, and the overbearing silence drove him to shut his bedroom door, finally.

"Mr. Grant, I'm afraid this is bad news," Dr. Acharya declared and then paused. Her doleful gaze remained firmly on him as if to establish whether Benedict was able or willing to hear what she had to say next.

Benedict glanced sideways, in the direction of the closed door.

"Please just go on." He spoke as evenly as he could manage.

"I regret to inform you that your mother suffered heart failure last night. She slipped into a coma."

Benedict sighed and ran his hands through his dark hair back to front, in relief. "She's alive," he breathed.

Dr. Acharya shifted in her seat, her eyelids fluttered rapidly. "Yes. But. I'm very sorry to say that she won't wake up."

"What do you mean?" His eye contact was unwavering then. "How can you be so sure that she won't?"

"Patients who show less than forty-two percent of normal brain activity, using a common brain scanning technique known as FDG-PET, never regain consciousness. Your mother's brain activity is at about five percent."

Her words rang out against the walls of his skull with the destructive power of a wrecking ball.

"Why keep her in a coma then?" he questioned, fighting a surge of curse words.

His eyes moved to the closed door again. And, why could she not leave the damned door open!?

Dr. Acharya advised on practical matters, before discussing organ donation and long-term care. She was sensitive in her tone, Benedict was straightforward in his decisions.

Alone in the restroom, Benedict splashed cold water on his face. How did people brace themselves for this? As he left the restroom, he glanced across the corridor to the children's ward communal kitchen. He saw a couple standing next to a wall covered with pictures of snowmen, bells, and Father Christmas. There was dry blood on the woman's blouse. *Not hers,* he thought. They had mugs in their hands and looked tired. They were silent. Yet, the doorframe seemed to pulsate from a blasting sound emanating from their internal thoughts.

Seconds later, Benedict found himself with his hand frozen on the door handle to his mother's room. The handle somehow felt akin to the executioner's axe, unnaturally cold to the touch. Looking through the glass-panelled door, he remained frozen in place until a presence behind him, stimulated him into movement. A nurse stepped aside. She smiled but said nothing as she entered the unpleasantly warm bedroom.

His mother wired-up to a plethora of medical machines, most of which he would never know the purpose of. The most obvious were the breathing tubes stuck down her throat, to carry out the most basic of human functions. Yet, take away the medical accessories and she looked no different to the last time he saw her. Her streaked grey hair held the remains of dark blond and graciously framed high cheekbones, a snub nose and a dominant forehead that seemed to celebrate the salient brain it contained. A clipboard hung on the end of her bed carrying all sorts of medical facts about his mother's state, but it was the family section that drew his attention. Only one entry was captured, filled with his name.

Despite the stifling heat, Benedict pulled up the thin blue waffled blanket on his mother. He sat down on the large leatherette armchair next to the bed and reached for his mother's pale hand. With her top half propped up by the articulated bed, she looked as if she was only napping. He wanted to rip out all these unnecessary tubes and wires. His mother was still practising law, "settling the score with justice," as she put it. Just last month she had done a five-mile hike. They had a weekend in Cinque Terre planned for the second week of January. His mother was not clinically dead... She couldn't be.

The nurse patted Benedict's shoulder on her way out. As she left, a repulsive hospital smell stirred, a mix of chemicals and machinery. Yet, the imprint of the nurse's motherly touch lingered like a beam of sunshine amid the howling gales.

"Please leave it open," Benedict requested. He wanted to add 'and stay with me a while,' but strong men do not solicit nor need to be comforted by nurses. Her fingers were still curled on the door handle. She looked mildly surprised by his request but did not question it and left the door ajar. Through the gap, Benedict saw a family of four holding hands followed by a bunch of brightly coloured balloons floating in the bright white, oversized corridor.

"Hey, mum," Benedict murmured gently, rubbing her soft bony hand with the tip of his thumb.

"So, you couldn't bear the sight of soggy tea bags in the sink anymore? A bit of an overreaction, don't you think? Are you really going to let me fight those ill-mannered wretches all on my own?"

He tried to muster a punchline harrumph, but the sound got stuck in his throat, forcing him to wait for the moment to pass before he could continue.

"Anyhow... I hope you've left me a note with what you want to wear on the day, what photo and all that. I won't accept any complaints once I follow you through the gate if you haven't, because you know I'll get it wrong otherwise." His voice trailed off. He looked at her hand again. She was still wearing her wedding band.

"… One thing is certain, though. I'm going to miss hearing about all those children I should already be having by now… And how motorcyclists are nothing more than living organ donors…"

Actually, you know what? I really will. I'm going to miss everything about you. Absolutely everything… He was going to crumble. But, he could not – would not – let that happen, not then. He breathed in, his lungs filling with air.

A medical consultant entered the room. Movements of air had loosened a strand of his mother's hair. Aware of how much she hated having hair on her face, Benedict brushed it off. And before he knew it, his lips were pressed against her forehead, murmuring his love for her at a barely audible volume.

With the exchange of one meaningful look, the old consultant exuding compassion understood their silent agreement. He promptly started to switch off all the medical apparatus that were keeping Benedict's mother artificially alive. There was no waiting on ceremony, no hesitation, he went for the 'ripping off the band-aid' approach. Benedict was quietly grateful for it.

Everything else afterwards felt out of focus. He heard people speak to him, yet nothing stuck. He signed documents but would not be able to tell you what they were. The administrator mentioned something atypical about a certificate, but her words escaped him. He felt on the periphery of a photoshoot, nothing seemed of consequence and everything was blurry and irrelevant.

Back in his car, he was dazed by how the world carried on spinning. He had this overwhelming feeling of déjà-vu. Everything, bar the inside of his own head, kept on going, just like when his father died. He dropped his mother's belongings on the passenger's side and turned on Radio 5 Live just like he would any other day. No newsflash about his mother's death or commemorations of her life. No minute's silence. He switched the radio station. Beyoncé's *Single Ladies* was playing. He drove so slowly, people who were overtaking him did that weird stern face scolding in his direction. But they may as well have been yelling at the tide to turn back for all the impact their efforts were having.

Yet, somehow Beyoncé's innocuous lyrics suddenly pierced his bubble of sorrow and found a way to offend him…

'If you liked it, then you should've put a ring on it. If you liked it, then you should've put a ring on it. If you liked it, then you should've put a ring on it'

… He thought about it, then thought about last night, switched off the radio and cursed at it, loudly. *No, Beyoncé. Whether I liked it or not, I couldn't have put a ring on it, could I? Life's not that easy. Maybe for the Vague n' Vogue of this world, it is, but not for the Ryan's n' Benedict's.* He slammed on the brakes. Despite his sluggish speed, the tires screeched on the tarmac. He avoided impact with a Spaniel by mere inches. His mother's handbag toppled, spilling its content on the floor.

As he gathered everything, he found an envelope addressed to him in his mother's handwriting.

Chapter 4

"No blood"

Manarola, Cinque Terre, Italy
Now, July 2017

Detective Giandomenico Paoli does not share the certainty of the press' speculation that the two corpses were illegal immigrants. Nothing he has observed, so far, would back up the assumption the reporters are jumping to. In the current climate, if you find a way to point the finger at 'illegal immigrants' the story would lead. The journalists knew this and the local guys were not going to miss a chance to get a by-line in a national by letting a lack of substance to their rumination get in the way of that. The Italian Carabinieri police force had made a different assumption regarding the dead bodies' presumed identity. Hence, Giandomenico was called over from Rome to oversee the case. And so far, Giandomenico would lean towards the force's theory.

Anyway, the dental records would be cross-checked, and their DNA samples sent for analysis, so with a little luck, they would know who they are soon enough. And when it turns up results that no longer interests the press pack, they would take their vulture-like gaze elsewhere. The boat should help to answer some pressing questions, once they finally managed to pull it from its resting place.

Leaving the two Corsican witnesses (if one could call them that), Detective Paoli goes to the attending forensic officer on site. A red-haired guy named Davide, who refers to himself as 'Dexter' – after the fictional forensic officer in the American TV series of the same name. The creepiness of naming yourself after a fictional forensic officer who also moonlights as a serial killer seems lost on Davide but is not on Giandomenico.

The detective climbs over the stepped wall across a steep curving lane used as a slipway to the sea by local boats. It is only a short jump onto the rocks from the wall, but they can be quite perilous and he does not want to ruin his suede loafers by accidentally falling in. So, pulling his trouser legs up to the knees, or trying to, as his jeans are so tight hardly anything moves, he bends down before lowering himself onto the rocky grey shore.

There is hardly any space to move. The sunken boat, a few metres away at sea, looks like a lurking killer whale from his vantage point on the rocks.

With a facemask over his nose and mouth, Davide is crouched over the bloated bodies lying face down, cold and very dead.

"So – what do you think, Dexter?"

"They're beautiful," replies Davide.

A shudder crawls up Giandomenico's spine at Davide's softly spoken words.

"I meant what's your initial take on this?"

"Oh, hmm." Davide rubs his hands together in a morbid yet animated way. "Their skin has been scorched by the sun and saltwater. But take a look at this." Using a pencil, Davide forms circles in the general direction of the two bodies, like a gruesome magician, before lifting one of the corpses' white T-shirt further up their back. Little crabs scuttle to cracks in the rocks away from the body. "There's no blood and no obvious sign of struggle dating back to their estimated time of death. And they were long dead before they hit the water… So, it's not looking like a straightforward case of misadventure at sea, Detective Paoli." Davide grinned at Giandomenico as if he had just informed him of the engagement of a mutual friend. "Rousing, isn't it?"

Yuck… How can anybody in their right mind find a case involving dead people rousing? Intriguing, perhaps; exciting, maybe; but rousing? Even then, that would only apply in the fictional context of a grisly detective or forensic-based TV series. Most of the viewers would never have seen a dead body at a crime scene in their life, meaning he was comfortable in his assessment that Davide, aka Dexter, is a creep.

"Do we have an estimated time of death already?"

"Not yet."

"But you seemed to think that they were long dead before they hit the water."

"Well, yes. Judging by their skin, bloating and odour, I'd say that they're in the early stages of decomposition. In this heat, maybe a couple of days or so, give or take a few hours."

"Drowned?"

Davide pinched his chin. "You think so?"

"No, I'm asking you."

"Ah. Well, they've been in the water. Yes."

No joke… Giandomenico takes a deep breath. His shoes get sprayed by a slightly stronger swell hitting the rocks. Annoying.

"Based on your initial examination, what do you think caused their death?"

"Hard to say, at this stage. The boat clearly crashed to the shore at some speed. But the crash didn't cause their death. As I said, I believe they'd already been dead for a couple of days before they landed here."

"Hmm. And a crash means that their engine was running."

Davide rubs then pulls at one of his protruding ears.

"Maybe other people were on the boat with them," Giandomenico thinks aloud. "But if these two had been dead a while, why would anyone choose to jump out of a moving boat, at night, instead of chucking the dead bodies to sea?"

"M-yeah, it seems unlikely. So, their motor was running with no one steering it. Is that even possible?"

"If jammed or deliberately set-up, maybe."

"Hmm." The forensic nods once, barely perceptible. "So, is your hunch leaning towards accident, suicide or murder?"

"I wouldn't dismiss murder yet. Suicide's doubtful. Accidental, maybe." Though ending up in such a touristic place by accident would be against the odds, yet not impossible.

Davide nods. "Well, sir, there's something very unusual going on there... Their death doesn't speak to me yet." The forensic smiles and makes a weird sort of waving motion with his slim fingers as if he was tickling thin air. "Yet it will, Detective Paoli. It certainly will."

Chapter 5

"You don't choose your family"

Marseille, France
Seven years ago, December 2009

Marie examined the lift. The plastic see-through on the lift door was chipped and cracked as if someone had repeatedly kicked it, which probably had been the case. The calling button was caved in. So, she opted for the staircase splattered with graffiti instead. Her journey up featured a different set of dominant fumes with each level, couscous first, mildew second, and weed third, finishing with a potpourri of indescribable stenchs. Accompanied the whole way by a commotion Marie was familiar with; yelling, loud TV, arguments, traffic.

At level four, she stood across from a broken front door, holding on only by its lower hinges and missing its handle.

Marie hesitated. She had decided to act on the call she received yesterday. It was not in her interest, but she could not ignore it. The words of the croaky voiced cop she had heard on the phone were still at the fore of her thoughts. She had to help, it was in her nature. Although she should have listened to the voices in her head telling her that it was a bad idea. Unbeknownst to her, she was reopening a door she should have kept firmly closed.

"Someone home?" Marie called in from the landing.

Nothing.

She stepped in, zigzagging between the debris of a much localised hurricane, showcasing lone shoes, broken knick-knacks, and a coat hanger seemingly holding-up a perforated wall.

"Vlora?"

Before hearing anything back, Marie spotted greasy, matted blonde hair on a skeletal frame wrapped in a dirty dressing-gown slumped on a sofa. Marie took a few steps forward, attracting a rheumy-eyed gaze to her general position without ever actually fully fixing on her.

"My baby. My sweet baby girl," the woman croaked, all smiles. Marie felt her throat tighten. This bag of bones with missing teeth grabbed hold of one of Marie's plump hands and slobbered it with kisses before rubbing a caved-in cheek against the back of her hand. She reminded Marie of an errand dog that was finally reunited with its owner, which, in a sordid way, was somewhat pertinent. Marie could barely recognise her own mother. Her face, ravaged by her lifestyle, looked just like a waxen witch. A lump formed at the back of Marie's throat.

"Hey, maman," Marie greeted gently.

Vlora wrapped her arms around her daughter's legs and started to cry convulsively. Marie really should not comfort her, she really, really should not. Her parents brought this on to themselves again, and again, and again, Marie reminded herself. They should have been the ones looking out for her, protecting her... She would not let her mum, and certainly not her father, back into her life. No way... Yet, her hand rested on her mother's back, rubbing her protuberant shoulder blades. Her robe felt sticky.

Vlora swept rubbish from the threadbare sofa onto the floor, then patted a stained space next to her. Very reluctantly, Marie sat down, cursing herself for being such a push-over, for not ignoring that damned phone call, for coming here... For genuinely caring for her mum, despite everything and for having to fight back the tears that were threatening to escape.

"My beautiful, beautiful girl." Vlora caressed her daughter's cheek. "I knew you'd come to take care of your maman."

Suddenly, a vision from the past came flashing back that hauled Marie out of her stupor. An image of her mum's bruised face pinned against a wall, a gun pointed at her face. Of course, this was a creation of her imagination, Marie had not been there when it all happened. She only witnessed the aftermath. Although she loathed the addition of the word 'only' to the previous sentence. Being a helpless teenage bystander to a traumatic event in your parents' life left haunted scars of the worst neurosis-riddled type. She wished Baul, Romain's dad, was there now. She missed him so much... No, she would not cry. *Think of something else*, she pressed herself. Why did her father put her mother through all that again? Anyway, why did maman not leave him? Argh, if it worked, Marie would have shaken her drunken mum by the shoulders until her brain cells would click into their rightful place, like a printer or washing machine in need of an effective whack.

The cacophony of the neighbouring noise, the smell, the dirt, and the tenderness of her mum's touch suddenly became too much for her. Marie stood up and started to clean up the mess around her frantically.

"So, what happened?" Marie enquired.

"Oh, honey, don't do that." Vlora grabbed Marie's hands full of junk.

"Please, let me."

"Honey, we've been evicted."

"What?! Then, what on earth are you back in here for?"

Vlora shrugged, still struggling to find eye contact, but Marie was not sure now if this was due to intoxication or shame, or even a combination of both?

Couldn't find a bar that was already open? Marie mused to herself whilst immediately chiding herself for the vile thought. She chucked everything she still held in her hands against the upended kitchen table. The burst of violence in the act took them both aback.

Marie breathed in. But she could not direct her gaze at her mum anymore.

"So, tell me, maman. What was it this time?"

She did not see her mum shaking her head which was smudged with tears, leaving clear trails down her grubby cheeks. All Marie could see was wrecked cupboards, flooring ripped opened, a ventilation system left exposed and dodgy stains of varying degrees of recency.

"What did they find here, uh? Drugs? Firearms? Filipino cockerels fighting Siamese cats for money? What?"

Loud sobbing.

Marie's frustration subsided. "Sorry, maman, please, don't cry…" More sobbing. "When will papa be released from custody?"

Vlora shook her head.

"Les Baumettes, again?"

Vlora was staring at the ground when Marie's gaze landed on her. Her mum was shaking. They both were, but Marie did not realise that she was, her teeth were clenched so hard as to mask the physical action even from her. She was left with a difficult choice to make.

Leave her homeless, ever-inebriated mum to her own devices, or become her guardian. The latter meant letting her parents, or at least her mother, back into her life. And nothing good ever came of that. It also implied an introduction of Romain and a postponement of her dream of getting him into a better home and fresher air. Argh, she was failing her sickly six-year-old on so many levels…

36

No. She had to do what was best for her son. If Baul were still there, he would have told her to stay clear of her parents. He would have helped and supported her through this difficult decision. Unlike most relationships, theirs had never reached the bruise-gazing stage. You know, the type of bruise that you notice one day, yet you can't remember for the life of you by what it was caused. But Baul was not here. He had not been for a while.

Marie's phone beeped. There was a message from Lavina, Baul's sister, filled with kind, thankful words for Marie's help with her job application. Marie would reply to it later, saying that 'it's what families do for each other'. And with that, Marie had reached a decision, but she delayed it by sending yet, another 'cute' text message to Dr. Edgy-Shoes instead

Chapter 6

"At the crematorium"

London, United Kingdom
Seven years ago, December 2009

It was 5:00 am when Benedict arrived at the office the following day. It was only him and the security guard for a while. By the time his secretary sat at her desk, he had already caught up with all his emails.

"Laure, set-up a meeting with Xiaosheng. And tell Lee I want his complete turn of a pitch for first thing tomorrow morning," he called from his desk by way of greeting.

"But Lee isn't meeting investors until next Tuesday, and your agenda is already brim-full. Are you s…?"

"Find some time," Benedict interrupted Laure. "Early in the morning or late in the day, I don't care. Just make it happen."

By lunchtime, he knew everything he needed to know. How his deals were progressing and what political and economic changes were likely to affect his operations or clients, everything.

Yet, he had left his mother's letter on his bedside table, unread, propped upright against the stem of a lamp. In a state of half daze, he stared at it while lying down on his bed until his body lost interest and forced him into sleep. The envelope had not been sealed, just folded in. The words on the front, *'To my blessed Benedict,'* had been formed with extra care. Her immaculate handwriting, as familiar as his own, seemed even neater than usual. The envelope was slightly creased, though, as if carried around a while. Perhaps she intended to use it as prompt to the conversation she kept meaning to have with him.

Benedict was in two minds about opening it. This letter was his last ever bridge to his mother. As she had been apprehensive about sharing this confidence with him, his hunch was that the nature of the revelation might be unsettling. And he did not want his mother's last words to him to be a disappointment. His childhood had been a happy one, if slightly overbearing, and he wished to remember his parents as he did now, private, but to his mind, near perfect.

Although tiptoeing in most walks of his life was not his thing, he was faced with a rare case of indecisiveness with regards to opening his mother's letter. He was bitterly aware that one thing was for certain, once her last words came to light, they could never be unknown. And he had been raised to believe that some things were better left unspoken.

If you asked him, everyone had secrets, even houses. Like houses, families could sustain the most hideous truths without falling apart. Even a leak from the roof running through a downstairs cupboard could go undetected for years, decades, without causing trouble. But once aware of said leak, suddenly the house becomes unfit. Its problem has to be fixed, and if laziness or material things get in the way of repair, one has to live with the idea that their home is substandard. The house is exactly as it always was, yet in the back of its occupants' mind, it is not adequate anymore. Could this truth ruin his opinion of his family?

Could it be about his father? His father had met his mother at a pharmaceutical convention. He was a new salesman, she, still studying, was one of the many young hostesses. Benedict remembered the many nights his father spent away, travelling for business. He would sometimes return and appear contrite when he looked at him. His parents would have discussions in hushed voices. It sounded to Benedict like his mother was trying to reason with his father, trying to keep him quiet about something.

"Benedict? So, which do you prefer?" His secretary appeared to have materialised a foot away from his desk in a puff of smoke.

"Pardon?"

She gazed at him, bemused. "Xiaosheng - 6:30 am our time tomorrow, or 8:00 am Thursday?" Laure repeated. He found her peculiar pronunciation of the Chinese name particularly galling today. Where did she get tchyo-tchyoung from? A cartoon from the post-colonial era?

"6:30 am tomorrow is fine." Scrolling down his Outlook calendar, blood rushed into his neck. "Why is my diary blocked out from 3:00 pm onwards tomorrow?" he snapped. How could she know? No one was made aware of his situation at work. He would sue the hospital for their indiscretion. This was unacceptable…

"The Christmas party?" Laure replied sheepishly. "Hugh has you down for the company speech to the troops. Would you like me to cancel?"

Crap. He forgot… And, of course, Hugh had him down for the company speech. The creepy old fart could not string two words together in public without alienating a string of people… And did he imagine it, or did Laure just use a condescending tone?

"That won't be necessary," he sputtered unapologetically. Turning his attention back to his computer screen, Laure was dispatched to her desk without another word. Maybe he should get her to work for Hugh for a bit, remind her of what leering felt like and why she asked to work for him in the first place. Give her an inch, she'll take a mile... Although she did get work done. And all the other secretaries on his floor seemed to share a brain between them. Anyway, this was all a giant waste of his time. He had more pressing matters to focus on. His ungrateful secretary was not one of them.

∞

Word of Benedict's mother's death spread fast and wide amongst her profession and community. Benedict's house was infested with bouquets of overpowering, smelly flowers, every sideboard covered with half-opened condolence cards – some from people he did not even know – offering trite platitudes on how he should feel.

On Tuesday afternoon, the day of the funeral, a crowd of people overflowed outside the synagogue. Benedict wore his usual bankers' uniform – blue suit with white shirt. While everyone else sported expensive black outfits, most men had to borrow a kippah from the basket at the door. Out of respect or compliance, they now boasted stranger's dandruff on the crown of their heads.

Diane looked like she'd stepped off a catwalk as she sat beside him. Benedict almost resented her (newish) appearance and mannerisms, but not today. When they first met, Diane stood out for the wrong reason. She joined his college for Sixth Form, she struggled to make any friends amongst long-established cliques. While others poked fun at her, sneering at her Primark clothes and accent, Benedict was drawn to her, to her difference and resilience. Until Diane burnished her style and his lot joined him in his admiration of her. Though, Benedict sensed that Diane's efforts to gloss her background had the opposite effect on his late mother. In her opinion, Diane's achievements were all the more remarkable for it, but his mother never openly commented on it.

The ceremony started, and a few people brought their hands to their face. Benedict wondered if it was only out of sadness. The synagogue had suffered a minor arson attack a few months back. It had been repaired since, but the lingering fume of smoke mingled with the sharp smell of fresh paint made the place barely breathable. Benedict found it particularly unbearable while the coffin was being carried toward the bema. However, not everybody could fit inside the synagogue, so the doors were kept open. Benedict was quietly grateful for it.

He only just recognised his mother as they opened the casket. She was wearing a dress that Diane bought for the event. Her face had been heavily, and yet subtly, made-up. She looked feminine and colourful rather than her sober, scholarly self. Incongruously, she looked better dead than alive, thought Benedict. The open casket had been Diane's idea, along with virtually every other detail and the handling of paperwork. Diane had stepped up to the role with graceful selflessness and the same superhuman efficiency she applied in the management of her own tech company. Some were surprised by the open casket. Benedict overheard them murmur 'how refreshing' or 'interesting' when they clearly meant 'what nonsense.' A lot of tears were shed, but none from Benedict, even under these circumstances he wouldn't let his emotions rise to the surface in public. His eyes remained on his mother the whole time. He did not give a eulogy or partake in the singing of any solemn hymns.

At the end of the ceremony, he shook hands with dozens of people he barely knew. They murmured the invariable 'what a shame it was,' 'a great loss,' followed by kind words about his mother, the ferocious lawyer, the charity trustee, and keen hiker. All of it was impersonal and insipid. Benedict wondered whether some of them showed up to pay respect to his mother or just to network. Diane kept mostly quiet, her arm delicately wrapped around Benedict in support.

There was no procession to the cemetery. Benedict made it clear that no one should follow the hearse, not even Diane. Anyway, he was headed to the crematorium, at his mother's wish. The ceremony should have been held there in the first place, which would have been disapproved of by some traditionalists, again. So cheques were written, exceptions made.

The clock fitted above the cremation chamber on a thinly cracked wall marked the passing of time loudly. Tick, tick, tick... He fought the urge to rip it off the wall, smash it onto the floor and violently stamp on it. Tick, tick, tick. As it read 5:00 pm, the coffin was moved through a small door shaped much like the type you might find on a pizza oven. Rollers transported the casket into the cremation chamber in slow motion. The door shut, a moment later a gushing sound broke through in what felt like a sudden, surreal assault, startling Benedict from his stupor.

Remaining still, unable to move, think, or it seemed even breathe properly, he felt unbelievably trapped, as if confined in the cremation chamber with his mother. His hands were balled up inside his jacket pocket, involuntarily scrunching-up his mother's letter. He had forgotten he had it there. As his heart rate slowed down, he pulled the letter from his pocket, smoothed it down against his lap for a long time, and eventually opened it.

Chapter 7

"Vlora meets boy"

Marseille, France
Seven years ago, December 2009

Children were starting to pour out of the open gate. As always, Romain's pale complexion and blond curls were immediately noticeable. Among the vast tutti-fruity mix of heritage his classmates had to offer, Romain looked the exotic one amongst his peers.

"Bonjour, *ma petite puce*, (Hello, my little flea)," Marie cried with opened arms. Romain flung his book bag and coat in her general direction and stuck his cheek out, in anticipation of a kiss that always welcomed him, This was their most rehearsed choreography and yet Marie never took it for granted.

"Bonjour, maman."

Bending down to retrieve a runaway book, Marie lost her balance. Luckily, a boy grabbed her just before she hit the ground. He had a youthful face yet he was already Marie's height, and his grasp on her arm was surprisingly strong and firm.

Once steadied, he slowly pulled his hand away from Marie's arm, his eyes locked with hers. "Thank you," Marie said with glee. "That's quite a grip on you, young man! What's your name?"

"I'm Gabin, Mrs. Boulanger." Gabin's accent was unusual, hard to place, mostly Marseillais but with a hint of somewhere else.

Marie straightened her blouse and refastened a button that had come undone.

"Lovely name. And unusual. Are your parents' fans of the actor?"

She felt Gabin's gaze lingering on her. This immediately prompted her to tightly wrap her jacket and arms around her hourglass figure, which was silly on her part. But the protective motion came instinctively. Her body had morphed into that of a woman at the tender age of ten, and soon, way too soon, followed an introduction to men's habit of conversing with her cleavage.

"I don't know. But I'm glad you like it, Mrs. Boulanger." There was something a little affected in the way Gabin kept saying her surname as if voiced for his own entertainment.

Romain tugged at his mum's sleeve.

"We must go," Marie declared. "It was nice meeting you, and thanks again for the quick save."

Gabin bade his farewell and smiled at Romain, although only his lips stretched, his eyes conveyed an entirely different message. Romain cowered behind Marie, unbeknownst to her.

"How was your day?" Marie asked Romain.

The six-year-old shrugged. Two young boys waved bye to a boy from his class as they passed by but not Romain.

"Did you learn anything interesting?"

His bottom lip stuck out, he raised then slumped his shoulders.

"What did you have for lunch?"

"Can't remember." The mechanical response delivered while he started to walk on the edge of the pavement as if on a tightrope.

Marie pulled him further away from the road. "Play with anyone new?"

Romain shook his head while staring at the thin, dishevelled woman walking by his mum's side.

Following his gaze, Marie breathed in even though she did not need to. "Romain. This is Vlora."

Vlora's hands were pressed against her small chest, her eyes filled with tears. Marie's chest tightened at the sight of her mum's reaction.

They stopped moving and Vlora lowered herself to be at eye-level with Romain. "What a sweet little angel you are, as handsome as the most charming picture I've ever seen." Her voice broke a little.

Vlora stuck a hand out. But the six-year-old burrowed himself against his mother, peeping at Vlora from behind her, a hand covering his mouth. To Vlora's credit, she had not stared at the large scar under his nose and along his mouth. And Marie appreciated it.

"Vlora'll be staying with us for a little while. Is that okay?" Marie queried Romain.

Vlora had let the floodgate open when Marie announced Romain's existence. She professed that she felt no resentment towards Marie for keeping her grandson a secret. Instead, she voiced her profuse apologies, remorse, and wished to reset the clock to do everything differently. Albeit, her words had an odd ring. Fake. Yet, Marie graciously depicted a collage of her life to her mum. Vlora smiled contently at the mention of her daughter becoming a nurse and a mum. But repentant tears were shed at a reference to Romain being raised single-handedly. So, to spare Vlora further guilt, Marie kept moot about the net of support her sister-in-law, Lavina, and grandfather-in-law, Pépé, had weaved around her after Baul's death.

Marie eventually made the offer for her mum to come and stay with them. Vlora insisted that after everything she put Marie through, she did not deserve her daughter's help or compassion. Marie suspected it to be a bit of an act at first. She remembered the reverse psychology her mother used to exploit and twist Marie round her little finger in the past. But something, it seemed, had changed. The low burning light that kept Vlora going all these years had vanished. Marie could feel it and could not ignore it.

Romain craned his neck up to check if his mother was serious. Truthfully, their home was not fit to host guests.

Romain eventually nodded… Neither he nor his mother could have foreseen how grim this situation would eventually turn.

Chapter 8

"Confession"

London, United Kingdom
Seven years ago, December 2009

Benedict smoothed the paper, caressing it against his lap. A moment was spent looking at the beautifully formed letters on the page. He breathed in, the way divers did before taking the plunge.

My dearest Benedict,
As this letter has found its way into your hands, it can only mean one thing. I'm no longer able to tell you, in person, what you're about to learn, which I deeply regret.
But first things first, I'd like to take a moment to say that you were without a shadow of a doubt the greatest blessing in mine and your father's life.
I'm aware that I wasn't the best mother you could have hoped for, old, unavailable, and unable to lay bare my feelings – amongst other things. I wish that I did. I wish that I could tell you how much I love you, right this instant. Benedict, I would add that I loved you when you could see it, and even when you couldn't. I loved you when you were the nicest and even when I was the only one to see it. I loved you when you were against me, just as much as when you were resting on me.
I vividly remember how my heart swelled for you every step of the way. The first time your tiny hand curled around your father's thumb. Holding your hand walking into school. Hearing you tippy-toeing into our bed when you were still scared of monsters. Feeling your small body go heavy against me. Seeing you fail but never admit defeat. Hearing your first word, in English, and in all those foreign languages I wish I'd learned, too. Listening to your well-formed arguments, challenging my views and beliefs. Seeing you win all those trophies, graduate, get all those promotions and setting up your own firm. I loved you in absolute unconditional terms, and yet, you've made it entirely redundant. Your father and I were intensely proud of the intrepid boy that you were and the accomplished man you've become.

46

I wish that you'll have the same joy experiencing what your father and I have been blessed with. And know that I'm so incredibly sorry I won't be around to meet your own children. When you do, not if, because I know you will, please go a little easier on the accelerator of all those terrifying engines you live for. This is the last you'll hear of it, so indulge me on this. Please.

Yet, my precious son, my dear, dear boy, and it is a terrible 'yet.' I must confess that I broke many laws to have you in my life. As in the eyes of the law, you are not, strictly speaking, mine.

Your father and I were holidaying in the South of France and Northern Italy when a desperate young woman's life crossed paths with ours and left her infant twins in our arms. You were brand new, still had your hospital tags attached around your ankles. You were both creased and had jaundiced skin. Yet, you both seemed a divine gift. I could almost hear angels singing when I looked at your little faces.

It's no excuse, but I had always longed for a child. Even as a child myself growing up, I had to learn to live without the baby brother or sister I pestered my parents for. Then, I never imagined a life without the creation of it. I longed to feel life inside me, and I tried everything. I would have done anything. If someone had said that I had to do naked headstands, three times a day, in the middle of Trafalgar Square, I would have struck that deal in a heartbeat. But nothing worked.

When I eventually realised that it would never happen, it didn't bring acceptance. It brought sadness, anger, and guilt. I still ached for the weight of a little life in my arms that I could call my own. I wanted to be this irreplaceable steppingstone into adult life for someone… To the point, I think I lost my sanity for a while. When I crossed path with a pregnant woman in the street, I had this horrible, burning desire to stab her glorious belly over and over. Not that I would ever act on these impulses, but I tell you to show the level of desperation to which I had sunk. So, I buried myself into work. But I felt tried, tired, and guilty. Guilt over my terrible thoughts and guilt that your father, who was so good with children, would never have one of his own because of me. So, when he said to me that he wished he was the infertile one so that I would stop blaming myself, I tried to pull myself back together.

At forty-four, the pain was still furiously sharp, pernicious. But I had found a way to lock it up, hide it. Because this sort of pain, my son, had to be kept hidden. It is expected of women, even in this modern world, to not voice or manifest this kind of pain. It makes others feel uncomfortable. I learned that barren women, like me, are not allowed to grieve the way a mother of a stillborn child can. The old saying, 'it's better to have loved and lost than never to have loved at all' doesn't apply. For women like me, whose desire to love a child was eating them away from the inside out, we had to pretend, keep hold of our dignity, and hide our heart's unspeakable agonies. There is nothing to complain about, 'you're lucky to have a good life, Rochele, carefree. Indulge yourself.' They saw me as the captain of a majestic ship when I was in an outboard dinghy buffeted about in the ship's wake, trying to stay afloat. Nobody wanted to hear that every time I got back home, to a house full of hopeful bedrooms, to me, it was an obsolete empty shell. Like me.

And there she was, this young girl, running away from us, leaving us with her babies. It felt like God's plan. When she came back, I made her an offer. A decadent offer. A lawless offer.

I had no right to do that. I know. Perhaps you will resent me for it. And I'm sorry you had to learn about it this way. Your father and I didn't tell you because I was afraid. Afraid, you'd feel rejected and lose your sense of belonging if you knew. Yet, you have a fundamental right to know about your origins. I don't know your birth parent's names. We didn't speak a common language, and I think we all knew that it might be better not to exchange names. All my apologies for the unintended torments this may cause, were you to decide to look for them.

However awful all this sounds to you, I can't say that I regret having you as my own or that I'm sorry for what I've done. As to be sorry would be to experience the pain of remorse which truth be told, I have not. No matter how amoral and self-serving this act might have been, I would never change or forego the time we've spent together and the immense joy you've brought your father and me. I will be forever grateful for it, the memories we created, the love we shared. And I hope you have it in your heart to forgive me for the way you came into my world.

Love you, always

Your mother.

The colour drained from his face. It could not be true. His mother was a lawyer, a law abider. These could not be her words. He was going to talk to someone official, and they would tell him that it was all a big mistake, that something like this was not possible. That his unwell mother was delirious. How could it be anything otherwise?

He had never felt different from his parents, not even from the lesbian aunt he has never met. He had quietly blamed his father many a time for his supposed likeness to his aunt. He assumed it ran in the family and with reasons. People had often commented on how similar in personality he was to his parents, particularly his father. They even shared the same passion. His first word was allegedly 'bike.' Before Benedict was big enough even to reach the car pedals, his father would sit him on his lap opposite the steering wheel and let him "park it". Admittedly, he did not look like him, but he always felt they shared a family resemblance of sorts… Or had this always just been a case of his mind filling in gaps he had not even realised were there?

The faint melody of 'Magpie' by The Unthanks suddenly came to him,…

"One's for sorrow. Two's for joy. Three's for a girl. Four's for a boy. Five's for silver. Six for gold. Seven's for a secret never told. Devil, devil I defy thee. Devil, devil I defy thee. Devil, devil I defy thee. Oh, the magpie brings us tidings of news, both fair and foul. And she steals the eggs from out of the nest, and she can mob the hawk…"

Black and white anger suddenly came knocking at his door. Benedict's hands began to shake so badly, it turned the piece of paper into a musical instrument. He felt sick. Waiting thirty years to tell him, via a letter, what a cop-out. How cruel.

"'Afraid I'd feel rejected or lose a sense of belonging,' then why now?" Benedict shouted at the chamber like a lunatic. "What's changed, huh? What's changed, mother?" He barked the last word, like a dog at a taunting magpie perched in the safety of the tree canopy. He was pacing.

"Let me guess. Could it be that rather than being afraid of hurting my feelings, you were…" he jabbed a finger mid-air, "… a coward?"

He closed his eyes. Suddenly, he was not standing in a crematorium anymore. He was at the edge of a cliff. Behind him, there was nothing, a bottomless abyss of dark matter, his whole past. His entire childhood was a web of deceptions, leaving him unsure of who he indeed was. All the parts he had never questioned about himself; his name, being English, being Jewish, his medical history, his family history, etc. They were all tipping over the edge of the cliff, threatening to take him with them.

And yet, his mother and father felt no less his late family than before. His vision of abyss was replaced by a very mundane one, of his mother asking him if he was confident he did not need a wee before he left. Something she would do every single time he left her house, without fail, despite turning thirty, three days ago. Three days. Two, since you left me.

Back in the windowless, shut door, white crematorium room, the walls were closing in on him. He had to get out or he would end up smashing every chair in here against the wall.

∞

Laure was standing outside the manor house rented for the occasion, smoking despite a drizzly winter rain. Meaning that smoking was not done in an attempt to look cool anymore. No, nicotine was ruling her brain cells. Hail to the Queen Nicotine.

But her frigid break was interrupted by an angry boy on his toy, riding the last stretch of the very long driveway far too fast. Until he purposefully screeched to a halt on the gravel, spraying tiny stones in its wake. Laure gasped. In a fury, she flounced towards the biker.

As Benedict removed his helmet, she stopped in her tracks. A halo of light coming from behind accentuated the copper in her hair and her enviable silhouette in a decidedly tight, non-wintery dress.

"Darling. You look ravishing," he declared, staring at her from a stretched arm's view.

"Hmm. Thanks." Laure's eyes widened then narrowed, some of her anger dissipating. "Benedict… Huh?" She rubbed a finger between her nose and upper lip. Benedict parroted her. There were traces of white powder on his finger. He wiped it off while smothering a small voice in his head begging him to go home. However, the substance he'd taken to numb the grief had tampered with his free will and was now puppeteering his brain cells. So he strutted into the building, heedless of people on either side of him.

Laure immediately caught up. Trotting ahead of him, she deliberately barred his way into the main room.

"I'm afraid you've missed the meal…" He tried to go around her, but she kept positioning her body in front of him. "… Perhaps I should take you home?"

"Why?" Benedict smiled at his secretary audaciously, spreading his arms on either side of the door's archway. His face was only a couple of inches away from Laure's. She swallowed noisily. "Are you suddenly aching for my babies?"

His attempt at flirting was met with a gaze filled with concern from his secretary.

"Aah! Look who's finally decided to show his face." A voice broke through from the main room.

It was Hugh, the firm's co-founder, his partner, ironically raising his glass in Benedict's honour. Benedict pushed past his secretary.

"Ready to give your speech, mate?" Hugh prompted.

Mate? Benedict thought back, imitating Hugh's pompous voice in his head. Though, perhaps, it did not strictly remain in his head, judging by Hugh's belligerent and shocked expression.

Who cares? Benedict went to stand unnecessarily close to Hugh. The old prick. Does he think he scares me? Benedict's face had an expression of unnecessary defiance. Hugh blinked furiously as if a series of confused thoughts were being shuffled before his eyes.

Laure stepped in between them, all smiles and light-heartedness, shoving a glass into Benedict's hand. An arm crossed in front of her like a battering ram and Benedict was subtly forced a foot backwards.

She was beginning to get on his nerves. It was at this point Benedict noticed a tall man hovering near her. He did not recognise him from the firm. Benedict took the glass from Laure's outstretched arm and jumped up onto the nearest table. He whistled for everyone's attention. Laure stared at him with pleading eyes, mouthing something or the other to him. He was not interested.

"Yeeehaaa!" Benedict stretched his arms up in the air, spilling his drink everywhere to cheers of response.

"Up twenty-six percent. Twenty. Six. Percent." Benedict punched the air. More loud cheers in response. "And that's all thanks to you…" Benedict started to point at individuals. "… and you, and you, and you. You, not so much." He made a wavering hand movement at someone, and everyone laughed. Laure's knitted face never looked so terrified. The tall stranger placed a comforting hand on her forearm.

"And I'll tell you what." Benedict swirled, a pointy finger pivoted with him, full circle. "While all those suckers are falling like dominoes. Clonk, clonk, clonk. I want you to continue to pluck them to the bones. There's no room for any other hunters than us. Do you hear me? I want you to take them to their graves and plough their fields." Benedict thrust the air with his pelvis several times. "Do you hear me?" he shouted, cupping his ear and still thrusting.

Everybody whooped, whistled, and clapped, the way teenagers would cheer the class bully, in the hope of shielding themselves from unwanted attention. This Wolf of Wall Street kind of speech was not the company's mojo. Stressball-Laure could not take it any longer. She freed her arm from the tall guy. Short of ideas, it was her turn to raise her glass and yell, "have a drink on us. Merry Christmas!"

Before Benedict could add anything else, Laure forcibly yanked him down from his pulpit.

"Great speech," she lied, trying to manhandle him away from people.

"You bet." Locking arms with her, he shifted their route.

At the bar, Benedict ordered drink after drink.

Laure placed a hand on his back, "let's take a breather, eh?" Benedict had forgotten she was there. "Shall we grab some air for a minute?" she insisted.

He laughed it off. Laure gave a jittery look around. *Why was she being so uptight?* He thought and placed a filled glass in front of her.

The whisky burned like fire in his throat, and he was getting light-headed when he heard a voice.

"Look at the big gay over there."

He remembered when Ryan had recognised him the other night. He turned to look for the source of the voice – someone who'd seen him in the bar?

Three analysts, one of them being Frank. Of course, Frank was amongst them, Mr I've-Got-One-Over-You. *Always thought that he was a phoney… maybe friends with Ryan. Maybe they talked about me. Laughed about me. He's still laughing now…*

"What did you just say to me?" Benedict whispered in a shouty way, taking a stance close enough to Frank's face that he could feel the warmth of his breath on him.

The analyst's eyes went wide. "N-nothing." Frank took a step back.

"Did you just call me a big gay?" Benedict spat out.

"No… No… I said nothing." The analyst took a few steps backwards.

Benedict laughed a less than humorous laugh, his blood-shot eyes unwavering from Frank's.

"We, he…" Frank nodded to the analyst next to him, "… said, look at that big A… I…"

"So, you were calling me an asshole, then?"

The analyst swallowed. His Adam's apple bobbed. "No, your friend. Y-your secretary… We… They…"

Laure was still at the bar, looking over with concern in her eyes.

"What about her?"

"We… They were… They were talking about her ass…"

Before he knew it, Benedict's clenched fist flew at Frank's face. But instead of hitting his analyst, Benedict punched the shoulder of Laure's friend who had materialised between him and Frank. In a swift movement, he immobilised Benedict, locking Benedict's arms behind his back as if he was arresting him. All eyes were on them.

"Nothing to see here," Laure addressed the gawkers, pivoting with raised hands.

"Glad we got that settled, without anyone having to get physical to defend a lady's honour," she concluded in a hushed passive-aggressive tone while glaring at Frank and his pals, before turning her gaze to Benedict. "Alright, let's get you home."

Benedict was still overflowing with a drug and booze-fuelled anger. A type of rage he had never experienced before, never even knew existed. A murderous rage. He wanted to claw at everyone in this room, rip their smug faces off. But the arms of Mr. Justice League felt steely against his, making resistance futile.

This time, Laure did not give Benedict a choice. She exchanged a subtle signal with his captor, and off they went with Benedict as their prisoner. The rest of the room stared on open-mouthed as their boss was frog-marched from the bar. Yet, there was no more resistance on Benedict's part. His rage died as quickly as it had flared. Through the substance-fuelled haze, something told Benedict that his captor was Laure's plus-one for the evening. While Benedict grew new-found respect for the guy, a sudden panic flared up about this man's intention towards him. Was he burrowing bugs under his skin right now? It surely felt like it. And his arms felt ever so steely… A burning wonder at what this man's plush lips would feel like against his had emerged. *For heaven's sake.* Benedict became annoyed with himself.

Benedict took the next day off. He expected his return to work would be sobering. He expected office chatter to suddenly grow quiet at the sight of him. Good, he had suffered their yapping long enough, a rest from it would be bliss.

He tried to ignore the debilitating mix of depression, anxiety, and wariness he was feeling. No doubt it was the side effect of what he scored after the funeral. It had to be, right? It could not be the loss of his mother, as it turned out she was not even his. It would pass. After a sleepless night, he went from staring blankly at his computer screen to staring blankly at his open fridge, to staring at a shrivelled slice of ham in an open packet. He wanted to eat with his mother like he always did when he was feeling unwell. He wanted to hear her debate over what they should eat and invariably decide on beans on toast. He wanted to follow their lunch with a walk or a swim as they often did. He settled for a bottle of Sauvignon Blanc and shut the fridge door.

An hour later, he found himself at his mother's house anyway, testing the water and checking the filter of her swimming pool. He dipped his bare feet in. A blurry reflection stared back at him, exposing him like a mirage of Benedict Grant. Appropriate. He took a swig of one of his mother's Château Latour. What kind of person would do such a thing? Put another human being up for sale? Hand their child over to strangers for cash? But, moreover, who would take them up on it?

Maybe the same sort of people who set their first boss up. Faking documents and transactions over a year, whilst ensuring he would be moving up the minute the fellow was cleared out of his way – based on a paper trail he swore he knew nothing about. In fairness, Benedict did the guy justice. This maverick was not made for the finance world. Always going on about saving the bees, eating sardines out of the can for lunch to better appreciate his wife's evening dinners, and his children writing poems to the Queen, his trusting face, the corduroy trousers, and the smell of herbal tea in his breath. Benedict did not look up to him, but saw through him and straight to the summit that was his goal. Later, Benedict got wind through a mutual contact that after being sacked he had gone into teaching, a much better fit. Although many might find what Benedict did distasteful, he viewed it as doing the chap a favour in the end. Clearly. He helped him find his true calling in life. So maybe he did get some things from 'his parents' after all, his willingness to bend the rules to get what he wanted while helping others.

Benedict brought the bottle of red to his lips again, but there was nothing left.

Anyway, they did it for the money. Of course, they did. Where there's a will, there's a way, eh? But then why sell only one of the twins? And what happened to the other one? Were they identical twins? Fancy seeing another one of him in a Soho nightclub. Benedict shuddered in revulsion. He would have to dig out his birth certificate, although it was now safe to assume that his mother had falsified it. It was well within her remit. It would not be a quick search. Although he was aware of how quick his brain could work compared to most, he also knew that his mother's had spun faster.

But wait, did he really want to know? Open another can of worms… He kicked his feet in the water as fast as he could, producing an explosion of white splashing water.

And why was his phone so quiet? No series of text messages from Diane. This was weird. He had a sharp recollection of calling her last night, well technically it would have been this morning. But he could not bear to think about what was said. He had finished the night in Soho and woke up in Peckham on an inflatable mattress next to two very young-looking guys. He remembered spending a lot of money, but he was quite sure that these two were not escorts and they were all legal… The whole of the day before was one big fat mistake after another. The letter, the drugs, the fight – well the half-fight thanks to Laure and co., the night... What was he capable of next?

Chapter 9

"A well-stocked wreck"

Manarola, Cinque Terre, Italy
Now, July 2017

The tow truck gets stuck. Too big to negotiate the narrow streets of Manarola, it is sent back to the station. On its way out, its wing mirrors scratch bright paint off the quaint buildings.

The hold-up is making Giandomenico feel impatient. The sunken boat carrying the two dead men to the rocky shore of this Cinque Terre village has information to unveil. And the sooner it happens, the better with these sorts of cases.

After a couple of hours and a lot of guided manoeuvres from a little army of people, the second tow truck manages to reach the harbour without any major hiccups. Despite its compact size, it looks grotesquely big in its surrounding.

The driver steers the tow truck to the edge of a stony stepped wall, halfway through the village's winding slipway to the sea, with great precision. The mechanical arm is articulated towards the seashore before unwinding the steel rope. Two firemen secure the hook at the end of the rope to the sunken boat. Everyone is asked to take a few steps back in case the steel rope snaps or springs into someone's face.

The driver presses a button. Giandomenico mouths a silent prayer, asking for the boat to not win this battle. The rope tightens and a small part of the wreck starts to poke out of the sea. The driver stops the process to let the water out, then repeats.

"Wow, stop stop stop!" someone yells at the driver.

The tow truck is pulled backwards, stopped from tipping over the edge and into the sea only by the small stepped wall.

Although disappointed, everyone agrees that it will not work. A tugboat is requested instead. It will pull the sunken boat to a more accessible bay.

A fireman jumps onto the rocky shore and into the sea to unhook the steel rope. Another comes to stand alongside Giandomenico by the edge of the stepped wall. They both silently examine the sunken boat, their hands in their pockets.

"Riva's latest model," the fireman declares in a deep voice, nodding to himself. He looks like an action figure, with a square body and very square cleft chin. As far as firemen go, he does not 'look' the part, he is the part.

"Come again?"

"That's a Riva 63 Virtus powerboat." The fireman points at the sunken boat with his Buzz Lightyear's head. "Her line's based on the classic Vertigo model but she's a bigger beauty."

"Expensive?"

The fireman lets out a guffaw and gives Giandomenico a friendly pat on the shoulder whilst making his way back to his crew. *I'll take that neither he nor I could afford her,* thought Giandomenico. *So, no illegal immigrants then.* However, if those two men were at sea for a couple of days or more, as Davide the forensic, suggested, then they could have come from far.

The detective takes his phone out and checks how along a ferry from Sardinia to Genoa would take. Only half a day. So maybe they were not alone in this boat after all. He would have to interview a few more people, perhaps local fishermen.

Once the boat is finally pulled out of the water, they find that the handle controlling the engine has been jammed. Meaning that the boat was not manned manually. It could have sailed away on its own carrying its dead crew members for miles.

However, a dozen litres of bottled water and food cans had been stored. All labels had been removed from the bottles and cans, like the clothes of the two corpses.

Chapter 10

"Thanks for the socks"

Marseille, France
Seven years ago, December 2009

The mistral was blowing so ferociously that Marie could not light the candle of her birthday cake. Romain had insisted they should all go to the beach for a picnic. He could spend hours meticulously balancing rocks on top of one another, creating beautiful stone-stacked pyramids.

The past few days of co-habitation with Vlora have been weird but unexpectedly enjoyable at the same time.

It was weird, because Marie had forgotten what it was like to live with her mum. But it came back to her in bursts. Her quiet and undemanding nature, her lack of initiative and leaving all decisions to whoever was in charge – Marie now, her dad then. Yet, the most impressive thing was that Vlora could make herself invisible, even in a home the size of most people's living room.

It had also been enjoyable because Romain had embraced living with her. A mum who did not get out of bed early enough in the morning to see her daughter to school for months on end. A mum who served dry cereals for most meals when she was there at all. A mum who did not get involved when the cruel side of Marie's dad, Fatos, flared up against his little girl. However, Vlora seemed quite good with Romain… More of a mum.

"We'll have to go in a minute," Marie announced, her curly dark hair fashioned into a Tina Turner's mane by the wind.

"Nooo. Please, can we stay a bit more?" Romain whined.

"Alright, two more minutes."

"Two hundred minutes?"

"Three."

"Five?"

"Deal."

Vlora walked towards Marie at an angle akin to the Leaning Tower of Pisa, risking a seventy-percent chance of being swept off her feet by the mistral and deposited across the sea in Algeria.

"If it's for my benefit, I'm fine to stay a little longer, you know," Vlora spoke quietly, to avoid little prying ears and sat down on an uncomfortable honeycomb rock next to Marie.

"Thanks. Actually, I was worried about Romain. The wind's no good for him."

"How so?" wondered Vlora.

"It'll make him cough, sometimes worse. And he doesn't always respond well to regular asthma treatments. So, it's best to avoid it."

"Poor lad." Vlora rubbed her upper arms as if the thought gave her the chill. Or, more likely, she was just cold. "Romain's a lovely child.... You did well by him."

That came out of nowhere, thought Marie, bracing herself for a 'but'. As it did not come, Marie murmured a self-conscious "thanks."

"Yep. You're a good mum…" Vlora added as if to herself, looking at her foot "… A very decent person all round."

A charged silence settled. Marie shifted her sitting position on the prickly rock.

"Has it caused him any problem at school? You know, with sports and all that." Vlora queried tentatively.

"No… I don't know… I hope not. He doesn't tell me much, and I'm so bloody busy all the time." Marie started to peel inexistent cuticles.

Vlora nodded empathetically.

"I worry about him. His health's one thing. But where we live…" Marie shook her head. "… I mean, it'd be so easy for him to mix with the wrong crowd… And without a dad…" She trailed off. "I need to get him out of there."

Vlora carried on nodding, like one of those nodding dogs. "Hmm. And, his size won't help either."

"What do you mean?"

"Well, he's small for a nine-year-old, isn't he?"

"Romain's only six. Turning seven next month," Marie replied, perturbed by her mum's confusion on Romain's age despite living with them for a couple of weeks.

"Oh, right."

"Anyway, it's just…" Marie sighed heavily. "I worry."

"Of course. It isn't ideal."

Once her relationship with Dr. Edgy-Shoes was more established, Marie hoped that he would love Romain and they would form a family unit of sorts. She wished they could just get on with it. Annoyingly, Dr. Edgy-Shoes only had time to share a couple of whirlwind coffee breaks since their first date. She didn't hold it against him, though. She of all people knew he had to work incredibly long hours. Yet, she had hoped for more by now. She sent him another doting text message, urging him to see her.

"Have you given some thought about what you'd like for your birthday?" Vlora enquired.

Marie looked at her mum, confounded, having never received a birthday gift from her. Birthdays did not bring the best of childhood memories to mind. For instance, when Marie turned eight, Fatos had a muffled argument with Vlora when her mum brought out Marie's pink birthday cake. As Marie brought a slice of the cake to her mouth, Fatos pushed her hand against her face and emitted a series of pig's grunts, pink icing covering her small nose, quivering chin and lips.

"I, ah, don't need anything. But, thanks for the thought," Marie finally mustered.

"I intended to buy you a new phone. One with a good camera."

"No-oh. One of those would cost you an arm and a leg. Where would you find that kind of money?"

"I've started working shifts at a café-tabac."

Okay, that was news to Marie. But good news.

"Well, that money's yours."

"But you're having me stay with you for free. I'd like to give something back. Show my appreciation and support." Vlora looked down at her knitted arms wrapped around herself for warmth.

"Well, in that case, you could write a cheque for Romain. I haven't been able to set anything aside for him so far. That would be the best birthday present I could ever wish for."

"Sure. Done." After a moment, Vlora cleared her throat. "And... hmm. Have you given it some thought?" she asked Marie tentatively.

"Given what some thought?"

"Will you come with me... to see him?"

Oh, so her questions about Romain and her birthday had actually been a preamble to what really was of concern to her...

Marie laced her fingers together. She stared at Romain bossing around a toddler-cum-assistant. Hands on his hips and rolling eyes, Romain took his role of pyramid-foreman very seriously. With the wind spraying fine cottony droplets of the sea in the background and his blond hair sweeping in all directions, there was an air of a Viking wilding about him. But going back to Vlora's question, did she want to visit her estranged father in prison? Well, no. The fact that he was in jail was not the issue. If anything, rather guiltily, Marie felt a pull of curiosity at setting foot in there.

Marie let out a sigh. "Maybe."

"Okay." Vlora nodded energetically.

"I'll need to give it some thought."

"Okay."

"Okay." Marie concluded their ping-pong of Okays.

More nodding. Then, silence.

"Maybe, I could look after Romain for you today when you're at work?" Vlora offered.

More silence filled by the smashing of waves against the rocky shore.

Marie rubbed her face with the palm of her hands. The offer seemed surreal, even though Vlora was Romain's grandmother.

"Alright," Marie asserted with a knot of apprehension settling in the pit of her stomach.

∞

At 7:00 pm, Marie hopped onto bus A30. The bus wound past motorways, factories, and unofficial rubbish tips that had sprung up where padlocks proved a scant deterrent to determined fly-tippers. After a short walk, she reached home, located on camp Saint Pierre, infamous for its noise and odour. Yet, it was still a step up from the camps that formed her childhood memories. The sort of illegal makeshift camps packed with ramshackle huts made from litter and roofs weighted down with tyres.

A little boy and his big brother loitered near her home. Once they caught sight of her gaze, they became immediately restless, gawking at this and that as if they had been standing in the wind, next to litter and dog poo, for touristic purposes.

"Hey, Dr. Quinn medicine woman," quipped the big brother, in a 'fancy-seeing-you-here' kind of way. Marie chuckled inwardly wondering where he had picked up his quaint reference from.

"Hello, Hamed," Marie greeted Hamed with a kiss on both cheeks, before crouching down to be at eye level with his little brother, Samir. "What's happened to you, sweetheart?"

His lips firmly sealed, Samir carried on holding a bloodied paper towel against his knee and shin bone, eyes to the ground. Hamed nudged his little brother.

"I fell off my horse," Samir grumbled.

The insolent reply sparked off a slap to the back of the head by Hamed, immediately followed by a whack from Samir.

"Oye, knock it off, boys," Marie ordered gently, a hand pressed against Hamed's torso.

Hamed gave Samir a scolding glare. Reciprocated by the little brother, the way yapping dogs do when emboldened by their owner's presence.

"He stuck his nose where it didn't belong, is what's happened," Hamed mumbled.

"Never mind what happened." She had learnt that it was often better not knowing, anyway. "Samir. Let me take a look at your leg." Samir winced as Marie peeled off the bloodied swab of paper towel. "It'll need stitches. Come on in."

The boys took off their dusty trainers at the door of Marie's as if entering a temple.

Inside the narrow trailer, where the heater barely worked, the fierce mistral wind buffeted against the aluminium walls, rattling anything that hung by a hook. There was no sign of Romain nor Vlora, they were not there, Marie noted.

"Can you boil some water for me?" Marie requested.

Hamed promptly rose from the threadbare sofa-bench. "The stove isn't working," he informed.

Zut. Marie had to make a choice this month between paying the land rent, the service charges, and the instalment on their new fridge, her loan repayment or the electricity bill. She could not remember which one she had decided to skip in the end.

"Next-door must be having a shower. Can you be a sweetheart and reset the power charge? Ours is to the right." Fingers crossed.

In two steps, Hamed had the entrance door opened, holding it firmly so that it did not bang against Marie's small vegetable patch outside.

It startled Amina, another neighbour, who was about to knock on it. The infant in her arms started to cry.

"Shhhhh," Amina soothed, before shoving her little finger into the new-born's mouth. It worked. Amina pointed with her head at an Aldi carrier bag to Hamed before shouting out to Marie. "Bibi baked you barazeks, to thank you for yesterday."

"Sounds yummy. Thanks," Marie cried back, a needle wedged between her lips. On another positive note, the electricity had come back on again. Yeah.

As Marie saw the two brothers out, the widow next-door was out in her garden, well, a square of AstroTurf bordered by a knee-high white plastic fence. The nimble woman was fixing an old-fashioned watering can onto the flimsy aluminium wall of her mobile home, next to her front door. The watering can had a lightbulb inside it, so once switched on it looked like light was pouring out onto her. Kitsch, but clever. Marie raised her arm in acknowledgement, but her neighbour was too preoccupied with her home improvement to notice her. As far as neighbours went, the old woman was alright, quiet as a mouse. Actually, the whole camp was mostly quiet this time of year. Unlike in the summer months when it gets invaded by hordes of tourists, partying all night on rosé, littering the communal bathroom with tampons, and making the whole place reek of grilled meat night 'til dawn. Yet, if their beach towel went missing, their sunburnt fingers would immediately turn on the permanent residents.

Down the curved alley, Marie noticed the familiar snow-white skin and shock of blond curls bobbing towards her. Her six-year-old son walked towards their trailer, passing to the right a group of teenagers chasing another group with pieces of wood with nails poking out of them. Future patients no doubt. Romain kept his head down, holding a folded piece of paper in his hand.

"This for you." Romain handed Marie the piece of paper. Marie waved at Lavina, standing in the doorway of her own trailer, to confirm his safe landing.

Lowering her gaze to the drawing in hand, Marie pondered. Colourful cats with elongated bodies? Hearts? An alt-modern-figurative-expressionist rendition of the universal paradigm of life? ...It had to be the latter, right?

"Awww, thank you, Romalovely. I love it. Where's Vlora?" wondered Marie, her arms wrapped around Romain in an unrestrained bear-like embrace.

"Dunno."

"Didn't you spend the rest of the day with her?"

"No, she left me with Lavina and Timo."

Marie was surprised, not that Vlora did not honour her engagement, but by the depth of her disappointment in her mum.

"Oh. Alright. So, what did the three of you get up to?" The words struggled to pass through the lump in her throat.

63

They did nothing, heard nothing, saw no one, all day, apparently. Now, reading anything proverbial about Romain's monkey-see-hear-speak-no-evil approach to life would be a mistake. He was not an early adopter to a gang's style code of silence, either.

Though looking at him playing with his WWE figures with such gusto on his bed might have given you a different impression.

"Teeth first, mister," Marie directed.

"No time for that. I'm on a mission." Romain pulled the little curtains separating his bed from the kitchen-lounge-dining area closed.

"What kind of mission?" Marie re-opened his curtains.

"I'm an invisible spy, protecting us against monsters."

See maman, you're missing out on quality time with your only grandson. Just like you did with your only daughter…

"Well, they may not be able to see you, but they sure will smell you, if you don't brush your teeth."

Yep, this counterargument made sense to him.

He was smart, which was great, and he knew that chatting after story-time would let him stay up longer. So, Marie lingered. As it turned out, he learned about the digestive system from Pépé, his great-grandfather. Timo, Romain's cousin-slash-best-friend, never passed him the ball when they played football with the others, 'so unfair'. But, Aunty Lavina played the guitar in the evening, so all was good in the world. And like a superhero with narcolepsy for a superpower, Romain dozed off halfway through reeling of his aunt's playlist.

The following morning, the little boy found a gift, wrapped and addressed to him from Vlora on the table as if Santa had left it there himself. Given its shape and size, Marie readied herself to give Romain a brief lecture about the value of money and how they should return this expensive phone in favour of a savings account. Marie was a little miffed at her mum for putting her in this position, however, she also recognised that it was an incredibly generous gift and it had been a little unfair of her to suggest a cheque. What six-year-old would get excited about a cheque, eh? After eagerly unwrapping the gift, a pair of socks with shiny patterns of bats and masks was unveiled. Oh. Romain beamed while Marie thought some things never changed.

Chapter 11

"The blumin' thing"

London, United Kingdom
Seven years ago, December 2009

Thursday morning was as expected. Eyes dropped to mugs as Benedict walked past the communal areas in the office. Even Laure had joined the trend. He was not greeted with her usual nod as he passed her desk. By lunchtime, she still had not addressed him verbally but fired over to him dozens of passive-aggressive emails instead. Nearing the end of the day, Benedict sent her an email, in which he urged his secretary to send herself an extravagantly expensive gift from him, as an attempt at a ceasefire.

"A Lamborghini then," she shouted, without lifting her eyes from the form she was filling out.

"The instruction manual comes in Italian only, I'm afraid."

Laure walked over and handed Benedict a contract requiring his signature.

"Oh well, never mind. I'll think of something else," she offered with a reconciliatory smirk.

"In all seriousness, please do." Benedict's voice conveyed an unprecedented level of qualms.

Laure nodded. She was studying him with a touching level of concern. "You haven't seemed yourself lately... Is everything okay?"

Silence.

She lingered. He grabbed a pencil and began to swivel its pointy end against his glass desk.

"I've lost my mother," he eventually uttered, his eyes never leaving the pencil. "Her funeral was on Tuesday."

Why did I just say that? He suddenly felt like one of those abusive husbands, who tried to justify their bad behaviour through seeking sympathy. Except, Laure was neither his wife nor his shrink.

"My goodness, Benedict. I'm so incredibly sorry to hear that." Laure walked back to his desk and crouched down. Her hand rested on his arm. He flinched. Would she use this information to

65

her advantage at a later point? His face closed up. "Why didn't you say something? Why did you come to the party?"

Benedict was not comfortable discussing this any further. "Anyway. Hmm, please send a gift from me to your boyfriend as well," Benedict blurted out shifting his arm from under her comforting hand.

Laure looked puzzled. "What boyfriend?"

"The chap who escorted me out and into a taxi the other night?"

"Oh, that's just Yoki. We're not together. He's a friend I met at a sculpture workshop."

"Sorry, I assumed..." Benedict never knew Laure was into sculpting. Actually, thinking about it, he did not know much about his secretary's life, despite spending the most substantial part of the past five years in her company. "Well, it doesn't change things. I'm pretty sure I punched him and... well, you know. Just send him whatever."

She giggled. "Like I have time for a boyfriend with the hours I work for you. I'm not sure he even noticed your punch in the melee, to be honest." He gave her a look. "But sure, I'll send him something lavish on your behalf", she exited the room knowing better than to argue with him.

∞

A few days later, a large delivery man with a red potato for a nose headed straight to Benedict's office. Laure was not at her desk, so he knocked on Benedict's glass door. But not waiting for an invitation, he barged in with one of those sideless trolleys.

A heavily tattooed hand held out a form on a clipboard to Benedict. "Sign here, mate."

A smallish parcel was unloaded onto his desk with a reverberating 'plonk.'

"Watch your back with this one, mate. 'Tis blumin' heavy."

"Are you sure you've got the right person?"

"You Benedict Grant?" The stumpy tattooed hand pointed at Benedict's name on the door then at the name on the parcel.

Benedict nodded.

"Then, there you go." As he was leaving, he turned his head around, waving at Benedict's name on the door again. "Your mum must have a thing for eggs, innit?"

Benedict raised an eyebrow.

"Benedict." He raised the palm of his hands in the air before adding, "Eggs Benedict, innit?" This triggered a barking raucous laugh forged by a packet a day. Benedict could still hear him chortling away half-way down the corridor, whilst wondering what his birth name was.

The burly man was right. The thing was blumin' heavy. It did not look any bigger than a box of cereal. Still, Benedict reckoned it must weigh half his own body weight.

There was no name or address on the parcel that indicated who sent it. The laminated invoice read, '10" dia bronze disc - £2,180.22'. What the heck was this?

And then it dawned on him. Laure had met her escort from the other night at a sculpture workshop. But there was no note in the box or stuck to the outer case. Nothing that said, *'I appreciate the gesture. Thank you for your bountiful generosity, and the thought put into it But I can't possibly accept this gift. P.S. You're not as much the asshole I took you to be the other night. Have a great life.'* Anyone decent would have left something along those lines, right? Admittedly, not in these exact words, but still. There only was a sticker, highlighting the fact that he paid £80 to post the blumin' thing. What a prick.

"What's this?" quizzed Laure, dropping her handbag on her desk.

"My guess. Your pal returned his gift."

Laure took a few steps in and caught a glimpse of the bronze cylinder inside the cardboard box. There was no attempt to lift it on her part.

"Hmm. Looks like it. But that's strange, that's not the company I ordered it from. Is there a note?"

"I haven't had time to check."

Laure rummaged through the box. Nothing.

"Yukinobu Wada!" she exclaimed, hands on her hips, using a weird disapproving playful tone as if this guy was her toddler, and she caught him fingering a tub of Nutella. "I'm surprised, Benedict. Yoki's usually so polite, painfully so."

Makes an exception for some, he thought.

"I'm happy for you to keep it. If you want it," Benedict offered.

Laure did not hear the irritation in his voice such was her excitement at the generous offer for her to keep it.

The rest of the day went exceptionally well. Benedict closed a deal that trivialised all others done that year. It would swell his bank balance grotesquely. Yet, for some inane reason, his mind kept going back to the returned gift. How rude. He thought of Diane. She had been maintaining radio silence since the funeral. Well, not exactly since the funeral, it was since his call after his office Christmas' party. But he did not want to think about that… He sent her a 'what's up' text message a couple of days ago. Yet, nothing. Admittedly not a particularly eloquent message, it undoubtedly justified a response to a grieving close friend, right? Even if said close friend had said deeply regrettable things to her. He cringed. Actually, forced to think of it, Benedict realised that the only contact, whether virtual or actual, he had had with people that week were all through work.

Benedict felt like he could hear Yukinobu cackle at him through the streets of London. The cheek on this guy to return his gift. Tapping on his keyboard as if his fingers were drumsticks, Benedict discovered that Yukinobu was a pretty prevalent Japanese name, adding Wada next to it did not help the matter much. So, Benedict kept expanding his search. Eventually, a solemn photo of Yukinobu stared back at him, as if defying him. There were a few others. One grabbed his attention, so he enlarged it. Yukinobu was at an art gallery, wearing a t-shirt with a picture of a Japanese flag peeling off to reveal a rainbow flag underneath. It would appear that as well as being a budding sculptor, Yukinobu Wada was a martial arts instructor. Without noticing it this internet sleuthing was proving an excellent way to stick a fork into Benedict's indignation. Yukinobu's dojo was in Benedict's neighbourhood. Benedict had inhabited it for half a decade. And yet, he had never seen that guy in his life before the Christmas party. Although, it was not like he took much interest in the people around him or even in his neighbourhood. So, maybe it was hardly that surprising that Yukinobu's existence had gone unnoticed despite being under his nose.

Benedict's search revealed that Yukinobu's next Aikido class was at 8:00 pm, half an hour from now. Before thinking it through, Benedict was stomping off down the corridor. He waved goodbye to Laure, who looked surprised to see him leave so early. Well, not exactly early *per se*, but early for him.

A series of grunts could be heard from the other side of the door. What Benedict intended to achieve or say to this guy was still unclear. Between his mother's revelation and work, on his high-speed journey over here his mind had not spared him much time towards his complaint with Yukinobu. Yet, Benedict's irrational irritation had propelled him forward into the dojo. He let the door slam behind him and for a moment, over a dozen pair of eyes focused on him. 'What are you looking at?' instinctively ran through his mind, although, probably wisely as he faced a room full of trainee martial artists, he refrained from giving voice to his thoughts.

As his stare met Yukinobu's unreadable gaze, he became even more acutely aware that he was not even sure what had brought him here in the first place. A vision of himself, tapping on Yukinobu's shoulder and petulantly saying 'why didn't you like the gift I had my secretary send on my behalf? It's so unfair!' sprung to mind. So, he just stood there, looking cross and... well, dumb; the way people do when muttering angrily to themselves while peering at the station monitor that has notified them of a delay to their service.

Yukinobu came to him once he had paired up his students in an exercise. The grunting resumed, echoing against the mirrored walls.

"Ben, am I right?"

"Benedict," he corrected unnecessarily, with embarrassing childish pettiness.

"Welcome, Benedict. Have you done Aikido or any other martial arts before?" His English was accented with a slight clip of his original Japanese intonations. Its cadence sounded efficient and reassuring, like the staccato of a Swiss clock.

"No." Benedict crossed his arms. And why was his sporting history any of this guy's business?

"Alright, that's not a problem. Are you interested in joining the class, or would you rather just watch?"

Neither. I came here to... Well, I came here to throw a wobbler about a returned gift and tell a perfectly reasonable man the errors of his ways... Argh...

"I'll just watch." Benedict uncrossed his arms... *Yep, it would appear that I came here to watch people dressed in pyjamas grunt loudly...*

Yukinobu nodded in a way that could only be described as a bow. This took Benedict by surprise. He found himself responding involuntarily by head bowing in return. Searching for something in a very wide black sack, Yukinobu came back with a brand-new uniform still folded in its transparent plastic bag. It read "White Kimono size M" on the front.

"In case you change your mind. This is a beginner's class."
Yukinobu held the small package in front of him with both hands
and nodded once. What could Benedict do? Eh? He took the
plastic bag.

"You're welcome among us, any time," Yukinobu added. It
came off weirdly staged.

Inexplicably, it dawned on Benedict that Yukinobu knew
about his interest in men. Something about the Japanese man's
choice of words, his demeanour, his tone of voice, or something
else that would be hard to put into words, or perhaps a
combination of all these. Nevertheless, it was as clear as day, he
knew.

But, how could he? Has he been gaydar-ed? Was that what a
gaydar was? Mind reading, but effective only for one specific
purpose. Benedict had always been a man's man and a boy's boy
before that. He liked bikes, cars, trains, diggers, any sports that
involved kicking a ball... and blue. He was boisterous. His father
often spoke in praise about his adventurous spirit and competitive
nature. It also seemed that when school complained about a fight
in which he partook, his father's reprimands were tinted with
concealed pride. As a teenage boy, his bedroom was draped with
posters of motorbikes. Growing up, he became more and more
into extreme sports. His fleeting girlfriends were more
cheekbones than bum and breasts, yet they had all been
unquestionably beautiful, admittedly with a turnaround to match
his bike's acceleration speed. He was, to the outside, the classic
macho heterosexual alpha male. So, what gave it away? How
could this guy presume he knew this part of him that he even
struggled to admit to himself was there?

Benedict stood there like a flowerpot for a minute. He was not
sure whether he wanted to punch him in the face or put on the
white pyjamas and have a good grunt. Not that Benedict was
afraid, but based on hazy memories from the party, he did not
think the odds of the former working out well for him were in his
favour. So, he put on the kimono and grunted for the next hour.
And he realised it was precisely what he needed; exhausting,
physical, and competitive. In sum, he lost himself to the exercise
and felt better for it.

At the end of the session, he did not mean to linger. Yet, while
everybody was chatting their way to the door, he found himself by
Yukinobu's side. As Yukinobu lifted himself up from his bags,
Benedict felt caught in the limelight.

"Weren't keen on the gift, then?" *What?! Why did I just say that?* For the second time tonight, Benedict felt a level of childish embarrassment that he usually strived to produce in others.

Yukinobu gazed at him with those enigmatic eyes of his.

"The gift was very generous, Benedict. Thank you."

Huh?

"Do you not sculpt anymore?"

"I do. Do you also sculpt?"

"Uh, no, I don't..." Why did he find himself discussing his hobbies or lack of it with this guy, again? The tangent this conversation had taken was confusing. "If you do, then why did you return it?" Benedict continued.

"Japanese traditions."

"It's traditional to return gifts in Japan?" Benedict's remark sounded sceptical.

"Yes. In Japan, if you receive a present, you're supposed to give a similar gift in return." Yukinobu nodded again as he imparted the information. There was a disconcertingly gentle way about him.

Aah, thought Benedict, he had not returned his gift, he had reciprocated. And, there he was, getting off his high horse, feeling idiotic about his reaction.

"Well, you're the first guy I punched who rewarded me with a two-thousand-pound gift afterwards." Cringe! Nonetheless, a smile accompanied Yukinobu's nodding response. What was the deal with all this nodding? Anyhow. Back-pedal, quick! "It, uh, made Laure's day, though." Great, and now, you just told him you re-gifted his month-worth of salary's gift to somebody else.

"She's gone back to sculpting?" enquired Yukinobu.

I don't know... "Yes. Would you fancy a drink? I'm paying." The invitation came out of nowhere and in a blur.

Yukinobu hesitated. "I can't, today. Another time maybe? Did you enjoy today's session?"

Benedict was surprised by the strange disappointment he felt at Yukinobu's response. Why would he care whether this over-the-top polite, middle-aged man wanted to go out for a drink with him or not?

"I did. How much do I owe you for it?"

Yukinobu waved it off. "Nothing. Just pay for your next session."

"I, ah." He was not intending to come back, but then again... "Alright, see you next week."

"Maybe not next week?"

"Why's that?"

Yukinobu lifted his bemused face while pulling the strings of his sack. "Christmas."

Benedict nodded, staring blankly, contemplating what his lonely Christmas would be like this year. Not that they celebrated it much in his family, but still. Yukinobu was gazing at him funnily.

The Japanese man glanced at the clock on the dojo wall. "You know what? I have got time for one if you're still game."

They went to a pub two steps away from Yukinobu's dojo, ergo Benedict's house, yet Benedict had never set foot in it before. A cosy, old man's pub with heavily patterned red-ish carpet and dark wood-panelled walls that managed to hold fort amongst its surrounding snooty neighbourhood – like Gaul village holding out against the Romans from the Asterisk stories Benedict had read with his mother as a boy. A warm feeling washing over him for the first time in days. *Good for them,* he thought.

Yukinobu only had time for a couple of sips by the time Benedict brought a second pint to his lips.

"Have you been in the UK for long?"

"Nearly thirty years. I was twenty when I moved here."

"The extent of my life." The comment escaped Benedict, in surprise. It felt like a smug remark though it was a genuine shock. But Yukinobu smiled back. So that meant Yukinobu was nearing fifty. Looking good on it! All the same, he felt it would be better if he changed the subject. "And, ah, have you always been an Aikido instructor?"

"No. I've had many lives," divulged Yukinobu, shaking his head cryptically.

"Cat to the Queen?"

"Uh?" Yukinobu frowned then instantly lightened up. "Ah. Ha. I wish."

"So, what did one do before being paid to kick people?"

"I studied palaeography and art."

"Palaeography?"

"The study of ancient handwriting, its systems, and the deciphering and dating of historical manuscripts."

"Hence the need to kick people in your spare time?"

Yukinobu laughed mutedly. Benedict liked his unassuming manner.

72

"I wish I had known how to kick people then." Yukinobu gave a rueful grin. "I moved to Oxford to complete my studies. I ended up staying and became an art dealer for a time. Then something else..." Yukinobu cleared his throat. "After that, I became interested in martial arts and drifted into private investigation." Yukinobu patted his chest, then side pockets. "PI's my primary job. Teaching martial arts is mostly for fun."

Held in both hands, just like he did before with the plastic-wrapped kimono, Yukinobu handed his business card to Benedict.

"We're only small," Yukinobu added. "It's just me, my partner, and eight others, but we cover everything, both private and business matters. If you ever need us." Although confused by the business-like turn their meeting had taken, Benedict faked interest and grasped Yukinobu's business card.

Benedict wondered what happened to make him pivot from art dealer to martial arts and private investigation, he could sense something in the way Yukinobu had brushed over the transition from one part of his life to another. Yet, he did not dare probe him. He feared his nosiness would not be seen as charmingly un-British. So, although Benedict had hoped for more than just Yukinobu's résumé, he went with the flow and walked him through his own résumé, omitting all the unflattering parts. He dwelled on his academic and professional successes with a false sense of modesty, followed by his hobbies, hinting at his wealthy lifestyle. Why did he want to impress this guy so much? He did not need anyone's approval, least of all from a middle-aged part-time coach.

As he stepped into his home, Benedict threw his keys into a large bowl by the front door. The vast entry hall magnified their clattering against the china. C-cling, c-cling, c-cling. His footsteps echoed throughout his empty, silent house. His home was exactly as it always had been – pristinely clean and tidy. The sort of house that people would look at in lifestyle magazines, browse with envy, and yet struggle to project themselves living in their lifeless perfection. He felt exactly that way about his own home on that day. All in all, and despite Benedict's best attempt, his conversation with Yukinobu had made for a cursory evening. Benedict did not manage to break through Yukinobu's walls. And it bothered him. He always managed to snare people in one way or the other, if he wanted to. So why hadn't it work this time?

He stared at his reflection in a bauble hanging from the tree. His housekeeper had put up the Christmas decorations of her own accord. The menorah was not out though. Maybe she was not sure what it was meant for. Anyway, it was late in the season for all this, with only eight days to go until Christmas and Hanukkah passed. His mother got him Christmassy crystal ornaments a few years back. They strolled the streets of Stratford-upon-Avon on Benedict's birthday when a little crystal crab stared back at her. 'How peculiar,' Rochele observed, claiming that the universe was determined to remind her of her cancer relapse. Until Benedict pointed out that what she took for a crab ornament had a lower part hidden by a decorative grate over the window, which as a whole formed a reindeer. Oh, how they had laughed and laughed, and Rochele bought the whole set. Ever since then, Benedict always got the 'crabs' out for Christmas. But he had not seen the point in doing so this year. In-jokes were great, but only if the person with whom they were shared was still there to impart a smile. Now, it just looked delicate and sophisticated, and like everything else in this house, it was neither warm nor inviting. It even looked intimidating, too expensive to come near it, in case the crystal broke. It seemed that this was what the festive season would be like from now on, intimidating.

Sitting at the bar of his kitchen island, Benedict stared vacantly at the food on display. The perfectly positioned bread and fruits looked almost artificial. His thoughts took him to weird, dark corners. His existence made no odds to anyone. But then, on a plus note, he would make an ideal MI5 candidate; no attachments, a forgettable face, no significant ethical inhibitions, an above-average intellect and multilingual with a nerd-breaking level of knowledge of all things James Bond-ish.

He set aside his hunger for a second, aware that he would probably fill his empty stomach with booze. He flicked open his laptop instead.

Now, how did the average, adopted John and Jane Doe of this world trace their birth parents and twin sibling? Obviously, contacting adoption registrar or post-adoption centres would be all but redundant.

His mother had obviously been extremely artful at concealing her crime, his birth certificate and history indicated nothing outside of the norm. According to the law, Benedict Grant was just that. A Grant, born at home, in London England, son of Aaron and Rochele. There was, obviously, no record of the transaction his parents made thirty years ago. The only pieces of information he had to go by were written in his mother's letter. And they did not add up to much.

He was born either in Southern France or North-West Italy. And assuming his birth date was relatively accurate, give or take a week, about 14,500 babies were born in France during that time and roughly 9,500 in Italy. But it could be assumed that only a tenth of those births would be located in the regions of Southern France and North-West Italy. So, it was down to circa 2,400. Still, not a great start.

But he was one of two, and as it turned out, twins accounted for just under one and a half percent of births. And presumably, roughly two-thirds of these would have a male in its set. So that brought him down to about twenty-four births. Now that was a more manageable number. Although they still had to be found.

Also, he had been born from a young woman, perhaps even a teenager. And from what he could gather, thirty years ago, mothers giving birth at twenty-five or below accounted for only about sixteen percent of the population in France and Italy. Hence, this should, in theory, narrow his find to only three or four sets of twins.

Okay, but how would he go about finding these statistically relevant three to four births out of twenty-four thousand?

Benedict leaned against the back of his barstool and grabbed a shiny apple off a perfect pile in a Murano glass bowl. He stared at his screen again, rubbing his chin. It was late, but his mind was still racing through probabilities and statistics. It will take an enormous amount of time and several trips to France and Italy to collect all this data. He would need help. Perhaps, the sort of help a private investigator could provide.

Chapter 12

"Good ol' Saturday night in A&E"

Marseille, France
Seven years ago, December 2009

In her effort to dodge the projectile vomit spraying like a fountain from a child, Marie nearly walked straight into a stretcher carrying a young man with a thirty-six-inch fire poker sticking out of his biceps.

"Hand and head injury," Marie read out-loud from her clipboard, as she entered the curtain-walled cubicle of her next patient. "Thank you for wai…"

Marie froze at the sight of the patient. He was the spitting image of Baul – Bohemian, dark-haired, golden skin. In fact, he might even be a better-looking reincarnation of Romain's dad. She felt her grip tightening on her clipboard. He was wearing a white tank top and uniform-type trousers with clumpy boots. Armed forces? No, they all had short hair, didn't they? His was not. Policeman, maybe? Thinking about it, Marie had seen many patients in uniform that evening, more than usual anyway.

"…ting…" She eventually finished her sentence. She felt her cheeks grow pink. So, following a line of action renowned for its efficiency, Marie did her best ostrich impression, lowering her eyes away from his bare arms and fixing them onto her clipboard. "Hmm, Officer Paoli?" She read from his form, vigorously tapping the tip of her finger against his name as if to prove a crucial point. What point? That she really was a nurse and not some random woman looking for an excuse to talk to distractingly attractive men? An inaudible groan of embarrassment echoed around her mind.

"Please call me Giandomenico… and you are?" His Italian accent had the deep purr of a fine-tuned Ferrari engine, which, combined with his silky voice, made for a delightful melody. Yet, it threw her a little. Despite having a very Italian sounding name, perhaps the most Italian sounding name in the history of the world and neighbouring planets, Marie had expected him to sound more like Baul. Well, no, she had expected him to sound, precisely, like Baul. His accent was supposed to have a hint of Marseille on a dollop of Romani gipsy. Not Italian. Nonetheless a hot accent, to her ear.

"Ah, uh, Marie. I'm, ah, Nurse Marie. So, uh, you may call me that. Marie." Smooth. Not.

She could barely look at him even though she craved to stare, so she pointed at the nametag on her chest instead.

"Nice," he declared.

Silence.

As Giandomenico realised where his stare had lingered, he hurriedly added. "Nice name. Marie. I like the name, Marie." This made them both laughed. She could finally relax. Lewd looks would usually make her feel uncomfortable. But she realised she quite liked his gaze, welcomed it even. It flattered her sense of femininity and objectively she knew she was ordinary looking, so it felt nice not to be completely invisible once in a while.

She checked his blood pressure, directed a small light into his brown eyes, asked a few medical questions and refrained herself from pouncing on him as she lifted his top up to listen to his heartbeat. Oh, there it was, a heartbeat. So, he wasn't a figment of my imagination after all then.

A doctor, nicknamed by the hospital staff as Dr. Apocalypse, came in, exchanged a few words with Marie, took her notes then proceeded to conduct further examinations.

Meanwhile, Giandomenico remained quiet. There was a charm to his quietude. He gave the impression that he was silently appraising her. And, she wished, really wished, that she could hear his thoughts. She did not feel any inclination to ask direct questions, though, not by a long shot. No, she wanted to find out what he thought of her, and whether the attraction was mutual, without him knowing that she knew what he may have wanted her to know. Easy, right? This was not the first time this desire for telepathic powers had struck her, and inevitably it had been in conjunction with desire for certain men. The type of men that she could, maybe would, even though she probably should not, fall for. Anyway, how could you fail to fall for someone with an Italian accent, an enigmatic gaze, and Bohemian hair?

"No concussion. The cut on your head won't require stitches, and your hand is just badly bruised. A bandage will help decrease the swelling," Dr. Apocalypse concluded, then nodded to Marie with his hands clasped behind his back as if instructing her to proceed and just left.

"Okay." Marie nodded to herself.

Giandomenico smiled at Marie. Why did he smile? Could he have sensed her agitation? Was he trying to comfort her with a pity-smile?... Oh. Perhaps he was just happy to hear that he did not have a concussion or any broken fingers.

"What happened?"

"I was working on a case," he responded vaguely.

"In Marseille?"

"In Marseille."

Why was an Italian Officer working on a case in Marseille? Would it be too nosy to ask? Though, did she really care to know... Could she ask him whether he had a girlfriend instead? Maybe not entirely professional.

"Hmm. And how did you injure yourself?"

"The bistro was down to one ham and cheese baguette and filled with hungry Frenchmen. 'Twas tough, but victory was tasty."

She was put off her stride for a moment before she realised that he was joking.

"Haha." Idiotic laugh, but nice save anyway. "And was it worth the effort?"

"Absolutely. French cuisine and French men in revolt. The full experience, eh?"

"Not quite." But she was not going to think about some of the obvious things the French were also famous for. No, she wasn't. "Kneading dough and grunting for freedom aren't the only things the French are good at, you know." Oh, it had been too tempting to resist, but she immediately regretted her attempt at double entendre... Too crude. No class. Men liked sophistication. Didn't they? Though, why should she care whether he wanted class or sophistication? She could not flirt with patients. She should not flirt with patients, should she? And, two people in uniform flirting was way too much of a cliché, wasn't it? Besides, her heart was set on Dr. Edgy-Shoes, was it not? He had been playing hard to get, though, which had been upsetting.

But, Giandomenico grinned like a Cheshire cat. Actually, there was nothing wrong with having a bit of fun, uniform or not, Dr. Edgy-Shoes or not. Window shopping, not shoplifting so to speak.

"You're referring to the very reputable French medical care, I presume," he quipped with a seductive undertone.

"What else?"

Marie finished bandaging Giandomenico's hand.

"I have to admit, I felt in good hands the minute I saw you, Nurse Marie."

"Why, thank you, Officer Paoli."

She smiled then looked at her watch clipped to her breast pocket. She ought to have left his cubicle by now. As she lifted her gaze back up, Giandomenico wore the same flustered teenager's expression as he did when she pointed at her named badge earlier. It amused and flattered her again. Okay, so based on the national reputation, he was as Italian as Italian could be. Whatever that meant.

"Can I ask you a question?"

Marie's heart skipped a beat. "Shoot," she muttered.

He leaned a little closer to her ear, which made her heart skip one more time. "What's the deal with the doctor who examined me?" His whisper had a jokey undertone.

She laughed a lot louder than it called for. "So, you've noticed. It took you nowhere near as long as the rest of us."

"I'm in the right field of work, then?"

"Yep, I'd have you in my team… Well, you know. If I worked for the police… And if I were your superior… And we had the budget for a new recruit…" *Argh, make it stop…*

He placed a hand on his heart and did a little bow with his head.

"Well, I'd much rather take orders from you than my pocket rocket of a boss. So, what's up with Doc?"

"I must say he's lovely, really. And an excellent doctor. He's just… eccentric."

"How so?"

"At a social event after a couple of glasses of wine he recently shared the fact that one of his motivators in joining the medical profession was to do with a theory he had on the possibility of an apocalypse. All based on sound science, obviously…"

"As one does." Giandomenico smiled, and their complicity felt a lot cosier than it absolutely ought to have done. He was the type of man who got laid a lot, Marie thought. The sort who could, therefore, afford to play with their food, the way fat orcas played with a seal before completing the kill.

"Well, I'm all done here." Marie collected her clipboard back. "Hope you feel better soon… And try not to rub many Frenchmen up the wrong way over baguettes again." Innuendo bingo, here she was again. Yet, this time, she owned it. No regrets.

He let out an Italian laugh. A sexy laugh.

"I'll try not to."

"Your level of French is excellent by the way."

"I've had a good teacher." He smiled in a bittersweet way that Marie could not quite understand. "I could do with improving my vocabulary, though. If I had the time."

"You could sign up to one of those word-a-day app thingies."

"Yes, I suppose I could. Thanks for the tip… And Nurse Marie…" He paused and looked bashful. The way they did in a romcom, after a jokey-flirty exchange, right before asking somebody out. Would she have wanted that? Maybe. Yes. Definitely, yes. Yes, yes, yes.

"… It was nice meeting you."

And that was it. Humph.

Once in the corridor, she checked her phone for signs of text messages from Dr. Edgy-Shoes. There was none. She then looked down at the patient notes, at the top of the page read a phone number starting with +39.

Chapter 13

"Ciao Bello"

Rome, Italy
Seven years ago, December 2009

Giandomenico's chief had been speaking to the press all week about last Saturday's arrests. The investigation had lasted years and spanned three countries leading to the arrest of Ditmir Petrioni, the head of the Mapula organised crime group, and an army of crooks linked in one way or the other to the Mapula's many trades. But this day was his. Giandomenico was receiving his promotion to the rank of Marshal. Everybody had been gathered in the precinct's main meeting room to hear his praise. It felt as though Giandomenico had been waiting for this moment his whole life. Yet, it did not feel as blissful as anticipated. It could not. His freshly dry-cleaned uniform felt very itchy, particularly around his you-know-where area, to the point of agony, though, his threshold for discomfort was low. Alas, it was hard to reach a satisfactory level of relief through the private and surreptitious use of his pockets. No, what he needed was a quick scratch in a fashion more akin to Baloo the bear than an upcoming star of the force.

Hence, Giandomenico registered only snippets of his Chief's speech. "… Giandomenico's significant contribution…" scratch through his pocket "… the dismantling of the main arms trafficking operation in Southern Europe" peep at the people in the room "… Marseille port…" subtle friction movement of his thighs "… deserving, capable officer…".

Applause.

Yes! Nearly over. God, he would never have expected that 'curtain' would be his favourite part of this particular gig. Life chooses funny moments to remind us that we, humans, are animals after all, with physical needs, urges and small yet all-encompassing problems like the rest of the natural world. Some of these needs may very well be at the bottom of the pyramid of needs for some self-important thinkers. Yet, they felt dominant right in the instant, even amid the most significant 'self-actualisation' moment in Giandomenico's existence. Or would a promotion be part of the 'esteem' need? He could not remember. Actually, he was not even sure whether he understood its principles correctly. Gosh, this suit was so itchy! Anyway, this got him wondering how many people in the room were genuinely listening to the Chief's words right then. Undoubtedly, the majority were pondering what they would have for dinner tonight, or if they remembered to clean the cat's litter tray before leaving the house.

∞

She was ten minutes late, which, by her standards, meant that she was about an hour early. It also meant that Giandomenico had been sitting at the café for a quarter of an hour watching the world go by. During that limited window of time, he fell in love. No *boffola*, love at first sight. He had never fallen so hard and fast before. She was foreign and the most fetching creature he had ever set eyes upon. Her very presence on the piazza offended people from the get-go. But Giandomenico was mesmerised.

She had everything going for her, that classic look, minimalist style, and muscular stance. Bellissima. She was a triumph. A Triumph 1200cc Bonneville Bobber that is, the latest in a long line of Triumph Bobbers stretching back to the 1940s. A thing of beauty, before angry café managers ousted her and her lucky owner, Giandomenico had his photo taken next to her. Perhaps one day he would treat himself to one he daydreamed about.

Anyway, back to his date, she was not apologetic about those ten minutes, why should she be, considering it was early for her. And she looked radiant, objectively beautiful. Being an old fashion geezer and always aware of his surroundings, Giandomenico spotted her from across Piazza Navona, despite the Triumph distraction. She immediately stood out as a local, amongst the ebb and flow of tourists. Regardless of the hot winter day, she was tightly wrapped up in an oversized furry grey coat, short enough to show off her slender legs. Her long shiny black hair rippled behind her as she trotted on high heels. She had the sort of gait that captivated people's attention and turned heads, regardless of their gender.

Giandomenico pulled out her chair, but she was not in a hurry to sit down. She placed one hand on his arm, the other around his neck and gave him a hearty kiss. She pulled away to take a good look at him, flashing her dazzling smile at him. Her red lipstick had smeared a bit from the kiss, and her large sunglasses had left two little pink dents where they sat on across her nose. She looked lovely. As her gaze rested on the glass of Prosecco on her side of the table, she tenderly stroked his cheek. He had done well.

"Ciao, love," she greeted in a gravelly voice.

"Ciao."

"I'm so pleased to see you." She squeezed his hand lovingly while placing her phone on the table.

"And I, you." The flashing light on her phone was beeping.

"How's everything, Doni?"

"Not bad."

"How was your week?" she asked distractedly, phone in hands.

"Mama, stop fiddling with your phone, will you!"

The somewhat teenage-ish, resentful, crabby irritation he often felt in her presence suddenly bubbled up to the surface. He had vowed to himself that he would put a lead on it from now on, but it managed to escape his grasp again, despite his best effort not to let it.

"I'm so sorry, love. It'll only take a minute. I promise." Giandomenico's mother just raised a finger to indicate that it was essential that she replied to her text messages right there and then. "The girls are coming over tonight, but Monica's dog has diarrhoea, and you know what Matteo's like. A nightmare."

"Is Matteo her dog?"

"No-oh. Matteo's Monica's boyfriend. You've met Matteo a few times, haven't you?"

"Nope."

"Anyway, he leaves his dirty clothes everywhere. So, of course, the dog ate one of his socks. So, Matteo's the one who caused all that mess, really. But of course, he's got no intention of looking after the dog tonight and giving Monica a break from all this. Very selfish, if you ask me."

"I'd say, dump him and dungarees."

"Very funny, Doni," she remarked sarcastically, before groaning. "Actually, it's terrible," she suddenly understood the *dung*-arees part. "But apropos, considering," she conceded with a smile and a roll of eyes.

"Anyway, can a dog get diarrhoea from chewing on a dirty sock?"

"O'course, they can."

Really? Anyway, who cared? He took the phone from her hands and chucked it into her oversized handbag. They childishly tugged on her bag for a couple of seconds until she let go, a pack of cigarettes in hand, but the phone still in her handbag. Small win.

"Mama, I'd thought you'd quit."

"Of course, I did. For a whole month, then…" She clapped her hands once. "Your papa called in." She vigorously waved her hand with pinched fingertips into the air.

Nope, he was not going to take the bait.

She lit up her cigarette and took a long, savoured drag, then flicked her shiny slick black hair.

Argh… Fuck it.

"What did papa come to see you for?"

"Money, of course. What else? Don't know whether he's dead or alive for three years. *Bastardo*. Then, he comes crawling out of the woodwork, tail between his little legs, whining that he's in debt, asking for a loan." She tutted.

Giandomenico sighed and slacked against the back of his chair. He glared at her. She looked away.

"And did you?"

"What?"

"Lend him money?"

"I, ah, me? No…" She shook her head, stubbing out her cigarette, avoiding his stare.

"How much?"

"H-his house was going to get repossessed. There…"

"How much?"

She lit up another one.

"I did that for you." She pointed at him, the cigarette pinched between her fore and middle fingers. "Sons are liable to their father's debts. You know that, right? I…"

"How. Much?" he reiterated through gritted teeth.

"Fifteen grand."

"Fift… MAMA! Are you out of your flipping mind?" He slapped his lap. Heads turned in their direction. "Where did you even get that kind of money?"

"Oh, you know. Here and there. Savings… *Nonno*'s inheritance."

"I don't bloody believe it. You've spent… No. No, I don't want to discuss this anymore."

There was a long silence. So long in fact, that he had worked out about five alternative ways he could try to get the money back from his father. Even though he knew he would not. He would let them work this one out on their own, like good little independent parents.

Most people understood that, as far as the split of parent to children duties go, it was the parents' responsibility to look after their children in their early-ish years, and that those roles would be reversed later on, much, much, much later on, hopefully. So, teaching one's child to function independently was one of those things that good parents would aim to achieve, right? Well, on that front, it would appear that somehow, Giandomenico's parents had done a particularly great job. Because their parent-child role reversal meant his independence happened much earlier than it should have. If he had to pinpoint when it was, he would probably say the day he stopped his mama nearly burning the house down by repeatedly setting off the smoke alarm to torment his papa. The night before his drunken papa had woken up the whole neighbourhood singing, if you could call it that, into the night air whilst stumbling home. To really cap things off, in his mama's eyes anyway, once he finally managed to get his keys in the door, he promptly peed all over an open umbrella in the hallway whilst giggling and humming loudly to the tune of 'Singing in the Rain'. Ironically, the only song he had chosen not to give flight to lyrics for. It was this final indignity that had prompted his mama's smoke alarm led revenge on his hungover papa. Giandomenico would have been nine, no eight, hold on, no, he was seven, damn.

His papa was full of sorry(s). It was a word that came easily to him. Most people like to hear that word, 'sorry', some even fight for it. Whole nations, as it happens, fight for it. Thinking about it, sorry is the verbal equivalent of a dry cloth. It brushes crumbs off the table. The problem is, when it's something more persistent than just some crumbs, dry cloths, much like 'sorry', do not cut it anymore, tables get smeared, stains are spread, and no amount of cloth-rubbing is effective. Nevertheless, some of us accept the stains, learn to live with them, accommodate the reality of the stained table, cover up the stains sometimes when they have company; but for others, the stained table must go, it turns their stomach merely to look at it. Let's say that despite the multitude of cloth-rubbing, the number of stains left by his papa's 'sorry-go-round' eventually drove Giandomenico's mama to show his papa the door.

During Giandomenico's formative years, his mama worked as a waitress, cleaner, and receptionist for a hotel she later ended up managing. His papa was regularly doing bits and bobs to make it through to their next pay cheques. His mama always shared the money she made, but when his papa got his pay cheques, he would disappear for a few days and come back with nothing. Giandomenico would go to get his cereal in the morning, and his papa would have invariably finished them the night before. His mama would drive him to school, and there would be no petrol left. His papa would say, "but I would never raise a hand to either of you," and that was his excuse for everything. He could rob them of their money, disappear for days, eat all their food and use up all their petrol, but he would never raise a hand to either of them. So, there you go, he was all good, at least in his book.

Any sane person would wonder why his mama did not kick him out sooner, this pisstaking *bastardo*, but he was good in other ways. These other ways did not make up for all of it, but, you know. He brightened up their days when he was there. He showered them with compliments, left tender words written with food on the kitchen table for his mama. He was an epic storyteller, the life and soul of every party, and a happy soul. His love was exuberant while being utterly irresponsible, unreliable, and, well, a total pisstaker.

Giandomenico's fifth birthday was a classic example of what his papa was like as a father. Giandomenico could remember that day as vividly as if it were yesterday. His papa took him to school one Sunday. He said that a surprise awaited his treasured boy there. Giandomenico tried to guess what it might be, pestering his papa with questions the whole way. But not a peep escaped his papa's lips. As they arrived, his papa spread his arms wide and shouted, 'happy birthday.' Giandomenico's friends were all there, in fact, most of the kids from school were there. The entire playground was covered with zany bunting and beautiful lanterns. There were dozens of fun activity stools, a table full of cakes, even a pony. Giandomenico let go of his father's hand. Seconds later, his chin covered with fluff off his pink candy floss, he gave his papa a toothy grin. It was the best birthday party that a five-year-old Giandomenico could have wished for. Until a year later, a now mature six-year-old Giandomenico realised that what his papa had sold to him as his fifth birthday party, had actually been his school Christmas fair. And yet, inexplicably, Giandomenico still loved him for it. The *bastardo*, cheapskate, was inventive and the feelings of joy he had felt at the time had been real, so it was not all bad.

His mama was chewing her nails with her cigarette still wedged between her fingers.

"I was promoted to Marshal today," Giandomenico finally declared, changing the subject.

"Why, that's wonderful! I'm so proud of my baby." She grabbed his face into her hands and kissed him like one would a baby. "Let's call *nonna*."

Before Giandomenico had a chance to protest, his grandmother was on the phone. Her congratulations were profuse, yet, nowhere near as long as his mother's opinion piece on Matteo's responsibility in depriving her friend Monica of a fun night out. His grandmother was living with his mother, so why this could not wait until his mother got home was lost on Giandomenico, but there you go.

"So, is this promotion the reason for my seeing you in the middle of the week?" his mother finally queried, putting her phone down.

"Oh, you know."

"And there I was, thinking you were going to announce your intention to make an honest woman of some lucky lady."

"It'd take more than marriage to make women honest."

"Ooh, ouch. Should I take it that… What's her name, M-something? Ah, yeah, Maelys, isn't up for giving you some tonight?"

"I've got no idea who you're talking about… And anyway, ugh, yuck, mama?"

"Oh, you know exactly who I mean." Yep, he knew exactly who she meant. "Your high school French teacher – do you think I'm stupid or something?"

Maelys had been in his life for fifteen years, on-off.

"How did you know?"

She looked at Giandomenico from above her sunglasses pointedly. "Anyway, why her? You could have a-ny-one you want."

He shrugged.

His mother shook her head, slowly. "You're still chasing after her, aren't you?"

There was silence. Actually, he was seeing Maelys this evening. But this time would be different… She had filed for divorce, you see. So, it could only mean one thing, right? She had finally chosen him over her husband. Hence, Giandomenico was adamant that it would work, this time, but he would not talk about it with his mother.

"Don't you want to get married and have children?"

Giandomenico had been summoned to meet the latest addition in his best friend's life over the weekend. Within minutes of crossing the threshold, a snotty, floppy infant was flung into his arms. Whether he liked it or not, he was made aware of all the latest developments in the life of their bundle of sleep-deprivation-inducing-misery. It was already bad enough that his friends were slowly but surely morphing into ten-pm-curfewers and daytime entertainers. But why did everyone have to assume this should automatically be the kind of life he would aspire to? So, did he want to get married? Maybe. The old romantic in him liked the idea, somewhat… Children? Hmm, not so much. Though, he had learned to keep quiet about not wanting children as whatever his reasons, they were all deemed inherently selfish or bad by people with kids as if his life choices were interpreted as a criticism of theirs.

Could this be the root of his attraction towards older women? Surely not. A psychiatrist would have many theories about Giandomenico. But he was fairly sure it was all a coincidence that the women in his life had always been more senior than him. Maelys was a sculptural nymph, the thought of her always brought his soldier to attention… Actually, putting aside the debasement brought upon by his parents, Maelys could have given him beautiful children, the United Colours of Benetton, mixed heritage kind of way. A perfect blend of Maelys's French-Caribbean caramel glow with Giandomenico's mother's beauty and personality, his father's genes would have to be set aside, too many loose cannons in there. However, for this to be a reality it would have had to happen when Giandomenico was a freshman. And even then, medically speaking, the term 'geriatric mother' would have been used to describe Maelys.

"So, who's coming to yours this evening? Apart from Monica, well, if her dog stops being quite the party-pooper." Another dodge from Giandomenico, in an attempt to keep the conversation civil.

While his mother launched into a lengthy monologue, he felt his pocket vibrate. A text message from a foreign unknown number.

Chapter 14

"Even monkeys fall from trees"

London, United Kingdom
Seven years ago, December 2009

It was bitterly cold out. Yet, Benedict could not bring himself to ring the bell. There was no sign indicating the presence of any kind of firm in this building. Yet, in amongst a list of surnames one of the doorbells said simply '3rd floor'. He was staring at it as someone exited the building. Seizing the opportunity, Benedict sneaked in. Wearing his usual confidence, the distraught-looking man did not question him. He even held the entrance door open for him, as this is how a life of privilege affects others' perceptions. In this instance, it seemed obvious to this man that Benedict was well within his rights to be entering this building.

His balled hand froze in mid-air when the door to the third floor apartment swung open.

"You've forgotten your c..." A petite woman with shiny black hair and a dark-green trench coat draped on her forearm was staring back at him. "Oh, hi. Can I help you?"

Through her frown, Benedict could tell that her brain was trying to compute whether she had already met him before or not. He had one of those faces, and she worked in that line of work.

"I'm here to see Yukinobu Wada."

"Sure. What's your name?"

"Benedict Grant."

"Have you used our services before Mr. Grant?"

"No."

"I'm not sure if Yoki's in. Have you got an appointment?"

"I haven't."

She made a sort of non-descript movement to the receptionist, yet the young guy seemed to understand this non-verbal, barely gestural communication correctly anyway. He sprung up, took the coat off her arm, and sprinted down the stairs to return it to the distraught-looking man.

"Not a problem." She extended her hand and shook his firmly. "I'm Yoki's partner, Prisha Khunt. We work and operate in exactly the same way, and we have been for over twenty years. We conduct high quality, discreet, and cost-effective professional investigations to solve a variety of problems, both private and commercial. Our agents are trained to the highest standards. And we always operate within the law, with our clients' needs as a priority. We could perhaps take your matter into my office." She concluded her well-rounded speech with a commanding sweeping arm movement in a direction, which he could only assume, would take them into her office.

Oh, she was good. But…

"I'd rather speak with Yukinobu. Please."

The receptionist came back in, short of breath.

"Sure, wait here, Mr. Grant." She and the receptionist shared a brief, telepathic exchange again.

"Hi. I'm Fred." He shook hands with Benedict in a disconcertedly clone-like way. "I'll see if I can find Mr. Wada for you. It'll only take a minute."

There were magazines in the newspaper-rack sandwiched between two small armchairs lined up in a pocket-sized reception hall. Amid those dated, battered magazines was a brochure about *Khunt-Wada Investigations*. After an obligatory childish, albeit private giggle at the obvious choice of name ordering for their agency with 'Wad'a'kunt' not really being viable, he read on that they supplied services for presumed infidelity, theft, tracing, and due diligence. Under tracing, they boasted a 98 percent success rate for missing persons and debtors. This somewhat appeased his qualms about his request.

Khunt-Wada Investigations had tracing examples ranging from ex-partners skipping out on owing money or outstanding child maintenance to tracing missing family members. Their most expensive option, Historic Trace, mentioned that '*family history trace also includes overseas traces. Across the team, we are fluent speakers of Hindi, Urdu, Punjabi, Japanese, Korean, French, and German. We endeavour to return the results within ten working days, but please be aware that the older the information, the longer the trace may take.*'

Yukinobu seemed to materialise into the room. If he were surprised to see him, only an expert in reading facial expressions would have been able to interpret it.

"Hello, Benedict."

"Hey. I bet you didn't expect to see my old face again so soon, did you?"

"It's alright. I'm a professional stalker myself."

Ah! So, he might not be a robot after all, Benedict thought, pleasantly surprised.

"Let's go in my office." And there it was, the clone-like handshake, followed by an exact replica of the sweeping arm movement Benedict had seen his partner, Prisha, perform earlier. Maybe they learnt it at Private Investigators School.

The office they stepped into was incredibly stark. The murky grey walls of exposed concrete, as was the modern trend lately, had been left bare. An ugly and idiotic trend in Benedict's opinion, but there you go. His metallic desk was also bare, apart from his opened grey laptop. Next to it, stood a tall and grey rectangular mass; if Benedict had to guess, an oversized safe. In front of his desk, two chairs, behind it a large window, and that was it. Maybe Benedict spoke too soon about Yukinobu's lack of robotic lineage.

"Have you recently moved into this offi… ah, please, leave the door open." Benedict sat on one of the, you've guessed it, metallic grey chairs opposite Yukinobu's desk, which was exactly as uncomfortable as it looked. It felt like it was made of a recycled radiator.

"Hmm, sure…" Yukinobu hesitated but left the door ajar. "No, we've been here twenty-odd years. But Prisha had the space freshened up this year."

"It looks, ah, modern."

Benedict could not help but notice that Yukinobu's fitted suit looked distractingly good on him. He was struggling to picture the body of a nearly fifty-year-old under this suit.

"Thanks. So, what brings you here, Benedict?"

His name sounded better when said with Yukinobu's accent. But that made no odds, Benedict felt unsure about the whole thing. He had since he found himself staring at their office building. Could anybody get straight to the point with something like this?

"Well, ah, it won't be an easy one."

"They never are."

"Ahem." Benedict cleared his throat. "How do you treat confidentiality in your line of business?"

Yukinobu could not help but glance at the opened door. They were alone, and it was after hours, yet he lowered his voice and leaned in over the desk. "Very seriously. As private investigators, we promise confidentiality and discretion to all our clients. Would you like us to sign an NDA?"

"Yes, please."

"Sure, I'll have it sent to your solicitor first thing."

Benedict grabbed his set of keys and stared down as he started to fiddle with them. Perhaps he should just leave.

There was a pause, which Yukinobu did not attempt to fill. Benedict appreciated it, and that was probably what kept him going.

"It's personal… Family business." Benedict tapped the back of his pen against the piece of paper. He knew that a Non-Disclosure Agreement would not be legally binding in his case. "I'll need guarantee of your absolute discretion… I mean, beyond this NDA."

"I see." Yukinobu rested his hands on the desk and knitted his fingers. "You have my word. It's all I can give you. But I can assure you that my word is more reliable than contracts."

"It's my biological parents. I'd like to find out who they are."

Yukinobu nodded, but in a way that spoke of a readjustment of thoughts rather than confirmation. Perhaps this was not what he had anticipated this meeting would be about.

"Have you got a copy of your original birth certificate with you?"

"Well, no, and that's the thing, I won't be able to get one either. At least not the real McCoy."

"Everyone who reaches the age of eighteen has a right to get it."

"Not if their parents bought their child illegally and procured fake documents."

Benedict looked away, unwilling to watch Yukinobu's reaction to his revelation. He glanced at the depressing grey London sky out the window, before lowering his eyes to the quiet street. A dog owner was walking away, feigning ignorance about the litter left behind by his Collie… What the eyes doesn't see, the heart doesn't grieve over… God, he hated when dog owners got away with doing that sort of thing.

"I see. Do your adoptive parents know the name you were given at birth?"

"Not that I'm aware of. And my parents are both deceased so that avenue of information is closed to me." Benedict's gaze dropped back to the keys in his hands. "My mother left me a death bed letter, unburdening the news onto me."

"Hmm. How long have you had it for?"

"Two weeks."

Benedict glanced at him then. If Yukinobu was computing these turns of events in relation to the evening they met at the Christmas Party, there was no evidence of it conveyed through his facial expressions.

"Would you let me read it?"

"I've discarded it." He had not, but on the same note, he did not want to share it with a stranger. Well, he did not want to share it, full stop. Not yet. He wasn't ready for that can of worms to be opened.

"Ah. Okay. Did she pass on any useable information?"

"Yes, and to be honest, I think it should lead us somewhere."

"Excellent. What makes you think that?"

Benedict told him about the assumed location, date, the fact he was a twin, and the presumed age bracket of his birth mother. He went on to share his Google search statistics. Yukinobu silently nodded, the same way he did the night before, throughout the all-encompassing recounting of his own research. Benedict found it a little off-putting last night, but he was finding it comforting today, slightly hypnotic.

"Right. I can't promise you that I'll be able to narrow it down to two or three prospects within ten days. However, I think there is a good chance that we'll be able to establish what your birth name was and find some information about your birth parents, or at least mother, and twin, eventually."

Benedict leaned back in his chair. It was his turn to nod. That very instant, he wondered why he did not consider going anywhere else for help. There were bound to be much bigger private investigation firms in London, perhaps with more credentials. At work, or with other aspects of his private life, he would have considered what his options were. Yet, here he was, with no intention of taking or even exploring other options with the matter at hand. A matter that certainly was the most personal and sensitive he'd ever had to deal with.

"If you don't mind me asking, what are you hoping to get from this?"

"What do you mean?"

"What would you like to know about your birth family? Their medical history and such, or would you like to meet them?"

"I, ah, I... I don't know." He hadn't really put much thought into what the next steps would be.

Yukinobu nodded in compassion.

"Have you ever done this sort of tracing before?" Benedict continued.

"I'll be honest. This will be my first involving the purchase of an infant from overseas, but historic tracing cases often have similar characteristics. The crunch often comes with the efficiency of record-keeping and the level of digitisation of old information in any given place."

"Alright. And by the way, if you need any help in ways of translation, let me know. I'm fluent in French and Italian."

"I speak French, too, but I'll take you up on your offer to translate Italian if it's needed."

Yukinobu turned up at Benedict's doorstep a few days later. Neither of them realised it was Christmas Eve until a group of bright-eyed folks sang terribly mangled carols at them. Benedict hurriedly shoved a tenner into their bucket to make them stop. Actually, he would not even have bothered opening the door if he had not had a guest. He always was a better person, particularly a better neighbour, when he had guests. But Yukinobu stuck his nose out the door and politely listened to the wreckage of much-loved carols until they were done. It was strange for Benedict to watch this grown man standing in his doorway, listening intently whilst looking like a deadpan Japanese beefeater enduring a phonic detention.

Yukinobu returned nearly every evening after that to share progress and get Benedict's help translating a few things. Even though Benedict suspected that his help might not have been essential (Google translate anyone?). It was just as well. Because, despite his window ledges being covered with holiday season's greetings cards, none of his friends or colleagues had cared to ask how or with whom he would be spending the 'festive period'. Not even Diane. Why had he said what he did to her the night of his company's Christmas do? He regretted it bitterly.

Benedict cracked open another bottle of beer and handed one to Yukinobu. There were already a dozen empty bottles dispersed across the kitchen.

"I still can't believe that she could be so deceitful and manipulative. It's such a freakish thing to do," Benedict spluttered, as he slumped back into an armchair by one of the kitchen's bay windows.

"I guess you could say that. Or… you could see it as an act of love."

"What?"

"Yep. Your presence in your parents' life was no accident. You weren't the result of a nine-month-old drunken night. Your mother was a lawyer, she risked everything for the chance at loving you."

"I suppose that's one way of looking at it." Benedict shrugged and started picking at his beer bottle's label.

"As far as your parents were concerned, you were a baby that fell from the sky and into their arms. You're one of the lucky ones who knows what true, untampered, exclusive love feels like. Not many people have that chance." Yukinobu pocked Benedict's chest with his bottle, leaving a wet ring mark on his shirt. "And believe me, if you haven't experienced it as a child, then, pfff, you're stuffed." He laughed without humour. "Hell, you've got more chance of the Queen shooting rainbows off her royal pout than finding that kind of love in a partner."

Benedict's lips curled up at yet another crack in Yukinobu's walls. "Not one of Cupid's disciples, then?" He teased, enjoying the company of a drunk Yukinobu.

"Cupid," Yukinobu scoffed. "Cupid will get you into someone's bed, alright. But that's it, my friend. After that, it's just deceit and manipulation, deceit and manipulation, deceit, and manipulation." Yukinobu moved his head left then right with each iteration. "Selfless, unconditional love between partners doesn't exist." His choice of the word 'partner' caught Benedict's attention. "Nah. People will keep their affection going for better, for richer and until lust do them apart."

Bitter much? This whole speech sounded a tad out of character, although he had only known Yukinobu a few weeks. Could the mystery around his time in Oxford simply be about an ex? Benedict wanted to ask but was not sure how to phrase it without sounding nosy or insensitive. *So, got ditched, did we?* Perhaps not that way...

"Amen to that." Benedict clinked his bottle against Yukinobu's to lighten the mood. Yukinobu smiled, but it seemed forced and stiff. "Still, I wish my mother had shared more about my birth parents."

"Maybe she didn't know more than what she has written to you."

"She must've."

"Not necessarily. If your mother had asked for personal info, they would've, too. But think about it, your parents had a lot more to lose by sharing theirs."

"Hmm. I suppose."

"Love. *Genau*."

Benedict raised one confused eyebrow.

"*Genau* is 'indeed' in German," Yukinobu clarified. And with that, he started a series of lunges and stretches.

Although wonderfully random, Benedict felt a tug of endearment towards the disillusioned Japanese man flexing his knees in the middle of the kitchen, while teaching him German. His mother would have liked him. And *genau*, Yukinobu had made some good points. Too busy resenting minor flaws in his education and unconsciously measuring his accomplishments against his parents', Benedict had missed their evident devotion for him. Perhaps his quest for fast-love and aversion to anything meaningful have not entirely been driven by his personal qualms over his sexual preferences. Maybe the all-encompassing love and attention he received from them had been enough. What's the need for a true connection if you already have one?

"What happened to you in Oxford?" Benedict suddenly asked, out of nowhere. "You go strangely vague whenever you mention it".

Yukinobu stopped mid-genuflection. His head turned to Benedict like a meerkat gauging danger. "Even monkeys fall from trees." And with that, he resumed bopping his fit body up and down in the middle of Benedict's kitchen.

Uh? What kind of response was this? Well, the type of response a man unused to siphoning barrels of booze every evening would make, right? But maybe it made sense, sort of... If desperately hungry, even a banana perched on an impossibly brittle tree might be worth a shot, hence a monkey toppling over. His guess, the same mistake would apply for a desperately horny monkey or a monkey running for their life or just a clumsy one... Or, perhaps, a monkey driven mad from maternal urge could fall from that flipping tree. Everyone makes mistakes. Benedict vaguely remembered seeing a documentary where a mob of broody chickless penguins fought to steal a chick, severely injuring said chick in the process. So, no one got to mother that poor chick. Sad, really... But, on reflection, *'even monkeys fall from trees'* was an adequate answer, after all, admittedly evasive, nonetheless interesting. It made Benedict wonder what drove this particular monkey, still genuflecting in his kitchen, to fall from a tree and what happened to him when he did.

Chapter 15

"Les Baumettes"

Marseille, France
Seven years ago, January 2010

Marie and Vlora reach the three-story-tall, windowless, circular wall by 12:04. Their appointment was at 13:30. They were wildly early but needed that time to appease their nerves. An idle mind is the devil's workshop, for some of us. But like mother, like daughter, getting the lie of the land in advance worked in their favour.

Paper in hand, Marie came up to the ageing bulletproof booth. She had been momentarily struck dumb, and just showed the stoic female official their documents, whilst carefully avoiding eye-contact.

"Please, wait here ma'am," responded a polite voice, amplified by a microphone, echoing like a nineties wedding DJ.

Marie frowned in incomprehension but then noticed a small group of people waiting to the side of the ten-foot tall fortified doors, heads down, and hands clasped in front of them like a herd of shamefaced goalkeepers.

Of course, there was no waiting room, it was not a beauty salon. Just as well, since Vlora had vomited behind the leafless plane trees posted around the intimidating wall next to which they were waiting.

Marie sent another text message to Giandomenico. His French phrase of the day would be *'J'attends patiemment'* (I wait patiently). Apropos. She was glad to have summoned the courage to initiate this electronic epistolary relationship. It was fun and took her mind off things, if only for a few seconds at a time.

Minutes later, a prison warden started to call the roll, on the street, in full view of passers-by. Aoun Fatos was the first name on his sobering bingo list, half an hour earlier than their allocated time. This had to be a first in the history of French administration. Though, it was not an administrative visit *per se*. And they probably did not have a lot else going on, thinking about it. Then again, it frequently seems it is those with the least demands on their time or those who live the closest that are late.

They were led into the bowels of the prison amongst a group, primarily made up of women, who as a group seemed to be intent on the study of various points on the concrete floor.

Then through a yard, before being crammed into a small, antiquated, and neon-lit room.

The Baumettes unique odour hit them for the first time; sweat, tobacco, grime, loneliness, boggy terror, and some other acrid smells Marie could not place. She was terrified if, guiltily, a tad excited.

Vlora took Marie's hand and pressed her bony shoulders against her daughter. The wait, while they all handed over their ID cards for inspection, was not long, and yet interminable. Once they eventually took off their shoes, bags, belts, and the heavy metallic barred door clunked shut behind them, it felt as if they were actually imprisoned.

A different prison officer called the roll again with the same staccato tempo as his colleague before him. He informed them of their booth number and gestured to the next room. The sound of mooing cattle taken to the abattoir sprang to mind as they proceeded.

The prison officer was about Marie's age, clean-cut, and had good posture. Marie felt a sudden urge to grab his arm and take him with them to wherever they were sent. He must have sensed Marie and Vlora's hesitation, as seconds later, he wished them a "good visit", in a manner that gently told them to 'clear off'.

Marie was taken aback by the courtesy and overall genteelness of the whole affair. So far. Were they not supposed to be barked at, scrutinised by judging eyes, and bad-mouthed by mustachios with acne-scarred skin chewing on gum? It was unexpectedly civilised.

When the final door opened, they strolled the length of a corridor, looking for their number.

The booths were the size of a cubicle, but with a see-through thermoplastic door to allow the guards to observe proceedings. The walls on either side were not transparent but were flimsy, making any pretence at privacy nothing more than that.

Marie was dragging behind her mother, her heart beating fast. Unsure what they were or were not allowed to do. Dirt draped the walls of their boxy booth, chewing gum was stuck to the splintery chairs, and the glazed doors were covered with finger marks. Scraps of food, dirty clothes or things that Marie did not care to examine too closely hung from the wire net above their heads.

The smell was not great before, but here, it was positively repugnant, and the spray of a skunk had to be better in comparison, the perfume of pure desperation.

They got a sense of movement from the detainees' side of the transparent thermoplastic barrier and heard greetings from neighbouring booths.

Vlora and Fatos had not exchanged any letters since the start of Fatos's incarceration, nor phone calls, as far as Marie was aware. He probably had no idea that Marie was going to be there. Suddenly, Marie heard a familiar voice talking to a guard. Her heart began to beat even faster.

Fatos's double take as his gaze met Marie's face had been barely perceptible, yet Marie caught it. If he was nervous or happy to see his daughter after nearly a decade, he did a great job of concealing it.

His appearance was a galaxy away from what Marie expected. There was none of the initial shocks she felt when seeing her mum for the first time after a decade and a half. Fatos had remained slim, ironically. He had not aged much either. The lines on his forehead were more prominent, and his hair more grey than brown. Other than that, he was very much the same olive-skinned man he ever was, and rather unexpectedly, he was cleanly shaved and cleanly dressed. If anything, Vlora and Marie looked paler and scruffier than him.

Standing in one of the corners of the booth, Vlora kept her eyes to the ground as he entered the room. She seemed to be shaking. After voicing a quiet greeting, Vlora smoothed her shirt against her slender body. Without uttering a word, Fatos looked Vlora up and down and again, with wanton lust. Marie would have blushed in discomfit if puzzlement did not reach her face first. Vlora might have been alright looking in her days, but by then, she would have been no-one's safe bet at a beauty contest.

"Hi, dad." Marie took the plunge.

He snorted. "Look what the cat dragged in," Fatos rasped, a predatory edge to his voice, before slumping on a chair, his legs spread wide apart.

Silence. The proverbial cat had got all of their tongues... A busy day for said cat.

"You look good," Vlora eventually offered in peace, attempting to break the ice.

"Yeah. What did you expect?" His lewd stare had remained on Vlora the whole time. "Whip marks? Ball and chain?"

"It wasn't what she meant," Marie hurried to say.

"Fuck off, ya fat gypo-ho." His protuberant Adam's apple hopped up and down with each word.

Precious father-daughter bonding moment right there. Making a memory... Marie crossed her arms. What did she expect? Warm apologies for all the harm her father had caused? A shaky embrace and hot tears? The truth was... She did. She knew better, yet she always did.

Vlora tried again. They eventually talked about a lot of things. He spoke about his incarceration, cellmates, daily activities, and TV programs. Then, they all spoke about white vinegar. Reviving an on-going debate, where Vlora sang its praise. She used it for everything; in salads, as a cleaning product, as a fabric conditioner, etc. While Fatos did not like its hair penetrating smell. Anyway, a side-track to the white vinegar conversation revealed that Vlora had been living with Marie since Fatos's arrest. If this came as a pleasant surprise to him, he did not make a show of it. However, he started to address Marie directly for the first time.

Marie warmed to him after all, despite her best attempt at staying cross. He seemed pleased to hear that she had become a nurse, but made his familiar judgemental low sucking noise when she mentioned that she lived in camp Saint Pierre.

They then ran out of time for Marie to ask the questions that brought her here in the first place. Why? She wanted to ask. Why did he do it again? Fatos might not care all that much about his daughter's wellbeing, yet he had always been concerned and protective of his wife... And, come to think of it, why did he loathe his daughter? Eh? What had she done to deserve that? Marie had always been a model child, yet she had felt nothing but resentment and contempt from her father, indifference from her mother. He always had big ambitions for her and said things like 'then, it'd make it all worth it.' Make what worth what? But explanation had never been forthcoming from her father.

Suddenly, a guard materialised by Fatos's side. As they parted, Fatos asked Vlora to come alone next time. The lurid 'up and down' he gave Vlora again left no doubt as to what his expectations were for their next visit. It then dawned on Marie that her mother had not pressed her to come along with noble ambitions of reuniting her daughter with her estranged father.

Vlora used Marie as a shield to fend off Fatos's amorous advances.

Vlora and Marie were left alone in the smelly boxy booth, alone with their thoughts, impressions, and stirred emotions. No panic resulted from being locked up this time. They were still dazed by the surreal and overall mundane encounter with Fatos. Most visitors coming out of their booths were in snotty tears, but neither Vlora nor Marie were.

However, Marie's phone was furiously bleeping on the tray of belongings that were handed back to her. She had dozens of missed calls, voicemails and text messages, but none of the fun kind she received from her new Italian pen pal. Romain had been admitted to her hospital.

Chapter 16

"The arrest"

Marseille, France
Twenty-two years ago, April 1995

Marie was skipping back home from school to an actual house with its own little garden. She had enlivened it with a border of fragrant sequences of lavender and rosemary bushes the moment they moved in. Her dad had promised her mother she would put a roof over their heads so many times it had become a sort of catchphrase. But he finally did it.

Up until three years previous, they still lived in a crowded ramshackle shantytown offering no privacy, bringing together more nationalities than a UN summit, but without any of the luxury of such an event. As part of the camp's entertainment, current affairs re-enactments were often performed. Their Yugoslavian corner, for instance, had brought back the ethnic splintering seen in their imploding country. With such complexity that nobody understood the knot of the issue, apart from them, and even then, only some of them. Marie certainly couldn't fathom it. But, to be fair, there were numerous sub-plots to follow involving all the factions her parents had left behind in the Balkans; Serbs, Herzegovinians, Croats, Albanians, etc. Too many. Vlora certainly had adopted the right approach, a perfectly pitched level of Don't-Carism. She faded into the background, by taking no initiative, co-operating and humming general consensus-opinion whilst committing to none. If you were too quiet, paradoxically, it made people talk more. And nothing good ever came from that…

Anyway, Fatos eventually did it. The house was only small, not much bigger than their old trailer. Nevertheless, Marie loved it. Even the simple act of heading home, knowing that the safety of bricks-and-mortar welcomed her at the end of her journey, filled the sixteen-year-old girl to the brim with joy.

Sadly, this short respite came to a brutal end on that very day. That afternoon she was greeted by flashing lights when she arrived home. Shoulders slumped and she stood motionless amongst the gawkers. Her lavender borders had been trampled by a herd of elephants, it appeared. And the front door had been kicked down. There was the noise of on-going commotion emanating from the house.

It was hard to tell what was going on. But then her father, his hands handcuffed behind his back was led from the house flanked by two police officers, shortly followed by a drunk or concussed woman and two more officers. It took a moment for Marie to realise that the woman with a swollen face covered in bruises and cuts was, in fact, her mother. Still shell-shocked, Marie caught her dad's red gaze. Were words of remorse thrown in Marie's direction? Maybe a show of concern for his pride-and-joy witnessing this unsettling tableau? No.

"What you're lookin' at?" he snarled at Marie as if she was a nosy neighbour rather than his only child.

Before the police had a chance to suspect who she was, Marie escaped the scene. Not knowing what to do or where to go, she found herself heading back to an illegal campsite where they had lived for a while. She remembered picking figs for a couple of summers in a nearby field. She was way too young to be legally employed but the grower took pity on her. He had spotted her gorging herself on his harvest and figured that letting her work for her meal was a better option than calling the authorities. The police had cleared out the slum a few years back. It looked entirely different. Smaller, somehow. Greener. The ghost of precarious lives remained in the vestige of dents on the ground, other than that it could have been any Mediterranean grove.

Marie was alone. Night had fallen. Her back pressed against an umbrella-pine tree, she slid down to the earthy ground and wrapped her arms around her knees. Head down, she started to cry, and cry, and cry. She cried for her parents, for her simple dream of a house, a home and what that actually meant to those who were never certain about where they might lay their head next. Lost to her thoughts, she did not hear the muffled footsteps heading towards her in the dappled moonlight dark.

When she felt a hand on her knee, her heart jumped out of her chest. He was crouched down to her level, his shadowed face merely a foot away from hers. She immediately scampered away like a crab looking for the safety of hollow rock.

"Marie?" he uttered, a hand on his chest, the other stretched out in front of him, trying to soothe her nerves. "It's me. Are you okay?"

Her heart, back in her ribcage, started to beat like a bongo drum. She stared at him, dumbfounded. They heard crickets chirping for a moment – literally, and figuratively.

"We go to the same school," Baul finally added.

Oh, she knew who he was alright. Everyone at school knew who he was. He was part of a new group of teenagers who had joined Marie's school at the beginning of the year. Gypsies. They were at the epicentre of most conversations, yet rarely interacted with anyone outside their group. Baul was a charismatic, handsome figure amongst this group, often apart from them, and yet at its centre. He was often seen alone during recess. His back leaned against the wall with a folded leg up, surveying the place with his hands in his pockets. The sort of troubled soul who gives teenage girls goosebumps, whether through excitement or fear, or perhaps a bit of both.

Marie carried on blinking away at Baul, confused about everything. What was he doing here? But more importantly, what had just happened to her? And why had the police taken her parents away? As she later found out, Baul had spotted her clearly distraught meandering apparently aimlessly. He followed her to the old campsite. He wanted to make sure that she was alright. Next, she would learn about the crimes of her parents. Her dad would be found guilty of facilitating an arms deal through the less salubrious end of the Marseille docks – there wasn't really a more salubrious end, to be honest. And her mum was unlucky enough to be married to her father and as a result, got caught in the middle of a deal gone wrong, subsequently being charged and convicted for aiding and abetting.

But that was still to come. For now, the two teenagers spent the night talking. The air got cold. Baul gallantly wrapped his black bomber jacket around her shoulders. Its warmth and scent enveloped Marie's teenage senses with a vision of Prince Charming. It did not occur to her that she was in a particularly vulnerable position. One that could have been easily exploited to disastrous ends.

They both knew of a little disused chapel nearby. Baul picked its lock.

The following morning, Baul brought Marie back to a camp used by his family and friends. It could not have been more different from the sort of shantytown camps she had become accustomed to over the years.

There must have been about thirty state-of-the-art caravans and trailers attached to expensive cars. Yet there was no direct evidence that anybody lived there. To all intents and purposes, it could have been an open-air dealership. Every vehicle was spotless, orderly positioned, and in obvious working condition, not one speck of litter was in sight, and only the rustling of pine trees filled the air.

"Have you just moved to this site?"

"Nope. We've been here for nearly a year. They're all working on Fos's construction site."

After walking past a couple more caravans, they reached a cluster of four people sitting in a circle on folding chairs, playing cards. So, the place was occupied, after all.

Baul nodded to everyone in acknowledgement then kissed the only woman in the group on the forehead. Noticing that Baul had company, the older woman winked at Marie as she played her hand. In contrast to her fierce, heavily lined face, her blue eyes seemed to twinkle with laughter and sparkle with an intelligence sharper than crystal's splinters. Mémé. Marie had no idea, then, of how significant a role this little old lady would play in her life. She was about to become Marie's first and last shot at being on the receiving end of rare motherly attention.

Marie and Baul remained quiet until they finished their round. Mémé won it. She, apparently, won every round.

"Is she cheating?" Marie whispered to Baul.

"Eh, that's my grandmother you're talking about there!" Baul fussed back.

"Oh, I'm so sorry, I didn't mean to…" she started, embarrassed.

"I'm only joking. Mémé's a cheat. Everyone knows it. But, no one's ever been able to catch her which makes her moves legitimate," Baul murmured back, close enough for Marie to breathe in the smell of church on him. She imagined she probably smelled the same – must and mould – albeit she rather liked that thought, more than she perhaps ought to.

"Why aren't you two at school?" Mémé probed. It was a voice and a face to listen to or obey, never to condescend to or ignore. That much was evident. Marie would later realise that Mémé unofficially ran the camp.

"We, hu…" Baul, by contrast, sounded uncharacteristically sheepish.

"Ah, I'd rather not know," Mémé interrupted dismissively. "Have you had breakfast yet?"

"No," replied Baul.

Mémé stood up from her chair with difficulty, leaning heavily on her cane. She gestured for the two of them to follow her. Baul locked arms with her, and she did not brush him off. They made their way up to her trailer at the pace of a Marseillais accent, slow. Just as everything else, the inside of Mémé and Pépé's caravan was immaculate as a show home.

Marie squeezed herself on one of the two facing benches with sixties flowery patterns. Baul sat across from her while Mémé placed bread with a selection of jams, butter, and cream on the articulated table in the middle. The teenagers opened their half-baguette turning them into doughy butterflies, spreading them with butter and ate ravenously. It felt nice to be looked after by an adult. Marie could not remember when someone had last shown concern about whether she had eaten or not.

The wince Mémé tried to suppress as she lifted her legs onto the sofa, brought Marie out of her reveries. The old lady's ankles were bandaged.

"Let me do it," Baul urged with a full mouth, in anticipation of what Mémé was about to attempt.

However, Marie beat him to it, "no, let me. To repay you for breakfast and…" Marie wanted to add 'last night' to Baul but thought better of it, "… everything else."

Kneeling at Mémé's side, Marie unpeeled the bandages. They revealed swollen, inflamed, and bruised ankles. Mémé explained everything that needed doing, and Marie performed each step with gentle care.

Marie later discovered that Mémé ought to be under the daily care of a nurse, but no medic ventured to the 'gypsy camps', or when they did, they came once, and once only. Marie could imagine why that would be once life started to mill about in the campsite. However, the teenage girl had been raised in no castle. So, the implicit, brooding menace didn't faze her.

Even though she was placed in an adolescent care home after her parents' arrest, she chose to spend all her spare time at the camp with Baul instead. She became good friends with Baul's sister, Lavina, and Mémé's unofficial nurse, a precursor to Marie's vocation in later life. In turn, Mémé granted the teenage girl her protection in camp. Though that proved entirely redundant, as everyone it seemed had adopted her. "You have a talent for bringing out the best in people and making their lives better for it," Baul once told her. Marie fell head over heels in love with him, his bohemian charm, his unusual sensibility, and his matchless artistic gift.

To Marie, 'love' had been like *'That'* song. When you hear *That* song being played for the first time, it stops your thoughts in their track, gives you goose bumps, makes you; turn up the volume, tap your feet to its beat, and then search everything there is to know about it. You'll listen to *That* song over and over and over again, marvel at its perfection. Then, after a while, you'll know all the words to it, every little note and hook. Eventually, you'll start to listen to it with less passion. Yet, its pleasant familiarity will continue to embellish the moment you spend with it or accompany your thoughts with comforting predictability. Baul had been *That* song. Later on, Marie would sometimes wonder if she would ever stumble upon *That* song in her lifetime again. Yet, looking back Marie felt grateful to have loved and been loved by Baul, she felt comfort in knowing that at least one man had wanted her above everyone else.

∞

Seven years had passed since the arrest of her parents when Marie's life took an unexpected turn.

All smiles, Marie waved at Mémé and Lavina from afar. They were sitting under the shade of Mémé's caravan's striped awning and Marie hurried to their side. She was about to tell them her good news, however, their sombre faces sobered her up. It was explained to her, in confidence, that the *gorjio* (non-Romany) boy who dumped Lavina a month ago had left something baking in Lavina's oven. Lavina was only two or three months pregnant. Marie was about to ask Lavina what she intended to do with it when Mémé squeezed her forearm and nodded to her left. Baul was coming back from his day's work and, incongruously, there was a definite spring in his step. The conversation ceased and Marie walked to him, meeting him several feet away from Mémé's caravan out of earshot. But before she could ask him about his day, she had to tell him about hers.

"I've got news!" Marie beamed quietly, her hands around his neck.

"You've gotten engaged?"

"Very funny."

He fake laughed.

"Phew. Lavina's ex-boyfriend turned out to be a girl?"

"Stop it. Besides, that's definitely not funny."

"What then?"

"I've been offered a permanent position at the hospital, effective from today."

Baul lifted her and span her around. "That's fantastic." His body had changed immensely in the past few years since he started to work in construction. It was not the skinny teenage boy's body Marie first met. He had morphed into a man. The work on the building sites put food on their table but his real passion was music. He was always found with a guitar strapped over his shoulder. He spent his evenings playing the guitar and singing in the bars and clubs of Marseille and the wider Provence area, building up a dedicated following in the local area and no small amount of national buzz. But no matter the number of swooning fans he met at the foot of the stage, he only had interest in Marie.

As he lowered her down, Baul added, "I've also got something of an announcement to make." But Marie's face closed up. Following her worried gaze behind his shoulder, Baul saw a middle-aged man, dark, with a handle-bar moustache walking towards them.

A moment later, the man was standing in front of them and his hard stare locked with Marie's.

"Here you are," rasped the man, pointing at Marie with opened palms, his breath stinking of alcohol. "And there was me thinking that you'd sailed away." To better yourself, Marie could finish the man's train of thoughts. She could also hear the resentment in his voice, the reproach. She knew where this was going and was dreading it already.

"Bonjour, papa," mumbled Marie.

"Couldn't be bothered to greet your dad on his first week out, could you? And your mother. Not once, did you try and see your poor mother in the four years since she got out." He tutted. "After all she's done for you. Not once." Fatos thrust a pointy finger in Marie's direction.

There was a pregnant pause as he nodded to himself. "Y' think you're better than us, don't you?" He sucked air through his front teeth, looking her up and down appraisingly. Her middle and thighs were chunkier since the last time he saw her. He would disapprove of that, considering weight gain as a weakness shared

108

amongst lazy, common people. Despite herself, she recoiled, feeling self-conscious.

Baul took Marie by the arm, pulled her back a couple of steps and planted himself in front of her. Lavina and Mémé rose to their feet.

"And who's this?" Eyes still locked with Marie's, Fatos pointed at Baul with his thumb.

"This is my boyfriend, Baul."

Fatos looked him up and down, a mixture of disapproval and scorn, before turning his attention back to Marie.

"Mixing with gypsies now, eh?" Fatos didn't bother pretending that he had any interest in getting to know the guy or past his prejudices. He grabbed Marie by the wrist. "Let's get you to your mother."

It was an argument Marie could never win, full of absurd contradictions. He criticised her for being a snob and yet according to him she mixed with people below their standard and did not live up to the sacrifices and risks he and Vlora made for her. However, Marie had long realized that what her father thought of as 'love' had never been that. It was possessiveness. No, less than that. He had a proprietorial, controlling hold over her and Vlora, they were 'his'.

Fatos managed to pull Marie with him a few paces before Baul set her free from his grip.

"Leave her alone." Baul marked each one of his words and blocked Fatos's line of access to Marie with his body. But Fatos moved so close to Baul's face that their noses were practically rubbing. Lavina and Mémé moved up to Marie's side. She wished they hadn't, she would rather get hurt than place either of them at risk.

"And you can shut the fuck up, pikey." Fatos spat, jabbing Baul hard in the shoulder with a grubby finger. "This is between me and my *princess* daughter." He spat, bringing a vision to the forefront of her mind of the only other time Fatos had ever referred to her as 'his princess'. She must have been nine, all geared up for the school's end of year dance show. She wore a shiny purple leotard, her face all made-up with glitter and her hair tied into a high bun. She had never felt prettier. Then, minutes before she went on stage, Fatos rubbed her round tummy and pointed out "it's going to be hard to hide that up there, *my chubby princess*".

"I'm not going anywhere with you right now, dad," Marie asserted from behind Baul, feeling her heart starting to pound. "If you tell me where you live, I'll come and see you… soon."

Making another unattractive sucking sound, Fatos swivelled on himself taking in his surroundings like a tourist at the zoo.

"Where *I* live… And do you live here?" Fatos probed.

"Yes."

Fatos started to prowl, circling them. "How long?"

"A while."

"With this man?"

Marie nodded. Fatos nodded back, grinning without humour.

"Are you his lookout girl?"

"No-oh. Dad, please just go."

"Your pimp?" Fatos' tone was deliberately provocative.

Before Baul had a chance to do something he would regret, Marie pressed her hands against her father's torso, forcing him to take a few steps back.

"Da-ad, please."

"What? Just trying to figure out the living arrangement around here." Marie pushed Fatos away a little further. "Maybe, I'm in debt to McPikey over there for my daughter's stay?"

Fatos shoved Marie's hands out of the way with such force that she tasted the hard-packed ground.

His eyes bulging out, Baul got into Fatos's face. "You heard her before, get out!" Baul yelled, shaking with barely contained rage.

Fatos glanced at Marie still down on the ground and shook his head. Exchanging one last stare with Baul, he staggered his way out. Without ever turning his head back, Fatos shook his index finger in the air while walking away.

A few weeks later, Baul struck his last chord on his way to sign his first record deal. The car's brakes failed him. He crashed against a wall and never woke up. Marie was twenty-three years old and, unbeknownst to her, a couple of weeks pregnant with Romain.

Chapter 17

"Dr. Cognizant spoke sense."

Marseille, France
Seven years ago, January 2010

Out of breath, Marie tried to pull open the curtain of Romain's hospital cubicle. It caught on a dent on the delimiting rail. Not entirely registering where she was, or with whom, being able to open the obstinate curtain seemed of critical importance. Until she snapped out of her flustered state and just stepped around the curtain. His small chest heaved rhythmically, emitting a Darth Vader pant into the oxygen mask. Tucked under a flimsy blanket, his red-rimmed eyelids and phantom-skin made him look like an auditioning extra for a part in The Exorcist.

Out of breath, but suddenly back in control of her senses, Marie took his pulse, checked his blood pressure, his oxygen levels, and carried out all the tests she normally would on any ordinary patient. Until her reverie was broken by Médélice placing a comforting hand on her shoulder.

"Marie. He's okay. He's just resting." The sound of Médélice's voice stopped the centrifuge in which Marie's mind had been spinning. She patted Médélice's hand which was resting upon her shoulder.

The sudden metallic ringing caused by the rattle of the curtain being opened with ease caught them by surprise.

"You're here!" Lavina, Romain's aunt, exclaimed with relief. She appeared with a plastic cup of water in hand, smelling like a stale clogged drain. While Timo, Romain's cousin, followed awkwardly behind.

Lavina engulfed Marie in a tight hug.

"What caused his asthma attack?" Marie murmured through Lavina's hair.

There was a pause.

Letting go of Lavina, Marie contoured her son's temple and jaw, before resting her hand on Romain's. Lavina flicked a ping-pong gaze between Marie and Médélice.

"I don't know," Lavina finally responded also in a murmur, even though she was not sure why they were murmuring. "One minute everything was fine, he was playing football with the others. The next, I heard Timo shouting for me. Romain could not stop coughing, you know. He couldn't speak either. His inhaler didn't seem to do anything for him. I wasn't sure what to do," Lavina spoke hastily. "So, I called you, but you didn't answer. Then, he started to clutch his chest. So, I got Pépé to drive us to the hospital. We were so scared. His lips had turned blue... I didn't know what else to do. I thought he might..."

"You did the right thing," Médélice interrupted, before Lavina uttered worries about 'death' in relation to Romain. "Romain's alright now. That's all that matters." Médélice eased Marie's crushing grip on Romain's hand.

There was a pause.

"How bad was the smell coming from the refineries?" Marie eventually queried.

"The what?" Lavina frowned for a second. "Oh, yes, it was pretty bad. The wind picked up at lunchtime. It smelled even worse than usual."

Marie nodded. "Lavina, you..." Her voice quavered. "You did well. Thank you so much... So much."

"No. Please, don't thank me. Thank Médélice and the doctor. They were amazing." Lavina shook her head in relief.

Marie nodded again and turned her gaze at Médélice. "Who has seen to Romain?"

"Dr. Cognizant."

"Who?" Marie frowned not understanding.

"You know, Mr. Cogni... Dr. Alain Lafarge."

"Oh."

Crumbs – Dr. Edgy Shoes. Long gone was her ambition to have a life-long relationship with him. Marie wished she had played it a little cooler. She machine-gunned the poor guy with text messages straight after their night together. Probably making him feel he was being stalked by a needy wretch shambling towards him, slurring "hug me, hug meeee." Argh, why did it have to be him? Of all the doctors in this hospital, it had to be him...

"Do you know where I can find Alain now?" Marie swallowed loudly.

Thinking about it, there had not been any tiresome corridor encounters for a few days. And no text messages had been fired off in a while. So, it did not have to be awkward, did it?

Oh, but awkward it was… Awkward, clumsy, cack-handed, and however else you wanted to put it.

The door to the consultation room was wide open as Marie arrived. Still, only polite to knock, she thought, seeing that Alain was engrossed in what he was doing.

"Come in," Alain responded mechanically, examining medical documents held against a lamp.

"Hi, Alain. It's only me. Marie." She waved self-consciously from the doorway.

Sitting on a rolling chair, his legs were tucked under the table. But his immediate recognition of Marie's voice acted like someone flipping a robot's power-switch, jolting it into sudden unexpected life. Without rolling backwards first, he tried to jump onto his feet. His lap bumped against the inside of his desk, causing the articulated desk-lamp to topple over, knocking him on the head and emitting a metallic 'clonk' noise worthy of a cartoon. He failed to look down as he attempted to go around the desk. Tripping over a cable, he stumbled headlong towards Marie and medical documents fluttered down to the floor. As they both leaned down to try and scoop up the liberally distributed papers, they ungraciously clashed foreheads in the process.

It was hard to believe, or rather accept, that this bumbling mess had overseen Romain's health and ensured the survival of hundreds of patients every year.

"Good afternoon," he muttered to the ground and presumably Marie, still flustered.

"Are you okay?" They both spoke simultaneously, mirror images of each other rubbing their foreheads.

They both grimaced and gestured for the other to go first.

"To what do I owe…"

"I've been told that…"

They both spoke in unison again and laughed. Well, Marie laughed. Alain produced a ventriloquist-like cackle, until he mimed zipping his lips with a pinched thumb and forefinger.

"I was told that you tended to Romain's care earlier this afternoon," Marie remarked.

"Pardon?" A frown of utter confusion veiled his expression. Whatever the presumed reasons for her visit, this was obviously not one of them and he clearly didn't remember she had a son.

"My seven-year-old son, Romain. He had difficulty breathing. You left him with Médélice."

Earth calling Mars…

And there was light. "Oh, Romain. Yes, yes. Romain Boulanger. Yes."

"How is he doing?"

"Please have a seat."

Oh no. Sitting was not good. She had offered a seat many a time to her patients. No, no, no, she wanted to stay right where she was. Standing.

She cleared her throat. "I'm good standing, thanks."

Alain sat down on one of the plastic armchairs, beckoning her with his bulbous green eyes. She could not stay standing now. She capitulated.

"Good," Alain affirmed. His large forehead was pearled with sweat. Why was he breaking into a sweat? "He's good. For now. A strong little fella, he is. He was brought to the hospital in the nick of time."

For now? Brought to hospital in the nick of time?

"Then why is he still using the oxygen mask to assist his breathing?"

He crossed his legs in a rather camp fashion and tapped the tip of his fanned fingers on his lap, like an old-fashioned university professor.

"Marie, I know this will be harrowing for you to hear, but your son has suffered a life-threatening asthma attack. Short-acting beta-agonists didn't work, so I decided to use a bronchodilator and put a breathing tube into his upper airway whilst his asthma was brought under control."

Silence.

"Marie, he reacted well to all this. He'll recover. He's doing well," Alain added.

Marie suddenly remembered to breathe. His tone of voice was full of compassion but confident, there was none of the ungainliness he displayed earlier. Alain locked his eyes with her and breathed rhythmically, like a midwife doing her best to help a mother-to-be during delivery. But he did not sound quite as demented as some of those midwives demonstrating breathing techniques, more like a Pilates or Yoga instructor. Anyway. Harrowing… He did it again. Who used words like these? Well, the sort of man who knew a lot – a lot of words, a lot about medicine, and a lot about treatments. The sort of man who saved the lives of charming, inventive, wilful young asthmatic boys. The sort of man Marie was suddenly incredibly grateful to have in front of her, speaking about her son's health. She could have kissed him right there in this instant, kissed his disappointedly normal-looking shoes even, but she refrained from it, sitting totally still instead.

"Oh, good God," she finally exclaimed, and it could have been in direct reference to Alain as far as she was concerned.

"The oxygen mask is just to help him while he rests. There's nothing to worry about. As I said, Romain's doing well now."

Romain's doing well, Romain's doing well, Romain's doing well... She breathed out loudly with relief.

"Thank you."

"You're most welcome." His posture still exceptionally upright, even when seated, Alain wrapped his knitted hands around his folded knee.

"What do you think caused the severity of this attack?" questioned Marie.

"Well, I'm afraid it's hard to say, for sure."

"I think it might be air pollution. I've started to notice a pattern," she interjected.

He resumed his old-fashioned university professor's fingertip tapping. "It may well have been. Airborne particles of any kind, pollution, dust, smoke, etcetera irritate the lungs and airways, as I'm sure you already know. It makes asthma worse, both long and short-term."

"So, what should I do to avoid this monstrous sort of attack from happening again?"

"Well, if pollution caused this very severe attack, I'm afraid short of single-handedly improving air quality, there's not much that can be done."

She struggled to keep it together. "Hmm." There was nothing that she could do. *Nothing*, she thought helplessly.

"The only thing you could do..." Oh, there was something she could do. "... is relocate somewhere with better air quality."

She could picture a stone cottage, the cool breeze coming off the sea on the headland where the cottage sat miles from the nearest building. Wouldn't that be nice? But alas, she could also picture her finances, or lack thereof. In her mind, when she opened her money-drawer a cloud of dust dispersed, followed by rolling tumbleweeds and the sound of crickets.

Alain's compassionate attention still rested on her. How much did doctors make? His place looked rather nice... No, she had to stop thinking like that. She was not like that. She was an independent, hard-working single mother who would get herself and her appendages into a house without anyone's help. Besides, Alain clearly had no time for her anyway.

"Thanks again, Alain, for everything. I'm truly grateful," Marie breathed, a hand over her heart.

He waved it off as if to say that he was only doing his job but spared her the clichés of false modesty. Instead, he seemed weirdly preoccupied with something. Intently looking at his hands, now firmly placated onto his lap, he opened his mouth to say something before thinking better of it. This made Marie slightly nervous. Was there something else she needed to know about Romain's health? Something upsetting that would make a doctor nervous about sharing it with the mother of his patient.

"Could I ask you a question?" he attempted.

Oh God. no. no. no. "Sure." She frowned in anticipation.

"It's, ah, rather personal."

She sighed. He blushed. She instantly realised that he had mistaken her sigh of relief for boredom or worse.

"No problem. If I can be of any help, I'd be more than happy to offer it," she hastened to declare to clarify matters.

He cleared his throat. "Obviously, you'd be under no obligation to answer."

"Okay."

A flashback to his roundabout indirect way of asking her out flashed before her eyes; his rambling followed by her decision to do it for him to set his nerves at ease. She had found it charming rather than irritating... Though thinking back, maybe she shouldn't have been so forward and then served herself on a platter to him, perhaps he found it all emasculating... An educated, well-to-do man like him could have been such a good father figure for Romain, she thought regretfully.

"It may sound silly to you," he pursued.

"I'm sure it won't."

"And please, feel free to be perfectly honest with me."

"Look. Alain, just ask."

"Okay. Did you enjoy yourself?"

"Enjoy myself?" *What? Now?*

"Yes... I mean, you know, with me, on our date."

Ah. That. "Sure. You're a kind, intelligent man."

116

He looked at his hands again.

"No, I meant. Did you enjoy yourself… You know…"

Alain made a hand movement in continuation of his sentence. *Oh.* "In bed?" Marie queried for clarity.

He blushed but nodded. *Gosh. Men. Really?* Her son nearly died, and he was preoccupied with his performance in the bedroom.

"Yep." *A bit.* Marie could almost hear the tension in Alain's body whistling out of him. His shoulders looked distinctly more relaxed, for a start. Despite herself, she felt a little tug of endearment towards him again. And although there had not been any fireworks, she had felt safe and cherished. Yet, like dogs who can smell fear, Marie had his nerves. It had not been off-putting as such… No actually, that was it, his sweaty nerves had been off-putting. Weirdly, she had felt like a sport's coach, too busy encouraging him to really take part in the game. Anyway. "Why do you ask?"

"I've met someone, you see…" Wait what? Met someone? It took him a decade to get on it, and he was already on to the next within a couple of weeks. What to say? Congratulations? Too condescending. Good for you? Too patronising. I'm happy for you? Embittered. She had to think of a different answer. But he spared her the effort. "Well, not met, not as such, because we were in high school together. But as you know, my experience in that area has been quite limited. So…"

She mustered a strained smile.

"Well, you've got nothing to worry about. So…" good luck? And, with that, she slapped her knee. "I better get back to Romain."

He jumped back up on his feet with a bolt. "Of course. Right, and I better, you know…" He waved his scrunched-up medical documents as a prompt to let her know how busy he was.

Romain was awake when Marie returned. His breathing bore similarities to a purring cat and he still looked like a spectre, or in his mother's eyes, a heaving porcelain doll. She ran her hand along his arm.

"Where were you?" he enquired with difficulty.

Marie looked for something to say, anything other than where she actually was, but could not bring herself to lie to her boy. "I went to see your grandfather with Vlora."

"Oh. I would've wanted to go..." he wheezed into his mask. "Why didn't you take me?"

"Maybe next time."

"Tomorrow?"

"No. Not tomorrow."

"But I wanna meet him... Ask him to come here. Pleeease."

"*Ma puce*, you're not well. Have a rest."

"Please?"

"Argh." She sighed. "He wouldn't be able to."

"Why not?"

"He's... He wouldn't... He just can't."

His breathing worsened. "...He doesn't want to know me." His small chin began to tremble.

Marie took a deep breath. "No, *ma puce*, your grandad is in prison."

Romain's eyes widened. "Did grandad rob a bank?"

It sounded odd to hear her son's say the word 'grandad' in relation to her dad.

"No."

"Did he stop eating veg and brushing his teeth?"

"No-oh. The police don't actually arrest anyone for that, it's just something I say. You know that, right?"

"Yeah, I'm just joking. So, what did grandad do?"

"He helped bad people do bad things."

"So, he didn't do anything?"

"No."

"Ahem."

"But 'taking part' is just as bad. Anyway, have some rest now."

Within seconds of making her promise that she would take him to meet his grandfather, Romain fell asleep. Yet, she could not quiet the little voice in the back of her head warning her that this would be a mistake, that her reasons for keeping him away from Fatos were justified. Seven years from now, she would bitterly regret not having listened to that little voice.

As she leaned in to kiss Romain's forehead, her stomach rumbled loudly. She realised that she hadn't eaten anything for the past nine hours.

On her way to a café, she slowed down by the entrance of a small chapel, the stone façade was covered in a black crust from pollution. Marie was not a Christian, neither born nor reborn nor Joan of Arc-ean. However, Baul had dragged her into churches, often. And, it was where she felt his presence the most. Say what you want, but to Marie, entering a church was like picking up a direct line to her missing half.

"Hi, Baullywood." She dipped the tip of her fingers into the murky Holy Water. The chapel was empty, cool and dingy. She lowered herself onto one of the nearest pews. It creaks under her weight. As always Marie felt slightly insulted by this moan of resistance from inanimate objects, particularly in the presence of Baul.

"I'd say that this morning would have made you turn in your grave, but…"

Baul's body was donated for scientific research and his organs for transplant.

"… Thinking about it, this isn't even the right use of the phrase. I meant that this morning must have given you a fright. Obviously, I'm not talking about mum's sneeze, splattering toothpaste all over the mirror… Although that made me jump too. Ha."

"… It was good to hear Romain and mum laugh afterwards, eh? They've got such a funny laugh those two." Marie shook her head, smiling. "I think they're the only two people who could create an earthquake with their chortles."

The echoing sound of the entrance door closing silenced Marie for a moment.

"Anyway… I wanted to say thank you, as I'm sure you kept Romain safely away from those pearly gates. That was nice of you. Especially as you're probably dying to meet him… Perhaps not dying... But, ah…"

Marie cleared her throat.

"So, hmm, I've got to get him out of here. Romain. Living in camp is no good for him, you know? And I know that your family will be a bit disappointed in us, for giving up… On your way of life… But, it's not like we really ever travel anywhere anyway…" Her own words didn't ring true.

Silence.

She eventually shakes her head.

"… I guess you're right, it isn't just for Romain. He's obviously my absolute main priority. But, yes. I do… I'd love to have a house. I always have. A little house, on the heath, far from the dirt of the city, where the wind wouldn't carry the smell of oil refineries. Somewhere a little cooler in the summer, where I could have my own little vegetable patch, and eat food grown directly from my own ground… The postwoman and I would be on a first-name basis. She'd ask how we're getting on out there. I'd flick my head towards our view of rolling hills and quip that we're on top of the world... Oh, and the old couple nearest to us would comment on how great it is to have a young family bringing life back into the area. They'd notice what a lovely boy Romain is…" A feeling of helplessness washed over her, she felt useless, worthless. She wiped the tears from her freckled cheeks and runny nose, making an unattractive, unladylike snort.

"Something like that. Anyway. I miss you. I miss you so much. I wish you were here with us…"

She tried to picture Baul but couldn't. In these moments, she would usually get a photo of Baul out of her purse. Tears would invariably roll down, looking at his happy and handsome image, a guitar in hand. But, for some reason, a fleeting image of Giandomenico pushed past. Pink warmth coloured her cheeks. It felt like a little betrayal on her part. He was good fun. His text messages never failed to make her smile and she wondered how long it would last until he got bored.

Once Marie arrived back at the hospital, she contacted the number on one of the ads pinned to the corkboard at the café. She applied for a second job as a part-time cleaner. Her shifts as a nurse were already long, but there was no other way for her to carry on saving a bit each month while having her mother stay with them. She owed it to Romain. As soon as she paid off all her student debts, and saved up enough money, she would get them out of the trailer and into bricks and mortar. That was a promise.

Chapter 18

"Down to two"

London, United Kingdom
Seven years ago, May 2010

Although laying inert, the closed folder may as well have been a flat screen transmitting the World Cup final at ear-splitting volume. Benedict was transfixed.

Yukinobu, on the other hand, was not. So, after several unacknowledged offers to go through its content with him, Yukinobu disappeared into the kitchen and put the kettle on to boil.

"Tea?" Yukinobu shouted out.

Benedict made a negative grunt, the sort of hissy grunt a teenager would make upon being asked to play the recorder at a family gathering.

Yukinobu fixed himself some toast while waiting for the water to boil. The way he buttered the golden piece was very meticulous, every millimetre was covered by a thin, even layer of melting butter, no blobs, and no dry bits. A precise and effective completion executed by someone who knew exactly what he liked and wanted.

The findings in this folder had consumed Benedict for the past few months. So much so, that he had not stirred a single fight with colleagues the whole time. The thirty-year-old was unsure what to hope for when it came to his biological family. The probability of disappointment seemed as high as Mount Everest.

He did not even know what he wanted the findings to say. In the past, it was well known that a high number of adopted children came from unmarried girls from religious families until a few decades ago. Babies were sometimes forcibly taken from their mothers. To Benedict, there was a romantic drama to those circumstances, and he wondered if French and Italian unwed mothers faced similar quandaries in the eighties, as other places in the sixties. Unlikely. Yet, he knew that he had been traded for money, his mother's letter implied as much. This may have been his birth mother's only choice. Maybe she wished there had been another way and regretted her decision ever since. A part of him expected that whenever the day would come that they would reunite, she would tell him as much. Call him her lost son, grab him into a warm embrace, well, if Italian… If French, she would put her cigarette to one side and give him a peck on the cheek, if feeling overcome with emotion.

Yukinobu returned to the library and sat across from Benedict. As if nudged, Benedict silently and slowly pulled two files from the folder. Yukinobu let him read through them. One was based around findings from Italy, the other in France. The first file made sense, the latter not so much.

"With this one, as I'm sure you can tell, it wasn't straight forward," Yukinobu chipped in.

"Why's that?" Benedict enquired whilst continuing to peruse the file in question.

"I did a lot of digging, and I'm afraid that's all I could find."

"Hmm." Benedict nodded distractedly, still flicking through the documents.

"I thought you'd still want to see the progress, though. It'll require more research to pin them down, but I think I'll manage it."

"It was bound to happen given the circumstances of my adoption. Please investigate further."

"Will do."

"Shall we make contact with the possible Italian family first?" Benedict was aware of the affliction in his own voice and his choice of the word 'we'. He did not particularly like it, but truth be told, this was not something Benedict wanted to do alone. And he wanted Yukinobu, especially Yukinobu, to hold his hand through it.

"Sure. Would you like to call or email them?"

"No, I'd like to meet them."

"Establishing first contact in person can be… tricky. Are you sure you want to put yourself through…"

A second helping of rejection? Benedict finished Yukinobu's thought without voicing it.

"What's the point?" Benedict interrupted. "DNA tests can't be done over the phones or via an email, can they?" There was an edge to Benedict's tone, so he forced himself to stretch his lips into a smile for good measure.

"Alright. I'll arrange it."

Chapter 19

"Fatos meets boy."

Marseille, France
Seven years ago, May 2010

The family section of the visiting rooms was hardly different from the other boxy cubicles they had used for their previous visit. It was a little bigger, perhaps, and there were a few tatty toys in a box in one corner of the room. Other than that, it was in the same dishevelled state.

Romain had been uber-excited about meeting his grandfather in prison. Or, more accurately, excited at the 'idea' of entering prison, while genuinely looking forward to seeing his grandad for the first time.

The reality of prison came knocking whilst in the family waiting section. There were four glowering families with them. Romain, Marie and Vlora sat near a single mum with two young girls. They seemed okay at first. But it became apparent that, for this woman, the way to teach her daughters that hitting was wrong, was by enthusiastically smacking them as they moved away from her. Well, as much as one can do in the caged-in environment they found themselves in. Romain's hand was crushing Marie's.

"We don't have to stay," Marie whispered to him. "Would you like to go home?"

Before he had a chance to answer they heard movement. Romain did not meet his mother's eyes as he simply shook his head in response. His mum was looking at him funny, he thought. Maybe she sensed something he did not even realise was there at his young age. His conflicting emotions; his reluctance to be here layered by a contradictory yet stronger desire to stay put. The way some people read horror stories, holding the book with one hand and fearfully covering their eyes with the other, but incapable of putting the book down.

Marie turned, the noise had been his grandad entering the room, Marie and Vlora stood but Romain remained seated, his hand still firmly interlocked with Marie's.

A broad smile on his face, Fatos kneeled to be at eye-level with the seven-year-old. Romain brought a hand over his mouth, to cover his scar.

"Now, who's this beautiful boy?"

There was a proud, paternal tone to his voice that Romain warmed to. But most of all, Romain was pleased that much like his grandma, his grandfather had failed to notice how he really looked. No one had ever called him beautiful before, apart from his mum. In fact, he was so happy he had forgotten about his mum until he heard her hiccup, only just once though, strange.

"I'm Romain," he mumbled back.

"Romain, a good French name just like Marie. Your mum chose well, didn't she?"

Romain shrugged and granted Fatos a bashful smile, still covering his mouth. His mum tensed even more, but of course, this went straight over Romain's head again. He could not have guessed that his mother almost heard the implied 'for a half-gypsy boy' but decided not to take the bait.

"Get that hand away from your face, boy, and toughen up."

This time Romain felt Marie stiffen, as he impulsively did as he was told.

"Isn't he handsome?" Fatos continued turning his gaze to Vlora, slapping his thigh then pointing at Romain. Suddenly, he leaned over, a hand curled behind Romain's neck. "Don't let anybody tell you otherwise. Alright?" Marie stood but Fatos took no notice. "See that?" Fatos asked, drawing the boy's attention to the little finger of his right hand. Its nail was nearly as wide as a thumbnail flattened and split along its length with a scar running all the way across its hand.

"This is what gives men character. Wanna know how it happened?"

Romain's hesitation had returned with clashing dread and yet an eagerness to know, butting up against each other.

Fatos went on to regale Romain with all the fantastic tales of the antics he was up to when he was the same age. How he and his cousins would create maze-tunnels with straw bales, how he would steal quinces from his grandmother's neighbour's tree and helped her prepare the most delicious quince paste anyone's ever tasted. "What? You've never eaten quince paste? When I'm out that's the first thing I'll do for you."

As for Fatos's hand, it was quite the heroic story. Vlora was on her way home from school when she walked into the path of an oncoming vehicle about to swerve, tip and rollover. If it was not for Fatos, Vlora would have been squashed underneath. However, the impact was such that a few parts went flying up and one came crashing down on Fatos, injuring his hand.

Their time spent in Fatos's company felt nothing short of a sprint to Romain who immediately asked his mother when he could visit again. Even at his young age, he could sense that it would require coaxing. But he was so excited that it did not take much effort on his part and he was certain that his grandma was on his side. She did not say anything, but he could tell.

And he was right, because his mum let Vlora take him again. Which became something they would do on a regular basis, for a while anyway.

On their way to school, Romain told his cousin Timo all about his day at the prison. Timo was impressed that Romain had been inside an actual prison and asked loads of questions. But as always, Romain had to reign him back to the subject regularly. For example, a question about the number of keys the guards had clipped to their belts somehow deviated to a list of reasons why Frank Ribéry should not have left Olympique de Marseille.

However, once they passed the school gates, Romain turned mute. As always, Timo started playing football with his friends while Romain made his way to the edge of the schoolyard, his stomach clenched, trying to become invisible until first bell. But it never was easy to turn invisible with bright blond curly hair and a large scar left from when his cleft palate had been reconstructed. Gabin, a boy who was much bigger than him and flanked by two other boys, slapped the back of his head for no reason whatsoever.

"Fly on your hair," Gabin taunted, whilst the others laughed. Cruder versions would see him being pushed over, wrestled to the ground, or lured into strange places. But this particular day was not so bad.

None of these things ever happened in Timo's presence, but for some reason, Timo did not see Romain as a weakling and Romain intended to keep it this way. When his cousin had once spotted something, he interrupted his game, kicking the ball at his feet right into the face of one of Romain's tormentors. On that particular day, the tormenting stopped immediately, but Timo got himself into serious trouble with school at the same time for giving the boy a pretty bad black eye. So Romain just kept out of sight, well as much as he could, it was easier this way for all parties.

Chapter 20

"Burn after reading."

Rome, Italy
Seven years ago, June 2010

"This is it." Yukinobu looked up, beyond the arched entrance doorway. Located in the historic centre of Rome, the narrow, cobbled street of sixteenth-century terracotta-coloured buildings could have served as a set for a *Romeo and Juliet* play.

The buzzer to the building was right there within easy reach. Suddenly, it all felt very real. Benedict ran his hands through his hair an excessive number of times, a nervous tic that he rarely let slip in front of other people. If he had been less nervous he might have noted the significance of him being this vulnerable in front of Yukinobu. But his nerves had robbed him of any self-awareness.

It was not lost on Yukinobu, who gave Benedict a sympathetic head-bow as if querying whether he was okay, immediately annoying Benedict. He did not need Yukinobu's sympathy, and he was not anxious. Never was, nothing could phase him. He was not procrastinating either. No. A sudden and acute interest in one of the leaves of the bougainvillaea growing by the building's entrance had just arisen. Such a beautiful green leaf, he turned it over to inspect its other side.

Yukinobu cleared his throat. Alright. Benedict released his grip of the leaf. Feeling Yukinobu's gaze on him, Benedict took a deep breath, raised his eyebrows, and rang the bell.

A moment later, a wooden shutter on the second floor creaked open. A bottle blonde woman glowered down from above.

"What do'y want?" She crossed her arms as she asked in Italian.

Blimey. Someone missed school on the day they were teaching the sunny-Italian-disposition, thought Benedict. At least she did not have any of the false kindness that people of a certain age tend to couple with their prejudice.

"Ciao. My name is Benedict Grant, and this is Yukinobu Wada. There is a personal matter we would like to discuss with you. May we come in?" Benedict enunciated every word, conscious that his accented Italian was probably not the easiest to understand.

She silently glared at them, gauging their character like a farmer at a livestock auction for what felt a very long moment. Long enough for Benedict and Yukinobu to seriously consider whether they should just leave. Whatever consideration she had been carrying out must have been completed as she then suddenly slammed the shutters with a decisive flap. Bam. The verdict she had reached remained a mystery.

Benedict and Yukinobu frowned at each other.

"Right. That went well," Benedict quipped, and they both chuckled. There was fondness in the gentle creases around Yukinobu's eyes, which Benedict could not quite interpret. Yet, he liked it. Their relationship had evolved over the case into a friendship. Though Benedict started to wonder whether it was evolving into something else again, at least on his part. Which he did not like. He had managed to navigate his life without ever getting overly attached to anyone other than his parents and Diane, though he had well and truly alienated that relationship. And so far, so good. Perhaps he should try not to enjoy this fondness he had spotted in the private detective's eyes, for fear it might get in the way.

Benedict and Yukinobu had moved a few steps away when they heard a whisper coming from behind them.

"Psssst, psssst."

The woman's head was poking through the gap in the entrance door. She waved at them to come back while she peeped at every corner of the street.

"*Avanti!* (Come on in)." She hurried them in a hissy whisper. She looked a lot older than expected, either in her late seventies or she'd had an incredibly tough paper round for someone in their fifties. A blotchy finger in front of her plump lips, she beckoned them through a small hallway and up a narrow staircase. Her frizzy blond hair flickered around her like the flame of a candle disturbed by uncooperative currents of air.

Once inside her apartment, she turned a plethora of keys in locks, slid many bolts and latched many latches. If this was a horror story it would be the point when the protagonists would start to worry that they had entered the monster's lair. Her five-foot-nothing body swivelled in one swift movement. Sporting a hunched posture and one raised eyebrow, she pointed her forefinger and raised thumb at them, as if directing a gun to their chests.

"Are you the police?"

"No."

"The CIA?"

"No."

"Americans?"

"English and Japanese."

"MI5?"

"No."

"Interpol?"

Of course, she had to be a freaking weirdo. Of course... Did he really expect a loving Catholic Italian lady who had turned her life around after giving g up one of her babies? ...Well, yes, he did actually. Having his hopes dashed via a list of security services was a new one though.

"No."

"My grandson is a police officer, okay?" *Her grandson was old enough to already be a police officer?* "So, no funny business, okay? Or he'll have you two behind bars before you have a chance to draw breath, okay?" She jerked up her finger-gun with every 'okay.'

"Okay," Benedict agreed.

She walked down the hallway into an insanely cluttered room with pile after pile of papers, notebooks, folders, etc.

"Say your names again."

Benedict spelt out their names for her, while she flicked open her laptop. A layer of security film blurred her screen, and there was taped paper on the camera. After a little while, she gave Yukinobu a stern look from above her reading glasses. As if challenging him to a stare-off, she brought a glass of cloudy water to her lips without breaking eye contact with him.

"Who sent you?" The question was directed at Yukinobu, who did not react as he had no notion of Italian.

"No one," Benedict replied on Yukinobu's behalf. "Look. Ms. Ginevra Cannavero, right?"

"It depends. What personal matter are you two here to talk about?" She arched one eyebrow higher than the other.

"Your..." Benedict massaged his chin for a second, then decided to cut to the chase. She was clearly a crackpot anyway. "...Sons, or possibly grandsons." Benedict emphasized the plurality of the nouns.

"I've only got the one. Grandson, that is. And one daughter."

"Is Ms. Ginevra Cannavero your daughter?"

"Yes."

"But am I right to think that your daughter gave birth to twin boys?"

"Huh." She slit her eyes.

"One of whom died a couple of days after being born."

"Huh."

Her huhs neither confirmed nor denied it, so Benedict pushed on.

"I'm gonna give it to you straight. We're not from the police. And we're not here to cause trouble. But there's a chance that I might be your other grandson."

Her facial expression did a 180 degree flip.

"*Mio nipote*! (My grandson!)" She jumped out of her seat and smothered Benedict into a tight embrace, whiffing of potpourri and mothballs.

Before Benedict had a chance to say another word, she was covering him with wet kisses. Her cheeks were drenched with tears as she scurried to one of the tallest towers of binders and folders that were scattered throughout the small living room.

"I KNEW IT! I knew it! I knew it! I knew it!" She waved one of her massive folders at Benedict and pointed at several others.

Convinced that the hospital had faked her grandson's death, she conducted relentless searches and investigations for the past thirty years. It had been a quest for her. Her daughter had obviously omitted to tell her that she actually sold one of her babies, if it came to that... She then went on to explain her monumental conspiracy theory about how thousands of babies were taken from young mothers every year, to be sold to the highest bidders. To these people, her daughter would have made the perfect target as she was young and poor and had given birth to not one but two perfectly formed boys. So, they presumed that her daughter would not grieve the loss of one of them. Yet, she had never, ever given up on him. Her late husband tried to dissuade her from it, but who else would do it? Not her lowlife son-in-law. Nor her beautiful daughter, bless her, she already had to work like a dog to make ends meet and raise her son single-handedly.

It was what Benedict had hoped to hear, nearly to a T, and yet, he was disappointed. If this woman was anything to go by, Ms. Ginevra Cannavero would not be the self-possessed, elegant mother he had pictured. More like a hedgehog on crystal meth. Though, one cannot judge the children by their parents. Then again, maybe he was expecting to meet someone like, well, his mother, his dear Rochele Grant.

The mention of running a DNA test insulted her. There was no doubt in her mind that he was her grandson. She could feel it in her gut the minute he walked in. Post-rationalisation much? Yep. She explained that she was living with her daughter. This was her daughter's apartment. She then showed Benedict a picture of her daughter with her grandson and highlighted all their resemblances. Which was flattering, as these people had clearly been dealt a very good hand when it came to the attractive genes, certainly more so than Benedict. Though, to be fair to her, her grandson did look a bit like Benedict. Then again, Benedict had an appearance that bore similarities with a higher than average number of people. In fact, if his look were a key, it would be one of those skeleton-keys that opened a set of several locks.

His name would have been Gioele, to complete a 'Gi' set; Ginevra (mother), Giorgio (father) and Giuliano (brother). She then talked about how hard life without Benedict had been. Not a day went by without thinking of him, she declared. She knew in her heart of hearts that he was still alive. There was a worthy inflexion in her voice that got up Benedict's nose. She asked him about his childhood. The happy recounting of Benedict's tender years did not seem to please her particularly, so he went on a little longer than he initially intended to. It was petty of him, and he knew it, but he would have lied if he had said that he did not enjoy it... at least a little.

The old lady tried to get them to stay longer. But after securing a DNA sample and hearing that her daughter wouldn't be back until the following day, Benedict was quite happy to put an end to this exhausting visit. After they finally managed to leave, Benedict and Yukinobu had time to kill before their flight home. Rome was familiar to both of them. So, instead of visiting the main touristic attractions, they found themselves sauntering down side streets visiting lesser-known art galleries.

Well, Yukinobu was, Benedict politely accompanied him. Anyway, even if it had been standing in the pit lane at Silverstone during the British Grand Prix, Benedict's head would have been too preoccupied to take anything in. He enjoyed spending time alone like this with Yukinobu, though. It was restful like entering a temple and finding it empty of people and blissfully cutting off all external noise. A safe haven. Benedict did not have to switch on his public persona in Yukinobu's presence or watch what he said or even say anything at all. Pretences would have been futile in any case, as Yukinobu possessed levels of perceptiveness that would have made Sherlock Holmes glance sideways with envy. Also, his code of honour meant his cranium operated on a level akin to a confessional stall, conversations and information being processed within its confines remained confidential from the wider world.

Yukinobu spent about ten minutes on every sculpture, painting, and… things that passed for modern art, always reading whatever morsel of insight had been provided by the artist to help the general public see what the artist saw in it when they 'birthed' it. Despite these insights, now and then Benedict could have sworn he saw speech bubbles floating above people's head, saying things like, 'Yep, I could have done that myself,' or 'what the fudge am I looking at'. One of those particular works featured a series of silver butt plugs fused onto a metal slab alongside a selection of metallic graters. The artist's notes indicated that it could be taken as an allegory of the impact of human vices on the planet. To be fair, it did look like a mini city, a sort of cursory architect's 3D rendition of Manhattan. Although not a particularly attractive piece of art, it had the merit to distract Benedict for a fleeting moment. And, in all fairness, this would not have been achieved by any of the old plates, pots, and amphoras whose only merit were to be old. So, on that front, the battle between Roman antiques and new crapola-Coppola had been won by the latter. Then, something happened.

As Benedict started to get seriously bored and in desperate need of a Peroni, he caught sight of Yukinobu silently sobbing in front of an impressionist painting. Frozen into place for a second, Benedict was faced with two choices. Pretend that he had not seen Yukinobu and stealthily retrace his steps back to the butt plugs until Yukinobu pulled himself together, or, offer some support. He definitely had more experience in the former. Could even win awards for it. Yet, the latter option pulled at him. If anything, he was startled by the avidity of his own compassion towards Yukinobu.

Lately, he had found himself increasingly wondering about what was on Yukinobu's mind. About his thoughts, what made him tick or recoil, who he was seeing when they were not together.

131

What Yukinobu truly thought of him or if he thought about him at all when he was not there…

Yukinobu had mentioned he had worked as an art dealer until something happened to him in Oxford that changed his line of work. Maybe something reminded him of that moment? Although… maybe, Yukinobu had a sensibility towards art that Benedict could not fully comprehend. Goes to show that you cannot trust a stereotype, thought Benedict, but maybe in Yukinobu's case, the stereotype rang true. Either way, Benedict wanted to comfort him, show concern. Yet, he could not think of anything to say or do other than 'I know how you feel, mate. Not a fan of grey myself… There, there.' So, despite himself, he waited until Yukinobu got a grip of himself, feeling frustrated with his own impotence.

Three days later, a courier delivered the results of the DNA test to Benedict's house.

Chapter 21

"One Caucasian, one East Asian"

Manarola, Cinque Terre, Italy
Now, July 2017

One of the police officers in Giandomenico's team points at someone. Giandomenico moves his head to one side then the other and still cannot see the relevant person for the heave of people in uniform crowding the place. So his colleague grabs Giandomenico by the arm and points directly at an old man. He is wearing a flat cap that has seen better days and a beige shirt with rolled-up sleeves revealing bony lumps the size of golf balls on the outside of his elbows. His curved back leans against one of the small boats parked on tows. He is staring at his age-spotted hands stacked on top of the curved handle of his cane. The placid dog beside him looks like an Italian Pointer, with a powerful, compact body, pendulous upper lips dribbling spit, and long, floppy ears. They look a poster-picture of the old continent.

Giandomenico introduces himself and shakes the arthritis-riddled hand.

"I was told that you discovered the bodies this morning."

The old man nods his head, his grey skin resembles that of elephants in its creased texture.

"Would it be okay if I ask you a few questions?"

The local man is forthcoming. He discovered the bodies at dawn whilst walking his dog through the empty streets of Manarola. The dog chased after some birds down the slipway into the sea. As the old man took a seat on the low, stepped wall by the inlet, he saw two bodies being buffeted against the rock by the swell of the sea. The old man asserted that although his dog went and gave the corpses a good sniff, she did not at any point scratch nor touch them. They were left undisturbed. And an hour later, when the police arrived, the bodies had been deposited on the rocks, discarded by the Mediterranean Sea's micro-tide.

Giandomenico bids his goodbyes before being directed to another set of witnesses, an Italian couple, and tourists from Milan. They look the kind who proudly announce that they 'could murder a drink right now' or 'haven't been wearing socks for months' – boring with a side of conformist, but agreeable. They are spending their 'mini-moon' in Manarola. Giandomenico had to have the term 'mini-moon' explained to him, which is a romantic weekend away after one's wedding but not quite the full McCoy in terms of honeymoons. They nailed their timing with that one. Thinking about it, this couple probably ought to give Pompeii a miss if they planned to spend their honeymoon on the Amalfi coast. This momentarily took Giandomenico back to a wedding he attended, where a bird defecated on the bride's veil, before flying straight into the venue's window and promptly dying at the groom's feet.

Anyway, the couple said that they saw a man carrying what appeared to be another man on one shoulder from a distance. This happened the evening before, sometime between 11 pm and midnight, while they strolled along the coastal path back to their hotel. They presumed that the person being carried was inebriated. Although it was dark, they remembered that both men were dressed in white T-shirts and dark jeans, like the two bodies draped across the harbour's rocks. This, therefore, throws up the confusing possibility that one of the unidentified deceased may have thrown the other into the sea before perishing himself rather than having died at sea as so much of the physical evidence currently suggested.

But as for everyone who has been interviewed so far, the old man and the couple did not know nor recognise either of the dead men.

The unidentified corpses remain in a fairly good state. From what Giandomenico and his team can tell so far, they do not appear to have suffered any obvious traumatic injuries. Their decomposition was also relatively limited at point of discovery. Both can significantly distort facial features and prevent identification, including fingerprinting. However, the hot temperature and long exposure to the sun have accelerated their decomposition. Internal gases have caused the corpses to swell and discolour, though their tissues had survived the initial, limited decomposition. All this meant their fingerprints and dental records remained a viable source of identification and would hopefully prove conclusive.

Yet, one aspect of their identification has been established. The smaller corpse appeared to be Caucasian, the other East Asian.

Chapter 22

"Poop Gate"

Marseille, France
Seven years ago, September 2010

The hospital was in a busy, urban area. As Benedict stepped out of his airport taxi, it took great effort to keep the contents of his stomach in. There was something about the sight of a hospital that did not agree with him. The jerky ride amidst sweat fumes and other fetid odours, punctuated with tire-screeching brakes, hand gestures and (creepy) catcalls, certainly did not help matters either. What was it with catcalling? Did it ever work? Or was it a mere occupational hobby, done to entertain micro-audiences? At one point, Benedict's hairy taxi driver, repeatedly yelled "rhmm rhmm rhmm" at a woman, making precisely the sort of sound one would expect a chubby child to emit while eating chicken nuggets. 'Thanks. I'm gagging to go on a date with you now', did not transpire from the woman's indignant side-eye.

Back in London, Benedict once heard a man throw out "you're pretty." To be blanked, and try again, "hey, what would a smile cost, babe?"

To which, the young woman replied, "equal pay and respect would do it, *babe*." Benedict felt like clapping her comeback, which (surely) would not have been received as patronising in the slightest. So, he had refrained.

Anyway, Benedict knew that neither the hospital nor the taxi ride was the real culprit here. His stomach was churning because he was well and truly apprehensive about meeting this woman, a nurse. The DNA result had been clear, Benedict was not related to the Italian family. Phew. Bullet dodged.

However, this time around, he could not use Yukinobu as his crutch because, rather inconveniently, the man had caught a nasty gastroenteritis… Oh, bugger. Could this stomach churning actually be the start of a stomach bug rather than nerves? He did not think so, or hoped not. Yet, it was the very first time a woman had ever had this effect on him. Of course, his last encounter with the intense, distrustful Italian woman did not help matters. But it also felt very final. There was no other lead, and Yukinobu went through an absolute ordeal to trace her. Although Yukinobu had not been able to find an address for her, the fact that she worked for a hospital made it a tad easier.

Still in the spot where the taxi had dropped him, Benedict took everything in. The hustle and bustle around the major Marseille hospital was dizzying with lights, noises, and activity. Its building was sandwiched within walking distance of two motorways, a commercial port, and topped by a tango of aeroplanes and helicopters. In sum, a peaceful haven for convalescent patients, right?

Maybe it was not such a good idea to show up unannounced and dump the potential news in person. He wished he had taken more notice of Yukinobu's advice and called or emailed first. This would have given this woman time to digest and adjust to the situation. However, it would have also given her control over 'if' and 'when' they would meet. A magpie flew past and the black and white bird never failed to bring his late father to mind. His old man would always salute them, murmur something under his breath, and then wink at Benedict. How did the saying go again? One's for sorrow, right? Could the old superstition hold? Benedict was not one for old wives' tales. No, he certainly was not. Another magpie flew by. Two's for joy, isn't it? He could picture his father winking at him right then. Benedict suddenly felt a little more optimistic and marched through the entrance. He asked for the nurse he was there to see at the reception. Minutes later, a sweet curvy brunette greeted him.

It had been easier than anticipated. In fact, easier than he ever imagined. She asked him out. He claimed that his mother had been a patient here and extremely impressed by the care she had received from her. As he was passing by, he could not resist thanking her in person. She had blushed and sweetly enquired who his mother was. Yukinobu had pre-empted the question and given Benedict the name of an elderly patient. The nurse did not remember her, but she was very gracious in her 'pretend' recall. The funny thing was, she averted her eyes and blushed a fair bit as if she was the one fibbing. Benedict found her bashfulness very endearing.

Coincidently, except it was not, her shift was ending. Before he had a chance to take the initiative, she stalled him by offering to take him to a nearby café. On the way, their conversation had flown seamlessly. From a simple question about how her day had been, Marie made him laugh almost continuously, through work anecdotes and amusing observations about everything and anything. While she punctuated their walk with the occasional pick-up and dumping of rubbish from the pavement and into bins.

"This is what I imagine life in Southern France is about," Benedict commented, gazing at the food and wine served to customers on the outdoor tables. They were on a square with a fountain, the corner café was dappled with light pocking through plane trees and delimited with colourful flowerpots. Very Amélie Poulain.

"A double-parked FedEx van keeping its gas on and the laundry lines hanging out of windows, is how you imagined the South of France?" she quipped.

"Of course, and this." Benedict nodded to a dog squatting down. A few paces ahead, the dog's owner pretended not to know what was being deposited behind him.

Marie's expression changed. Her ears seemed to stand.

"Pardon me?" She beckoned to the dog's owner, the type people would not usually dare to accost. Crumbs… Benedict had aimed for 'funny' not to ignite a fight. A thread of regret nipped at him.

"Monsieur?" She trotted across to the shady guy. A Mickey Mouse's head embroidered on the back pockets of her jeans bounced with her every step. This did not help in making her look street, nor did her pink butterfly handbag. "Monsieur?" she insisted, louder. Benedict took a few paces in her direction, in case he would have to back her. Sizing up the other guy, Benedict decided that he could probably take him after all, well, 50/50 odds, maybe, and an occasion to put his recently acquired Aikido moves into practice.

As Marie finally caught up with the dog owner, everyone sitting out at the terrace of the café goggled at them.

"I think you forgot something back there." She pointed at the brown dollop.

Much to Benedict's surprise, the shifty guy flapped his hands in the air and put on a good show of thanking her for bringing it to his attention, before obliging to his duty of scooping up the steaming poop. The excitement over, Benedict felt a mix of relief and a tad of disappointment at the outcome – he had psyched himself up for a punch-up.

As Marie dashed back a little red-faced, Benedict pulled out a chair for her. He had officially fallen for this unique little trooper of a woman. Truly and utterly fallen for her... Well, not in a romantic way, that went without saying. But so far, she had been nothing other than charming, witty, warm, and damn committed. Superb. Plus, he had absolutely loved the thrill of this mini drama, which he rarely got to experience in real life. Confrontation was something he relished but rarely got to experience out in the open. Sure, he stirred the pot at work, within his social circle and whenever an opportunity arose, but it was nearly always submarine ops, bar last Christmas' scuffle.

"Back in England, this guy would've gotten away with it, with a hard stare. At most."

"England. Is that where you're from then?"

"Yep. London."

"Wow, your level of French is amazing. I mean, I knew you weren't from around here, but I just thought you came from somewhere up north."

"And you were right, only slightly further up," Benedict quipped.

"Oh yeah. Haha... And what do you do to pay the bills?"

"I work in the city."

He could tell that it was lost in translation but did not see the follow-up question coming.

"You're a civil servant?" At least, there was a hint of incredulity in her voice. Still, the assumption was, quite frankly, a little insulting. Civil servant? Him?

"No. I'm a partner at a trading firm. Co-founder, actually." Pre-empting a question about what he was trading, he chipped in. "I work in finance. Whitehall is where civil servants work. The city is where people with pound signs in their eyes work."

"Oh, right. Fancy then, eh? That'd explain the 'hard stare' approach in comparison to my way of dealing with poop-gate head on earlier. I bet, that 'hard stare approach' applies to only a certain breed of British people." She was right, of course – that'll teach him for making sweeping statements based on his own social background, he thought. "You must think of me as a right peasant," she continued rather self-consciously.

"Well, if you were, I'd think of you as an incredibly charming peasant."

Marie blushed again. A blasé waiter appeared and she looked down at the menu for the first time and stalled for a few seconds, her eyes darting to the price of each option. She settled for a Margherita pizza, the cheapest option on the menu, and so did he.

Once, their sloth of a waiter was gone. Benedict leaned across the table towards Marie.

"I've got a confession to make. I didn't come to see you because of my mother."

"Right."

"Well, actually, I did. But. Not for the reasons I mentioned earlier."

After a small pause, she managed a quiet "oh. Hmm. Okay..." She looked at her plate, looked at her hands, then used the prongs of her fork to swivel it. "Why are you here, then?"

Benedict cleared his throat. "I've got reasons to believe that you may be my sister... My twin sister."

Marie choked a little, stared at him, then burst out laughing. Her reaction puzzled Benedict. He would usually take offence, but remarkably, not on this occasion. In fact, her laugh was infectious. He ended up joining her. It was, after all, an impossible situation. Plus, it felt good to laugh.

"I'm sorry. I'm sorry, I'm sorry..." She avowed after a while, waving her hands in front of her. "We may well be..." Benedict could tell that the words did not match her doubtful expression. "... It's just ... the last thing I'd expected you to say. No offence."

"None taken. What did you expect?"

"Well... You know." Her eyes moved sideways, eloquently.

"Oh. You thought my mother tried to set me up with you?"

"Pretty much." She smiled and shrugged as if to say, too bad. "So. What makes you think that we're related?" There was a smile in her voice, that he did not mind. He would have been impossibly sceptical of this declaration as well.

Benedict explained everything. Her initial reaction was to just stare at him, silently and rather intently. This made him a tad uncomfortable, but he understood where it came from. He had been there not long ago and, to her credit, it did not cause her to inhale something nor punch anyone. She then, and without any prompting, suggested a DNA test. She was brilliant.

"Wow. Pardon my French, but that's batshit crazy... And, I'm sorry, but I don't think my mum would have it in her to do something like that... Well, she isn't perfect, for sure, but I don't think she would, you know, sell her son." She stalled. "I think..." Marie, who had shaken her head the whole way through, suddenly placed her fork back down and looked away pensively. "Mind

you, I wouldn't put it past my dad." She took a swig of Panaché.
Before Benedict could say anything back, she added. "Did you try
to reach him? My dad. Fatos Aoun."

"Yes. And, I understand that he's in prison." Benedict trod
lightly, gauging the water, but there was no awkwardness on her
part. "I sent him a letter, pretending I was a family friend. But
ah..." He was incredibly rude and opportunistic, leaving me with
no taste to meet him whatsoever. "... Getting a visitation order
can be quite hard."

A smile without humour brushed her lips.

"Probably best to leave it at that anyway, to be honest." She
swirled the ice cubes in her drink with a straw, making them clink.
"My mother?" she queried without looking up.

The sudden pang of resentment he felt at the mention of 'her'
mother surprised him. In the past few months since his mother's
revelation, he had wondered why his birth parents chose his
sibling over him. At first, he had imagined that they might have
sold both of their twins. But when this assumption was possibly
negated by Yukinobu's findings, a feeling of rejection nagged at
him. Benedict buried this sentiment as it would have proven his
mother right for not telling him her shameful secret, and he did
not want to give her that just yet.

However, what he realised just then was that the resentment he
felt towards his birth parents had little to do with being rejected.
He resented them for taking his sibling away from him. He had
had a privileged upbringing. A happy one even, until his father
died. And although he had daydreamed about having siblings as a
child and forever felt envious of the bond that siblings seemed to
share, after his father's death Benedict went through a period that
could only be described as 'grievance' over the absence of a
sibling in his life. The anguish of losing his mother was gut-
wrenching, yet one he neither would nor could share with her. He
craved a sibling then. And the sad thing was, he fantasized about
someone with grit, humour and altruism... He had fantasised about
a sibling like Marie.

"Not yet. It was hard enough to trace you, but your mother is
Vlora Aoun, right?" Benedict checked.

"Correct."

"She's impossible to locate."

"She's, ah... Well, let's see how the DNA results turn out,
first. Then I'll introduce you." Marie took another sip. "By the
way, I absolutely hate this expression," she vowed with a smile.

"What expression?"

"Pardon my French." She mocked-crossed her arms.

Benedict chuckled, though he could not help but think that this was said as a confusing attempt to change the subject.

"Well, at least, it's not the first thing that sprung to mind about the French. Imagine being Brazilian, and having your nationality eclipsed by pube-waxing."

"Granted." They both shared a giggle.

Their food arrived.

"I'm very sorry about your mother passing, by the way."

"You and me both," Benedict responded, meeting her eyes. Marie swallowed a mouthful then managed a meek, sad smile.

"And you learned all this from a letter?" she traded gently.

"Yep." His thumb ran on the label of his Kronenbourg 1664, before starting to roughen its edges with his nails.

"Do you have it on you? The letter."

"I do." His eyes drifted back to the label he was peeling off, shred by shred. Oh, heck… "Would you like to read it?"

"Only if you're comfortable with it."

Somehow, he was, entirely so. Benedict handed his mother's letter over… Followed by a paper towel, a few minutes later. Without peeling her eyes off the letter, she dabbed her cheeks and blew her nose like a Piccolo trumpet.

"Gosh, that was your mother's last words to you?"

Benedict simply nodded.

"I bet my mother's last words will be something like 'who knew bus 22 had so many stops'…"

"I would've preferred that. It was hard enough to lose her. But this is…" He rubbed his face with both hands and sighed.

"I can imagine… Though, on the plus side, we wouldn't be speaking now, if she hadn't said anything. And based on what I've read, it would've been a shame for me not to meet you, whether we're siblings or not."

Benedict made an unattractive snorting noise although he agreed with her on the last part.

"When life gives you lemons?" Marie volunteered encouragingly.

"Make lemonade," he grumbled despite himself.

"I'd make limoncello. But, yeah."

A faint smile escaped his lips. She placed her small hand on his, gently rubbing his skin with her thumb. The shape of her gnawed nail looked like his, he decided. His first instinct was to retrieve his hand from under hers, but he surprisingly did not want to. Her motherly touch had an inexplicable soothing effect on him. It eased to some degree the sad knot of anger that had taken residence at the nape of his neck since his mother's passing.

When Yuki mentioned the name 'Marie' as his potential sibling, Benedict remembered being a little shocked. He had heard of men called Jean-Marie, but Marie, for a man, was a bit out-there. Or so he mused until his thought had finished its lap around the block. And he cogitated on the possibility of his sibling being a female. Somehow, he had been convinced that it would be a man.

Over the past few months, Benedict had imagined this man to be named Vito, living in Italy, or having immigrated to America. An identical twin. Identical to such an extent that if it were not for the scar on Vito's right cheek, it would be impossible to tell them apart. Vito had had a rough childhood. After his parents were murdered, he'd bounced from one foster home to the next. He grew tough and ruthless. There was no one to talk him out of the bad company he was keeping, which, combined with a cold-blooded demeanour and ambition, led him to a criminal life. Instead, Benedict was sitting opposite a doe-eyed, freckled-nose, rosy-cheeked lady nurse, full of compassion.

"Going back to your mother's letter, if we may?" Marie offered. Benedict nodded for her to carry on. "Obviously, what she did is wrong and reprehensible. But..." Marie stumbled for a moment, clearly trying to make sense of her tumbling thoughts. "And, I mean, I can't fully relate with her, as my son arrived pretty quickly but..."

"You've got a son!" Benedict interrupted, eyes widened and bright.

"Yes. Romain."

"How old is he?"

"He's seven." She waved away the side-tracking. "Anyway... But, I'm aware of the odd and unpleasant things that happen to childless women."

"What do you mean?"

"Well, a close friend, Médélice, had a ruptured ectopic pregnancy. It was all very traumatic, and she ended up being barren. But it's what she went through, afterwards, that opened my eyes to a lot of things, actually. Her first marriage collapsed. Then, some of her friends fell away, because her sadness over her infertility made them feel awkward, and because their social lives became centred on families. And, the way people at work take advantage, it must feel like not only can she not have kids but she's almost being punished for it, in a way…" Benedict crossed his arms, but Marie was not finished. "And a Bangladeshi patient once told me of her infertile daughter's tragic suicide and explained that in her country, barren women are sometimes cast out from their community as a harbinger of bad luck to others. It's awful."

The turn that their conversation had taken made him feel inadequate. He wanted Marie to feel sympathy for him, not his baby-snatching mother. He did not know who he was anymore. And his mother was entirely to blame for it. Quite frankly, it spoiled his appetite…

"This is tasteless," he declared, pushing his ice cream bowl away.

"Vanilla ice cream that isn't handmade from Madagascan vanilla pods isn't worth serving, quite frankly." Marie tutted in jest.

"You think me a snob?" It came out harsher than necessary.

"No, I think of me as a right peasant, remember? Besides, what would be the point of being wealthy if you weren't even a discerning eater?"

She placed her hand on his again. It felt warm and candid. Also, the way her forefinger and thumb were positioned formed a half-heart shape, waiting to be completed by his. He repressed a smile, he did not want to give her the satisfaction, yet he enjoyed her motherly benevolence… And everything else about her.

143

Chapter 23

"Results"

London, England
Seven years ago, September 2010

Three days later, just as it had happened before, a courier arrived with the DNA results.

Benedict had found himself staring with dead-fish eyes at the unopened envelopes in a vegetative state of anticipation on three occasions previously. Well, four, if his mother's last letter was to be included. As a matter of fact, that fourth occasion undoubtedly counted, as the sucker-punch news it divulged to him had ruined all future 'letter opening' moments, for the rest of his life. The first time Benedict had procrastinated over the opening of a letter was after his university applications. Although only one truly mattered to him. Yet, when he read the good news, he still, somehow, managed to feel a tad disappointed. The content of the letter was fine. Naturally, he was pleased to be accepted. Problem was, it read like all the others. It was printed and sounded administrative. An entirely handwritten letter would have been a ludicrous expectation, but a personal accolade would not have gone amiss.

You see, since his bowel movements were enthusiastically cheered during his potty-training days, it seemed only fair for his London School of Economics admission letter to live up to the level of adulation he had grown to expect from achievement met. Confetti falling from the card would have been entirely distasteful, it was not a sixth birthday card after all, but still, something was amiss.

The other two occasions were inconsequential in the end. STD results came back negative, and so did the DNA results to the Italian family. Yet again, he had hoped for more than just a wave-off from both. It was ridiculous for him to feel that way, and he knew it. But as Yukinobu would frequently say, you can't change the spots on a leopard, can you? The way he still slightly rearranged the words of old phrases was one of the things that Benedict had grown to find endearing in him.

Benedict took a deep breath, but he could not bring himself to open this particular envelope.

They had not met for long. Yet that was all it took for him to develop a bond with the bubbly French nurse. She was the sister he'd never had but always yearned for. There was an authenticity to Marie's character that made a refreshing change to what Benedict was accustomed to. No game, no intent to impress, no ambiguity. She even came with her own child. He wanted her to be in his life, in a significant way, a thicker than water, blood relative kind of way. He wanted to write her name in the next of kin section of official documents. He wanted to be tangibly grounded to her, another human being. But this craving to have Marie as his true sister felt needy and weak. And he was not a weak man, no, he was the opposite of that, right? The lack of human contact he'd had over the past few months was his choice. His decision. He did not need others. Yet, he checked his personal phone for his last contact with Diane. Nothing, for over eight months. His school friend was not holding a grudge anymore, she had written him off her life altogether, he thought. He sighed, scrunched up the unopened envelope into a ball, and lobbed it out of the opened front window.

A moment later, Yukinobu made an unannounced appearance. Letting himself in, he found Benedict on the landing, sitting on the hardwood floor, his back against the wall, staring at his knitted fingers perched on folded knees.

"Is this what I think it is?" Yukinobu lifted the crumpled envelope that he'd picked up outside the front door.

Benedict met Yukinobu's gaze and nodded his head slowly.

Yukinobu smoothed the sealed results against his lap.

"Shall I hold on to these for now?"

"If you want."

Benedict picked himself up and headed to the kitchen. Yukinobu tagged along.

"I thought it went well? Your meeting with Marie."

"It did go well." Benedict opened a beer bottle. "Great, in fact." He took a sip and stared at his bottle on the kitchen counter. "She'd make the perfect sister."

"Okay… Then, why the dramatic littering?"

"I'd rather talk about something else." Benedict cut him short, heading out to the garden.

"We certainly can. But…" Yukinobu flapped the letter.

"No, seriously. Please," Benedict pleaded as he walked off.

145

A little disconcerted, Yukinobu left the sealed DNA results on the kitchen counter and followed Benedict outside.

Gazing off into space, Benedict buried his hands deep into his pockets. After a moment of hesitation, Yukinobu placed a comforting arm around Benedict's shoulders. The weight of Yukinobu's arm felt alien, so much heavier than that of his late mother or Diane, and yet familiar, even if somewhat of a distant memory. It felt like solid warmth, a human's touch, bringing him back to thoughts about Marie. But Benedict would not let the heightened emotions this simple gesture had stirred in him to rise to the surface. He was not that kind of man. Sentimental. He was a man's man.

Yet, he patted Yukinobu's hand where it rested on his shoulder in acknowledgement. It was only polite. But this clasp morphed into an embrace. Then, one thing led to another… And, Benedict woke up the next morning to the smell of an egg-white omelette being cooked in his kitchen by an extremely fit Japanese private investigator-cum-martial arts teacher. Benedict noticed that the sun was shining outside, birds were chirping in the trees, and it was the latest he had ever woken up on a Wednesday morning.

∞

The next day, Benedict knocked on Yukinobu's front door. He had been here before, a few times, but only to talk about progress on the retracing of his family. Although each of these visits eventually turned into dinner, sharing a few drinks and watching a game. This time there was no pretence, he was just here to see him. A mix of conflicted emotions surged forward, nerves yet excitement, glee yet guilt. Benedict braced himself for an awkward greeting.

But there was none, Yukinobu bawled "hi" and immediately rushed back to his frying pan. This stalled Benedict, who found himself wiping his feet on the mat for a decade longer than necessary. He hung his coat inside a neatly organised hallway unit and placed his uncomfortable leather shoes next to an orderly row which was sorted in ascending order – starting with flip-flops at one end and boots at the other. He walked across the open-plan living room to the kitchen. Yukinobu poured beer into a pint glass that he brought back specifically for Benedict from a weekend spent in Dublin with Laure. Benedict seemed to inhale the whole pint in one gulp.

146

"What are you cooking?" Benedict sat on one of the two stools by the small kitchen peninsula. His kitchen was sleek and functional, nothing out on show. He finished his beer, Yukinobu poured him another.

"Teriyaki salmon soba." Yukinobu added curry oil to one of the three pans he had on the heat.

"My mother would have loved it." He did not mean to say that. It just came out.

"I would have loved to have met her."

Benedict walked over to the long windows. It was half-past eight and the sun was setting, but the small courtyard was too enclosed to display much evidence of it.

"I've got to be straight with you. I'm not gay," asserted Benedict.

"Alright." Yukinobu did not look up from his cooking.

"Okay."

"And I'll be straight with you, too. I am." Yukinobu chopped spring onion, his knife banging fast and methodically on a wooden board.

Was he poking fun at me? wondered Benedict. "Alright," he mustered, begrudgingly.

"Glad we cleared that up." Yukinobu smiled at Benedict from over the pans.

"So you're happy with just a casual thing?"

"Sure."

"Because, to be completely honest with you, my goal right now is to have a family. I mean a child. And a wife, of course, the biological link to the child is important to me."

"Okay."

"Would you like to have children, yourself?"

"I'm a little too old for that now."

"Men never are."

There was a pregnant pause.

Yukinobu's lip curled up at one corner. Benedict was mystified by him. He found him so difficult to read, so different from everyone else he knew, so full of contradictions. There was something about Yukinobu that pulled him in but at the same time kept him at arm's length. He was straightforward, yet impossibly private, wanting but never pressing and always composed, bar momentary cracks in his wall exposing a passionate soul.

"I'm surprised you're not already married or engaged at least," Yukinobu volunteered, looking at his pans.

147

"I've been focusing on my career."

"Well, their loss then." The food was ready. Yukinobu looked up before adding. "For now." He smiled at Benedict again, in a way that Benedict did not like, as if Yukinobu knew something he did not. But there also was something calm, a quiet confidence that Benedict found irresistible.

The Japanese man moved up behind Benedict's stool and ran a finger along his spine ever so lightly. Benedict automatically arched his back in response, the two of them moving as one. Like the night before, Yukinobu was leading that dance. Until he suddenly broke it off. "Shall we eat?"

Benedict mustered a nod and washed his mouth out with more beer.

"Have you looked up the results from the DNA test?" Yukinobu enquired as he served them up.

"Not yet."

"Maybe you should spend another weekend in the South of France anyway."

Benedict tucked into his food. "This is very good," he added pointing at his plate.

"Perhaps have another drink with Marie whilst you're at it? Spend some more time with her?"

Yukinobu insisted, his eyes on Benedict. He had not touched his cutlery yet.

Benedict stared at the fork in his hand for a moment as if the pink salmon on the end of it held some unspoken secret or greater wisdom. "Maybe." He breathed, finally, nodding to himself.

Chapter 24

"Watching the news"

London, England
Twenty-two years ago, March 1995

It felt surreal to be heading back to Jacob's place after what had come to pass between him and Jacob's brother a few weeks earlier at the cinema. Yet, this was, precisely why Benedict had sort of invited himself over. He was not sure if he was ready or even wanted to come to terms with his sexuality, but he could not shake away the intense memory of that day. It was half-term again, so Benedict was hopeful that Sacha might be back at his parents for the break.

"Hi, mum," greeted Jacob.

Mrs. Goldman turned around, wiping her hands on her apron as they entered the kitchen.

"Oh, hello," she carolled. "Lovely to see you, Benedict."

"Can he stay for dinner tonight?" asked Jacob.

"Of course, he can. We might even have some of that Indian skimmed milk knocking around somewhere." She playfully winked in a pantomime fashion, in the sense that you could not miss it in the back rows.

Oh no, here it comes again... Benedict would have been all of five, playing cars with Jacob in their living room whilst Jacob's mother had some travel documentary about India on the TV. At one point, Benedict looked up from his cars and pointed at a herd of skinny cows on the TV and said, 'those must be the ones that skimmed milk comes from'.

Hands resting on her stomach, Jacob's mum chuckled at the rehashed memory, before wiping tears from the corner of her eyes and sighing.

"Yep. That was me," Benedict acquiesced.

Jacob exchanged an 'I'm sorry' look with Benedict, before declaring, "right, mum, we'll be in my room."

"Have fun. Dinner will be ready by six. I've made lasagne since you're asking." She pursed her lips at Jacob, before cooing, "Sacha's favourite." At the mention of Sacha's name, the sixteen-year-old's heart skipped a bit. "Doesn't agree with their dad, mind you," Mrs. Goldman added, a hand cupped by the side of her mouth in a conspiratorial tone before making a circular gesture over her guts. Benedict took a mental note for later, 'do not sit next to Mr. Goldman at dinner.'

At six o'clock on the dot, Jacob's mother yelled, "dinner's ready!" up the stairs, setting the whole house quaking.

The older brother settled at the table a good five minutes after everyone else. As Sacha sat down, Benedict received no acknowledgement or greeting.

"Jacob, have some greens too." Mrs. Goldman frowned at the disappearing mountain of pasta and bread that had been piled on her son's plate minutes ago.

Turning her attention to Benedict, her facial expression changed. "Oh darling, you've hardly eaten anything. Don't you like it?" she queried, worried, or perhaps vexed.

Benedict forced himself to eat a mouthful as he spoke. "I'm just a slower eater, Mrs. Goldman… It's delicious." And it was, but his appetite had been spoiled by something else, or rather someone else.

Jacob's father turned on the news and Mrs. Goldman frowned at her husband's initiative. Yet, they all turned their heads towards the living room. After a little while, a photograph of two men with bloodied faces appeared on the screen. A reporter stated, over the still image, that four teenage boys had been charged with an aggravated hate crime after a homophobic attack on two men on a Cardiff train.

"Isn't that sad?" Mrs. Goldman tutted, shaking her head in dismay.

"Awful," Mr. Goldman agreed.

"Mind you. Those two shouldn't have flaunted their lifestyle like that. I know that we are all more modern these days, but still, they put themselves at risk. Like the French say, to live happily, live hidden." Moving the main dish by Mr. Goldman's side, she then offered, "want some more, dear?"

Jacob's father nodded, whether out of reflex or in agreement that much was not clear. All the same, Mrs. Goldman served him an extra spoonful of lasagne.

"And imagine learning that your son is… one of them…" She could not even bring herself to say the word. It was as if it would cause a disaster like an actor enabled to say "Macbeth" aloud in a theatre. "… And on the news, of all places, for the whole world to see." The horror of that thought brought tears to her eyes, where there were none upon hearing of the attack.

Benedict glanced at Sacha, but he seemed to be taking little notice of anything other than his plate.

"Muuuuum," Jacob, however, moaned with appalling disgust at his mother as if she had just declared that he was still being breastfed.

"It's not their fault, Jacob. It's a mental illness. All the same, thank God our four sons are normal, eh?" She patted Mr. Goldman's forearm, who suppressed a belch into his hand, which seemed to bear no relation to the conversation. "I can think of very little else that would cause greater disappointment," Jacob's mother continued before turning her gaze to Sacha. "Speaking of which..."

Sacha choked slightly on his food.

"Are you alright, dear?" She placed a hand on Sacha's back.

"Uhu," Sacha grunted as he cleared his throat.

"When will we meet this Maya of yours?" she quizzed.

"Soon," Sacha answered with a barely audible sigh.

Jacob's mother beamed at her eldest. For the first time since he sat down, Sacha lifted his eyes, met his mum's gaze, turned up the corners of his mouth, and met Benedict's eyes. The complicit denial in this smile had a destructive force that shocked Benedict and instantly brewed up a proliferation of difficult choices that the sixteen-year-old would have to make.

When Benedict returned home that evening, he found his mum at her desk as he always seemed to since his father passed a few months ago. He certainly could not recall a night when he had not found her here.

"Hi Benedict." The tone of her greeting as he stepped into her office suggested she had not realised he was not home when she got back from work.

"Hi, mum."

"How are you?"

"Alright. You?"

"Not bad."

"Have you heard the news about those two men who got attacked on a train?" questioned Benedict.

She shook her head before adding without much interest, "What happened?"

"Hate crime. They charged four teenagers with the attack."

"I see."

"But, these two homos rubbed it in. I'd say, they brought it upon themselves." Despite his best efforts, Benedict's provocation came out as a question rather than a statement. He hated that he was talking this way. But he wanted to glean his mother's reaction.

"You're wrong. In the same way that no level of allure or state of undress gives anyone grounds for rape, people's sexual orientation can never excuse acts of violence."

"But what these two guys do, is disgusting, isn't it?"

Rochele's steel-blue eyes were appraising Benedict with more focus.

"Nonsense. The attack is disgusting and bestial, nothing else. If anything, entering a homosexual relationship is brave."

Her answer confounded him. "Why would you say that?"

"Well, these two men have acknowledged and acted on a love, knowing that it may draw hostile attention, but they've done it anyway. Also," she looked down at her hands, "I'd imagine that entering a relationship knowing full well that no children will ever result from their love could be very saddening... for them... perhaps their parents too." Her voice trailed away. She tried to hide the pain these words clearly carried for her. But it cut so deep within her that its violence seemed to shoot directly through Benedict's heart, knocking him down as if a life architect had thumped him on the head with a 3D map of his future – a future of repressed identity.

The reading the sixteen-year-old Benedict took of his mother's sentiments was to shape his mindset on his sexuality. To carry on being the 'perfect son,' he would have to perfect his pretence. And just like that, he knew what he had to do. He would not let his mother, nor the memory of his late father, down because of what, surely was, a mere quirk in his personality. Not knowing it meant crippling all his relationships; family, friendship, or otherwise, with lies... Isolating lies, pernicious lies, self-confining lies. He made himself a subconscious promise he would not be a source of disappointment to his mother. He would be the *perfect son*, who would produce a grandchild to honour his parents.

It would be many years before he would have the self-awareness and understanding of his mother to look back on her words that defining day and realise just how badly he had misread what she was trying to say. Discovering what causes an inhibition does not always lubricate the entanglement of conflicting desires between one's creed and raw impulses. However, Benedict had learned something profound about who he was. When it came to his family, his wants would always come after their needs.

Chapter 25

"The marks on the wall"

Marseille, France
Seven years ago, September 2010

Romain was chasing pigeons on the esplanade of Marseille's old port. He was trying to catch them with his jacket fashioned into a lasso, whilst Marie was left cooling her heels, or more accurately burning her forehead, in the late summer sun.

Her stomach was filled with butterflies at the prospect of seeing the preppy English man again. His coming back must have meant that the DNA results had proven to be a match. She could not believe it. A brother. And a fancy brother at that. How would she broach the subject with her mother? Why did she do it? How? Fatos must have coerced her into it.

Alone with her thoughts, she tried to change their course, but instead she started to fret that she had not made a particularly good first impression on her new brother. He was so well-spoken, better than her, and in his second language. So well-dressed and well-mannered and generous, he had paid for their meal before she even had a chance to see the bill. He could become such a good role model for Romain if things were to go well. *THE* male role model. But her little crusade against the dog owner, albeit a despicable human being as far as she was concerned, had been a definite low. She feared it had the whiff of the hysterical to her new brother – it felt weird to think about having a brother. But she was determined to make up for it, and for the upcoming news that on top of having a birth father in prison, his birth mother was a self-absorbed pathological addict. His sister lived in a trailer park, and his sickly nephew had a dead 'gypsy' father. On consideration, she might want to keep quiet about certain things, for now. Maybe dole them out like small packages so as not to send fancy Benedict running. Plus, Marie had no intention of inviting him back to where she and Romain lived, that went without saying. Yet, the butterflies in her stomach had turned into moths.

As she took a bite at her already well-gnawed thumbnail, she spotted Benedict. Strolling down La Canebière and about to cross over Quai des Belges, he was only a few paces away from them and precisely on time. She turned her head away, back towards the boats, and inhaled sharply. Most things tended to make her feel nervous these days. And the more she did, the more stressed she became. She had to get off the bus three stops earlier than necessary the other day, for no reason whatsoever other than a feeling that the sides of the vehicle were closing in on her. It was like her heart had started beating at a hundred kilometres an hour, her palms became sweaty, and her head began spinning, she had to leave the bus before she keeled over. Bent over double with her hands resting on her knees, she panted for a few minutes before she felt ready to walk the rest of the way home, feeling stupid. Thanks to the Provence sun, she was sweaty in more places than just her hands by the time she opened the door to their trailer. She knew all too well what it meant, and she could not afford to go through it. There was no space in her life for panic attacks, agoraphobia, claustrophobia or whatsoever-phobia. She was determined to fight it… People with a safety net could afford the 'luxury' of panic attacks, people in her circumstances had to 'pull themselves together and get on with it'. And yet, it was happening again. Oh no, not now. She started to hyperventilate. Why was this happening to her? She did not have time for this. She dragged herself and her palpitating heart to the nearest bench, closed her eyes, and tried to slow her abnormally rapid breathing.

This was when she heard a splash and screams which were shortly followed by another splash and more screams. As she opened her eyes, she sobered up instantly. Romain had fallen into the murky port water. Benedict was in the water with him, one arm was wrapped around Romain's chest as Benedict swam through all that the city port of Marseille could throw at him. The stuff that could be identified consisted of oil patches, floating McDonald's wrappers and a dead pigeon. Those that could not be identified were best not to linger on for too long. He was making his way towards the ladder of a yacht docked at the port. Romain knew how to swim and yet did not wriggle himself free from Benedict's grip.

Marie leapt onto the boat, ran to them and enveloped Romain into a very tight, wet embrace from which he desperately tried to escape.

"That was one acrobatic leap you just took onto the boat," Benedict praised Marie.

"And a very silly one!" Marie began scolding Romain, who finally wriggled free of her arms.

"It was the pigeon's fault, maman," the boy bellowed back, pointing at the dead pigeon floating in rainbow oil slicks. "Didn't you see it pouncing on me?"

Marie and Benedict exchanged a baffled look, looking again at the dead pigeon, then back at Romain's sullen pout. They peeked back at one another, and guffawed at the excuse which clearly had less life in it than the pigeon itself.

"Argh!" Romain slapped the side of his trousers and stomped off with a piece of slushy McDonald's wrapper stuck in his hair. Slosh. Slosh. Romain grabbed hold of the sides of his dripping trousers. Slosh. Slosh. To his chagrin, his grand departure was spoiled by his soggy state. But he was committed, as only a seven-year-old can be, so he carried on, wheezing and coughing as he went.

"So, I take it that I've just met your son?" Benedict nudged Marie playfully.

Marie nodded and rolled her eyes, but thanked him for diving in after Romain.

Back on the port, a boat owner who watched the whole scene and had access to running water, hosed Romain and Benedict down and wrapped them in towels while Marie went to a store to get them some dry outfits. She went for the cheapest options she could find, yet it blew all the money she had set aside for the afternoon. Thankfully, Benedict did not turn his nose up at the 'I heart Marseille' T-shirt and lurid coloured shorts and insisted on repaying her, which she point-blank refused, obviously.

However, it meant that she had to make some adjustments to her plan. Instead of taking the touristic train – more of a luggage cart from an airport done up in the livery of a train but you get the point – from the old port to the height of Notre-Dame de la Garde, they had to walk up the steep streets of Marseille, laboriously.

Romain obviously loved her for it. "But mamaaaan..." he whined and grouched, his head turned to the magnificent basilica that dominated the bay like a beacon.

Halfway through their walk to the peak, continuously serenaded by Romain's moaning, Marie pointed out that "true pilgrims crawl up the stairs to Notre-Dame de la Garde on their hands and knees to get the Bonne-Mère's protection... So, walking is authentic, whereas taking the schmuck-stroller of a train isn't. So think yourself lucky." Judging by Romain's glare in response, she could tell she had definitely won him over with this line of argument…

Seconds later, Romain turned his head towards Benedict.

"You're English, right?"

"Correct."

"Do you like mint sauce on your meat?"

"Hate it."

"See." Romain's head turned to his mum. "Neither of us is into being authentic," Romain claimed, waving his pointing hand back and forth between Benedict and himself.

Marie spotted Benedict suppressing a smile, at least someone was finding Romain's whingeing amusing. And when had Romain ever learned about something as British as mint sauce?

Running out of incentives, Marie used her hail Mary, "Zinedine Zidane walked up rather than taking the tourist train."

Romain snorted an 'as if.' And yet, he resumed his ascent a few paces ahead of Marie and Benedict silently, albeit rattling a wooden stick against the cobblestones.

"Is Zidane your trump card with Romain?" Benedict whispered to Marie.

She winked and thanked him for taking the heavy bag of wet clothes off her hands.

" "So, uh, the DNA results were positive then?"

Benedict pursed his lips slightly and looked down. Why?

"I haven't received them yet."

Pressing on, Benedict joined Romain's side, leaving Marie somewhat puzzled and with a multitude of questions still running through her mind. They had just spent their first hour talking about nonsense. When what she really wanted to know was: when were the DNA results due? Has he ever been married? What had his childhood been like? Did he drink red or white?

They were all left breathless, in the literal and figurative sense of the term, when they finally reached the foot of the highest point in the region. As they sat on one of the outdoor benches, Marie dragged Romain closer, wrapped her arm around his shoulders, and stole a smile from him.

The seven-year-old spotted a few sets of swivelling spyglasses. His battery clearly recharged, he ran to them, and Benedict paid the required donation to unlock them for viewing. They giggled together. It was nice to see. As they started up toward the stripy basilica, Marie decided to leave them to it. Romain seemed to have taken to Benedict the same way she did. The banker's confidence had drawn her in immediately, before a guarded and somewhat cryptic side of him had poked through.

Taking in the stunning panoramic views across the city and the glittering sea beyond, she felt a twinge of guilt for not doing more with Romain. She could not believe that it had taken a virtual stranger for her to take her son here for the first time. Though, in her defence, there were days when she barely had enough time to sleep. She suddenly realised that she had left her schoolboy in the hands of this virtual stranger. A thread of panic, meshed with guilt, built up. She ran up to the Basilica and entered. She ran around like a maniac, searching every face, looking behind every pillar. People glared with disapproving looks, but she did not take notice. As she stepped out, she stopped a family, asking the mother if they had seen a small boy with blond curls and a large scar under his nose with a man around her age. They had not. Her anxiety continued to creep up. She hurried to a vista point on the cliffside and pushed past tourists taking selfies. She asked the same question again and again, but they shook their heads every time. Two middle-aged women started to look for Romain and Benedict with her. They went around the Basilica.

As she reached the city side, her tension immediately gave way as she spotted them. Their heads were turned away from the spectacular views of Marseille and beyond, staring at bare walls instead.

They took no heed of her presence behind them as she approached. Bullet holes and marks littering the limestone walls of the basilica had drawn their attention. A commemorative plaque explained what they were, but Romain hung on Benedict's every side-tracked word instead.

"… and this Basilica bears the scars of the Battle of the Liberation of Marseille," Benedict finally concluded.

A faraway look in his eyes, Romain nodded to no one in particular. He noticed his mum and smiled broadly at her as if he had forgotten that she was there at all. His acknowledgement of her was only brief, though. But this did not vex Marie. She welcomed Romain's interest in his new uncle. She just wished she had kept up to them a tad closer.

"How much will it cost the Germans?"

"What do you mean?"

Romain shrugged. "To repair all they've destroyed." The boy pointed in the general direction of the bullet holes on the Basilica. "And for that."

"Nothing. They pay for their stuff. We pay for ours."

"Hmm. That'll never get fixed then." Romain put his finger in one of the bullet holes. "We're poor in Marseille…"

"Shall we see the inside?" Marie cut Romain short, nervous about the sinuous turn this conversation could take towards their own financial standing.

For lunch, Marie was worried that Benedict would want to eat in a sophisticated place that she could not afford. But he insisted that all he wanted was to try the most traditional food Marseille had to offer.

"Are you sure?" Marie fretted.

The look Benedict gave Marie could only be described as 'bring it on.'

Alright then. Marseillaise grub, here we come…

Tapenade for appetizer, an inky black, grainy mush made from capers, anchovies, olives, and garlic. Marseille tapenade is quite a thing – take a sniff at the contents of a compost bin left to ferment in the sun for a few days, add salt to it, and you get the idea, delectable though. Benedict ate it, his eyes locked with Marie as if to say 'pfff, tapenade. Not. Even. A. Challenge… Been there, done that'.

She followed by ordering a pissaladière for starter, which is best described as similar to a pizza topped with onions, and more anchovies – you are never far from an anchovy in Marseille. Salty, but yummy was the consensus. But then…

Benedict's spoon hung firmly above his bowl of pungent broth. He had tried bouillabaisse in a fancy London restaurant but that was a pale imitation, failing to prepare him for this true Marseille bouillabaisse. The odour was stronger than sweaty socks rubbed against a pig's backside. And if that was not enough, it was served with aïoli, a smelly garlicky mayonnaise; rouille, a smelly garlicky mayonnaise mixed with cayenne pepper; gruyère, a smelly Swiss cheese; and croutons, not smelly at all, just cubes of dried bread. Benedict munched on a crouton.

"Bouillabaisse uses fish or seafood scraps that cannot be sold," Marie imparted with a smile.

"Sounds delicious."

Benedict pressed his tongue in front of his teeth, briefly pushing out his lips in uncertainty. Romain chuckled. To taunt him, Romain started at his bowl with gusto, like a kid snapping their fingers at some other kid who could not manage to produce any clicking despite a series of attempts.

Marie had hesitated between bouillabaisse and pied-paquets – lamb's feet and slimy sheep's tripe. She was glad she went for the former. Although they both sounded revolting, pied-paquets was not actually much of a challenge once you got past the mental image. The full bouillabaisse experience though was capable of overwhelming even the hardiest of foodies. That said, despite his slow start, Benedict ate most of it.

Benedict took care of the bill, claiming that it was his treat – hmm, she doubted that. Still, Marie had to give it to him, resilience was on the order-of-the-day in *his* restaurant. As they left the brasserie, Benedict was still very much game for trying what Marseille had to offer in terms of dessert.

And she decided that he had to try the oh-so celebrated navettes from 'Four des Navettes.' Romain practically floated there when he heard his mum utter the word.

While Romain raced ahead, Benedict scratched his head and looked at his feet then into the distance, carefully avoiding making eye contact with Marie.

"Curious about mum and dad?" Marie prompted. In all fairness, it was his turn to share but as always, she was eager to please. Even if it was at her own expense sometimes. She could be 'over-eager', 'too nice', and it could have the effect of putting people off, much like the bouillabaisse she could overwhelm in her efforts to please. On reflection, she was now sure this was what had happened with Dr. Edgy-Shoes. But she could not help herself.

Benedict nodded.

She nodded back and went on to tell him about her dad working as a docker and her mum going through life much like seaweed, carried by the currents of a crowded city, dazed ninety percent of the time. Their uphill battle to get naturalised. And how they obtained their French citizenship at the start of the Balkan War. She skipped the part about their living arrangements, embarrassed to be, and have always been, poor. But she revealed some of the bad facets of her dad's personality and the bad choices he made, which led to his and her mum's original imprisonment and then again more recently, for him. And how she had the presence of mind to cut herself off from them at sixteen, which led her to meet Romain's dad and eventually fight her way uphill to become a nurse.

Wrapped in the conversation, they did not notice that they had caught up with Romain, who was practically dribbling in front of a pile of biscuits displayed in the Four des Navettes boulangerie.

"What happened to Romain's father?"

Marie placed her forefinger over her lips, pointing at Romain with her eyes. But Romain did not react. The orange flower scent diffused by the little biscuits, shaped like rowing boats, lured him closer. Yet, looking at Benedict, Marie could tell that it was difficult for someone who was not from Marseille to understand all the fuss about a treat which, objectively, looked like a dog treat.

Marie eventually responded to Benedict's question about Baul with a Gallic shrug, hunching her shoulders up and putting her hands out, the French equivalent to 'shit happens.'

The shop keeper handed a bag full of navettes to a beaming Romain.

"That'll be €14.97, please."

Benedict paid for it, ignoring Marie's protestations, as per their new norm.

On their way out, Benedict repeated the last two digits the shop keeper had just voiced. "*Quatre-vingt-dix-sept...* four-twenty-ten-seven." Benedict shook his head at the absurdity of French numbers. "I still can't get my head around that. What's wrong with just a plain ol' ninety-seven, *nonante-sept*?"

Marie cleared her throat, pointedly. "Can you remind me how many feet and toes tall you are? Or is it stones and pebbles you weigh?"

"Okay, fair enough. Though we don't use toes and pebbles. You know that, right?"

"Oh yeah, sorry, my bad, you use dollars, right? Oh, no wait, pounds." She smiled.

"Oui-oui. Oh, no wait, is yes really wee-wee in French?"

Childish but funny... So, Marie stuck her tongue out at him. Benedict touched the navette she had in her hand with his as if clinking glasses in a toast. After one nibble, Benedict's eyes opened wide before exclaiming, "what did the people of Marseille do to deserve navettes?"

"Good, eh?" She smiled.

"Divine," Benedict mumbled with a mouthful.

"Now, let's get down to brass tacks." Marie raised an eyebrow at him as she spoke. "Is there a Mrs. Grant?"

"No." Benedict shook his head, with an expression on his face that Marie could not quite place. "Well, actually, there's a Ms. Grant... But I've never met her."

Marie gave him a look of perplexed amusement, so Benedict continued.

"An aunt." Okay, this was not the point of Marie's question. Anyway, let's roll with it. "My parents and grandparents didn't condone her lifestyle. So, I've never met her."

The dark undertones affecting the word 'lifestyle' clearly denoted a sticky point for him. But before Marie had a chance to voice some sort of nonsense to steer clear from the subject, Benedict added, "the official reason for their schism was my aunt's lack of respect for my parents, but I suspect this wasn't the only nor the main reason. Because, from what I could gather, my short-haired, trouser-wearing aunt only ever had female housemates." He put the word 'housemates' under quotation marks with his fingers.

His gaze met hers. An appraising gaze. A gaze assessing her reaction, maybe even her character. She had seen this gaze on him during their first encounter when they spoke about his mother's letter. Deep down, Marie believed everyone was entitled to have a shot at happiness. And as long as it did not impair anyone else's, then who cares? However, she was not sure what Benedict's views on the matter were. Whether he was a liberal or of a similar opinion to his adoptive parents... or would you say abductive parents in this case... wait, was abductive even a real word? Anyway... The latter was more likely, as people often are the product of their education. Like accents, education takes a dozen years to forge. But once it has taken shape, no matter how hard one tries to shake off its vestiges, it has a tendency to float back to the surface. Ultimately, she did not want to upset him. What she thought did not matter. She also acknowledged that a part of her was seeking approval from Benedict. He was not from her standard set. He was above it. He was polished, well to do, and had his act together. She wanted him in her, and (especially) Romain's, life. So, she remained silent for a moment, pondering what she should say next.

"And, hmm, did you try to get in touch with your aunt now that you're..." an orphan, no, that's not the best word to use, "... an adult?"

"Do you think I should?"

"I, ah, don't know..."

"Would you? *Les-be* honest, why wouldn't one want to meet their deviant aunt if they had one?" There was a dark quip to his tone.

Not funny, she thought. And did he really use the term deviant, in reference to his aunt's homosexuality? *Was it to provoke me, or was he serious?* Marie recognised the tension clenching at the back of her jaw, but she could not do anything to ease it or stop what was bubbling up. She was not even particularly committed to the gay cause, but just like she had not been able to hold back at the dog poop-gate…

"Deviant, really!? You know what. Yes. Yes, I would meet my *deviant* aunt. And I bet she'd…"

Benedict raised his hands in surrender and laughed an easy laugh.

"Alright, alright, I will then. You can even come and meet her with me if you want." Marie did not understand what was so funny about what she had said. But she was glad he'd cut her off mid-sentence, as she was not so sure he would be laughing otherwise. Also, she liked that Benedict was already thinking about a 'next time.'

"Can I have a bite?" Marie asked, pointing at Benedict's navette, the last one in the bag.

"I'll let you bite my elbow off before I'd give away this little fellow," he replied with a smile.

∞

On the flight back, Benedict took a deep breath and opened the envelope with the DNA results. It told the same story as the last time, no DNA match. Marie was not his sister, raising with it a revolution of bitter disappointment in Benedict.

Chapter 26

"Waiting game"

Marseille, France
Seven years ago, October 2010

It had only been ten minutes since Marie last checked her cellphone. Still no message. The cafeteria was empty. She sat at a table where a copy of *Côte & Provence* magazine and *Elle Decoration* had been left by a previous customer. Like second nature, she instantly began to peruse the real estate section, whilst waiting for Médélice. She would barely be able to afford the front door of the places she gazed at on the glossy pages in front of her, but all the same, there was no harm in looking. Also, even if she had that kind of money, she would not spend it on some of these places. Giraffe-patterned wallpaper – I don't think so. Animal skulls – gross. Old ladders leaned against interior walls – fancy being the painter and decorator who lied to his wife about leaving his ladder out on purpose in their living room, then finding out that it had become a design statement in the homes of those with more money than sense. She was reminded of a no doubt apocryphal story she had heard of a kid who, on realising he had dropped his glasses on the floor of a modern art exhibition, returned to find them surrounded by an army of art lovers. They had begun taking pictures of his spectacles and commenting about the simplicity of this particular 'exhibit.' The shock followed by embarrassment in the air must have been thick enough to cut when he reached down to pick them up off the floor and put them back on his nose, she thought.

"I'll have that one." Médélice peeked at the page with the most expensive mansion listed in *Côte & Provence* over Marie's shoulder.

"I'm afraid they've already accepted my offer."

"Shame." Médélice pulled a lopsided pout. "Well, if you need a pool cleaner, I know of one who's available as of today."

"Oh, no. Has Gus lost his job?"

"Don't 'oh no' him. Mr. The-World-Is-Against-Me doesn't turn up to his appointments, doesn't bother to cancel in advance, yet blames his boss for his lack of understanding."

"He'll find something else soon. He always does."

Médélice snorted.

"Or he could start his own business?"

Médélice snorted even louder.

"Anyway, how did it go with your new-found brother?"

"Well," Marie muttered, rearranging the magazines into a neat pile.

"You don't look so sure."

"I still can't get my head around it… It's mad."

"I can't either. But why the long face?"

Marie gave her a detailed account of the day she and Romain spent with Benedict in Marseille.

"It all sounds fab, apart from the near-death experience in the harbour. So, what makes you think he wouldn't want to do it again?"

"He still hasn't called. Or texted. I thought…" Marie shrugged, looked down at her hands, and started picking at her nails. "… I thought that he'd have tried to arrange another visit by now. I don't know if he really liked us. I've tried to reign in Mrs Uber-Keen-Ready To-Please, but you know what I'm like." She shrugged again. "He was friendly enough, mind you, but always careful about what he said, you know, business like." She paused, before adding, "we're so different."

"Don't be silly. You've only met twice, and he's only been gone five minutes. You sound like an infatuated teenage girl."

"I wish I could be more chilled."

"I know, but you're lovely as you are. Anyhow, why are you so hung up on seeing him again?"

Marie thought about it for a moment. Some of her family members, and by that she meant her parents, had hardly any positive impact on her life. Her small group of friends had been ring-fenced for a while. Marie hardly had time to maintain the relationships she already had. Just the thought of building a new one seemed hopeless. So why did she want Benedict in her life so badly?

And then she remembered. She remembered the way he shadowed her when she went after that dodgy guy about his dog's poop, ready to take a punch for her if it came to that. She remembered how his food order had put them on an equal footing and how he took care of the bill before she even had a chance to see it. She remembered how his hand did not twitch or slip from under hers when she yearned to comfort him. It had felt as natural

165

as if it had been Romain's hand under hers. She remembered how his mother's original letter came with a copy, where every slicing word had been translated into French, for her. Benedict had not even met her and yet he had already thought about ways to put her at ease. And of course, she remembered the way he behaved with Romain. Benedict did not strike her as the sort of person who would go out of his way to help or please others, and yet he made an immediate exception for Romain, his presumed nephew. He seemed to be a family-first type of person, without a shadow of a doubt. She also remembered the instant connection she felt, the immediate ease in each other's company. It was like being reunited with an old friend. The basis of their encounters was, at best, bizarre, and yet Marie had already felt the brotherly blanket Benedict had wrapped around her, whether he did it intentionally or not. And she slipped into a sisterly act just as readily.

"I don't know..." She laced her fingers. "It's hard to explain and you'll probably think I'm mad..."

"No, I already know you're mad. But in the best possible way."

They exchanged a smile.

"But honestly, I swear that I felt a sort of sibling connection with him before he even revealed anything to me... Besides, he'd be such a great addition to Romain's life. Someone to look up to, you know?"

"Romain's already got you to look up to."

"Oh, you know what I mean. Like, a male role model with a family connection. A sort of father figure."

Marie swiped her screen to bring it to life. The only new message was from Giandomenico, the preview telling her he was requesting his French word of the day. But she was saving it for later. She liked to be extra witty for those.

"I bet you've been checking your phone every two seconds." Médélice teased her.

"Pfff. No."

"Yeah, right... Girl, as Kung Fu Panda would put it..." Médélice raised her forefinger and put on a silly, deep voice. "Yesterday is history, tomorrow is a mystery, so enjoy the now. Because today is a gift, which is why it's called the present."

Marie glared at her.

"And you're welcome," Médélice quipped whilst putting her hands together and bowing her head in a Namaste gesture. "Anyway, what did you mean by 'we're so different'?"

166

"He's about ten stories above our station. He's well-educated, well-travelled. His French is impeccable. He's got a fancy job, and I bet his home isn't owned by the council…"

"Wow, wow, wow, young lady. Hold your horses right there. A) there's nothing wrong with living in a council flat…" Médélice cleared her throat and pointed at her chest. "B) you're well-travelled too. The only difference is that the world has come to you, rather than the other way around. C) Your French is impeccable too, baby." Wink. "D)…"

A ping from Marie's phone interrupted them. She did not waste a millisecond to check it, '6,655€ IS STILL waiting in your name. It's for the accident you had, which wasn't your fault! To claim this ASAP, fill out the form at http://…' She let out a sigh of disappointment, while Médélice snuck a peek at her screen.

"Awww, did you have a pee-pee accident on the bus and it wasn't your fault?" Médélice cocked her head to one side and pursed her lips in mock sympathy.

This brought a smile to Marie's lips and she felt blessed to have Médélice in her life.

"If only it were true, I'd have 'accidents' on the bus every day for that sort of money."

"Bet you would. Anyway, never mind that… And D) we've got a great job, too… We get to see old people bits, have a little prod, spend minutes checking patients' blood pressure just for an hour of filling out forms…"

"Eh, I love being a nurse. Stop it!" She laughed.

"Glad we agree then… So, he was brought up as a posh-boy?"

"Yes, but he told me something funny. Kids were jumping in the sea from the rocky dykes by the Fort Saint-Jean museum, you know the one I mean?"

"No. But I'm with you. Kids jumping in the sea… Did he get PTSD? Oh no, the dead pigeon, the floating McDonald's wrapper, it all came back to him!" Médélice brought her hand in front of a faux oh-face.

"Argh, behave! Or else I'll leave."

"Sorry. Carry on."

"So, I told him this was how I spent most of my summer holidays as a child. Well, his were also spent by the beach, but windbreakers, waterproof jackets and camping were his lot. He tried to make it out as if all Brits thought that comfort on holidays was for wimps, but it made me wonder whether his parents were as wealthy as I thought they were."

"Either way, does it matter?"

"No. Of course not. I…"

Marie trailed off, the head nurse locked eyes with her from the other side of the canteen. The authoritative glasses-on-the-tip-of-the-nose type of a woman tapped her wrist where an imaginary watch was meant to be then swirled a forefinger in the air. With that, Marie and Médélice scampered back to work.

Chapter 27

"Persuasion"

London, England
Seven years ago, October 2010

There was something about the way Yukinobu's uniform bunched against his body, contouring his taut muscles with each movement, that caused a stirring in Benedict's pants. His Jiu-Jitsu class was coming to an end. Benedict had only caught the last five minutes of it. While everyone was heading to the door, a young, attractive guy, who was not a natural martial artist – Benedict was only thinking that because it's true – came to speak to Yukinobu. Benedict could not make out what they were talking about, but as they laughed, the young blond placed his hand on Yukinobu's arm, and Benedict was seized with a sudden burning pang of jealousy.

For the first time, options did not matter. Only Yukinobu mattered. All Benedict wanted was to share a lasting intimacy with this man. He had mixed feelings about the novelty of this sentiment, particularly as he never envisaged himself feeling like this, nor that he would be able to admit to it, even to himself. Benedict had only ever experienced what he liked to call 'Fast Food Love' until now. You know, the sort of love that is convenient and indulgent, yet cheap and unmemorable. And this had worked perfectly for him – the way a cheeseburger left him feeling satiated, if a little grubby.

But this was different. Yukinobu was undeniably more than a cheeseburger, and weirdly it made Benedict feel angry at Yukinobu... Angry for hogging his thoughts, for becoming indispensable, for being so perfect and yet so ineffectual to his grand plan. Every time he caught sight of Yukinobu, Benedict wanted to rip his clothes off or knock his socks off with all he had to say to him. Still, part of him also wanted to drive Yukinobu away. Old habits? Or a nagging feeling that Yukinobu would never be right? He did not know. Actually, he was not even fully aware of what this new repressed feeling really was.

"*Sayonara*," the blond guy cheerfully cried as he parted from Yukinobu.

169

Naff... Benedict grumbled to himself.

As Yukinobu got closer, an uncertainty flickered through his face. Perhaps he was unsure of how to greet Benedict. Their new status quo was still fresh, after all. Or maybe something in Benedict's expression was somewhat uninviting. In Benedict's heart of hearts, an apology for the blatant flirtation he had just witnessed was in order. Even though it was a ridiculous expectation... and Benedict knew it. So, a stern welcome took form instead.

Yukinobu settled for a subtle head bow and something clicked. Benedict was not sure what it was; Yukinobu's uncertainty, the glisten of sweat on his golden forehead, the flush of pink on his high cheekbones, or the crinkles around his teardrop shaped eyes. Or maybe a combination of all these things, but suddenly his grumpiness over the 'sayonara' guy evaporated.

"How was Marseille?" asked Yukinobu.

"Alright."

"Just alright?"

"Well, I wasn't accused of being undercover MI5 nor Interpol not even the CIA, like in Rome. So, relatively uneventful in that sense. But, yeah, alright."

"So, not the fireworks of round one?"

Benedict replied with a vague head movement.

"Was it your nephew?"

"No. He was great. A little offbeat, but a good kid."

"What was it then? You don't sound thrilled."

"I don't know what it is..." He knew what it was... but felt stupid to admit he had gone because Yukinobu urged him to, only to be devastated by the DNA results afterwards. "Everything went well, and they were both sweet and fun... Maybe it just didn't live up to expectations."

"What were you expecting?"

"More... I think." Benedict sighed.

"What more?"

Benedict shrugged. "Anyway, how has your week been?" He took a step closer and ran a hand over the opening of Yukinobu's folded Jiu-Jitsu top. "Did you think of me much?"

"Let's finish up this conversation. What's brought about this change of heart?" Yukinobu sounded concerned.

Benedict sighed and flapped his hands against his sides in protest. "I don't know. Alright?"

"Really?"

"I shouldn't have done all that in the first place... I wasn't in the right frame of mind when I brought it up with you..." Yukinobu looked puzzled. "Let's just drop it. Okay?" Benedict insisted through clenched teeth.

There was a pause. Yukinobu stared at him while Benedict looked down then away.

"What are you afraid of?" Yukinobu finally asked.

"I'm not afraid of anything, what are you on about?" His voice went up a few octaves, ending up on the whingy side.

What would he be afraid of? The ugly truth was that Benedict just could not be bothered. And objectively speaking, these people would end up being a charity case. With a dead drug-abuser mother, a father in prison, and a husband out of the picture for some unknown reason which Benedict was not that bothered about uncovering. Admittedly, Marie and Romain had turned out alright. Well, more than alright, even. But he had always wished to have a sibling. He remembered writing words to that effect in one of his cards to his parents, just the once though, never repeated having seen the devastatingly sad effect it had had on his mother... But realistically, what would be the point of establishing a sibling-like relationship with someone who just happened to be born at a similar time to him? What would he get out of it? And maybe... just maybe, there was a slight chance that he did not want to get attached to people who would disappear from his life eventually, like everyone else.

"You were very invested in finding your birth family and thrilled beyond belief after you first met Marie. So, what's changed?" There was undeserved tenderness in Yukinobu's eyes.

Although it had not started like that, looking for his biological family had given Benedict an excuse to see Yukinobu regularly, even go abroad with him. So maybe, as Yukinobu assumed that Benedict's loss of enthusiasm was due to unspoken sentimental issues, he could just play along with it.

Benedict took on a faraway look and remained silent.

"Have you opened the envelope?"

Hands burrowed in his pockets, Benedict nodded.

"No good?"

Benedict met Yukinobu's gaze and nodded his head again slowly.

"I think you should arrange to see them again anyway," urged Yukinobu.

No reply.

"Have you kept the results?"

"At home."

"Would you mind if I took a look?"

"Be my guest."

When they reached Benedict's home, they headed straight to the kitchen. Benedict retrieved the DNA results from a messy junk drawer and handed them to Yukinobu.

Yukinobu's eyes were still on the letter when he took the cup of jasmine tea Benedict handed him.

"These... Ah..."

"Are very disappointing," Benedict interjected, before opening a beer bottle.

"I know... But..."

"Could we talk about something else?" Benedict cut him short, perching himself on a breakfast bar stool.

"Sure. But..." Yukinobu flapped the letter.

"No, seriously. Yukinobu, you did a hell of a job. This is no reflection on your work. I just really liked her and the kid. That's all... I may want you to start again, at some point. Just not now. Please." He pleaded.

"Benedict," Yukinobu said assertively.

"Yeah?"

"Can you fish out the results to your previous DNA test?"

"Sure. Why?"

"Please, just do it."

Benedict handed them to Yukinobu, who placed the documents side by side.

"Those results are the same as before. Exactly, the same. Look, they even have the same number reference. Call them."

The institute could not be sorry enough for the oversight. It had never happened to them before, blah blah blah. Verdict – his DNA and Marie's were a match. She was his sister with a 99 percent certainty.

Chapter 28

"Something that happened in Oxford"

Oxford, England
Twenty-six years ago, 1991-1992

Life was good. Great job. Beautiful flat. Dreamy partner. Teddy could have chosen anyone, but he'd chosen him.

Growing up, Yukinobu was the sort of child you could easily forget you had left in your car, only remembering on returning to your car after your shift at work was over. Not that it had ever happened. His parents were industrious and distant, not forgetful. Anyway, school was the main contributory factor in forging his self-effacement, not his parents.

During World War II, hundreds of thousands of Korean women were forced to live as comfort women in support of the Japanese military. Yukinobu's Korean grandmother it seemed could well have been one of them. This was not something he and his sister had learned from their parents or even from school history lessons, but in fact gleaned from school mates. A bit of history they were happy to share on a regular basis. They called them germ-girl and scum-boy. But it did not stop there. Being 'hafu' (of mixed heritage) made them *'Zainichi'* Koreans and second-class citizens. They were third-generation immigrants. Their ethnic Korean father had been born in Japan and so had Yukinobu and Rui. Yet, Yukinobu, Rui and their father were *Zainichi* directly translating as 'foreign resident staying in Japan' or 'dirty Koreans' to most of their classmates.

Yukinobu and Rui also sported an excess of -ers. They were taller, with squarer jaws and had a sturdier, more muscular physique. When his sister Rui, two years his senior, was eight, a new teacher took over their physical education classes and split the class into four groups. Each group comprised of all boys or all girls, bar Rui's group where she was the only girl. Her classmates did not fail to notice it. They giggled and whispered. The mishap was brought to the teacher's attention, bashfully. Later Rui was faced with a taunting "if you're a girl, then prove it" from her classmates. She did not. After that, her nickname changed to germ-boy.

Middle school was open season on rumours and insults about Yukinobu's presumed sexual orientation. Mind you, Yukinobu nipped the latter in the bud when as a fourteen-year-old he thumped the Billy-Big-Boots of school bullies. The guy cock-a-doodle-dooed 'faggot' across the school corridor on the day Yukinobu's beloved Korean grandmother had passed. Hence, his internal pressure-cooker went 'boom' most spectacularly. Years of hard feelings led to the breaking of the bully's nose. Yukinobu was severely grounded, but it also turned off the tap of insults directed at him and by association his big sister, too. So, all in all, there was no remorse.

By putting that episode aside, along with Yukinobu's natural inclination, confined him to self-effacement and silence, with books and homework as his only escape. It got him far educationally. His sister, too. She became a nuclear physicist. Which, ironically, confined her to all-male teams for the major part of her university and professional life. However, it also cut Yukinobu off from relationships in all their forms. But then, he met Edward, or Teddy, to most who knew him.

It happened on his very first day in Oxford for a one-year Master's in History of Art. Coming way too fast around a street corner in his father's Jag, Teddy nearly splattered Yukinobu all over the cobbles. As chance would have it, they were heading to the same lecture which was due to start minutes later. This came to Yukinobu's attention in the worst possible way. He was hunched over an opened book, avoiding eye contact in a crowded auditorium full of unfamiliar faces, when he heard a thunderous voice directed straight at him. All eyes turned to the orator of the flamboyant apologies. Teddy sat down next to a red-faced Yukinobu and took him under his wing. From then on, and almost under duress, Yukinobu was absorbed into Teddy's pack of friends.

It was Yukinobu's first taste at a social life, and, because of Teddy, he was thrown directly in at the deep end. Teddy's group of friends, mostly boys, was large and met on a very regular basis. Yukinobu was a cursory add-on at first, whose presence did not deter nor contribute to anything. Yet, he became a source of attention despite himself. In Japan, girls tended to gravitate towards him. He had done nothing to initiate or encourage it. He could not have been more disengaged if he had tried. Yet, his impossibly good looks worked against him. They did in Europe too, though, this time, the attention he received seemed to be more of the male kind. Which should have given him no reason to complain. Except, he had no intention to act on it. He had never felt a need to realise his attractions sexually back then. Maybe he was repressed, unconsciously denying himself of acting on his desire. Perhaps the childish mockeries of his youth had scarred part of him. Or maybe his compulsive desire to never draw attention to himself restrained his sexuality. Sexuality that would have set him apart from the norm, resurrected gossip and brought further shame to his family, or at least he thought at the time.

However, at that exact point in time, his rebuttal of male advances was caused by something altogether different. Something he had never experienced before. An obsession. His mind was consumed by someone. An unattainable someone, lost to girls. Yet, the compulsive, self-sacrificial monogamist in Yukinobu could not separate his mind from his body and he never would in later life. He was saving himself for the implausible. He was saving himself for Teddy.

Teddy laughed loudly, spoke confidently, flirted compulsively, and lived fully. He invited strangers to his table, drove fast, owned a slick new gadget – a mobile phone worth god-knows-how-much – and initiated drinking games. He voiced his opinions with passion, whether to one person or a hundred and whether you were interested in hearing about it or not. Yukinobu could not help but admire him from afar. Teddy was not conventionally handsome. His fair hair was shaggy, and his features looked more that of a prime minister rather than a popstar. Yet, his lap always featured a rota of girls, and pretty girls at that. Yukinobu secretly envied every one of them with bitter jealousy.

To spend more time with Teddy, Yukinobu would grab any opportunity available to him, including writing papers with him. Even though Yukinobu always ended up doing ninety-five percent of the job. Anyway, one day, after one of their papers was handed back to them, Teddy wrapped his arm around Yukinobu's shoulders and patted Yukinobu's biceps while congratulating him for the high grade. His smile was only inches away from Yukinobu's face. It happened for the briefest of moments and yet, the friendly act was so charged, that he promptly had to gratify himself in the nearest toilet. This left Yukinobu feeling depressed, with a hint of disgust, and lingering frustration, in sum, a groupie's disease. The type of disease suffered by people who have to

175

fantasise about someone famous to be able to climax when making love to their lovely partner.

But then, the impossible happened. It was the end of the school year. The night had been particularly heavy and Teddy was struggling to walk in a straight line. He was heading back to his hall of residence, unaccompanied which was a rare occurrence. Worried that he would not make it home, or perhaps, seizing a last opportunity to be on his own with Teddy, Yukinobu walked him to his room, well, half-walked, half-carried. Part of him wanted to confess to his gnarly feelings for him while Teddy's state of mind was hazy enough to be unsure of what he had heard the next day. Of course, he did not. But, as Yukinobu was easing Teddy onto his bed, Teddy span Yukinobu round, threw him on the bed and launched himself on top, his mouth immediately searching Yukinobu's. This was all Yukinobu had fantasised about for the past ten months. Yet, he peeled Teddy off him at once. It was surprisingly easy, Teddy was as light and thin as Yukinobu was wide and muscular. Yukinobu wanted to be certain that this was not a drunken oversight, that Teddy had not mistaken him for a girl. Teddy called him a wayward tease. Henceforth, the four (-midable) months began.

Yukinobu decided to stay in England after his degree to see where things were headed with Teddy. And they skyrocketed. Yukinobu landed a stellar job as an art dealer at a prestigious firm, whilst Teddy worked for his father's PR agency in London, Hampstead. They saw each other every other weekend, always at Yukinobu's place in Oxford. It was all wonderful. Yukinobu was the happiest he had ever been.

Then, on November 5th, Yukinobu got a night-time visit. He had spent the evening with some friends in Oxford's South Park for the bonfire night celebrations but had left before the bonfire sporting Guy Fawkes effigy was lit up.

He was house-sitting for his firm's owner so was making his way back there. He reached the residence's alley as the fireworks started to erupt. The night was loud and effervescent with multicolour illuminations. The narrow beams of light cutting through the darkness of one of the first-floor windows went unnoticed to his eyes, and so did the light footsteps above him as he locked the front door behind him. By the time he felt the burning pain slice through his stomach, which nearly sent him to his grave, it was too late.

Yukinobu became obsessed with his 'case,' as was his way of dealing with anything of significance. Piece by piece, an ugly truth came to light. The circumstances of this aggravated burglary were not fortuitous. He had expected as much. The burglars left with only one thing, a painting by Claude Monet worth more than the average person makes in ten lifetimes.

What Yukinobu did not expect was to find a link to Teddy. Teddy had inadvertently tipped of a criminal. This, in itself, would have been forgivable, he was not part of a criminal conspiracy, he had just let slip the location of a valuable painting. After all, Teddy was incorrigibly chatty.

However, the discovery that the information had slipped during pillow talk took Yukinobu a lifetime to swallow. The depth and ramification of Teddy's treason changed his outlook on life, impacted his personality, pushed his professional life into a very different path, and shut him down from anyone else. Or almost anyone…

Chapter 29

"Seen a ghost"

Marseille, France
Seven years ago, October 2010

On her way home, Marie felt a tap on her shoulder that made her drop her grocery bags.

"Hello, Mrs. Boulanger," greeted a boy, with a smile that didn't quite reach his eyes.

"Oh. Hi," Marie replied, putting a hand to her chest. He couldn't have been older than twelve, yet he was already towering over Marie.

"These look heavy, Mrs. Boulanger. Let me carry them for you."

"Oh, don't trouble yourself. I don't live far."

"That's no trouble at all. I've forgotten my keys, so I've got an hour to kill before someone can let me in."

"Alright, then. Thank you. It's very kind of you."

"Sure." There was something unnerving about him. The way he lowered himself to take the bags from Marie's hands whilst keeping eye contact with her could almost be described as sinister.

"Forgive me. Your face looks familiar, but I don't... Are you a friend of Romain?"

"Yes, Romain and I go to the same school."

"Oh, I remember now. You caught me as I fell once, just outside Romain's primary school."

"That's right. I'm surprised you recall it."

"I'm good with faces. How have you been?"

Marie felt a ping in her pocket as they were about to cut away from the main road and into a dingy path. It was from Benedict. He wanted to see them again. The DNA results came back positive. Marie uttered a joyful yelp before covering her grin with her hand.

"I need to respond to that." Marie pointed to her phone. "Thank you so much for your help, though." She reached out for her bags.

"I can wait."

"Are you sure? I wouldn't want to keep you."

"Certain."

"You're too good," she replied, her head buried into her phone, missing a subtle yet unpleasant air to the boy's stance.

As she pressed send, she heard the familiar sound of Pépé's roaring Citroën Visa 1980, followed by the horns of drivers making rude gestures as they went around Pépé. He manually rolled down his squeaky window. About a half-century later, Pépé asked, "wanna lift, sunshine?"

"Don't mind if I do." Marie beamed, unaware that was the best decision she made all day. "Do you want one too?" she offered the boy, half-heartedly.

"No, I'll walk." There was an expression on the boy's face that Marie could not quite place and yet for some reason it triggered a shiver.

"Thank you for your help," she uttered with an unexplainable quaver in her voice.

The boy opened the door for her.

"It was my pleasure." He smiled without humour.

Marie shivered again. "Oh, and, ah, what did you say your name was again?"

"I didn't. It's Gabin."

Marie was very excited to share with Romain the plan she had just made with Benedict.

"Maman, can I ask you a question?" There was a hesitation in Romain's boyish voice.

"Sure, shoot."

"Is he your boyfriend?"

Stopping halfway through putting boxes of cereals into the cupboard, Marie levelled her face with Romain's.

"I can assure you that Benedict isn't my boyfriend. However, he's someone I'd like you, and me, to get to know better."

"We should introduce him to grandma."

Marie hummed in agreement, already starting to think of ways that she could broach the subject with her. *Hey mum, remember my twin brother? The one you sold to strangers thirty years ago, well tah-dah, here he is again.* Maybe not that way.

"Can I invite Benedict to my birthday?" he asked eagerly.

Marie smiled. "Sure. Although you realise that your birthday is in four months."

Romain stopped to think about it. "That's over a hundred days."

"Indeed."

"Maybe, we could invite him to your birthday first."

"That's a nice idea. And you'd like to know something funny?"

Romain nodded eagerly.

"Benedict's birthday is on the same day as mine."

"You're exactly the same age?"

"Exactly."

Romain gazed at her in a daze.

"By the way, a school friend of yours helped me carry my bags home tonight," she added in passing while finishing putting away the shopping.

"Who?"

"What was it again? Oh, yeah. Gaby"

"Do you mean Gabin?

"That's it, Gabin."

Romain looked as if he had seen a ghost.

"What?" Marie questioned, staring.

"Nothing," Romain replied as if he had a lump in his throat.

∞

Lavina had been questioning Romain about the scrape on his forehead for about half an hour to no avail when they heard a knock on the door. The bloody scrapes had happened at school, a boy in Romain's class had dared his younger brother and friends to trip Romain up. But there was no way, Romain was going to admit it in front of Timo. Plus, it didn't hurt, he thought. Not really.

It was Vlora at Lavina's door. Romain ran to her and wrapped his arms around her bony body tightly. Vlora had promised to collect him from school, but as her word carried as much weight as the wind, Lavina had insisted that he walk back home with them. Romain felt almost teary at the sight of his grandmother. He knew it meant she would take him back home, ask no questions about his forehead and not make him do his homework.

"Mummy is taking me to England tomorrow," Romain declared whilst Vlora switched on the TV.

Vlora stroked the little pudge under Romain's chin. He liked when she did that. "Ma puce, I don't think you are. You must have misheard," she imparted kindly and handed him the remote control.

"No, she even showed me the tickets." Romain went to find the printed document from where he had seen his mum keeping it. "See."

His grandmother's eyes gazed at the information on the piece of paper. "So you are... And you're travelling in business class." She frowned thoughtfully and looked at Romain. "Did your mummy say why you're going?"

"Yeah, we're meeting Benedict. He lives there." Romain beamed.

"Who's Benedict?"

"Maman's friend."

"He must a very good friend of your mum."

Romain shrugged uncertainly. "I've only met him once."

Vlora asked a lot of questions about Benedict. Romain was quite happy telling her about the day they spent with him in Marseilles. He giggled when she enquired whether this man was his mum's boyfriend but mentioned that Marie said no when he'd asked her. His grandmother went all funny when he told her that his mum and Benedict shared the same birthday. She was completely quiet after that and took off once Marie got home.

Chapter 30

"Inquest in a nutshell"

Manarola, Cinque Terre, Italy
Now, July 2017

Whilst evidence is being packed away, Giandomenico records his account of the case so far.

On 3rd July at 6:27 am, the police were contacted after the bodies of two men were discovered on the rocky inlet of Manarola, about 120 kilometres southeast of Genoa, Northwest Italy.

The men were found fully clothed, both lying on their fronts, resting on the inlet rocks opposite a seaway, their legs partially submerged in the sea.

A search of their pockets revealed a set of keys, a half-empty packet of chewing gum, Euro coins and wet, illegible store receipts. No phone, ID, wallet, or anything else that would give a clue as to who they were or where they came from was found on their person.

A powerboat was immersed close by and was identified by a local fireman as a Riva 63 Virtus. This has subsequently been confirmed as her registration was readable. It was loaded with supplies sufficient to sustain two men for at least a couple of weeks. The state of the engine and undamaged parts indicated that she was a new boat. A request was sent to check the registration. If this were to prove inconclusive, an inquest of the recent buyers of this specific model should also be launched to identify her owner.

Witnesses 4 and 5 recounted that on the evening of 2nd July from 7:30 pm and 8:00 pm, during which time the streetlights had come on and they saw a man carrying another man. He was carrying him on his shoulders along the coastal path of Manarola.

The dead men's faces were clean-shaven but long exposure to the sun and salted water had damaged their skin and features beyond recognition. Yet, from preliminary inspection, it could be assumed that the smaller man of the two was about 173 cm, of Caucasian appearance with a Mediterranean complexion, and thought to be aged about 35 to 40 with brown eyes and hair which was slightly grey around the temples, slim. The other one would be described as East Asian and in excellent physical condition. He was measured around 186 centimetres tall, with broad shoulders and a narrow waist, harder to age but assumed to be 40 to 55. Neither men's hands nor nails showed signs of manual labour. Also, the Caucasian male had had extensive, elaborate, cosmetic dental work which might also indicate a higher socioeconomic status. They were dressed similarly in white T-shirts, dark jeans, and socks but no shoes, and all labels on their clothes had been removed and carried no identification. Their dental records and fingerprints have been sent for analysis.

With his thumb still pressing down on the record button, Giandomenico finds himself growing quiet. Staring at the corpses being bagged, he imagines them as somebody's son, father and husband, and having to deliver the news to their family. His stomach tightens.

Chapter 31

"Symmetrical potted-trees"

London, England
Seven years ago, November 2010

Marie and Romain's flight was delayed due to a 'terrorist' threat. Yet the armed response tended to the discovery of an idiot rather than an incendiary device. A passenger had joked about having a bomb in his bag. A hoot of a joke, really. Anyway, once the culprit had been frogmarched from the plane, protesting his innocence of anything more nefarious than a misjudged sense of humour, they were underway only two hours later than scheduled.

Unlike most first-time flyers, Marie and Romain were not apprehensive but mostly excited. Even the two-hour delay, the screaming toddler in the row behind them, the kicking, pushing and pulling of their seats from said toddler, the people trying to cut the passport line, and those stopping dead in front of them with their wheelie suitcases, did not temper their dog-about-to-go-on-a-walk level of excitement. They were both awake at dawn and at the airport three hours before departure. Romain took hundreds of photos of non-descript clouds, filtered by condensation trapped in the window. Marie had never left France so it all seemed surreal. And she felt ever so important sitting in first class, even though the only difference was marked by a threaded curtain pulled behind them and a tray of non-descript food that was weirdly burning hot and icy cold at the same time. Magical. She heard one of her first-class co-passengers muttering that you only noticed the difference on Trans-Atlantic these days in between quaffing mouthfuls of champagne and glaring at the excited toddler.

This weekend was one of the few Marie was not rostered on to spend at the hospital and so Benedict had offered a trip to London for them both. Pépé had driven them to the airport in his tilted Citroën Visa 1980, which he started in second gear in a puff of grey smoke and fumes as always.

Their arrival at Heathrow airport was disorientating compared to Marseille airport. They already felt the buzz of being abroad — everyone speaking English was their first clue. Benedict waited for them at the gate, looking as fancy as ever. His car was fancy, too. It was probably worth ten times Marie's trailer. Which made Marie feel like taking her shoes off before getting in, though there was no shoe rack in sight. She remained immobile most of the journey as if her movements could damage the car in some way. As they entered Belle Lane, guarded by crash barriers and iron gates, she was surprised by how green and leafy their drive had been. No concrete jungle in this part of London. Marie craned her neck to admire all the manicured mini front gardens and buildings.

"Your street's name sounds as lovely as it looks," commented Marie.

"And yet, if people had to guess what my street's name ought to be, I bet *Bell End* would be the popular choice."

This went straight over Marie's head, so she smiled politely in agreement. She had to look up bell-end on her phone and was left perplexed by it... Why would anyone think of him as an annoying or contemptible dick? He was so charming.

As they stepped out of the car, a flight of doves flew away. It literally did... Perhaps they were pigeons, but, in Marie's mind, they were doves.

"On which floor is your apartment?" Marie muttered in a reverent tone, her head turned up, taking a full view of the white building in front of her.

"All of them."

Although Benedict's answer was dead-simple, it took Marie a moment to take it in. This was all his... She knew he was wealthy, but who lived in mansions in capital cities?! It dawned on her that she was about to step into one of the mythical houses she spent countless hours perusing in those glossy magazines. She noticed that birds were chirping. Perhaps they were as surprised to find her here as she was to be here.

Outside, everything about Benedict's house was as pretty as a picture. The symmetrical lighting on either side of the front door, the symmetrical geometric forms of the greenery – very 'in' this year – and symmetrical potted trimmed trees, even the spiders looked classy and, well, symmetrical. Their long slim legs spoke of miniature hats, hands covering mouths when laughing, and no elbows on the table. Although not her usual inclination, she could not help the pang of envy she felt. Only a fraction of Benedict's house would suffice to Marie and Romain's contentment. She could almost picture a large knife, slicing a small portion of

Benedict's house, putting it on a boat and sailing it to Marseille. She should not think like that, she mentally scolded herself.

As they walked up a flight of perfect steps, Marie glued herself to Romain. They remained immobile and silent in the intimidating hallway, trying to take up as little space as possible and not to pollute the air with their beggarly breath.

Although a characterful house from the outside, the inside was modern, chic, and if forced to admit, austere. Benedict offered to show them to their rooms. There were sophisticated black and white photographs staring down at them from every corner. As they reached their bedrooms, Marie expected to see a Sheba cat with long white fur stretched out on one of the beds or kneading a plush pillow with sparkling clean paws. But there were none, how disappointing. Bet it would have been called Rockefurrller.

Overall, Benedict's house was a solid ten. Not the sort of ten written in glitter with the zero in a heart shape. Nor, for those with a filthy mind, a motioning ten with the one having its wicked, thrusting way with the zero. It was a domineering, frosty ten, a Versailles ten. In her mind, this ten was as evocative as Marie's home was a zero. No, not a zero, zero would be living on a cardboard box under a bridge. She felt grateful for her trailer. It had sheltered her and Romain for many years. It had to be a solid two, perhaps even a three. However, the gift she had bought for Benedict suddenly felt heavy and kitsch in her bag. A large zany candle holder ceramic in the shape of a clog featuring olives, fishes, and boats. She should have bought a bag of navettes.

Romain pulled on Marie's arm as she dropped her coat on a swish armchair and whispered in her ear to ask if he could stay with her tonight.

Sensing the diffidence, Benedict led them to the games room next. Romain raced past the pool and foosball table straight to Benedict's wall of unwrapped Xbox and PS3 games. And with a flick of the fingers, Romain was sold.

"So, this is how you spend your spare time?" Marie teased.

"No, but I had a feeling it would coax a seven-year-old boy into my house." He tapped the side of his nose.

Marie cocked her head to one side, a faint smile on her lips, then raised an eyebrow at him.

"That made me sound incredibly creepy, didn't it?"

"Yep. Great impression of Herbert the Pervert, though."

He smiled, but she could tell the Family Guy reference went straight over his head.

It took a little effort to drag Romain out of the house, but once out, he seemed enchanted with everything and anything Benedict took them to see, do and eat in London. Marie owed it to her boy, he was an easy kid to please, if a little undemonstrative. Although this aspect of Romain's personality did not come through in Benedict's presence. Romain was typically excruciatingly stern with strangers which came as a surprise to those who knew his mother and her incredibly upbeat, sunny disposition. Marie had even been called into the head teacher's office halfway through Romain's first school year, to reassure his teachers that her then five-year-old boy was not a mute wilding. Maybe Benedict proved himself to Romain by jumping into the swampy port water to save him. Or maybe, Romain was missing a male presence in his life. And what a stereotypical male figure Benedict made.

After they all faked interest in museums, Benedict took them for a walk to see the London Bridge. But, instead of looking at the sights, they spent half an hour discussing the red inflatable speedboats that went past - like the ones the police use, Romain had enthused. A discussion that ended with a promise that for their next visit, Benedict would take Romain on one of them.

As they arrived back at Benedict's house, they bumped into a smiley man dressed in martial arts apparel. He was only a couple of houses down from Benedict's house and it seemed as though he had just come from Benedict's house or had been waiting for them there, but Benedict appeared surprised to see him.

All the same, Benedict proudly introduced Marie as his sister and Romain as his nephew, before adding, "and this is my friend, Yukinobu." But it was imparted at such speed that Marie and Romain had to ask Benedict to repeat his friend's name a couple of times.

Yukinobu bowed his head at them and stated that he was pleased to meet them in impeccable French. But something seemed off.

Benedict was very complimentary towards Yukinobu and explained that his friend's help had been instrumental in finding them. Yet Yukinobu's face seemed to have turned into a mask of formality where there was initially an inviting friendliness to it.

After Benedict's unusually long monologue, both men simultaneously cleared their throats. A brief moment of silence punctuated the exchange, before Yukinobu excused himself and went his separate way. There was a hesitation in Benedict, but they eventually resumed their way into his monumental house.

Later that evening, Marie and Benedict shared stories about their respective childhoods. Incongruously, this left Marie saddened by the thought that she would never be able to meet Benedict's late father and mother while she seemed to have cemented Benedict's decision not to meet Fatos for now.

"Have you already mentioned me to Vlora?"

"Not yet."

"Hmm. I've been thinking…" Benedict trailed off.

"Yeah?"

"Well, I'd prefer to be there when you tell her."

"Sure. But, uh, it'll be quite a thing for her to face up to. She might not…" Embrace the news? Respond well to it? None of these were a delicate way to phrase it. Short of anything better, she settled for "you know?"

"I know. But I'm okay with it."

"Alright. However, if it's okay with you, I'd like to tell Romain once we're back in Marseille."

"Are you worried about his reaction?"

"Oh no, I'm sure he'll be over the moon. He's already been telling everyone about our new English friend."

"What concerns you, then?"

"It's just that some aspects of the story may be best to leave out, for now. And we really ought to keep quiet until after we've spoken to Vlora."

A frown of concern veiled Benedict's expression. "Do you think Vlora might have put two and two together if she's heard Romain mention your new English friend?"

"I shouldn't think so. I mean it'd be quite a leap, right?" Marie faltered.

"Maybe."

Chapter 32

"Oh brother."

Marseille, France
Seven years ago, November 2010

They heard the faint concerto of sirens before they reached the bumpy little lane leading to camp Saint Pierre. The blue and red lights reflecting against the sides of the caravans and trailers created an eerie light show. Once they set foot on the familiar pathway, clusters of people came into view. Marie and Romain's progression was finally stopped by an unfamiliar flimsy barrier of yellow police tape blocking the way home to their trailer.

Two silent fire engines were parked in front of them, with three police cars and an ambulance to the side. People gawked at the commotion from their vaguely delimited turf. There were a lot of crossed arms and stern faces directed at the police. Groups of young men, hovering in the background, were making unintelligible, taunting noises towards the officers. A teenager pulled wheelies on the edge of the taped-off area as if testing the boundaries of the authorities. Several police officers were posted to the taped perimeter. They were stern but seemed twitchy, staring back from the other side of the yellow fence, daring the youths to step out of line just once. However, once the locals spotted Marie and Romain, their eyes did not waver from them. Their appearance had caused a timeout. Something was *very* off.

"What's going on?" Marie asked a neighbour. Compassion veiled the woman's eyes, she put a sympathetic hand on Marie's shoulder and opened her mouth. But before the woman had the chance to say anything, a bulky figure whose enormous helmet still seemed too small for his head, reached them.

"Do you live in that trailer?" The fireman gestured towards Marie and Romain's trailer. Uniformed men and women were walking in and out of it, all the windows and doors were wide open.

"It's, uh, yeah, we live here. But. Wha-What's going on?" Everything felt like a film set of her neighbourhood rather than life as she knew it.

189

A small group of people started to gather around them, staying at a respectful distance but close enough to hear what was being discussed. Romain reached out for his mother's hand.

"Please come with me." The fireman placed his large paw on Marie's back leading her and Romain somewhere, away from prying eyes.

"We received a call about a smell coming from inside your trailer."

"A smell?" queried Marie, confusion in her voice.

"A burning smell, ma'am." The flammable materials used in constructing these trailers and mobile homes and their close proximity meant the local authorities took these calls very seriously. Marie knew that well.

Did she leave the gas cooker on by mistake?

Her trailer was clearly intact, no flames licking from the windows, or black mark of soot to indicate anything out of the ordinary. "It looks fine, though. So, nothing major's happened, right?"

"Not to your trailer. Though, I'm afraid we had to force open the door."

Marie took another look at her trailer and noticed the damaged doorframe, however, she was still too shocked and confused to be annoyed. A police officer joined the fireman's side.

"But my mum could have opened the door for you. Actually, where is she?" Marie asked as if to herself, prompting her and Romain to search the many faces still gathered outside for the familiar face. Yet panic still did not creep in, Vlora had a habit of disappearing, even when she was supposed to look after Romain.

With a subtle nod, the police officer who had reached their side sent the fireman jogging back to Marie's trailer. There was some kind of pecking order at play here that was possibly a clue to the nature of what was going on here, but Marie's brain seemed to be operating in slow motion.

"I'm Officer Nicolas Martin." The officer extended his hand and Marie grabbed it automatically. "Are you Marie Boulanger?"

"Yes, and this is my trailer." She pointed at it and tried to get closer, but the officer raised a hand in front of her implying that she and Romain should stay where they were.

"Where were you at four-fifteen this afternoon?"

"Where's my mum? Vlora Aoun, have you seen her?"

"Ma'am? Please answer the question."

"At Heathrow airport, in London, our plane was about to take off. There." Marie handed the officer the scrunched-up flight tickets that she had kept in her pocket. "I'm looking for my mother. Have you seen her?"

After a brief glance at the document, the officer took a sharp breath.

"Ma'am, I'm afraid your mother, Vlora Aoun, died this afternoon at approximately four-fifteen from carbon monoxide poisoning."

∞

The funeral was a small affair. Marie tried to reach Fatos but was unable to apply for a supervised release on temporary licence on his behalf as he had been placed in solitary confinement. Although she fought his corner, truth be told, his absence was a blessing. She wasn't ready to have him around Romain outside a supervised environment and it wouldn't have been the right time and place to introduce him to Benedict.

Benedict made the effort to be there. She could tell he was struggling with the cruel disappointment of never being able to speak with his birth mother, after being so close to finally meeting her. Yet, he barely let any signs of it bubble to the surface. He came with his friend, Yukinobu, even though Marie asserted that if he felt he had to be there for her it was not necessary. All the same, it was good to see him. Marie had not felt this inexplicable bond towards someone since Romain was born. Benedict's mere presence felt like a teammate had arrived, a feeling that someone's on your side without needing any words of confirmation. It must have been strange for him, let alone disappointing, to have lost two mothers in the space of a few months, she thought. One who he had known so well and one he had only just learnt about. Yet one for whom there remained so many questions that would now probably never be answered.

From an admin point of view, there was hardly anything of Vlora to clear out or close down, not even a bank account nor a mobile contract to cancel and her possessions had been meagre. Also, although Vlora had been living with them in close quarters for nearly a year, her absence was barely felt. This, in itself, made Marie sadder than her death. Neither the numbing feeling she had felt after Mémé's passing nor the burning pain caused by Baul's accident were there. It was as if she had never really existed, more a shadow than an actual person.

Marie was convinced she had loved her mother. Yet, Romain's tears and his questions – where's heaven? Can we call in? Send her a letter? – were affecting her more than the loss itself. Romain, unlike her, was genuinely and visibly distraught by the loss of his grandmother. When he heard the news from the police officer, the boy had another asthma attack. Marie was ready to take him to the hospital before it calmed down and eventually passed.

When Marie suggested going to a café after the funeral rather than back home, it did not seem to raise any suspicions in Benedict regarding her desire to avoid her abode. He seemed preoccupied with other things. It was just the four of them left, everyone else had to head back to something.

"May I ask how this concentration of carbon monoxide was strong enough to kill her?" Benedict attempted, his face still turned towards his tiny cup of café noir.

"She had the wood burner's door opened with charcoal burning inside it."

Benedict removed his sunglasses and examined Marie closely. But her eyes had lowered to her hands wrapped around a cappuccino mug. Yukinobu tapped on Benedict's wrist, meaningfully.

"Oh." With this simple exclamation, Marie understood that Benedict had clicked that Vlora's death had not been accidental.

"Sorry, I didn't mean to pry, I was just concerned for your safety."

"I know." Marie smiled a bland, humourless smile.

"Did she leave a note, or something?"

"Nope."

There was a moment of silence before Marie added.

"I'm sorry you've had to bury your mother" Marie mouthed the word 'twice' "this year…and that you didn't even get to meet Vlora like you wanted."

"Can't be helped." He leaned across and pulled on one of Marie's dark curls lightly. It sprung back up into a corkscrew. "I've got you, and Romain, now."

Marie pushed Benedict's hand away from her hair and looked at Romain sipping a mint diabolo from a straw.

She placed her hand on the top of Romain's head. "Romain, *ma puce*, can I tell you something?"

192

Romain blew bubbles from his straw but nodded. Marie exchanged a meaningful look with Benedict.

"You know how Lavina is your aunty because she was daddy's sister."

Romain gazed at his mum, lips still wrapped around the end of his straw, and blinked.

"Well, as it turns out, Benedict is mummy's brother. Which makes him your uncle," Marie continued.

The boy's eyes went from his mum to Benedict and back to his mum again. Letting go of his straw, the corners of Romain's lips curled up, he then grabbed Marie's arm and buried his face against it.

"Cool." They heard the boy say, muffled by his mother's jacket followed by a soft giggle.

∞

Romain did not go for their usual high-five when his grandad entered the family visiting booth, but wrapped his arms around his waist instead. Fatos crouched down to better hold him. Romain felt silent hot tears running down his nose and landing on his grandad's shoulder. From this angle, Romain could see healing cuts poking through his grandad's thinning hair, and resorbing bruises on his forehead and along his right eye.

"What's wrong *ma puce?*" asked his grandad.

"*Mamie*'s dead," Romain disclosed with disarming simplicity.

Fatos's hands were suddenly wrapped around the boy's upper arms pushing him at arm's length, staring at him. It hurt slightly, but Romain did not complain.

"What?" Fatos shouted, his glare now directed at his mum. There was something behind his grandad's eyes that startled the boy.

"I - I tried to call you," Marie stuttered. "But I couldn't get through... They said you'd been placed in solitary confinement."

Fatos straightened himself up and started to pace relentlessly, reminding Romain of an old lion treading the same spots afforded to him by the confines of his zoo cell.

"When?"

"A week ago."

"A week ago!?" His voice angered. Fatos stopped, glared some more, then resumed his pacing.

"Her funeral..."

"Her funeral!?" Fatos interrupted, his red eyes bulged. Romain took a few steps closer to his mother. He did not like it in here anymore. The air felt increasingly stuffy, like something bad was going to happen.

"We couldn't apply for a supervised release because of your... situation here. And the funeral..."

Fatos punched the flimsy separation wall, leaving a dent and startling the people in the next booth. It put an abrupt stop to the humming background noise coming from the other booths in a single act. Two prison guards entered their booth, batons in hand. Romain could feel his breathing worsen by the second. Tightening.

"It's alright. It's alright..." Fatos kept repeating, his hands high in the air, his head lowered and shaking it from left to right as he resumed his caged animal pacing.

"Are you okay, ma'am?" one of the guards enquired as his keys jingled loudly at his waist as he took a few steps closer to Fatos. Marie placed herself between the guard and Fatos.

"Everything's fine. Really. Just reacting to bad news..." Marie stretched her hands in front of the guard. "His wife died."

Romain drew in two puffs from his inhaler, attracting everyone's attention at once. After a pause, the guards nodded.

"Alright. We'll be behind the door if you need us," the other guard informed as they both left.

Silence.

"How did she...?" Fatos asked, head down, still pacing.

"By carbon monoxide..."

"In our trailer," Romain added to help his mother. But her expression was one he had never seen on his mother's face before. It looked like panic but why would that be?

Then everything happened in a blur. His grandad was right in his mother's face, howling "you did this! You did this!" and other words that should not be repeated by a seven-year-old. His mum had her arms wrapped around her head. Romain's heart started pummelling his small rib cage. He had never seen his grandad like this. It was scary. The guards took Fatos away. Romain had been too shocked to react, but he should have reacted, he wished he had reacted. What his grandad had done was not right. It was unfair to his maman who was then crying and saying 'sorry' to Romain over and over again while rocking him in her arms. Why would she say 'sorry'? She had done nothing wrong. But Romain was struggling to breathe so he could not tell her how great she was and he could not find the words to express how much he wished to have done something to defend her.

Chapter 33

"Brewing circumstances"

Marseille, France
One year ago, April 2016

Without any forewarning, Romain entered a turning point in his life. Later, this thin chain of events will be rehashed in Romain's mind. Most of the time, in repentance, wishing that none of it had come to be. At other times, he will look back in anger, thinking about the circumstances that led to all this. In those moments of anger, everybody and everything else will be the problem, not him. In his mind, he becomes the victim of his environment and the people who make it up. And finally, sometimes, although rarely, he would allow himself to think that it all happened for a reason. He believed in fate.

As for most afternoons after school, Romain, now thirteen years old, and other boys his age used to mess around in the park minutes away from school. The sort of park used by teenagers and younger children under the loose supervision of older siblings that doubled as a trading ground for weed amongst other items. A multi-purpose facility one might say.

Romain tossed his book bag to the ground to help form a corner of their makeshift football field. After twenty minutes playing and coughing up enough dust to blanket the Sahel, Romain went to sit in the shade, wheezing away in a concrete tunnel like a grumpy goblin – apparently children love a concrete tunnel to play in. Romain desperately wanted to score a goal, or at the very least, wished that his ineptitude as a footballer did not come across. The girls were out that day, you see, and for some reason that was not entirely clear to him then, this fact had recently started to matter to him a lot more. In fairness, it was always hard for Romain as a severe asthmatic in the Marseille heat and dust. His ineptitude was compounded further by the fact that in Marseille, football was everything to everyone, with Olympique de Marseille coming somewhere slightly above both God and country no matter who you asked.

A few minutes later, Romain noticed Sophie peeling off from the pack of smokers but did not think anything of it. The self-imposed age and sex segregation rendered him as relevant as a lamp post to her. So, when her womanly figure appeared in front of him, Romain very nearly inhaled his inhaler whole in shock. She giggled lightly.

"Do you have a light?" Sophie asked, a joint secured between two fingers. The sun behind her, made her look like a divine apparition, turning the contour of her caramel skin and dark ringlets into glittering gold. She looked lovely.

"Light? Uuuh? Light?" he stuttered, patting himself down, hoping that a lighter might magically materialise there. He looked at the ground and wondered if he could manage to ignite a spark with two of the stones around him.

But he shook his head defeated instead. Note for later, always have a lighter, just in case a Soph-ortunity represented itself. Though, he was certain he never intended to smoke, ever.

To Romain's utter bewilderment, Sophie crawled into the tunnel with him anyway. She was two years older than Romain, hence a worldly woman to him; she may as well have been a decade older in their universe, and in a perfect way at that. She was the older sister of Romain's classmate Eloine. They were from a good family, with a proper house and parents who were pro-social-mixing. She had been friendly to Romain, if not a little 'starey,' on the couple of times Timo and Romain had been invited over to Eloine's place. An invitation that neither Romain nor Timo would ever contemplate making in return, despite enjoying Eloine's company. In fact, Timo and Romain would always remain vague when questions were asked about their homes.

Anyway, Romain had developed a little crush on Sophie, along with half of the girls in his class, some of his other classmate's sisters, and girls close to his own age in camp Saint Pierre. But Sophie had never talked to him or even merely acknowledged him at school. So he'd decided that her ankles were hideous and unattractively merging into her calves.

Sophie sat right beside him. She was so close that her bare upper arm was pressed against his. The touch of her cool skin was electrifying. Only inches away from Romain, she smiled as she lit her joint. She had a lighter on her the whole time. It was the sexiest thing Romain ever experienced. He felt he was in the presence of a Bond girl. Hence, he remained immobile, petrified, sweaty, and unblinking, as if any movements on his part might cause this mirage to dissipate. Honestly, he might have dribbled a little, although he hoped he did not. He couldn't remember now.

"Everything okay there?" she asked, letting out a cloud of smoke through plump lips.

"There?" Wheeze. "Me?"

"Uh-huh… Why? Is there a holy spirit in here with us?"

"Oh. Ha-ha. Ahem, no. Ha-ha." Wheeze. "Yup. Yup." Wheeze. "I'm okay."

"You don't sound, okay."

"I'm ace." *Ace?* Could I be any lamer? Romain thought, before having a coughing fit.

"Good." She sounded entirely unconvinced. "So, you didn't come in here to sulk about football but to enjoy the scenery, right?" She giggled at her own wit, so Romain took the cue and laughed also.

"… I don't like to stay in the sun for long," he admitted, feeling a little embarrassed.

"Maybe you should. You look a little ill, you know?"

"I know." He sighed.

"I think a little colour on you would set off your blue eyes and blond hair very nicely."

"It would?"

Sophie placed her arm alongside Romain's. "Look how pasty you are compared to me! You're like a vampire."

"Vampires don't exist."

"Yeah, but I think you should be in the sun. You'd get a nice glow."

"I'd get a sunburn."

"Hmm. I don't think so. Why are you so stubborn about it?" She tossed her joint's stub through the other end of the narrow tunnel onto dry, unkempt, Mediterranean vegetation. They both watched it go out, while dry pine needles sparked and crackled, threatening for a moment to catch light. Romain imagined that this was precisely how fires in their region started and burned down whole villages. He opened his mouth to say something, but then, Sophie did something highly distracting. She turned to him, and a crucial part of her anatomy jiggled. "Are your parents Swedish or something?"

"Ah uh…" noisy swallowing, "are they?"

She giggled. "Can I touch your hair?" she requested, a hand already raised. Romain hated his hair being touched, everyone who knew him was aware of it. So much so, that he would regularly be teased about it.

However, having lost the ability to talk, he just made a weird little noise, a cross between a moan and a squeak. Sophie interpreted this as a 'yes' and ran her hand through his neatly gelled curly blond hair. Given their physical proximity, her bust stroked the side of his arm. So, funnily enough, Romain did not mind so much about his hair getting messed up and thoughts of her 'cankles' were nowhere near his mind anymore.

"You have beautiful hair," she breathed. Romain hated his hair, well, his whole appearance, in fact, but he would not push back the compliment. Anyway, he couldn't have as her words were now reaching his neurons as "blah ya blah blub ya."

Next thing his frazzled brain registered was her face tipping forward. His heart rate sped up to a level he did not recognise as having reached previously. Although his brain was not processing much at that point, his mouth instinctively found hers. The experience was slobbery, a soup of tongues of some description. She tasted like an ashtray, yet, not altogether unpleasant. Something Romain was already bragging about to Timo, if only in his head, and before it had even finished. Ashtrays were now the sweet taste of victory, finishing first in the kissing lane business. Tiny cheerleaders in the shape of joint butts were congratulating him, commenting on how the pasty vampire lad with a large scar and from an underprivileged background beat all his fellow kiss-virgin contestants to the poll. He even cupped-a-feel, if only by accident.

The spell was broken as they both heard her name being called from afar. And with that, the slightly irritating, foxy girl, two years his senior, was gone. Romain would have chased after her, but he had to wait for a specific something to calm down before he could go anywhere.

He eventually came out to reunite with his thinning pack of teen males, palms sweating, and knees wobbly but feeling triumphant as he re-joined the group. Sophie was standing by a bench of smokers, a guy on a bike had his arm around her shoulders. Romain said nothing, there was no point – nobody would have believed him. He kicked dirt whilst his friends spoke on top of each other about goals and decisive passes. But then, Romain felt a tap on the back. He turned around to see Timo flying past, the ball still attached to his feet. Timo went on to score before winking at Romain, shouting "tosser," making a rude up-and-down gesture with his right hand. He knew. Romain smiled and turned his stare to the ground. Of course, Timo had clocked what happened even though no-one else had noticed. Suddenly, it did not feel so important to let the others know. The main contestant in the kissing-race was aware, and somehow that was all that mattered.

On their way home, after boring Romain with all his exploits at football, Timo abruptly gazed at Romain mischievously. He had the sort of twinkle in his eyes that people have when an amusing thought is tickling their brain. So, he stopped walking for a second, turned his back to Romain and pretended to be smooching by moving his own hands along his back, asking Romain whether he 'stuck the ol' tongue down Eloine's sister throat.' Despite the teasing, Romain did not need to be asked twice. He quickly divulged as much bragging information as he could fit in, before Timo's short attention span would veer to something else.

"Good man," cheered a voice from behind.

Before they could turn their head round to see who it was. An arm was wrapped around Romain's neck, and knuckles were rubbing his hair very roughly. For God's sake.

Romain's heart sank at the sight of Gabin. He tried to wrestle himself free of his grip, but the sixteen-year-old boy's hold was too tight.

Gabin erected his arm, and Timo fist-bumped it reluctantly.

"You shoulda knobbed her. She's clearly gagging for it. Anyway, who's the ho?" Gabin questioned, a mixture of humour and menace in his weirdly accented voice.

Romain suddenly felt protective of Sophie. Not of her honour, it was not the fifties. Besides, Romain was not even sure that he truly wanted to repeat the experience. Though something told him that he would probably never have to make that decision anyway, as the likelihood of Sophie speaking to him again, let alone kissing him, was minimal. However, as always, Gabin brought with him brewing clouds of an insalubrious loom. Truth be told, Romain worried for Sophie's safety, withholding her name to Gabin in the context of what was being discussed and perhaps a tad exaggerated, seemed the right thing to do.

"Oh. Uh. You don't know her. Someone who lives on our street." Romain looked away as he uttered the words.

"Street? I thought you pikeys lived in trailers?"

Romain's gaze turned to the ground, yet he felt Timo's body tense up next to him.

"Where did you get the idea that we lived in trailers?" Timo spat.

Gabin took his arm away from around Romain's narrow shoulders, and with that, Romain could tell that he was a little more intimidated by Timo than by him.

"Well, you do, don't ya?"

"Why don't you just fuck off?" groaned Timo through gritted teeth.

Gabin shrugged and laughed. "Calm down, pansy. I just came to say 'hey.' It isn't my fault if Snowyknob pipped you to the post," Gabin taunted, stepping closer to Timo, forcing his cousin to look up. But Romain could almost feel Timo's blood boiling from where he stood. "Anyway, cheerio. And Romain, tell your gorgeous mum I said 'hi.'" Gabin pushed between Timo and Romain and went on his way.

Romain shuddered at the thought of Gabin mentioning his mum again.

After a long silence, Romain asked, "What do you think Gabin meant by 'tell your mum I said hi'?"

Timo turned his head around to check the street behind them. "Dunno. The guy's a creep." He shrugged and went back to picking his nose.

Chapter 34

"Flying kites and Aunt Yael"

London, England
One year ago, May 2016

"Ah, there's a rerun of Casino Royale at the Curzon on Victoria Street today…" Benedict commented as if to himself, his head hunched over yesterday's *Time Out*. "It's a crime that I've missed it at the cinema…" Benedict grabbed his phone. "There's a showing at 2:05 pm. Shall we all go?" he urged.

"But it's gonna be such a nice sunny day. Why don't we go to a park or something?" Marie suggested, poised in front of the toaster in Benedict's kitchen.

"Kew Gardens?" Yukinobu suggested, who had joined them for breakfast.

"Oh, I'd love to." Marie grinned. "Only the British could have a Queue Gardens," she quipped.

Benedict crossed his arms and let out an audible sigh.

Later that day…

"So, what did you all think of the film?" Benedict beamed.

"Loved it," Romain exclaimed before turning to his mother. "I know what you're gonna say, *maman*, and I'm sorry… but I thought it was sick." Trying out new English slang had become a recent development.

Marie pulled the straps of her handbag further up her shoulder, miffed.

Yukinobu met Benedict's equally confused gaze. "What is it?" Yukinobu asked Marie gently.

"Films like that one really don't help people with facial scarring, you know. They're always portrayed as weirdos or villains. Never the love interests or heroes. It's so… Anyway, it bothers me."

"No, you're right," agreed Yukinobu. "And it's a lazy shorthand on the director's part to identify the bad guy. Don't you think, Benedict?" Yukinobu prompted.

"Hmm. Still, it was a good film. And Mads Mikkelsen was great in the role of Le Chiffre... I-I thought," Benedict stuttered the end of his sentence.

Marie was glaring at him with a mixture of disgust and disapproval. Something that had not happened previously, unlike most siblings neither of them was holding tacit grudges over something that the other did when they were ten years old. However, Marie's stare was having the effect of making Benedict look uncharacteristically sheepish for a moment.

"Do you get a hard time for your...?" Benedict continued hovering a hand over his lips to indicate Romain's large scar while looking at the boy for support. "...Romain?" but Romain had stopped listening a long time ago and was engrossed by a game on his phone instead.

"Uhuh," Romain grunted, uninterested.

Benedict swivelled and pointed at Marie. "Oh, what about Harry Potter?" he remarked triumphantly.

Marie stopped to glare at Benedict. "Yeah. And he makes up for the dozens of villains with scars or disfigurements in all the Star Wars, Marvel and James Bond films?"

Benedict treated Marie to a smug Gallic shrug. As he glanced ahead, amongst the crowd in Leicester Square, Benedict noticed a slender, beautiful woman with bouncy chestnut hair holding the hand of a little boy eating a Fab ice lolly. The two of them so elegantly dressed they could have been walking straight out of a *Vanity Fair* photoshoot.

Benedict's grin vanished as his eyes met the woman's stare. He would have taken a different direction if he could, but there were only a few paces between them by this point.

"Hi, Diane," Benedict boomed, with all the sincerity of a campaigning prime minister caught leaving a brothel.

"Hi." Glacial politeness frosted her tone, conveying a (not-so) secret desire to stub out a cigarette against his face.

Suddenly, memories meshed with guilt, regret, and shame rushed back to Benedict. Diane had been nothing but loving towards Benedict, a love he had taken entirely for granted. Of all the things he had put Diane through, his drunken phone call on the evening of his mother's funeral had been a low blow. Halfway through the call, Diane inadvertently professed her bottled-up love for him. But instead of opening up to her about his own sexual orientation as others might have done with their one true friend to that point, Benedict became angry at her honesty and, perhaps, his own cowardice. Instead of gently rebuffing her advance, he launched into a vile mockery of her upper-class pretence and aspirations, hitting her where her insecurities were closest to the surface. He knew he had done wrong, but he had never reached out to apologise for his behaviour. Partly because he planned to deny any recollection of the phone call when she eventually contacted him again, which he would have followed up with an expensive bribe of a gift. But her call never came, and other than a couple of oblique text messages he had not made the first move.

Benedict felt a sharp tug of nostalgia peering at her. One day, you expect to see someone's name bleeping on your phone screen twice a day. You can pick out the sound of their voice, even their laughter, in any crowded room. And the next, they are nothing to you anymore other than a faint memory like the shadow of your silhouette disappearing when a cloud goes over the sun, as if it had never been there in the first place. As his gaze lowered to the little boy grasping Diane's hand, the realisation of how fleeting most things were by contrast to family ties brought a twinge of envy to the surface. This little boy could have been his. His mother's white trousers had a tiny hand-print stain on them. Benedict wished this mark was on him, that they were on their way to fly kites in the park, build castles on the beach, or dance in the kitchen listening to Katy Perry or something else poppy that kids like before they get 'cool'. Except, Yukinobu was the one who featured in his daydream of happy family life, not Diane.

Before Benedict had a chance to attempt small talk, Diane was gone, leaving Benedict staring at the back of her boy's head. He had ached to reach out to her innumerable times over the years; his strong, ambitious, lovable Diane. He had missed her immensely. He should have congratulated her on being a mother. He yearned to beg her to be a part of his life again, yearned to introduce her to Marie, Romain, and Yukinobu, especially Yukinobu. He owed her an explanation. But he remained immobile, left feeling like an asshole, but unequipped to do anything about it. He had trained himself to lockup deep-rooted feelings so well that he was a prisoner of his own making... Locked-in, unable to break free from his inaptitude to do anything remotely sentimental.

"Who was she?" Yukinobu asked.

"An ex," Benedict lied flatly. Diane had meant much more to him than the sum of all his fleeting exes put together, but it made for a more straightforward answer, save the explanation.

"Oh my gosh, Benedict! She was your girlfriend? And you let her *go*?" Marie murmured in a shouty kind of way.

"I've realised that I'd prefer someone more authentic and younger at heart," Benedict replied, meeting Yukinobu's gaze with twinkly eyes.

But Marie feigned a baffled look. "You realised that you'd prefer a younger 'tart'?" she teased.

Yukinobu got a fit of the giggles only made worse by Marie surreptitiously winking at him.

"No-oh. Younger. At. Heart," Benedict enunciated profusely and a little pompously. "Anyway. I've contacted my lesbian aunt and we've arranged to meet next week," he then announced without any apparent reason or, perhaps, pre-empting the regularly reoccurring conversation about his long-lost aunt and closing it at once and for all.

∞

A heavy silence impregnated their drive back from the airport. Sitting in the shotgun seat, Yukinobu propped his elbow up against the edge of the window, resting his cheekbone on his fist, gazing into space.

Benedict placed his left hand on Yukinobu's knee. "Is everything alright?"

Yukinobu muttered an unconvincing "uh huh".

After shifting onto the fast lane of the motorway, Benedict took his eyes off the road for a moment to look at Yukinobu.

"You don't seem yourself. What's the matter?"

A lorry overtook another lorry and a slow-ish car pulled right in front of Benedict's. Braking just in time, Benedict banged the stirring wheel in protest.

"Can you believe that?" Benedict barked, pointing at the vehicle ahead, before tailing it intimidatingly close.

Yukinobu didn't respond.

Benedict still felt that the idiot in the car in front of him should be taught a lesson and undertook it at the earliest opportunity.

"So, are you not going to tell me what's up with you?" he spat out. However, he refrained from slamming the brakes to scare the idiot now behind them. He would have if it was just him in the car or someone else with him, but he would not risk it with Yukinobu in the passenger seat.

"Who really was the woman with the little boy from earlier?" Yukinobu ventured.

"Oh, uh, an old friend. We used to be close…" The words caught in his throat. He wished Yukinobu would not notice, but he knew that he probably had.

"What happened?"

"She, hmm, it was silly, really. She professed her love for me, out of the blue, and…"

"And you didn't see fit to reveal yourself."

There was a long pause and Benedict focused on the car in front.

"I don't know what you mean…"

"Oh, come on." There was an uncharacteristic edge to Yukinobu's tone. "Is this…" Yukinobu waved his finger between the two of them. "… just a phase. Are we just having fun?"

"Well, we are, aren't we?"

Yukinobu scoffed and turned his head away from Benedict's.

"Why do you see your sexual orientation as such an identity flaw?"

"I don't. Anyway, I'm not…" Benedict wanted to deny his sexual orientation yet again, but it sounded ridiculous, even to him. "Can we change the subject?"

"When are you going to tell Marie and Romain?" Yukinobu carried on.

"I don't see how this is any of their business."

Yukinobu laughed a humourless laugh, they both knew they probably had already figured it out. Marie at least would have. "Anyway, what if I'd like to make it their business?"

"You want to claim me?"

"Would it be so bad?"

"Then, what? Tattoo a rainbow across my forehead?" Benedict sniped.

Of course, Yukinobu did not bite. He never did. Benedict's hands tightened around the steering wheel. He would have liked Yukinobu to ask him to pull over, to make a scene. He would have told him not to be ridiculous, made him feel unreasonable.

"What if I did?" Yukinobu looked straight at him, sternly. His tone was even… reasonable. "What are you so afraid of? It isn't the fifties, you're hardly going to be dragged to prison for it, are you?"

Benedict was tempted to explain, but instead… "we would in some countries."

Yukinobu grabbed the handle on the ceiling above the car door, staring out. "What if I told you that what we have isn't enough for me anymore? What would you do about it?"

Another heavy silence settled. Benedict wanted to say that what they had was not enough for him either. That he wanted, no *craved* a child. A child that looked like him and Yukinobu, not because he so desperately wanted to brag about them or hang a photo in his office the way others hang their Ivy League degree on the wall. He was past that phase. What he wanted was to cement their relationship by caring for a little being that they would both be responsible for and cocoon in their warmth, and stability, and unconditional love. The words lodged in his throat, he only had to open his mouth to let them free. But it felt incongruous to voice it, as if he was about to purposefully expose his flank in a knife fight. He could not do it.

As he slowed the car by Yukinobu's house, neither man could look the other in the eyes. No words or even goodbyes were exchanged. Yukinobu just got out and he was out of sight soon after. Yet, Benedict stayed put, hoping that Yukinobu would retrace his steps and they could make plans for next week. But this didn't happen.

As Benedict settled in his cold leather armchair, a bottle of beer in hand, he felt a gnawing weight settle over him, like grit on an icy road.

The *'je ne sais quoi'* he had, as Diane had once pointed out to him many moons ago, was the intermeshing of his exciting, fast-paced and egotistical sides. It made him the sort of person who would let a partner ride alongside him, as long as not a single whisper of need was voiced. The years spent with Yukinobu had opened his eyes to it, yet he wished they would also have taught him how to deal with it.

∞

Marie just missed her bus. Her cellphone rang. It was Benedict, returning her two missed calls.

"How did it go?" Marie inspected a row of four red plastic seats fixed on an iron bar fused to the concrete ground.

"*Bonjour* to you, too, dear sister."

Marie heard the slight echoed sound of a hands-free car call.

"Oh, alright, if you insist. *Bonjour*," she quipped. "Are you driving back from Oxford as we speak?"

"Yep."

"So, how was your meeting with Aunt Yael?"

"Not what I had expected."

"How so?" Satisfied with its lack of chewing-gum or any other suspicious stains, she sat down on one of the red squares. It squeaked, but did not wobble, so she felt reasonably confident that she was not about to taste concrete.

"For one thing, I wouldn't have thought I'd be playing ping-pong within minutes of meeting her."

"She owns a table tennis?" She got herself comfortable.

"Yep. Right in the middle of her living room. There's also a giant shark embedded head-first in the roof of the house opposite hers."

"I like her already. So, did she beat you?"

"She did. But, in my defence, she had a walking cane to lean on. So."

"Well then, that's technically cheating."

Magnified through the see-through plastic roof, Marie could feel the sun baking her already sweaty neck. It was going to be a long and smelly bus ride.

"Exactly my thoughts… But in all seriousness, it went… okay. She's mad as a box of stoned frogs and the total opposite of my father. Although, saying that, when she opened the door, her resemblance to my father was uncanny. His spitting image… Only two decades older…"

There was a charged pause, filled only by the humming of his car's air conditioning.

"I'm glad it went well, though," Marie comforted her brother, which was still odd for her to say. "Have you arranged to meet up again?"

"Not yet."

From Benedict's slight lapse of time before giving his answer, Marie knew that her brother had no intention of seeing his aunt again.

"Did she say anything about her dispute with your parents and grandparents?"

"Hmm," he acquiesced distractedly.

"Can I ask what her take on it was?"

"Yes. They got into a fight when she first met me, apparently. She didn't believe the miracle story. My grandparents got

208

involved, took my parents' side, and threatened to send her to a madhouse if she didn't calm down. So, she cut herself off from them... However, she also kept on calling me by my father's first name and beckoning a cat that didn't exist... So, I don't know quite how reliable her recollection was."

"She may have lost her mind, but she was right about the miracle."

"I suppose so."

"So, their falling-out wasn't about her sexual orientation, after all, was it?"

Benedict sniffed at that.

"You know, Marie, on the rare occasions my aunt's name was ever brought up, it was invariably followed by 'what a waste' and my grandmother shaking her face in disgust... My shady arrival may well have set the whole thing off. But..." Benedict let his last word hang.

"You're not sure if the crux of the matter really laid there?" Marie offered.

"Marie..." There was a question being formed in his pause which Marie did not attempt to fill or pre-empt. But before he had a chance to voice it, their line had disconnected.

Chapter 35

"Violence"

Marseille, France
One year ago, May 2016

Romain was alone in the changing room. He had to stay behind and tidy up after rugby practice. It was Timo's fault. So, Romain gave his cousin the passive-aggressive treatment throughout. Yet, minutes later, Romain could not have been more grateful to have Timo in his life.

What started as a misdirected box-kick opened up a box full of thumps, jabs, and thwacks, as it often did when Timo was involved. And, as always, teachers, or in this instance the rugby coach, would embroil Romain irrespective of whether he had anything to do with it or not.

Romain let the water of one of the showers run as he grumpily undressed. Lost in his crabby thoughts, he nearly jumped out of his skin when Gabin suddenly appeared from behind one of the rows of lockers.

"My dear, Romain," Gabin called arms spread open whilst looking Romain up and down, making him feel utterly uncomfortable. "Fancy bumping into you two days in a row."

"Well, we're in the same school," Romain grumbled.

"You got me." Swivelling on his spot, Gabin looked around him in an affected way. "But where are all your teammates?" And just like that, Romain knew he was in trouble.

"They'll all be there in a second," he lied.

"Oh, really? Coz I just saw an awful lot of them heading out of here a few minutes ago."

"Right. Well, I've got to catch them up, so, I'm gonna step in the shower," Romain stuttered, wrapping a towel around his waist.

"Don't wait up on my account," Gabin replied with a predatory smile, taking a few steps closer to Romain. Despite himself, Romain remained where he was, feeling an enormous dread coursing through his whole body and making him wheeze.

"There aren't many boys quite like you, are there? You're very... unique." Gabin ran a finger across Romain's cheek,

210

towering over him, turning Romain's legs into jelly. "Mind you, your mum is quite the number."

Romain tried to push past him and make a run for it, but Gabin caught his wrist. In one effortless movement, Romain was thrown to the floor, his head banged against a wall as his towel was stripped away from him.

The sound of a door being banged open was followed by, "look, I'm sorry mate, I, ah…" Timo's voice trailed off as he saw Romain rubbing his head lying naked on the floor and Gabin looming.

"What's going on?"

"I tripped and fell," responded Romain, his chest heaving up and down.

Gabin smirked but made his way out. "See you around. Romain," he vowed, with a barely concealed baleful undertone. "And tell your mum I said 'hi'… Although, I may just do that myself. Soon."

∞

The stench grew worse from one cubicle to the next. But it was the stains of dried urine that made Romain gag. As he came out from the last cubicle, he cleaned and wiped his hands as if a colony of HIV positive mosquitoes were stuck to him.

Inspecting every wall and door, Romain was satisfied he had covered or gotten rid of all the lewd graffiti Gabin had drawn and written about his mother. He seemed to have got to every cubicle in the school and all of them fresh today. Romain decided that Gabin was a sociopath and his hands balled into fists inside his jeans' pockets, glaring at a cubicle door. A complete sociopath.

"Ahem," grumbled a boy, pointing to the toilet. "Are you…?"

"No. Sorry. Go ahead." Romain stepped out of the boy's way, gesturing towards the empty cubicles.

It was bad enough that some of the kids at school made fun of where he lived and his appearance, but Gabin's threats towards his mother boiled his blood. He went to wash his hands again, to give himself an excuse to remain in the restroom.

He had seen Gabin bully other kids and harass girls to the point of driving them to change schools. Gabin was relentless, he knew that. But why did he have to target his mum? Romain could brush off any other type of insult, endure any amount of bullying or intimidation, but not when it was aimed at his mum. And, who knows what this maniac was capable of?

But what could Romain do? The schizoid was twice his size, erratic and unpredictable. Romain felt like howling at the top of his lungs, ripping off the soap dispensers and punching the hand dryers, but he settled for silently squashing the sides of his face instead.

He was pacing when the other kid left the restroom, looking sideways at Romain with something approaching concern. His rage was meshed with despair at how insoluble his problem was as, realistically, erasing insults from walls were neither here nor there regarding the knot of the issue.

The bell rang and Romain left his smelly den. And despite the commotion, he immediately spotted Gabin, who had been held behind by one of his teachers. Argh, no. Not. Him. He could not bump into him now, still drunk on fury. Romain dived back into the restroom, to let Gabin go on his way without any possibility of interaction.

But the door slammed open just before the second bell rang. "Here you are!" Gabin exclaimed in his weird sing-song way of talking.

Like a theatrical villain, Gabin took in the décor of his surroundings, or its lack of it, whilst clicking his tongue tauntingly at the censor of its 'art'.

Romain felt his heart rate speeding up and had to control his breathing. He felt cornered but he was *not* just going to take it this time. Before Gabin could launch into anything further, Romain was desperate and holding absolutely nothing back, and he pounced at him. Empowered by a mix of adrenaline, a total loss of reason and raw rage, he pummelled the stunned Gabin mercilessly. The element of surprise meant Gabin had lost the upper hand even before it began. In his scramble to escape the wild animal that had attacked him, Gabin cracked the back of his head against the edge of the bathroom sink with such force that Romain thought he heard the sound of a skull cracking.

Gabin slowly slid to the ground, as if his large body was made of ice cream and he melted along the bathroom sink to the floor. Stunned by the turn of events, Gabin placed a hand behind the back of his head and it came back smeared with his own blood. His stare met Romain's. But instead of Gabin's usual sneer, Romain was confronted by a facial expression and body language that he had not seen from the bully before. It could only be described as submissive, the way betas concede victory to the alpha. Though, it made no sense because Romain was still Romain and Gabin was still very much Gabin.

Romain silently recoiled. He did not relish the moment, but acknowledged, if only to himself, that the brutal outcome of this fight or flight situation had served a purpose. Before peeling away from one another, they exchanged one last look. A tacit agreement between them had been reached. Romain would not speak about any of it to anyone and Gabin would leave Romain and by extension his mother alone. She was safe from this lunatic, Romain thought... Against all odds, he'd done it. He'd protected his maman.

Such was the speed of the event that Romain's geography class had not even started when Romain attended. The loud noises felt weirdly normal. No one was giving him sideways looks. Arnaud was sitting on Romain's desk, flirting with Léa, well, doing what Arnaud's thought flirting was, from Lea's perspective he was being loud, annoying, and obnoxious. Arnaud's back was turned to Romain and his feet were propped on the chair in front. This would usually raise Romain's hackles, but not today. Romain barely noticed Arnaud or anyone else. He barely had an awareness of where he was. Everything that was being said, even words uttered directly at him, sounded inaudible as if his head was underwater. When Arnaud finally turned his head towards him, Romain placed his book bag in Arnaud's arms and pushed his feet off the chair. At the end of the class, the alarm rang, bringing Romain back to the real world for the first time since it had happened. When he saw Timo's friendly face and heard the homely banality of his words, Romain had to fight back the tears. At that moment he was sincere in his wish that he would never have to resort to violence to solve a problem again.

Chapter 36

"A decent proposal"

London, England
One year ago, June 2016

Benedict dropped his laptop bag in the hallway, with as much care as a schoolboy. He ran up the stairs two steps at a time to the playroom. The curtains were all drawn and the room smelled like a skunk had freshly marked his territory. Headphones on, Romain's back was turned away from the door. Romain was fully immersed in his computer game, speaking Pidgin English into his headphones, swinging his head between two screens and furiously tapping away on the keyboard.

"Hello, Lol_Haha_Dead666," Benedict greeted Romain using the teenage boy's username. 'Cool,' thought the middle-aged man.

There was no reaction.

Benedict tapped Romain's shoulder and sprung out of the way as Romain did an acrobatic flip from his wheeled chair. The thirteen-year-old immediately jumped back on the horse, so to speak, but his head turned down shortly after. Both screens read, 'You were killed by His_Royal_Flabness.'

"Oops," Benedict scrunched-up his face apologetically.

Head still theatrically down-turned, Romain wheeled himself away from the desk and hugged Benedict.

"Thank you for all this." Romain pointed at all the brand-new gaming equipment that filled the room. "And, that, is the best chair I've sat on, in my life. Look, look…" Romain beckoned Benedict to crane down his neck. "… It has Bluetooth connectivity and power sockets and a subwoofer and sit, sit…" Romain pushed him down and put on a game. "… do you feel the vibrations?"

"Yep…" *You really are your mother's son, no doubt there,* thought Benedict, looking at his teenage nephew on the verge of hyperventilation over a chair.

"How cool is that?" asked Romain.

"Well, I'm glad you like it. But it's under the condition that you carry on doing well at school. Got it? Your mum will tell me!"

"Yeah, yeah," Romain muttered.

"And ah," Benedict started to fiddle with the plastic wrapper of one of the new PlayStation games as he spoke. "How are things at school?"

Romain swallowed loudly. Or did Benedict imagine that?

"Alright." Before Benedict had a chance to ask any specifics, Romain hurried to continue. "Nothing much has happened. A guidance counsellor talked to us about careers and stuff."

"And, did something pique your interest?

"I don't know." Romain shrugged. "Sociology?"

"Hmm, well, if you go into Sociology, you'll be one of the rare unemployed people in the world who'll understand exactly why they're on the dole."

"Huh?"

"Nothing. Just promise me you won't go into Sociology."

Romain gave a perfunctory nod.

"Where's your mum?"

The thirteen-year-old pointed to one of the windows with his thumb while putting his headphones on.

Flinging open the curtains, Benedict saw Marie knelt in the vegetable garden under drizzling rain, doing God-knows-what to an already immaculate-looking patch. What had started as just a few pots had turned into the Manoir aux Quat' Saisons' vegetable garden over the past five years. She waved as he knocked on the window and headed towards the house to greet him.

After a peck on the cheek, Marie removed some scones out of the oven – Benedict's favourite treat. Her hands and shadows under her eyes hinted at the laborious few years she had spent juggling a full-time nursing job and cleaning houses she could never afford, although she had never mentioned the latter to Benedict.

"Smells delicious." Benedict beamed. "How was your flight? You made it here in record time today."

"Good, thanks. How was your week?" Marie pricked a scone with a knife, before placing them onto a large plate.

"Not bad. You?"

"Alright."

Benedict sliced a still steaming hot scone across its middle.

"How are things with Romain?"

Marie shrugged and raised her hands. "I don't know. He doesn't tell me much. Although, he's seemed less tense this past month. Has he said anything to you?"

Romain had called Benedict a couple of months ago, urging him to ask his mum to move to London. Actually, he had begged Benedict to do so. Benedict had felt incredibly flattered and touched by it, but he also liked how things were and had no intention of altering the status quo by risking getting Marie's back up. Marie and Romain had visited him on a near-monthly basis over the past five years and they had proved incredibly easy to get on with. Benedict had changed nothing of his lifestyle, and Marie and Romain just slotted into his habits seamlessly, providing the sort of undemanding, fulfilling companionship that Benedict would have thought obtainable only through pets but better. Actually, they had even changed his outlook on a few things. For instance, until they came along, Benedict had always agreed with his mother that 'the best houseguests are those who leave your house after a couple of hours.'

"Not much... But I'd picked up on it, too. He seems to be better now," he ventured.

Benedict piled more clotted cream onto his steaming scone as he spoke. He liked his scones extra creamy.

"Hmm."

"Do you know of anything that might have happened at school or outside of school?" He licked the cream off his finger.

"I don't think so. He did mention something about slapping a teacher's bum the other day."

The trajectory of Benedict's scone stopped mid-transit. A blob of cream, the size of a red bus, dropped onto the granite countertop.

"Only joking," Marie smiled.

Benedict scrunched his nose in affront.

"In all seriousness," Marie rested a hand on Benedict's forearm. "Thanks for having him here so often. It really does him good."

"Don't mention it." He patted her hand, before scooping out the runaway cream.

"I worry that the other kids are giving him a hard time…"

"You're his mum. It's your prerogative to worry," Benedict mumbled, his mouth full. "But there's no need. He's smart and interesting, he'll have his revenge later in life. He should just try to keep his head down and get out of people's way for now."

"Problem is, he'll always stand-out no matter what he does. There's no mistaking him."

216

"Hmm. He's quite pasty." Benedict nodded, deliberately omitting other aspects of his appearance. "He wouldn't stand out for that here like in Marseille, ha." He chuckled, before worrying he may now have planted an idea into Marie's head that he did not want to seed.

Marie responded with a sad, worried smile.

"Well, let's have a cure to all ills." Benedict grabbed a bottle of Malbec from his wine rack and filled up two glasses to the brim.

Later that evening…

"Amazing spaces," Marie scoffed at the TV, watching a show that claimed to turn small dwellings into big dreams. "Small spaces are just what they are, small, period."

"I don't know," Benedict contradicted. "What they've done with that caravan is pretty amazing, I'd say."

Marie snorted but gave him a gentle, conciliatory smile before swirling the red wine in her glass. Benedict stared at Marie's profile which was illuminated by the flickering light coming from the TV screen. She looked like him, but what the eyes could not see was better than him. Despite the difficulties she had faced in her youth, she had become a better human being for it; affable, engaging, spirited, he thought. Qualities, he did not presume to possess.

After a while, she met his stare with side-eyes. "What?"

He inhaled as if about to launch into a lengthy, heartfelt speech but instead settled for "nothing."

Unconvinced, Marie narrowed her eyes in jest, before turning her attention to her bleeping phone. From the grin on her face, Benedict knew the text message was from the Italian chap she had been texting for ages.

"How come you've never invited me to your home?" Benedict suddenly questioned.

He had an idea of why that might be, but he never cared for his suspicion to be confirmed, as he did not really care to remedy it, until now.

"Where we live is, ah, different from what you're used to, and we'll…"

"… You'll be moving soon. Yada, yada. You've already said that. But I'd like to see where you currently live."

"You wouldn't be able to stay the night. It's too, ah, cosy."

"Just for coffee then."

217

Marie took a deep breath. Her eyes were glimmering.

"I'm a little embarrassed for you to see it, is what's…" she murmured into her glass.

"You shouldn't be embarrassed around me."

"Ahem." She cleared her throat. "You know the old caravan on that show? Well, that's pretty much what my home is like."

"You live in a caravan?" Benedict queried tentatively, recollecting mentions made about Romain's father. Was he a gypsy?

"A trailer, but, uh, yeah." She nodded once, resolutely not looking at Benedict.

Okay. That he did not expect… He had pictured blocks of flats and loitering youth, not a dusty campsite or trailer park. Fuck.

"And there I was, dragging you both to choose a powerboat with me. Flaunting my money."

"Absolutely not. And Romain loved it, and taking sailing lessons with you. No. If anything, you've been incredibly generous with us. Besides, we've stayed at the site partly out of choice."

"Why?"

"There's a sense of community that we wouldn't get in a council estate. I don't want to downplay the danger. But ninety-nine percent of the time there's no danger, or less than in the projects, I think. We kind of share a life with our neighbours. When everyone sits out, and the kids play out, someone always watches over you. We help each other." Although, she wished the old Algerian couple living on the plot opposite them would stop barbecuing mackerel quite so late in the summer evenings. Leaving Marie and Romain with a choice to either keep their windows shut and sweat to death in their trailer-cum-sauna, or encrust the stench to their every pore and fibre. "Anyway, it's very hard to get a council flat. There's probably a hundred applications for every opening."

"What about a house?"

She sighed. "It's all I ever think about… Dream about… Well, that and meeting Prince Charming." She trailed off.

"Mind you, it can get quite lonely in ivory towers…" At times, Benedict caught himself wishing for material problems. A lack of them meant he had plenty of headspace for personal introspection, invariably leading to self-inflicted torture of the worst kind. Particularly since he started socialising with Yukinobu's and Marie's more wholesome minds. Benedict's lifetime of deceit intertwined with financial success left him with a profound aftertaste of remorse and regret. Very damaging feelings, which sucked joy and fulfilment from day-to-day life and achievements, leaving people stuck, looking backwards. Two of the seven plagues of the human mind, along with depression, thought Benedict. They eat you from within, even the strongest of people.

"… As we've started a sort of confessional here. I'll admit that my generosity towards you was not all that altruistic… Since the two of you have stepped into my life, you've made it more… more…" Benedict could not find the word at the tip of his tongue. "More…"

"Expensive?"

"Haha. Barely. No, you've made it less… lonesome."

He noticed her hazel eyes glistening in response, before she declared, "life's been much better with you in it for us, too."

He cleared his throat and readjusted his position in his armchair.

"As for Prince Charming… why don't you meet-up with this Italian chap who keeps texting you?" Benedict suggested.

"He lives in Rome." She shrugged. "Plus, I think he's seeing someone."

"Fair enough."

"On that note, what's happened with Yukinobu?"

Benedict's throat knotted at the mere mention of Yukinobu. He tried to conceal his emotions but the pain it induced ran too deep to be fully masked, prompting Marie to quickly blunder, "I mean, ah, we used to see him a fair bit, in France and here, but nothing in the past few weeks."

Benedict tensed up even more. He knew that she had sussed some things out, yet he never cared to discuss any of it with her. "He's just been a little busy lately that's all."

"Oh. Alright," Marie responded unconvinced.

"We may have exchanged some words. But he'll come around. Eventually." He hoped.

"That's a shame. What's happened, if you don't mind me asking?"

Benedict finished his glass and poured himself another, letting the question hang.

"He's just mad at me about something he doesn't understand."

There was another short silence, somewhat filled by the gibberish coming from the TV.

"Did you two…? Were you…? I mean…" Marie tiptoed, even though she had eluded to it a number of times before.

Benedict growled and rubbed his face with both hands. "A couple? Yes, Marie. We bloody were… are. I hope." Saying the words out aloud felt alien to him. Making him feel exposed. The way actors playing a nude scene in front of a fully clothed crew must feel.

"Oh." She did not sound surprised.

"Hmm."

"Were we the cuckoo in the nest? I mean, perhaps Romain and I got on Yukinobu's nerves? I'd understand if we did."

"No. Yukinobu doesn't do nerves. And, if I'm honest, he's the reason I stayed in touch with you two at the very beginning. He loves you both."

"Oh… So, Romain and I weren't the cause of dispute?"

"No… Well, yes. But only indirectly. He wanted me to tell you… about us."

"Why didn't you? This isn't the fifties! How did you think we were going to react? 'Oh, you sick, sick men, let's take you to a conversion clinic this very minute!'"

Benedict wished they would stop reminding him it was not the fifties as if it was some sort of transcendental argument.

"I was about to tell you."

"So, why didn't you?"

"Because of your shifts."

"What about them?"

"Because you often work at weekends, I end up spending a lot of time with Romain, alone, which I enjoy. But I didn't want it to become a problem."

"Benedict!" She pushed herself upright on the sofa, knocking her glass of red wine down onto the hardwood floor. "Did you think that had I known you were gay, I'd automatically assume you liked to fondle little boys in your spare time?" She punctuated every few words with a question mark.

"A lot of people do," he muttered.

"No one does!" she shouted on her way to the kitchen, outraged. "Of course, they don't!"

"Marie. You're too nice…" His voice condescended at her presumed naivety, as he followed her around. "What's being said behind closed doors isn't what people voice in public."

Benedict pointed at the misplaced kitchen roll.

"Ha. Thanks." Marie unrolled a mountain of paper. "Anyway, what are you going to do?"

"I'm going to open another bottle of wine, finish it up, go to bed and spend a lovely weekend with my shouty sister and loner nephew. Then go to work on Monday."

"Argh." She waved away the silliness. "Have you tried to win Yukinobu back?"

"I haven't lost him. He's just… taking some time to himself."

Marie gave him a look.

"No," he grumbled.

"Too proud?"

"No. Just no point."

"Don't you love him?" Marie cleaned up the spillage by spreading it around and leaving a dripping trail behind her all the long way to the kitchen.

"I do. I absolutely do. I've never felt like that about anybody else before…" Benedict rubbed his face with both of his hands. "But he can't give me children, can he?"

Marie swivelled in shock at the revelation, wine trickling down her hand from a soggy kitchen paper ball, like a witch holding a freshly ripped out heart in a sacrifice ritual. "Is that what you want?"

"What I really, really want. Ziga-ziga ah."

"Spice Girls?"

"Yeah."

"Cool," she sneered.

"Cool yourself." Benedict gave his best impression of a mean girl's face before sticking his purple tongue out.

"Oh-kay. Moving on… If you really want a child and love Yukinobu. Why don't you adopt? Or use a surrogate mother?"

"Or snatch a baby? Make it a family tradition?"

"Sorry… I know it can't be easy." She looked contrite but he was not about to show sympathy. He just wished she would drop the subject.

"Yukinobu and I are a gay couple, unmarried, one of us in his mid-fifties and Japanese with a Korean passport, the other British. Adoption would be near impossible, and surrogacy agreements are not enforceable by UK law. So, 'isn't easy' would be putting it mildly."

Marie put a hand on his arm. There was a pause before Benedict's gentle tap responded that it was all right.

221

They changed the channel to golf. A very long silence grew roots. So long, in fact, that they had time to watch one of the golfers actually take a shot.

"Isn't it funny that we seem to name girls after fruits, like Peach, or Apple, or Cherry? Even Berry... And boys after predators, like Bear, Hawk, Wolf, Fox and, ya know, Tiger." Marie pointed in the direction of the TV. "Funny, eh?"

Benedict understood what she was aiming for. But no amount of chit-chat would bring him out of the funk that alcohol, the turn their conversation took, Yukinobu's absence, and a decade of bottled-up frustration had infused. Albeit, he eventually mustered an "uh huh."

The camera cut away to the crowd, resting its gaze on a skinny woman standing next to an enormous man wearing a golf polo shirt, making him look like a badly stuffed sausage.

"Gosh, fiddlesticks! How big *is* that man?! The country of great outdoors has well and truly been defeated by the French... of the fried kind for that guy, hasn't it?" Marie exclaimed, putting down her packet of peanuts before resting her hand on her stomach pudge.

"Uh, huh."

Marie turned her gaze away from the TV and onto Benedict. "You know what, Benedict?"

"No, but I've a feeling you're about to tell me."

"We think of it as only a human thing, but it happens to other animals, too."

"What thing?"

"Homosexuality."

"As in lesbian cows?" he quipped, though a frown of incomprehension veiled his expression.

"Not cows! Pirates."

"Do you mean primates?"

"Yeah, like I said. Primates. Are you trying to be difficult? Or is this line of conversation offending you?"

"Should I be offended that there are gay monkeys? Or are you calling me one?"

"Don't be silly. Anyway, it's less noticeable with primates because the males simply don't compete for the females' attention or to become alphas. But there are gay pirates, ya know."

He was going to let the drunken 'pirate' reference slide this time. "Uh, huh."

"Actually, thinking about it, maybe some cows are into a bit of lesbianage as well. Who knows?"

"Not me."

"From what I've read, or heard, can't remember where I learned about this, something happens in the womb that makes animals, including humans, gay or straight."

"Are you telling me that looking at you in the nude for nine months put me off women for life?" Benedict teased, finally able to muster a feeble smile.

And then out of the blue.

"I could be the surrogate mother to your child, you know." Marie hiccupped, the alcohol taking hold.

Benedict choked on his drink. "I beg your pardon?"

"Well, not by using your soldiers or Yukinobu's ding-dong… or anyone's ding-dong. Although the latter would give me a sweet break from my Sahara crossing, if you get my drift." Hiiic-cup. "But, I could go to a sperm bank, or use Yukinobu's swimmers, and as we were made from the same batter," hiiic-cup, "then this baby would have both of your genes. As if you've made it yourself. What do you think?"

"Would you, really?"

"Yes, I would. I love you. And Yukinobu. And," hiiic-cup, "I enjoyed being pregnant with Romain."

"You do realise that you'll have to abandon your child to me at the end of it, don't you?"

"Yeah, but I'd get to be an auntie to your little Lychee or Tiger." Hiiic-cup.

"A bit of casual racism for closure, why don't we?"

"Maybe. But you've got to admit that 'Wad'a'grand Tiger' would make a fantastic name."

"Wada-Grant," he repeated as if tasting the ring to their hyphenated surnames.

"Is that you entertaining the idea?"

"I appreciate the offer. But let's talk again in the morning. When you're sober. It's too big a decision for you to make now."

"Righto."

"I'd be forever in your debt if you did, though."

"You won't have to be. Coz that's the beauty of being family."

"Oh, yes. I would. And I've got an idea about how I'd repay you."

"Like I said. No need… You know that old saying you like to quote to Yukinobu every time you do something annoying?"

223

"A friend is one who overlooks your broken fence and admires the flowers in your garden?"

"Yep. That one. Well, family don't overlook your sorry fence, they help you fix the damn thing, instead of admiring your flowers."

Benedict guffawed light-heartedly. "Alright, Plato. Let's see if you still fancy fixing my sorry-ass fence tomorrow." There was a giddiness in his tone that he could not repress. A lid had been lifted off. The sour aftertaste that life had been leaving behind had started to seep out.

∞

"I'm game." Marie declared, smiling at Benedict from above her mug of café au lait, the next morning.

"Are you sure?" Benedict checked.

"Certain."

He suddenly could not contain it. He pounced on his sister, giving her exuberant kisses on the forehead and cheeks, in a distinctly non-English fashion. Their mutter of amusement blossomed into an enormous belly laugh as she tried to fend off his affection, ending up wearing the contents of her mug instead.

"I meant, I'm gonna ask the Italian guy out," Marie quipped, giving him a teasing grin. "We were on the same page, right?"

"Of course! What else?" With that, Benedict grabbed Marie's unlocked phone of the kitchen table and ran off with it, pretending to be typing away.

"Don't you dare!" Marie exclaimed in a shouty giggle, catching hold of him.

Benedict raised the arm clasping Marie's phone in the air. But she pulled it down and snatched her phone off him.

Then something changed in Marie's expression. A girly rose tinted her cheeks. "Actually, let's do it," she asserted, to herself it seemed. She then stared at her phone for a bit.

"Well, go on then," Benedict encouraged.

∞

Posted in front of Yukinobu's entrance door, Benedict felt the same apprehension as he did on their first date. They had not seen each other or spoken in person for weeks.

"Hello stranger." Yukinobu looked surprised to see him but Benedict did not detect any hint of bitterness. That being said, Yukinobu had always been hard to read, annoyingly so. "Come on in." He stepped aside to let Benedict in while wiping his hands on his apron. "This is a nice surprise," Yukinobu added, which raised Benedict's spirit.

All the same, Benedict remained silent, too nervous to say anything.

"Would you like to stay for dinner?" Yukinobu offered, smiling. "I've just made a pasta bake large enough to feed a whole family."

Yukinobu removed his apron and Benedict noticed that his white t-shirt was clinging. He was as handsome as ever, yet he seemed somewhat leaner than Benedict remembered.

"I, ahem." Benedict cleared his throat. "… Wouldn't want to impose." Although he did. Very much.

"Not at all." Yukinobu hovered by Benedict's side, fussing over taking his jacket off him. He placed a warm hand against Benedict's back, leading him to the kitchen. Benedict suddenly wished his back was bare so he could feel Yukinobu's palm on his skin. The open space was filled with the homely smell of his pasta bake.

"Look, I…" Benedict wanted to say he was sorry, that he should not have left it so long to contact him again. That he missed him. That he knew he could be a selfish bastard at times, yet if he would have him, he would be *his* selfish bastard... But Yukinobu cut him short, holding a wedge of lime in one hand and a cold beer in the other.

"Fancy it?"

"Oh, hmm, yes, thanks."

Yukinobu's interruption made it harder to deliver his speech. Stalling for time, Benedict shoved the bit of lime down the neck of the bottle and swished the beer around.

"It's good to see you," Yukinobu volunteered, reading the mood of the room. His gaze enveloped Benedict like it used to, but unlike looking into a mirror, it saw beyond what the eyes can see. And not just saw, it accepted.

A flashback of the self-assured, perceptive man Benedict first met came to the forefront of his mind. A poised man, confident in who he was, a patient man, who took a repressed Benedict along in the long and tricky journey of acceptance of his own identity, a loving man… Benedict could not contain it anymore. "Have a baby with me," he blurted out. "Please."

Yukinobu laughed. A lot.

"I mean it." He kept his voice serious.

"I can tell you do. Sorry. Alright, let's take a step back for one second and think about things. What's happened?"

"What happened is that I love you. I told Marie about it yesterday, and I'd tell the whole world if you want me to." Benedict took a couple of steps towards the front windows. "I'll shout it from out here if you don't believe me." But Yukinobu stopped him.

"That won't be necessary, I believe you." Yukinobu chuckled.

"So, will you?"

"I don't know. I shouldn't think so."

"Very well." Benedict slapped the side of his thighs. "Okay, then. Shall we sit down and eat?" He continued in a thin peevish voice.

"Don't be like that. For years we've been 'friends' with benefits, while you carried on with your straight life…" Yukinobu simpered as he voiced the last two words, but Benedict refrained from crossing his arms in response to the little jab. "… And after a few weeks of not seeing each other, you've now decided you're gay, want to have a child with me and, I presume, move in together. What's brought all this on?"

"Various things."

"Very compelling." Yukinobu suppressed a nascent smile.

"You."

"Me? I merely suggested it was time to disclose our relationship to your sister and nephew."

"Shush. I'm trying to explain… And be romantic."

"Sorry. As you were."

"As you know, I've always wanted to have a family of my own and the biological link is important to me. I told you that on our first date."

"You did. I'll give you that."

"I just never thought it'd be possible to build that with you. And you're the only person I'd ever want to do that with. And I know that I've kept pretending otherwise, mostly to myself, but I do want you to claim me and I want to claim you. And I want to stay with you and see a mini version of us being born and raised by us."

"What's suddenly made it possible in your mind?"

"Marie has made an offer."

"Oh-kay."

"She's offered to be a surrogate."

"What?" Yukinobu exclaimed in disbelief.

"Yep." Benedict nodded for effect.

"Donating her egg or carrying it?"

"Both."

"That's, ah, an incredibly selfless offer. A very Marie-offer, mind you." A frown veiled Yukinobu's expression. "But it seems a little risky, don't you think?"

"In what way?"

"She'd effectively be carrying her own baby. So there's a chance that she'd bond to it quite strongly. Don't you agree?"

"I voiced that concern. But she said that she sees it as babysitting our baby in her uterus. Her words." He laughed.

Benedict was aware that, on paper, Marie would not be the ideal candidate for surrogacy. She would be turned down by any agency on the basis of her age and credit check alone. Irrespective of the added risk that using her own genes carried. Yet he would not further Yukinobu's misgivings by sharing this as, to his mind, Marie was the ideal candidate. He trusted her and would not contemplate putting the fate of his family in another woman's womb other than Marie now that the offer was on the table.

"But why would she put herself through it?" questioned Yukinobu.

"I didn't force her hand if that's what you're implying. Hell, I didn't even attempt to seed the idea. I know that I can be self-centred at times. But this idea was all hers."

"I don't doubt it, but did you ask her why she'd do it?"

"She simply replied 'I can't think why not'."

"Hmm."

"I'll obviously cover all medical costs," Benedict added quickly. "I'll also take up life and critical illness insurance for her and Romain… And I'm already thinking of a way to repay her."

"Hmm."

"What d'you mean, hmm?"

"Well, you're always like this." Yukinobu paused and Benedict did not attempt to fill it. "You make up your mind about something and then expect everyone else to fall into line."

Disappointment coursed through every inch of Benedict. He did not expect Yukinobu to hold up a mirror to him. He had expected him to, well, go along with it. But of course, Yukinobu was right. Yet, Benedict could not help who he was either, no matter how much he had grown into himself since having Yukinobu in his life.

"Let me think about it," Yukinobu added sweetly before Benedict had a chance to say anything back.

This gave Benedict an ounce of hope.

Chapter 37

"Matter baby"

London, England
Nine months ago, October 2016

The fertility clinic did not look anything like they expected. The walls were not white, and there were no spectacled scientists clutching test tubes full of sperm in gloved hands. Yet Marie, Benedict, and Yukinobu were in for a zany experience. The waiting room had two sofas, a few tongue-tied patients, a television on mute, and no inane music to break off the palm-sweating silence. It struck Marie as odd, as if the expectation was that she and Benedict should be keeping an ear out for the wind-up delivery of the masturbation rooms. Part of her felt unexpectedly turned on at the thought of what was going on behind all those doors, shortly followed by a little self-pity – she really had been in the desert too long.

Glancing around, Marie noticed a dwarf lemon tree in the corner of the room. Its leaves had seen better days, all pocked as if a gang of nefarious caterpillars had had their wicked away with them. And small greenish lemon-spurts had fallen in and around its pot. It did not speak of fertility or potency. Marie looked away. There were a few old magazines on the coffee table. One of them had George Clooney and his heavily pregnant wife on the cover. Expecting twins, at fifty-six and forty, they must have had help decided Marie, arbitrarily. Fancy seeing George Clooney coming out of one of those booths, instead of Yukinobu. She felt a little pulse beat downstairs, followed by self-pity again, before noticing that Benedict was bouncing his legs restlessly next to her as if a mini earthquake affected his small section of the waiting room.

"Hopefully, today will be our Yuki-day!" Marie nudged Benedict.

"Our yucky day?"

"Our Yuki-day. You know? Our. Yuki. Day." Nudge-nudge, wink-wink.

Benedict wore a what-the-heck-is-she-on-about frown on his face.

"As in Yuki-nobu who is in one of *those* rooms... It sounds like our lucky day. You know, our yuki-day... Sorry. It was lame... Nerves, you know."

"Aww. I get it. Our lucky-day, Yuki-day. Ha yeah. Funny." He tried his best to sound sincere.

Marie sighed, before taking his hand in hers.

"Are you all right?" he rasped.

"Yes."

"Having second thoughts?"

"None."

His hand was beginning to squash hers.

"There'd be no shame in admitting if you were. I wouldn't hold it against you. Not for one minute. Nor would Yukinobu... And there's still time to change your mind. Okay? Plenty of time. Plenty. So, if you do there's no harm, no foul."

What on earth? "Have you?" she squeaked.

"Have I what?"

"Had second thoughts?"

Snort. "No." He sounded overly affirmative. "Why would I?"

Benedict retrieved his hand, looked down and started bouncing his legs. Marie felt a pull of motherly endearment at his qualm. Something she had never seen in him before.

"Producing a child is fairly easy and quick. Raising it is the real difficult part. It's only natural to feel nervous about it."

He shook his head. Leaning back, he rubbed his forehead. "That's not it..."

"What is it then?"

He stood up, taking a few steps towards the exit door and stopped. He leaned against the wall and turned his gaze towards Marie. It was glacial. Marie swallowed.

Silence.

The way he looked at her reminded Marie of the way some patients reacted after being told they will have to leave their fate in the hands of doctors – strangers who supposedly have their well-being at heart.

"Are you worried that I won't hand the child over once it's born?" she asked tentatively.

He remained silent, banged the back of his head lightly against the wall, and stared at the ceiling, closing his eyes.

Marie drummed her fingers, opened her mouth, closed it, then reopened it... "This one time, when Romain was two, I remember holding him on the toilet seat so that he didn't fall in, you know.

As his solid business hit the mark, water splashed onto my face and all over my mouth. Thinking about it now makes me feel intensely broody."

Benedict offered a half-smile. Marie moved up to him and bumped her shoulder against his a couple of times.

"Look, I get it. Deceit and hidden agendas have been your daily bread. Being at the top of the food chain must mean you've mastered those rules, too… I haven't. I'm not like that, and you must know that by now. I WILL hand over your child."

There was tenderness in his eyes as he ruffled her hair in tacit agreement.

"Argh, get off!" Marie ducked out of the way and smoothed back her curls. "Are you mad? Curly hair don't do ruffling."

"Sorry." His voice sounded more relaxed. "I never asked," Benedict added. "Did the Italian guy ever get back to you?"

"He did. And said he wanted to meet up but…" She gave the thumbs down. "… He never followed through with it."

"Ah, that sucks. His loss."

"*C'est la vie.*" She shrugged.

A short, effeminate man entered the waiting room and lingered by the door. As his gaze met Marie's, he gave off the distinct impression of being lost and timid.

"For sperm donation you need to go down the corridor to the right," Marie informed quietly, giving him a sympathetic look before pointing him in the right direction.

He stared at her a moment.

"Thanks. If I go bald, I'll know who to call for a haircut now," was the eventual reply in an assertive feminine voice.

Marie scanned down the person's torso, flicked her eyes to inspect their face more closely and coupled with the woman's sarcastic statement, Marie's oversight of her gender became clear.

Benedict stifled a giggle into his fist whilst Marie's face turned bright red. The woman moved to a sofa, her eyes still locked with Marie's as she wrapped her arm around a woman covered in freckles, who looked absolutely terrified. The freckled woman clutched an oversized handbag tightly in her lap. She took out a bottle of mineral water with shaky hands, had a swig and then handed it to her friend. As she grabbed the bottle, Marie's new nemesis flipped Marie off.

"Right," Marie muttered and nudged towards the door to initiate a move elsewhere.

But Benedict remained immobile, his veil of concern returned.

"When I asked 'why', you said 'you couldn't see why not'…" He began. "But really, why are you willing to put your body through nine months of hormonal fluctuations, morning sickness, back pain and stretch marks, not to mention the bodily trauma of delivering a baby, weeks of recovery and potentially fatal harm?"

No pause for thought was required, as Marie knew exactly why she was willing to do it. Yet, she stalled a little for time by taking in a deep breath as she was not particularly keen to voice her reasons. Not only because they sounded a tad worthy, but she was also worried she would not be able to control her effusion of emotion.

"Because I love you. Because I find it cruelly unfair you can't fulfil your desire to have a family with Yukinobu. Because I had an easy pregnancy with Romain, so it is something I could do for you. I would have done it for your mum, too, had I been born a generation ago and had I known her. Being able to have children when they're wanted is a blessed gift. One that I wouldn't want you, particularly you, my brother, be denied of." Marie wiped the happy tears that had been rolling down her cheeks and laughed once, a little embarrassed by her outpour. "Besides, maybe this baby will grow up to become the British or Japanese Prime Minister. Who knows?"

Benedict pulled her into a tight hug, momentarily unable to say anything back.

"Maybe both. I heard that twins run in our family," he eventually quipped, a catch in his voice.

They chuckled and Marie felt the emotional tension that had been trapped in their bodies seeping out.

Chapter 38

"Blooming"

Marseille, France
Six months ago, January 2017

Marie took a deep breath before stepping into room 148b. Flavia glanced over as Marie entered, letting out an exhausted sigh, before staring back at her phone.

Flavia's fish-shaped green eyes magnified by glasses reflecting duck-face Instagram captions were 'true' windows to her millennial soul. Her hair had recently fallen out, but she found wigs itchy. So, she would only wear one around people that mattered. She did not wear one then. A web of wires was draped over her bare arms and around her neck. Intravenous drips stood next to her bed, bags filled with fluids dripped at the pace of bored teenagers and seeped through the feeding tubes into her veins.

"Morning, Flavia."

"Morning, Nurse Boulanger," Flavia muttered as Marie reached the heart monitor pinched at her forefinger and read the series of little bleeping disco graphs.

"You can call me Marie," she offered, not for the first time.

"No can do." Flavia did not look up from her phone screen.

"Why not?"

"You're too mature for it."

"I'm thirty-seven!"

The twenty-something-year-old smirked. Marie's body tensed up. Damn it! Marie had promised herself that she would not react to Flavia's digs anymore.

"A little old for this, then?" Flavia inclined her phone in the direction of Marie's stomach and arched her pencilled eyebrows. "I'm presuming you're pregnant, right? Not just a big lunch?"

"I am," Marie replied, annoyed that she looked eleven months pregnant when it had only been three.

"Was it planned?"

"Yes." Marie felt her ears turn red. Flavia was angry with the world, so weirdly, it made it better. Still… "It's my second, actually." Now, why would she care to add that? She had nothing

233

to prove to anyone, including a vitriolic cancer patient with a penchant for pouty, vacuous Instagram photos.

"Uh. Is your first a boy or a girl?"

"A boy."

"I bet you're hoping for a girl then."

"And hopefully, she'll turn out just like you." Marie bulged her tongue into her mouth.

"You should be so lucky," Flavia snapped back.

Whether it was a boy or a girl made no odds to Marie, obviously. It was not hers to keep. But what if it was? Why did so many people make this assumption? Just because she already had a boy, should the absence of a penis between this baby's legs truly be the primary driver of her greatest hopes and dreams?

Marie checked the bruising where Flavia's breast used to be. It was reabsorbing and scarring as it should.

"Same father?"

Oh, for God's sake!

"No."

"Ouch!" Flavia protested at Marie's involuntary rough touch. "That's not my fault! No need to take it out on me."

"Sorry." And Marie genuinely was. Despite Flavia's bravado, Marie knew she hurt on many levels. Life had dealt Flavia a cruel hand... No one should have to go through what she did, at such a young age. "Have you been taking your medicine?" she asked gently.

"Hell yeah. Are you kidding? That's the only perk from the blasted thing."

Marie caught Flavia taking a fleeting glance at her ample breast.

"All of them?" Marie double-checked, even gentler than before.

"Yes, Nurse Boulanger, all of them..." Flavia's phone was back in her hand, reflecting more pouty faces on her glasses. "So, do you know who the lucky father is?"

Rolling her eyes, Marie exited the room without uttering another word.

The first to guess about her pregnancy had been Médélice. And such was her excitement that Marie could not get a word in edgeways. When the details of her situation were eventually confided to her friend, Marie was met with an uncharacteristically frosty, judgemental reaction from Médélice. The idea that Marie intended to hand over her baby to two men had put a distance between them. And it was not clear which part was received worst – abandoning the baby or facilitating its adoption by a homosexual couple.

It went something like this.

'Babies are blessings. They should be cherished. God knows, I would.' Médélice dabbed her eyes. 'Babies needs their mother. A mother and a father just like God intended.' A pointy finger tapped the cafeteria's table.

'Then what about Romain? I'm his only parent,' Marie interjected.

'Well, that's different. Tragic. But, entirely different. Call it what you like, self-preservation maybe, certainly.'

But after that, Marie kept part of the picture (on her situation) private. The toxic reaction of her friend; her big-hearted, tender-hearted, everything-good-in-the-world-hearted friend suddenly brought home the ugly realisation that Benedict's worries had foundation. And that Marie's acceptance was not universally shared.

Still, she hoped Médélice would come round to it in due course, despite finding it decidedly difficult to reconcile this new facet of Médélice's personality with the woman with whom she shared countless hours of fun and giddy conversations. A woman as warm as warm could be, with a contagious laugh that never failed to brighten up a dull ward. A type of quaint soul who still uses Facebook to share photos with friends rather than a venting, political ground. Yet intolerant.

Marie's phone rang, displaying an unknown number.

"Marie Boulanger speaking."

Ruffles and tumbles came through on the other end of the line, followed by a long 'aaaaouch' and eventually a "hi, this is Brigitte, the estate agent."

"Are you alright?"

"Oh, I'm fine. Haha. This pussy of mine is just so eager, I nearly lost a finger," uttered an elderly female voice.

"You're talking about your cat, right?" She hoped.

"I am. The hungry beggar. Anyway, I received your message about the house. Great choice. Great, great. Huge parcel of land. And I'd be more than happy to give you a lift. Now, you're visiting on behalf of your brother. Is that right?"

"Actually, the house would be for me, but my brother is paying."

"How nice. Now, Marie. May I call you Marie?"

"Please do."

"I've got to warn you. There might be animals. Rodents, most likely. But rest assured, I'll have my umbrella with me."

"In case they pee on us?"

"Ha ha. You're funny. No, to bash their brains out."

"Right."

"Are you still interested in seeing it?"

"I am."

"Splendid. I shall be waiting for you by the hospital's entrance. Don't drop dead in the meantime. Haha."

"Thanks, Brigitte. See you at 5:00 pm."

"Toodle-oo."

Marie hung up and stared at her phone, uncertain how she was supposed to feel about the exchange. Other estate agents had made her feel worthless after finding out where Marie lived. Turning their noses up at her and refusing to help her, much like in the Pretty Woman scene when Julia Roberts is chucked out of an upmarket shop. So, on the one hand, this estate agent was unlikely to do that to her. On the other, she was clearly the type to start applying make-up, then forget about the other half of her face before going out.

"I've heard congratulations are in order," a voice called from behind.

Unbeknownst to them, Marie rolled her eyes and accelerated. She heard them speed walking to catch up with her. Marie was heavily tempted to speed up to a trot so that they never would.

"You heard well," Marie eventually responded. "I presume Médélice was your source?"

Nurse Lucie ran a pinched forefinger and thumb across her lips as if zipping them together. Marie wished they really did.

"You'll have your hands full soon. Make sure you get all the sleep you can get now!"

"Yep." Because that's something you can control and save up.

Lucie's eyes lowered to Marie's stomach.

"Oh my, you've already bloomed!" The middle-aged nurse exclaimed before rubbing Marie's belly.

"Thanks," Marie guessed. Is this really a compliment? Marie suddenly felt like pinching the woman midriff's roll and saying, 'good grief, so have you!'

It had only been a couple of weeks since people had started to be aware. But Marie was already fed up with the unsolicited

236

advice, nosy questions, and inconsiderate remarks. God help with what the next six months had in store for her.

"Aww, I'm so happy for you. Is this an IVF miracle?"

What?! Marie stopped and turned around to face Lucie. That was it...

"Nah, he took me from behind. I came twice. A real treat. So, tell me, were yours produced kneeling as well, or are you more of a ride-on-top kinda girl?"

Silence – even the crickets were shocked.

"Right," said the head nurse who had appeared out of nowhere and only caught the tail-end of Lucy and Marie's conversation. "Marie, your help has been requested in room 203. It requires discretion."

Their faces redder than a beach flag on a stormy day, Marie and Lucie scampered off, resolutely staring at their feet as they did.

There were armed guards by the door. A dark hair man swivelled on his feet as she entered room 203. His old-school bohemian look was accentuated by his navy-blue shirt, sleeves rolled up to the elbows. The top two buttons were undone, exposing his enticing Mediterranean skin. His lips curled into a dazzling smile as his gaze met Marie's.

"Hello, Nurse Marie," an accented suave voice greeted.

Marie instinctively brought her clipboard in front of her stomach.

"Hello, Officer Paoli." She beamed.

"Why. You remember me, Nurse Marie?" Giandomenico quipped, bringing a hand to his chest.

Marie treated him to a coy smile. What was he doing here? "Well, I'm surprised you do." She could not help the small jab but, judging by Giandomenico's smile, he did not register it as one.

"No man would ever forget such a beautiful face." Giandomenico took a step closer and enveloped one of her hands in his and softly shook it. Marie felt like sighing.

A hand waved in the background.

"Hello," was muttered tentatively. Marie craned her neck to see past Giandomenico. "Hello," repeated a small man in a French police officer uniform, lying on a bed. "Terribly sorry to interrupt. But could you possibly see to my neck, please?"

∞

237

Marie had given no thoughts to romance for a while. She had been so busy trying to stay on top of bills, raising Romain, and building a relationship with her long-lost brother that everything else took second stage. However, she would be lying if she said that the prospect of meeting Giandomenico in person again had not inflamed her imagination. Yet it had been seven months since she suggested it, and nothing happened, so life resumed its course. Then, of course, she had to be pregnant when Giandomenico finally made his move.

Giandomenico chased after her, stethoscope in hand. As he handed it back to her, he casually enquired what she was doing that evening.

"Not much," Marie admitted. "Why, do you need me back at the hospital to see to your colleague?"

"Good God, no." Giandomenico shook his head and smiled. He looked like a Mediterranean version of Jon Bon Jovi. "It's just a wry neck and the guy's already fretting about a wheelchair for life... No, I just wondered if I could tempt you out for dinner."

"Me?"

"You."

"For dinner?" Marie wondered if she heard him correctly. "How do you mean?"

"I'm envisioning you and I will be sitting down, preferably in front of one another, eating with a knife and fork, drinking and having a chat."

Marie blinked several times as if spinning a wheel in her mind on the number of occasions Giandomenico featured in her dreams. Yet none involved using a knife and fork or having a chat... He had made such an impression on her when they first met. Since then, they had exchanged an endless number of texts, but he had become a sort of fictional character with whom to trade funny one-liners. Until she took the plunge and asked if they could meet again. However, as he did not take her up on it, she reverted to thinking of him as a fantasy... Anyway, how could he look even more debonair and handsome than she remembered?

"You do eat dinners, don't you?" he added.

"Yes, otherwise I don't sleep well. No one does, sleeping on an empty stomach slows your body's ability to convert proteins into muscle."

Silence.

"Good to know," he assented while she felt like digging a hole in the wall with her forehead. "So. How about it?" he offered again.

"About dinner? You and me? Yes. I'd love to. Definitely. Let's have dinner. Tonight."

"All right then." Giandomenico smiled that his knee-weakening smile of his. "Drop me a line with a time and address, and I'll be there." He kissed her cheek and left, leaving her standing still, gawking at his departing, sexy figure.

She hid her face behind her clipboard, reliving the toe-curling exchange. How inventive would she have to be with her outfit to hide her stupidly fast-expanding midriff?

Chapter 39

"Rainbow-tears"

Provencal garrigue, France
Six months ago, January 2017

It took a while to reach the house as the road was sinuous and bumpy. The whole area looked like a rendition of a French resistance's hideout; desolate, arid and inhospitable. They were in the middle of a maquis or garrigue, Marie never knew the difference between the two. Anyway, it was hilly, rocky, filled with numerous shrubs, across vast open spaces framed by mountains to the north and glimpses of the sea to the south. Simply put – it was stunning and lonesome.

The car struggled to drive the unbeaten tracks. As it stopped, Marie came out to a breeze of wild rosemary, lavender, and thyme, accompanied by the sound of cicadas and real crickets. Behind a grove of Mediterranean trees, all Marie could see was a large pile of stones the same colour as the rocks freckling the evergreen area. The derelict building camouflaged perfectly into its surroundings as if whoever built this old sheepfold aimed to conceal it. Marie neared and beyond a disused chicken run peppered with fruit trees and beehives, she noticed an abandoned vegetable garden. An ingenious watering system still running strong and alleys of wildflowers detracting creepy crawlies had stayed there, illustrating the love and care that once went into creating it. Vividly, she could picture an old couple, their laughter, their contented hard work and ingenuity, their love.

A deafening metallic noise brought Marie out of her hypnotic reverie with a bang. Looking for its source, she found Brigitte, roaming the land. In a hunched posture that could only be described as Neanderthal-esque, Brigitte was clunking one pan against another. Her head was moving from side to side, with her snout up and eyes wide open. Marie felt as if a tinfoil hat on Brigitte's head was amiss.

Brigitte caught Marie goggling at her. Seeing it as a cue, she discarded her pans and brandished her umbrella instead.

"Now, do not worry, young lady. I'll protect you." Treating Marie to a broad smile or bared crooked teeth, who knew, the older woman karate-kicked the door of the converted sheepfold. As the door opened, she commando rolled against the outdoor wall, expecting rats to storm out, or perhaps a bear.

Peeping through the opening, the estate agent raised a balled fist and shouted, "all clear." She waved for Marie to approach.

"Well, that was all a bit exciting, wasn't it?" Brigitte declared, panting for effect and brought a hand to her heart. "Please come on in, Marie."

"After you." Marie gestured towards the house. It was safer to keep Brigitte in sight.

The walls were extra thick, keeping the temperature inside cooler than out. Marie went to open a set of shutters, but Brigitte beat her to it by switching on the light.

"Oh, I assumed there was no electricity," Marie said.

"Wrong!" Brigitte laughed, clapping her hands excitedly before pointing at Marie. "The previous owners, very, very, very clever hermits that they were, installed solar panels…" She pointed to the ceiling with her umbrella, "and a well, tapping water from an underground spring."

"Clever, indeed," Marie agreed. "Do you know why they're selling?"

"They died, the poor things."

"How sad. Do you happen to know how?"

"Yep. I should probably not say, but the female got attacked by a pack of wild dogs. They possibly started eating her while she was still alive, technically. The husband found her, and…" Brigitte clicked her fingers, "bam, dead. Had a stroke. The poor things." She slumped her shoulders and breathed out while pulling a face expressing sadness and a touch of the insane.

Before Marie could say anything, Brigitte clapped her hand once. "But fear not." The old woman raised a knuckly forefinger. "This could easily be avoided. If the situation ever occurs to you, find a tree or a wall and press your back against it. Always have a stick or an umbrella with you." She brandished hers as a prompt. "And wallop them with it. Aim for the nose. Beat them to the death. No room for mercy. They want to eat you and you don't want to be eaten. Simple as."

"Uh, huh," Marie groaned, moving back slightly.

Marie later did a bit of research and found out that none of that ever actually happened. The previous owners had died of old age and had no heir.

The visit inside the house did not take long; one communal room, one bathroom and two bedrooms. The floors and walls were bare and in need of loving care, yet they stood strong beneath the flakes, cracks, and dust.

Despite everything, Marie had fallen in love. It would need some work done to it, a lot of work, and she would have to learn to drive and get a car and accept that Romain would need a motor scooter. But her heart and gut had spoken.

On the drive back, it dawned on Marie that she had a lot to be thankful for. A lovely son, a golden brother, a nephew or niece on the way, great friends, good health, and the threshold to her dream home was finally in sight, along with a first date with Giandomenico. She was so happy she could cry. Which she did, leaving trails of rainbows in the tears' wake.

Chapter 40

"Vlora's story"

Menton, France
Thirty-eight years ago, December 1979

This was not happening. It could not be. The baby was not due for another eight weeks. Ideally, it would not be happening for at least another ten years, maybe never. She should have been more careful. It was all her own fault, though. She had insisted on leaving Albania, their families, school, and everyone behind. And for what? To have a baby, two babies, on her own, while Fatos was off on a wild goose hunt for a job in Marseille.

The babies had been born naturally, but Vlora lost a lot of blood. She was lying in bed, recovering. Except it did not feel like a recovery, more like her limbs were tied to each pole of the bed while she was interrogated by aliens. An old midwife uttered French words that Vlora could not understand. She was convinced that this square-faced midwife would be reporting her to the police. No one wanted them in this country or anywhere. Vlora could almost hear the menace in the woman's smile.

Vlora had to escape the hospital. The two newborns were next to her hospital bed. Both had tags attached to their ankles like lambs with clips attached to their ears. As soon as an opportunity presented itself, she made a run for it and found an unattended pram in the corridor. Her legs were still wobbly, but she pushed through it, the fatigue, the pain, everything. She had to act fast.

She sneaked out and walked and walked and walked. It was very early in the day, windy and cold, and yet, the sun dazzled her. There was no direction to her walk. She had to escape, and she was. She was determined not to let Fatos down, she had been nothing but a disappointment to him so far. It would cease.

The Promenade du Soleil was uncharacteristically empty, even for a winter's day. Vlora had always seen it full of people, strolling along the pleasant seaside, an excellent spot for pick-pockets. This was when Vlora spotted them, people in uniforms. She never got caught, but then again, she had never attempted to hide from them with two newborns in tow before.

A middle-aged couple sat on a bench looking out to the churning Mediterranean Sea. When Vlora met their gaze, she saw pity – or was it revulsion? – in their eyes. She surmised for the first time that she might look like an approaching cockroach. She had not adequately washed since giving birth. Her clothes were those she wore on her way to the hospital, smelly, and covered in unidentified stains. Her cheeks started to feel hot and wet. Stupid tears. Maybe it was the sun in her eyes or the wind that had triggered her tears. It must have been that. Because it surely could not have been the deep feeling of loss at what her life had become, nor despair at these newborns crying in the cramped pram. These babies could not really be hers. Could they? But they were, and it hurt, and not only metaphorically speaking.

Anyway, Fatos would be back with her soon in just a few days. A few weeks tops. He would know what to do. He would take care of her, and the twins as well. He would. Wouldn't he? The policemen were getting closer, only twenty meters away. She would get arrested. She couldn't afford to be.

Vlora hurried towards the couple and sat next to them on the bench. Vlora stared at them, then smiled with wet eyes. The elegant middle-aged woman said something Vlora did not understand. She reminded Vlora of the Virgin Mary. The morning sun formed a halo behind the woman's blonde head, and the comforting touch of her hand on Vlora's arm felt like absolution. Vlora heard her own sobs as she was stared into the Virgin Mary's eyes. The policemen were now ten meters away. Vlora dashed away from the awfully crowded bench, away from the pain and troubles, leaving both babies behind.

It was for the best. These people looked like they would know what to do with them. Better than her. Better than Fatos. She and Fatos could start over, make a new life for themselves. Fatos could start a building company, as per his plan when they left Albania. And she would figure something out. She could sing and play the guitar in cafés. She loved singing and playing the guitar. She would lose a bit of weight and do something with her hair and be spotted by an important someone. She would go on tour. She would get invited on talk shows. She and Fatos's love story, their close escape from their minefield of a country and their constrained separation from their own babies would stir people's raw emotion. Millions would buy her autobiography, which she would not write out of vanity or self-indulgence but as a therapeutic exercise, a way to exorcise her emotionally-opened wounds...

Wait, Vlora was pregnant when Fatos left for Marseille. Fatos would be expecting at least one baby when he returned. She had to get a baby back. No, she had to get both babies back. She could not abandon them or either one of them. Could she? She would never forgive herself if she did. Fatos would never forgive her either. Although, he did not necessarily need to know about both of them. And it would make life a little easier. It certainly would.

Vlora's attention got drawn to a convertible car that had stopped at a red light. The music playing on the radio sounded American. The brunette girl on the passenger seat was about Vlora's age, she giggled and sang the words to the song. Her hair-do looked expensive, her clothes looked expensive, her jewellery looked expensive. Making her laugh and keeping her happy would be expensive, too, Vlora thought. But it was not the difference in their state of wealth that tightened Vlora's chest. It was her air of carefree, easy happiness. This girl was not an illegal immigrant who had given birth to twins only a few hours ago. She did not have to worry about finding shelter or keeping herself and her babies alive. She was probably on her way to a picnic or to brunch with Princess Stéphanie of Monaco. Life was unfair. So unfair. Why did she have to fall pregnant? Vlora never wanted to be pregnant. She was not even sure whether she liked children or not, let alone have one, no, two of them. An urge to rip the cassette out of the car radio and pull its film out and strangle this happy girl with it flared up... Yet Vlora found herself returning to the bench.

A few hours had passed since Vlora left, and yet the couple had not moved. They were still sitting on the same bench, on the Promenade du Soleil, with their halos still shining bright. Except, they must have moved because one of her babies was cradled in the woman's arms drinking out of a bottle while the other was asleep in the pram. There were no police officers waiting to handcuff Vlora and extradite her to Albania. The woman had no apprehension of Vlora's approach as she was engrossed in what she was doing and nothing else seemed to matter. She and the baby made a tender image, considering. These people must be lunatics, she thought with a pinch of guilt.

Vlora had met their sort before. The 'great saviour' type that filled your hands with bags of rice and bottles of water when all you really needed was condoms. Yet, at that precise moment, Vlora wished she was the one drinking out of the baby bottle. She wished they were her parents and that eighteen years from then she would be riding shotgun in a convertible on her way to brunch with Princess Stéphanie of Monaco.

Vlora sat next to the couple in silence but the woman did not acknowledge her. Her eyes remained on the newborn cradled in her arms. She was singing a lullaby that Vlora did not recognise and the man had strolled towards the sea. He looked angry as if Vlora really had been his daughter, and he had better leave rather than give rein to an explosive scolding. The woman kissed and nuzzled the newborn's head and was clearly in a world of her own. A world where the baby in her arms really was hers, and she was determined to savour every moment she would have with it for the rest of her life. She was making it harder for Vlora to do the right thing. Fighting the urge to flee again, Vlora rested her hand on the woman's forearm to signal that it was time to hand them back.

Avoiding eye contact, the woman turned her body slightly away and pushed a bag on the ground with her foot towards Vlora. Nonplussed, Vlora stared at the woman whose gaze was still anchored to the baby. A tear landed on the baby's head, and this time, it did not belong to Vlora. What was going on? The woman resumed humming lullabies. The middle-aged man was walking further away with his hands behind his back. As Vlora raised her hands with the intent of relieving the woman of her burden, the woman shifted away from Vlora and tapped the bag with her feet. Vlora opened it. Wads of Franc notes were staring back at her. Could it be real?

Later, she became convinced that it had never happened or perhaps she convinced herself of it. Anyhow, she had been hallucinating. How could she have met the Virgin Mary otherwise? Vlora never mentioned any of it to Fatos or anybody. Because there was nothing to tell. She only delivered one baby, as most women do. And France's social security system for the necessitous is very well-known. As it happened, its charity extended to paperless Albanians, and this was how she got the money that paid for nappies, food and the campervan in which they lived for the following thirteen years. However, the decision she made that day progressively rotted her soul from the inside out. She would never forgive herself for what she did and no amount of alcohol would ever truly distract her from the remorse, guilt and shame. Her life entered a grove of which the canopy became gradually thicker, eventually shutting off all light and rain, entrapping her in a web of intertwining dark branches.

Chapter 41

"Ugly is as ugly does."

Marseille, France
Four months ago, March 2017

Bitch, and all her fucking lies. She killed my angel and now she tries to tarnish her name… He would have known if Vlora was expecting twins. Besides, Vlora would never have abandoned his son, the flesh of his flesh. The slut just found herself a new pimp. That's what's what. She'd opened up her legs for a house.

Earlier that day…

Fatos had a 'lawyer visitation' at 9:00 am with Marie Boulanger. Of course, he had assumed it was a mistake. First, a visit from his daughter would constitute a family visit. Secondly, the last time Marie visited him was years ago, right after his beloved Vlora had passed. He howled at Marie so ferociously that a prison guard dragged him away. They had spoken on the phone since then, but Fatos had assumed he would never see Marie, nor Romain, again.

He had no evidence that his daughter had been the one responsible for Vlora's death, but he knew she was. He knew it in his guts. He just did. Marie always had it in for them. She thought she was better than them. Being a nurse, she had learned to kill whilst passing it off as natural causes. It was precisely why she had pursued a medical career in the first place. No doubt about it. She could pretend to be kind and compassionate all she liked. It may well have worked with everyone else, but she could not fool him. No, it had to be Marie.

"The return of the prodigal daughter," Fatos scoffed.

The 'lawyer visitation' was no mistake. Marie had obtained the right to visit him on professional grounds because she was a qualified social worker as well as a nurse. Family visitations were an ordeal to get, only one number to contact and it was always busy. So, she had found a loophole. *Good for her,* he thought begrudgingly. Fatos did not know what Marie's angle was, but he would let her game play out, and destroy her, like she destroyed his precious angel, Vlora.

It was a lengthy procession of opening and closing doors, going up and down stairs and walking through flooded corridors to finally reach the waiting room. A tall, mixed-heritage inmate in his forties was already there. Fatos greeted him with a nod, but sat well apart from him on the wooden bench, which was nailed to the floor, avoiding leaning against wallpapers of black mildew. A drawing was carved into the bench, entitled 'Samy,' and pictured a man being hanged and sodomised simultaneously. Nice.

"Meeting your lawyer?" asked the tall man.

"Social worker," Fatos left it at that. He did not want to engage with an inmate he did not know. Less was always more in prison. The room quickly filled up with three more inmates.

A prison guard with tattoos up to his ears called Fatos's name and directed him along another corridor towards a small box room with a little white table and two dated chairs.

Marie looked surprised to see Fatos smile at her with presumed warmth. As she stood up to shake his hand, he pulled her into a warm embrace, enveloping her round belly with his own body.

"Sit down, convict," ordered the prison guard. "No physical contact allowed."

Tears were not far from Marie's eyes as Fatos pulled away from her. She was putting on a great show of being moved. He had to give her that.

"Are you alright, ma'am?" the prison guard questioned, pressing his baton against Fatos's torso as if he were a tamed lion at the circus.

Marie positioned herself between the two men. Fatos rolled his eyes behind Marie's back.

"I'm fine. Thank you. I'm his daughter, as well as his social worker. We haven't seen each other in a while, is all."

"Alright, ma'am."

Fatos dragged his chair noisily along the floor and locked eyes with the prison guard, before lowering himself onto it.

As the guard left, a heavy silence filled their first moment alone.

Marie reached into her pockets and placed chocolate and homemade échaudés on the table. It was a nice touch, and something she could not have done under 'family visitation.' *She was good,* he thought, but he was no sucker.

Fatos took a bite out of a hard-as-rock échaudé biscuit.

"Hmm, nice." Fatos smiled, displaying aniseed stuck between his teeth.

He caressed the hand she had left on the table and she accepted his gesture timidly.

She cried, so he cried, thinking that two could play that game. She looked surprised. It occurred to him that she had never seen him shed a tear before. 'Crying's for the weak and lazy' he always used to say. He had smacked Vlora across the face for sobbing, once. Not his finest hour, but it had been a long day at the docks and he couldn't bear the incessant drunken sobs anymore. Vlora's state of unhappiness felt like a personal insult to him. After all he had always been a great husband; faithful and a steady provider. What more could she want from him? It wasn't his fault if their ungrateful, snobby, fat daughter turned out the way she did.

Marie discussed the house she had bought in detail and depicted a vivid picture of what it would be like once fully refurbished. Her face lit up with palpable excitement at the prospect, which he interpreted as impish glee. She was gloating and rubbing it in. He listened patiently, making all the right noises at the right times.

"Congratulations, then," he finally exclaimed. "I would crack open the champagne, but they treat us like convicts here." He winked. She smiled. "And this doesn't appear to be our only cause for celebration," Fatos continued.

"Oh." She rubbed her belly. "Yes. Thanks."

"A new boyfriend?"

"Ahem, yes. Giandomenico. He's from Italy, so, we don't see each other as often as I'd wish, but it's going well. He's a very nice man. I'm not sure what he sees in me..." She spoke the last sentence almost in a whisper and lowered her head.

'An easy trollop' flashed through Fatos's mind.

"I'm sure he's the one punching above his weight. What does he do for a living?"

"He, uh," her gaze shifted downward, "works for the police. He's a detective."

A laugh escaped Fatos. "Is he now?"

"Yes… But, ah, he's not the father of my child."

"No?" Fatos voiced innocently while smirking inwardly. *Of course, he's not.*

"Actually, this isn't really my child either."

What? He scoffed internally. "How can it not be?"

"Well, this is the reason I came to see you. I wanted to tell you something in person." She started picking at the skin around her fingernails, her eyes resolutely not meeting his. "I'm carrying the child of a couple who is very dear to me, as they cannot conceive."

"How very selfless of you. Is this how you have been able to finance your house?"

"Oh. Hmm. Yes." She blushed. "I tried to dissuade them from it, but they insisted."

"Of course," he conceded, trying his best to mask the sarcasm.

"This couple…" She stalled.

"Yes?"

"They're both men. Lovely people. They love each other dearly."

"Okay." And I'm the one in prison? "Work friends?"

Marie pulled out a smiley photo of Benedict and Yukinobu. Fatos faked an interest.

She cleared her throat. "No. He's my brother." Marie pointed at Benedict in the photo.

Fatos chortled, in a loud, scornful way. "You don't have a brother. And don't try to tell me that some whore has been carrying a baby of mine that I don't know about, because I've NEVER cheated on your mother." He pointed his finger at Marie's face. "Never. Do you hear me?" His tone was menacing. His attempt at playing the game and keeping his cool evidently gone.

"I do. And I wasn't implying it. He, Benedict Grant is his name, was born on the same day as me. We are twins. I..."

"What. The. Fuck. Are you talking about?"

"Benedict is yours and mums. Mum gave him away, for money, the day after we were born."

Fatos wiped the table of the photo, stood up, and flicked his chair violently against the wall.

"How dare you insult your mother like that!" He jabbed a finger in the air with aggressive ferocity, spit escaping his mouth as he yelled, his bulging eyes as wide as the moon. "That woman was a saint to put up with a fat, good-for-nothing daughter like you. But that wasn't enough for you was it? Nah. Never enough…"

How dare she suggest that his Vlora would ever do such a thing? The disrespect. The craftiness. The scorn… Vlora had never been quite the same since giving birth. But depression after having children was common, or else why would there be a term for it. Was it, baby-bel? No, that would be the cheese. Baby blues? Yes, that was it, baby blues.

In that moment, his eyes must have screamed 'murder' because Marie stood up and stepped away from him until she was placated against the wall, her arms and hands protectively laced across her belly. His blood-red angry face with lurid eyes was right in hers. His pointy finger waved at her as he shouted a litany of insults towards her. Spittle foamed at the corners of his mouth in rage and indignation, or perhaps resentment and guilt. The sort of bitter feeling drawn from a place where deep love had putrefied into hatred.

It took two prison guards to manhandle him away from Marie and he spent two weeks in solitary for his troubles. In that time, the only thing he could think about was how he would get back at his daughter. He wanted to hurt her, and yet, despite all the ill feelings towards her, he was conflicted about physical, irremediable hurt.

When he returned to his normal cell, which, comfort-wise was, all things considered, even worse than solitary a small pile of letters awaited him, all from Marie. She was not apologetic about what she disclosed, one of the letters even included some sort of DNA test results that Fatos neither understood nor believed. Yet, she claimed to regret the way she had delivered the news. More ruses.

Several weeks later at lunch, Fatos sat with a group of inmates who he had an alliance with, or more accurately, to whom he was a subordinate. The head of this group, Ditmir Petrioni, was notorious, both inside and outside of the prison, for being a cold-blooded drug lord. Against the odds, Fatos had ingratiated himself with him, thanks to vaguely shared Albanian heritage even though Fatos's allegiance had been to a different organisation when he had been caught.

On this particular day the tension was almost palpable. Ditmir was pushing food around on his tray, not eating. It was evident that Ditmir was fuming over something, but it was never a good idea to inadvertently say the wrong thing or ask the wrong question. So, lunch was spent in silence. Later, Fatos got wind that several of Ditmir's safe houses had been compromised. Meaning products and money would have to be moved elsewhere.

As an underling, Fatos was neither in the know nor involved in anything significant. Fatos did the menial jobs. Although debasing, he found his groove, and other inmates left him alone.

So, he never had cause to challenge the status quo. However, Ditmir's situation had given him an idea to both help Ditmir and have his revenge on Marie. His ratty eyes glittered. Based on Marie's description, her isolated house would make an excellent safe house. He would tip Ditmir's guys. If they took the bait, there would be nothing Marie could do about it. Some lowlifes would squat in her dearest dream of a house for as long as Ditmir saw fit. No doubt, long enough for her to be stuck in her shabby trailer until the end of her brainless pregnancy, worrying she would never be able to move in. That'd teach her... The thought of taking a house away from Romain crossed his mind. Though, in truth, this was Marie's doing, not his, no matter how you sliced it. She was forcing him to deprive '*his*' grandson of a house. He would add that to her list of sins.

Chapter 42

"Dream house"

Marseille, France
Three weeks ago, June 2017

"How about a two-round trip?" suggested Romain. It had taken a whole day to move the contents of Marie and Romain's trailer into (and onto) two cars. Loading Marie's brand-new car, courtesy of Mr. Benedict Grant, had been like playing Tetris. So Pépé's good ol' Citroën Vista 1980 had been put to work again. However, once entirely tied up, Marie had to admit that the Citroën's rustic tilt had taken on an epic proportion. The tower of Pisa would have cast a jealous glance.

"Perhaps you should," Lavina agreed, wiping black oil from her hands onto her apron

"Perhaps we should," conceded Marie.

"Nonsense," Pépé exclaimed, patting his car like a mule.

Marie and Romain's imminent departure had attracted nearly half of camp. Gawking at Pépé's car, a clamour of incoherent opinions took form. Yet everyone eventually agreed on one thing; driving the battered old car through unbeaten tracks was a very bad idea. But before a verdict was issued, Pépé squeezed his cane onto the brimming passenger seat and drove off, leaving a puff of black fume in its wake.

Marie, Romain, and Lavina exchanged a puzzled look, while Timo laughed wholeheartedly. Carrying a large bin bag filled with everything he owned, Timo was still laughing as he headed towards Marie's old trailer which he was now moving into.

"Well, we better follow Pépé," Marie replied to Romain, rubbing her enormous pregnant belly. "He just stole away with everything I own," she smiled.

After hurried embraces, they were off. Despite the overwhelming amount of joy and excitement that filled Marie to the point of near implosion, tears welled up as she looked back into her wing mirrors and the dispersing crowd behind them.

Romain ran the back of his curved fingers along Marie's cheek. "You're the best," he praised.

253

Marie mouthed 'I love you', without taking her eyes off the road or her hands off the steering wheel.

As they eventually parted from the road and onto the long track leading up to their new home, she overtook Pépé to lead him to the right path. The lorries and machinery that had travelled over the past couple of months had made it easier to navigate. Still, it remained tricky to keep to it.

When they reached their little corner of paradise, Marie was surprised to see a 4x4 with blackened windows parked under the shade of their pine tree grove. Their contractors had finished everything they were supposed to. They had even helped build furniture. Marie felt uneasy. Something was not right.

She parked closer to the house and Pépé followed behind. As they stepped out of their vehicles, a short dark-haired man in his thirties, lizard-looking, came out of the house, eating an apple. He was flanked by a large Asian man that could only be described as a grisly bouncer.

"Can I help you?" asked the lizard man, between two mouthfuls of apple.

"I was going to ask you the same thing," Marie replied, a little out of breath from contorting her pregnant body out of her fancy but impractical car. Before she could get any closer to the house, the lizard-looking man planted his scrawny self across, stopping her.

"I'm afraid you can't enter." His accent was hard to place, a mix of Marseillais and Southern European, maybe.

"What do you mean, I can't enter? Of course I can enter. This is my house." Marie took a step to the side, but the man took one too, remaining firmly in front of her.

"Afraid not." He discarded his apple against Pépé's car, causing Pépé to spit on the ground defiantly. The way this man looked at Marie, Romain, and Pépé was more than just taking in their appearance. There was malevolence in his calculated, cold glare, a threat even.

"Who are you?" Marie asked.

"We're your lodgers, Marie Boulanger." The man broke into a reptilian smile. He extended a hand towards Marie, and despite herself, she shook it.

"What, ah…" Marie stuttered, turning her gaze to Pépé, who subtly motioned his stern head as if to say do-not-fight-this.

"We'll be out of your hair in no time, we're just awaiting orders. But, Marie, until then no words to the police. Or anyone."

He lowered his glare to Marie's swollen stomach long enough to make a statement. "Or we'll fall out."

There was a moment of silence. His reptilian eyes were on Marie, Romain, and Pépé, studying their faces for signs of comprehension. His expression became a creepy mask, conveying a very particular type of warning.

Marie felt her heart sink as Romain tugged her arm back towards the car. She felt a slight tremble in his hand. The two men remained where they were, glaring, as Marie and Pépé drove back from where they came only minutes ago. Seemingly satisfied that they had come to a form of understanding, the lizard-looking man shoved his hands into his pockets.

A few minutes had passed before Marie's eyes started streaming.

"Stop the car," Romain ordered in a calm, cracked voice. "Let's take a minute."

Pépé's car came to a halt also. All three stepped out of the cars. Marie felt her entire body heave and jerk from convulsive crying and Romain pulled her into a tight hug.

"What are we gonna do?" enquired Marie between gasps. "We can't go back to the camp. What will people say?"

At that exact moment, one of Pépé's car tires started to hiss until it was completely flat. Cradled against Romain's shoulder, Marie began to bawl her eyes out, louder than ever.

"Pépé, can you not have a word with the rest of the family?" queried Romain. "I know they don't have much to do with us, but surely if you explained the situation, they'd help us?"

Pépé made a weird sucking noise, hobbled to his car, and parked very slowly out of sight. As he stepped out of his comatose vehicle, he repeated Romain's words. "They'd help?" Pépé made the same sucking noise again. "What do y'have in mind, son? Have them come here, give those thugs a good kicking? Kneecap them maybe? For what? For you? So that you and your *gorjio* mum can move into your house?"

Pépé shook his head. No one spoke for a long moment.

"Pépé's right, sweetheart," Marie conceded quietly, wiping her nose with the back of her hand, sniffing. "We have to talk to the police." Even as Marie raised it, her voice trailed off.

Pépé gave her a sad smile. A smile that said they currently lived in a camp, where they were considered lowlifes, the scum of society, and the type other people preferred to pretend did not exist. The police would bury their complaint at the bottom of the pile and sit on it while the thugs find a way to teach them a lesson for disobeying.

"Let's sleep on it. We'll come up with something, don't worry. Or maybe they'll just leave soon, and we won't have to," Pépé proposed, probably not believing much of it.

Romain directed his mum's face to him. "We'll move back to our trailer for now. I'll make up some excuse… A problem with the roof or something," Romain suggested.

Pépé squeezed Marie's shoulder, while Romain wrapped his slender arm around her, guiding his mum back to the car.

"But believe me, this problem will get resolved," Romain added as if to himself. There was a fervour in his tone that Marie had never heard before. A promise.

Chapter 43

"An English boat"

Rome, Italy
One day later, July 2017

"The autopsy results, Sir."

"Any identification?" Giandomenico asks, flicking through the file.

"Afraid not. We've requested they broaden the search to other countries. So hopefully something will come up soon."

"Thanks. Let me know when it does."

Giandomenico hunches over the autopsy report and produces a satisfying clicking noise with each tap of his fingertips against his metallic desk.

The pathologist estimated the time of death at around 5:00 pm on 1st July. So, Davide, the forensic, had been in the right ballpark. The men had been dead for about two or three days before they hit Manarola's seashore.

Both of their hearts are of normal size. However, small vessels not commonly observed in the brain have been found. *Perhaps caused by dehydration or a heat stroke* wonders Giandomenico.

One of the men's pharynx is covered with a whitening layer of mucosa and a patch of ulceration in the middle of it. Both of their stomachs are deeply congested, full of blood mixed with their food content coupled with an acute gastritis haemorrhage. Their kidneys and livers also contain an excess of blood in their vessels. The centre of the liver lobules is destroyed, and their spleens are strikingly large about three times the normal size. *Okay, we might be on to something here* he thinks.

To ascertain his assumptions Giandomenico heads to the lab.

"So what's your take on all this, Dexter?" he utters, brandishing the file.

"Interesting. Highly unusual. If you ask me, it doesn't fit with your run-of-the-mill murder," replies Davide hands on hips.

"Are you ruling out murder?"

"No. Not at all. An odd one, though. Just saying."

"The clock is ticking. Cut to the chase. Please." There was a sobering authority in Giandomenico's voice that surprises both of them.

"As you read, tests failed to reveal any foreign substance in the body." Davide points to a section of the autopsy showing the men's last meal was pasta, eaten three to four hours before death, and nothing else. "But, I am quite convinced the death was not natural."

"What about these small vessels in their brains? Doesn't that suggest heat stroke or dehydration causing their collapse?"

"Unlikely. The pathologist agrees with me on that. We both believe it's just a side effect of an undetectable substance."

"You're leaning towards poisoning then?"

"It remains my prime suspicion, yeah. Perhaps JD-1434 or PY-2212. They're hard to detect and both cardenolide-type of cardiac glycosides."

Davide handed Giandomenico a university paper from a professor in pharmacology that testified to this theory, with the names of the two drugs entered as Exhibit B.18. This group of soluble sedative-hypnotic drugs are extremely toxic, and a fatal dose would be extremely difficult, if not impossible, to identify even if suspected in the first instance. The forensic expert also recommended the common names of these drugs were not be released to the public due to their easily procurable nature from a chemist without a prescription.

He noted the use of these poisons would explain the observations made about the men's organs. Therefore, the only fact not found in relation to the bodies was evidence of vomiting. He stated its absence was not unknown, but that he could not make an assertive conclusion without it.

"Do you think the poison was accidentally administered?"

"No, and although I can't say for certain whether it was administered by the deceased themselves or by some other person, I can certify that their death didn't occur on the boat. See these…" Dexter pointed at scratches and marks on the corpses.

"Hmm," Giandomenico acquiesces.

"These occurred after death. They had passed for a few hours when they were moved, probably onto the boat."

"Then why was the boat stocked with bottles of water and cans of food?" Giandomenico ponders to himself. "Maybe they were already there…"

"One more thing," Davide interrupts. "I'd guess that whoever dragged them into the boat didn't have great upper body strength, judging by the post-mortem marks on their bodies – it was probably a woman."

Chapter 44

"The man of the house"

Marseille, France
Three days ago, July 2017

There was nothing Romain, Marie, or Pépé could do to expulse the thugs. They learned that, under French law, squatters had rights. Plenty of rights. The internet overflowed with accounts of squatters staying months, even years, and the owners' uphill battles to evict said squatters after formal complaints had been filed.

In theory, if these guys had not been thugs and Marie's current living arrangement was different, there was a bureaucratic process to follow:

Step 1 - File a formal complaint.

Step 2 - Provide proof that the house was occupied and was, indeed, their main residence.

Step 3 - Provide evidence of illegal occupancy.

Step 4 - Wait for a court ruling.

Step 5 - Wait two months until an expulsion procedure could be set into motion.

Step 6 - Write a letter to their descendants to alert their great-great-great-grand-children that they were due to inherit a house somewhere in the garrigue once some squatters had been ejected. Notaries of the time would no doubt warn said heirs that once upon a time, a woman had been eaten alive by a pack of rabid dogs.

In truth, Romain did not mind being back in camp Saint Pierre. He did not think it was as bad as people made it out to be. Perhaps because his mum had made it so that he always felt safe and well looked after. But things had changed.

Since they returned, the sound of his mother's cries had become ever-present. A soundtrack to her disappointment. One afternoon, amid putting away the grocery shopping, he heard a stifled sniffle next to him. A half-rotten apple in hand, his mum was sobbing, her face concealed by an open cupboard door. At night, she would cover her head with a pillow to muffle the sound of her cries, or she would wait to be under a running shower. Still,

Romain heard the tell-tale signs. She kept reassuring him that it was nothing. "It's just my hormones," she would say, blaming it on the pregnancy. But Romain didn't believe her. She seemed very determined to do something about their situation at first. Two weeks in, she appeared to have thrown in the towel. She kept talking about fate, reflecting on all the hard luck she experienced throughout her life and how this would never change.

It broke Romain's heart to see his mum in ways he had never experienced before. She was everything to him, his classroom and playground, shield and wings, iron and feather, a woman with the heart of an angel tempered with a spine of steel. People had always tiptoed around the subject of his dad and the nature of his death as best they could. Yet, it never bothered Romain, to never talk or hear about his dad or the lack of it. His mum was there, and to Romain, that was all that mattered.

The teenage boy wished he could have met his dad. Of course, he did. His dad sounded like a fascinating guy, from all accounts. 'Baul was their ticket out of camp Saint Pierre,' Lavina had told Romain, or maybe herself, many a time. Baul had it all. The brain, the good looks, and above all, the talent. The day of his death, he had received a call from the record deal he had been chasing. The record deal of a lifetime. Although there was pride in knowing this, it did not make his dad anymore alive. Romain was the man of the house. Pépé or Lavina might have found it hilarious when he proclaimed the title. But he was. Hence, it was his role to protect his mum and the baby.

Besides, it was his fault… The accent, you see. Pacing around at camp, guilty thoughts kept swelling. He knew only one other person with this unusually hard to place accent. Gabin. In his mind it had to be Gabin. He could not figure out what Gabin's connection was to these two guys nor how Gabin had orchestrated it. But it was him. Gabin was behind it, end of story. He acted as if nothing was the matter whenever Romain observed him at school. Yet, Gabin had taken his revenge in the most spectacular way, Romain thought with anger and guilt. Anyway, he would find a way. He would shield his mum and the baby from Gabin or anything and anyone. He had done it once before and against all the odds, therefore, he could do it again, he would do it, he repeated to himself.

The fourteen-year-old rode his new scooter until there was no road left, then he walked through the garrigue, as he had done every day for the past few weeks. Hidden amongst the bushes, he silently observed everything he could about the house, its occupants, and their comings and goings, whilst trying his best to ignore the sabre-rattling, vicious ants invading his space. He was confident that a day would come when an opportunity would arise. And the day came sooner than he thought.

Back at camp, he heard his mum's voice as he approached their trailer. She was using that annoying gooey tone she reserved for Giandomenico's ears. So, Romain kept quiet and lingered outside for a while. He desperately did not want her to hand him the phone, as she randomly did. It was bad enough she did it when on the phone to her friends or Benedict.

"That's so very sweet of you to say…" Marie purred.

Romain wondered how long this was going to last. He had never known his mum to have boyfriends. As far as he knew, she had not dated since his dad passed. So, it was weird. Like *weird* weird. When his mum mentioned she had met somebody, Romain tried his best not to guffaw. Clearly, the guy had to be an oddball, or a sleazeball, anyway some sort of ball, to date a pregnant woman, who was carrying a baby for someone else. Then, when he found out that the guy was from Italy, it started to make sense. Most of them gelled their hair like lacquered ducks. But then, as he found out that Giandomenico worked for the police, he got a little alarmed.

"… Oh, you know. A friend from, ah, work." There was a pause. "They've, apparently, been squatting in her house for a couple of weeks. They're thugs, clearly, and she's on her own, with her daughter. She's beside herself and doesn't know who to turn to. It's…"

What was she doing? Romain barged in and shouted "*bonsoir* maman" at the top of his voice.

"Oh, hi, Romain." She moved her phone away, a hand on its speaker and mouthed, 'I'm on the phone'. But Romain stared at her with enormous eyes, urgently gesturing for her to hang up.

As soon as she did, he yell-whispered "I thought we agreed that we were not going to talk to anyone about this for now. Especially not the police!"

"Don't use that tone with me, young man! Anyway, I told him I was seeking advice for a friend."

"Oh yeah, 'a friend'. You told your detective boyfriend that you, who hasn't moved into your new home for unclear reasons, are seeking advice *for a friend*. However will he crack the mystery of that case?"

Marie chewed an already gnawed fingernail. "It's just that…" She began to sob into her hands. Romain wrapped her arms around her, feeling like a thug himself now.

"I know. But, stop worrying about it, we'll move in. Soon. Very soon." Mark my words… A promise, again.

Chapter 45

"Vicious"

Marseille, France
Four days ago, July 2017

Ditmir Petrioni's right-hand man walked across the prison yard in Fatos's direction. There was a slow pace to his walk, like a patrolling feline. Everyone took notice, yet Fatos made no eye contact. He had no reason to believe the man was coming for him, so he even moved away a few paces towards the edge. When he could not go any further, Fatos leaned against the wire fence. Torn plastic bags and pigeons' feathers trapped in the barbed wire above his head gave a semblance of shade. But the bald man with a broken nose and a scar around his ear, who was now flanked by two other equally handsome inmates, continued his course towards him. Fatos kept his head down, nervously.

Once planted in front of him, Fatos had no other choice but to raise his gaze from the cracked concrete ground to the guy's face. The blazing sun was blindingly bright and Fatos felt pearls of sweat breaking out on his forehead, but he held the man's stare as they acknowledged one another. Fatos could count the bald man's nostril hairs. After what felt like a frozen moment, the man extended his oar-sized hand to Fatos.

"You did well," the bald man asserted as they shook hands. "Ditmir won't forget."

"Thanks." Fatos was utterly confused. Was this sincere or a threat? "But w-what do you mean?"

"We're moving to another safe house. But your tip paid off. And as I said, Ditmir won't forget."

The bald man tapped Fatos's shoulder before taking off.

What? Already? So, whoever they had squatting in Marie's house had left after a mere fortnight.

Hands clasped behind his back, Fatos paced on the spot. He could not let that happen, could not let Marie off the hook so easily… However, thinking about it, he was now off the mark. Squatting or tearing down Marie's house was not the answer. He sent gravel skittering with the tip of his black trainers. A stone skipped on the uneven lake of concrete until it hit someone's heel. The large inmate with veiny eyes turned a steely gaze on Fatos who was too engrossed in his own thoughts to notice.

Actually, Fatos had not even aimed at the right target. He was not thinking of the gravel but the people on the receiving end of his punishment. It was those snakes' fault. They had polluted Marie's head. For years. Marie had met those perverts long before Vlora was murdered. They must have been behind it. It was to their benefit. With Vlora out of the way whilst he was in prison, the coast was clear to fill Marie's head with all their filthy lies about being siblings. They had manipulated his daughter for their sickening plans. Getting her to have their babies and whatnot. However, he could not let the ungrateful bitch go totally unscathed either. She had to be taught a lesson… It was the gypo situation all over again.

He would put his new plan into action as soon as he was allowed his next call.

Martin was a lowlife who would sell his own mother for a handful of spare change.

"I don't have any photos, but there'll be no mistaking them as the other two are a blond teenage boy and a woman."

Fatos made him write down the address of Marie's house in the garrigue.

"Right, mate. I'll do it," Martin agreed, his Belgium accent slurred.

"But listen, as I said, only the Mediterranean man and the Japanese fellow, not the boy and the pregnant woman. And wait until the two men are in the house. Make it discreet, it can't be traceable. Do you hear me?" Fatos stressed.

"Got it, mate."

Chapter 46

"Taking charge"

In the Provencal garrigue, France
Three days ago, July 2017

R omain was back in the garrigue, observing the house
crouched down behind his now regular point of cover. He
detected no activity neither in nor out of the house. Yet,
lights inside the house were on and the car with the blackened
windows still sat outside the front of the house. The two men were
in. Those who coerced his mum into leaving the premises. The
fourteen-year-old had studied them very carefully over the past
couple of weeks, watching them carrying boxes in and out of the
house, installing an alarm, infrared sensors, and other equipment.
He knew everything he could about their security system.

The sun had long set, but Romain was yet to witness any
movement. This had never happened before. Something was off.
He left it another half-hour, although it was starting to get late. He
ought to be getting back home. But he wanted to know what was
going on. Duck-walking down dry, gravelly slopes, zigzagging
from shrub to shrub, he quickly reached the edge of the two men's
'secure' perimeter.

His thighs were burning from the strain and his heart was
drumming against his chest, however, this was mainly in
anticipation about what he was about to attempt. He drew in a
sharp breath to calm his nerves, waited another minute, then
purposefully set off an alarm before bolting for cover. Hunched
over himself, his every step triggered mini avalanches of pale
stones, trickling down the steep hill as he scampered up.

A braid of adrenaline, debilitating buzz and intoxicating dread
pulsated into his fingertips and through the sweat soaking his
balaclava. A cocktail of emotions he had experienced before and
hated.

Leaning his back against the base of a large tree, he tried to
catch his breath. He was far from sight, but close enough to be
noticed. The sound of his own exertion and loud crickets made it
impossible to detect whether someone was chasing him or not. He

waited a moment for his own body to calm down before carefully casting a look towards the house.

No one appeared to check out the perimeter, let alone chase him off the grounds. A wave of relief washed over him, but he had to go back and investigate. So, Romain sneaked towards the house, careful not to set anything off this time.

Crouched down, his back against the stone wall of the house, he cautiously listened for any signs of life. Next, he peeped through the kitchen's window but could see little. He ought to get inside, however, he was aware that it might be the stupidest idea he had ever had.

His hands trembled as he reached the front door handle. He opened it very slowly whilst leaning against the wall. Risking a peek, he saw both men lying on the kitchen floor in contorted positions, one clutching his throat, the other his midriff. Romain wandered in as mutely as he could muster. The house was several degrees cooler than the warm night outside. It felt like stepping into a grim cellar. Romain shivered and ever so quietly, he checked the rest of the house. It did not take long, with only two other rooms to check.

Once confident that there was no one else, he nudged one of the two men with the tip of his foot. No reaction. Then the other. No reaction from him either. He surveyed the compact kitchen-living for any indications as to why these two were in the positions they were in. There were an awful lot of empty bottles and cans. And both men had collapsed near the kitchen sink, so perhaps they were drunk and about to vomit before they passed out.

Romain then pressed two fingers against one of the guys' neck. Panic crept in. There was no pulse... However, he reminded himself that he had never been able to find his own pulse either, so, it did not automatically mean anything. Folding himself at the knee, he touched the skin of their necks again. They both felt cold. Though, anyone would get cold from lying on cold tiles, right? Maybe they were still alive, perhaps in an ethylic coma, Romain thought. Either way, what to do?

He tried to calm himself down, he could not afford to have an asthma attack right here and now. If he called an ambulance and those two guys were confirmed dead, they would call the police. He and his mum, the gypsies, would be prime suspects. It would be easy to establish that these men had occupied the house. His mother had access to medicine that could just as easily poison as treat and send people to their graves and the house was isolated.

In sum, they had motive and poison would be a method of choice for people like them.

Hyperventilating and pacing aimlessly, Romain kept repeating the same question over and over in his mind. What to do? He could not let his mother go through this.

It then dawned on him, the car with the blackened windows, Benedict's powerboat... He would need Timo's help but it could work...

Chapter 47

"Click"

Rome, Italy
Two days later, July 2017

Giandomenico unmutes his computer and brings his first cup of coffee of the day to his lips. A news feed about his case aired a few minutes ago on all the major TV channels in Italy.

"… A prisoner [mugshot of the prisoner] and alleged associate of Ditmir Petrioni has escaped from the French prison where they are both serving sentences.

[A clip of Petrioni entering the prison is aired.]

Petrioni is believed to have succeeded the former head of the Mapula organised crime family, Lucio "The Drac" Conti, who himself ordered dozens of killings during a bloody reign of terror, ending only following his death at the age of eighty-one.

Petrioni is serving twelve years in prison, after his arrest, eight years ago, along with forty-five alleged Mapula's members. This marked the culmination of a cross-border investigation focusing on criminal activities centred on the port of Marseille. At the time, the arrests represented a significant blow to traditional organized crime across southern Europe. Jean Borell, Head of the European Defence Agency, declared 'there is no more room for this type of scum in our world.'

[The screen goes back to the news anchor.]

Police spokesmen have confirmed that the two bodies [two mugshots appear in the left-hand corner of the screen] found on the seashore of the Manarola village on 3rd July have been identified as small-time criminals with links to the Mapula.

[Clip of American tourists at the scene.]

It is unclear at this point if this relates to the escaped prisoner, Fatos Aoun. Police continue to investigate his links to…"

Giandomenico switches off the TV and sighs in contained annoyance. The significance of the escaped prisoner's name is lost on him at this point. Marie and Romain go by the surname Boulanger.

Someone knocks on Giandomenico's office door.

"Detective Paoli?"

"Marshal Seno?" Giandomenico looks up in surprise. "P-Please come in."

He immediately rises to his feet and invites her in, before shutting the door behind her. She smells delightful.

"You look... lovely," he blurts out. He cannot help himself.

She blushes. "Thanks. I, ah... have good news."

"Please, do tell."

"The boat in your case is registered."

"Excellent."

"But not in Italy."

"Of course, it isn't. It'd be too easy, eh? How long will it take to identify its country of registration and owner?"

"Already done."

"You're a star!" He could kiss her right now. But he would not, for more than one reason. "Let me guess. Albania?"

"Nope. It's a French boat. Registered under the name of a Brit. Benedict Grant."

A sobering shiver runs down Giandomenico's spine. Now this name rings alarm bells. Fuck. Fuck, fuck, fuck.

"Giandomenico, are you alright?"

He grabs his cell phone and runs out the door.

Chapter 48

"Tragedy"

In the Provencal garrigue, France
One day later, July 2017

If it was a movie scene, there would be shots of eerie movements amongst the low-growing vegetation, followed by a handful of stones trickling down the exposed limestone footpaths of those Mediterranean hills. It would be unclear what or who was progressing up those hills and this looming development would remain unknown to the main protagonists, but the premise of a terrible fate would undeniably be unfolding.

As it were, there was indeed a slow but steady motion snaking up the garrigue towards Marie's new house. The antagonist, breathing laboured, dry brambles crunching loudly beneath his feet, but the cicadas' chorus masked the noise he was making.

"Shall I crack open a bottle of rosé?" Benedict already has a bottle of Château Calissanne in hand.

Slouching against the back of her chair, Marie brings a hand to the front of her enormous, torpedo-shaped belly. "Tiger Wada-Grant says, 'a small taster glass for me,' please."

"Tiger Wada-Grant?" Yukinobu repeats, sitting upright on the white slatted, metallic chairs. The sort of chair that slices the pudge of one's back into three, but not Yukinobu's. And let it be told, this sort of leanness, at near sixty years old, requires discipline.

"Why? Don't you like Tiger Wada-Grant?" Benedict quips, trying to keep a straight face. He had been particularly giddy since Marie's pregnancy started. The rosé bottle nearly topples over after he places it on the wobbly outdoor table.

"It's, ah, different. But, perhaps we should wait until the baby is born to decide," proposes Yukinobu.

"Perhaps we should," Benedict agrees, before tittering with Marie, like two children.

"By the way, I love the new style." Marie waves her half-full flute glass in the general direction of Benedict's white linen, barely buttoned shirt.

"Cheers!" Benedict clinks his glass against Marie's. "Though, you'd expect nothing less from someone who spent so long in the closet, right?"

Marie takes a sip, whilst eyeing Yukinobu who is nodding with a content 'I concur' look to his face.

"Anyway. Thanks for helping us move in... I'm so glad you could make it." Marie raises her glass. "I truly am. I didn't think this day would ever come..."

Her phone pings. A text from Médélice:

Congratulations again on your new house! I hope everything went well with the move this time. Sorry, I couldn't make it this evening. xx

Marie made Médélice aware that Benedict and Yukinobu would be there today. So, she knew there was a chance Médélice would not join them. Yet, it saddened her to be proven right. Flicking through the screen of her phone, Marie notices that she received several missed calls from Giandomenico. She will call him back shortly, no doubt he just wants to check how the move is going.

Directing her head towards the opened front door, she shouts, "Romain! Quit setting up the TV and come and join us."

Romain comes out of the house, the controller in hand, as if under hypnosis. The cacophony of cicadas stops, marking the end of a sunny day. Benedict catches a sound that does not belong up in the garrigue hills, but quickly dismisses it.

"Can you hmm..." Romain mutters in a trance, points at the house with his thumb, and goes back inside.

Benedict and Yukinobu look at Marie, who raises her hands in a fan-like movement and pulls a face stating that she is just as confused as everyone else by Romain's Walking Dead impression. They follow him inside.

Gathered around Romain, whose pale face is reflecting the flickering glow of the TV, they all gaze at the screen. The late news blares from the TV.

Mugshots of two men found dead on the Italian coast are shown. One looks Mediterranean, the other Asian. A report is made about their affiliation to the Mapula crime organization, along with a mugshot of a prisoner who escaped Les Baumettes.

Marie gasps. Yukinobu nudges Benedict, who shakes his head in equal incomprehension.

"What's going on?" Benedict asks.

"That man, the one who escaped prison," Marie points at the photo of Fatos Aoun just as his name is uttered by the TV reporter, "is our father." She continues, but Benedict has already made the leap. His biological father's name and the content of the shady letters he had sent Benedict could never be easily erased.

"And the two dead men... I'm sure they were the ones who squatted in here." Marie could barely believe the words coming out of her mouth.

"What the hell is going on?" The mysterious deaths, her father escaping from prison, it all seemed too much of a macabre coincidence not to be related.

"The two men?" Yukinobu wears a frown.

"Yes. What is it?"

"It's just that..." A hunch takes form in all of them, before Yukinobu continues. "They look a little like us. From a distance at least." The Japanese man flicks his forefinger between him and Benedict and a dark suspicion settles.

His words act like an electric switch. Suddenly springing into action, Marie shouts directions. Romain bolts the front door, the others focus their attentions on closing all the wooden shutters.

Marie turns to Romain, alarmed. "Remind me, how did you find out that those two guys had left our house?"

Romain opens his mouth, but no sound comes out. He rubs his hair back to front repeatedly while shaking his head. The teenager was about to say something when he felt his shoulder being squeezed. He turns his head to see Yukinobu has his forefinger across his lips, gesturing for all of them to lower themselves to the ground and take cover.

Benedict hears the faint sound of movement outside. The house is surrounded by dry, stiff bushy plants and bramble. Someone is in them now, trying to look through the slats of the bedroom's shutters.

Benedict and Yukinobu scoot over to either side of the living room and listen. There's more rustling and a shadow walks past the shutters of the front window near the entrance door.

"*Bonsoir*, darlings, I know you're home." A heavily accented voice erupts from outside. "Open up." Marie and Romain go rigid. They recognise the penetrating voice even amid the panic.

"We're armed. Go away, and we won't shoot," Benedict yells before they get a chance to agree on a response.

"Now, don't be silly. Why would you want to shoot an old man like me?"

"What do you want, papa?" Marie shouts back.

"I just want to meet my… boy." The last word sounds as if it had been spat. "And his boyfriend." He adds, not bothering to conceal the disgust and hatred this time.

"Please, papa, I can hear that you're upset and…" *clearly drunk* "distressed. We were just about to go to bed. Please come back in the morning instead?"

They can hear glasses being swiped off the outdoor table, smashing against the hardpack, rocky, rough ground.

"Don't you want to show your old man around your new *castle*?"

Romain opens his mouth, but Marie immediately places the palm of her hand across it. Eyes wide, she shakes her head at him, silently imploring him 'let me handle this'.

"I do. I absolutely do. Tomorrow, over breakfast. Please?" Marie pleads.

"Open up. I'll do you no harm."

Marie grabs Benedict's arm and taps her nose. Before anyone else could register the smell, she murmurs "gasoline". They all exchange a petrified look from the various positions they took within the house.

"We don't have much of a choice. If we cooperate, we may have a chance. If we try to hold the fort, he's definitely going to torch the house," Benedict whispers hoarsely. You could slice the tension with a knife.

"No," Marie utters, before letting out a muted scream of sharp pain as the baby makes its presence felt.

"Are you okay, maman?" Romain asks.

Marie nods, grasping her middle, determined that it can wait.

"Now?" murmurs Yukinobu, eyes wide.

"No. We're good. False alarm," Marie asserts, not believing a word of it.

"Tick-tick-tick," Fatos groans from outside.

"I'll go and talk to him," Yukinobu commands.

But Benedict presses a hand on Yukinobu's torso and shakes his head. "No, I'll go. You and Romain make sure nothing happens to Marie. Alright?"

This brief wrestling argument layered with multiple shades of love opens Benedict's eyes to the evidence that everyone in this room would willingly sacrifice themselves for the others. He also sees with the purest of clarity that he loves Yukinobu, his unborn child, Marie and Romain more than life itself.

Leaning in, Benedict plants a kiss on Yukinobu's lips, the first they have ever shared in public. Such is Yukinobu's shock, he almost recoils.

"I'm coming out," Benedict yells to Fatos. Yukinobu attempts to protest, but Benedict pays no heed to him.

Another contraction races through Marie's body but no one notices. All eyes are on Benedict as he opens the door. Through the ajar door, they discern Fatos's slim frame and puffy red eyes, his loose clothes and bushy grey hair are covered in dust as if he has come from a day on a building site.

A gun pointing at Benedict, Fatos presses forward, forcing Benedict to moonwalk back into the centre of the living room.

"Tell them!" Fatos shouts, spraying spittle in Benedict's direction, his gun barrel only inches away from Benedict's chest. "Tell them..." He nudges his head at Marie and Romain. "...This is all a lie!"

Her arms spread in front of her, palms down, Marie breathes "papa, please calm. Put the gun down. Please."

"Not until these imposters..." There's more spittle as he stammers. "These..." He struggles for words. A string of unsightly saliva dangles from his five o'clock shadow. "... Frauds have set the record straight..." Fatos marches in Marie's direction. He only takes a couple of steps, yet everyone immediately holds their breaths at once. Fatos stops a couple of arm's lengths away from her, his gun pointing downward. "Can't you tell? Can't you tell it's all lies? Your mother would never, never..." Fatos jabs his forefinger towards the ground, "have done what he says she did. Can't you see that he's manipulated you? He's not your brother. And you're carrying..." He points his gun in the direction of her belly. It is a limp movement, yet everyone but Fatos takes another sharp breath.

Romain tries to step in, but Marie pops her arm before his collarbone, blocking his progress. She can feel his body trembling despite the tension in her own.

"Grandad!" It comes out as a plea.

Fatos looks at Romain for the first time and it derails him. His face scrunches up, his eyes glisten. He starts pacing on the spot, jabbing his temples with the butt of his gun on one side and the palm of his free hand on the other.

"It's happening again. I failed you again…" The sound of his self-inflected jabs grow louder and louder as he growls. "I've tried, and tried, and tried. But you've always been a soppy sentimentalist. Can't you see…" He stops the jabs to point the gun's barrel at the side of his eye. "That it was in these con-artists' interest to get rid of your mother?"

No one takes the bait, understanding it's a rhetorical question. But Benedict does wonder what Fatos means. How could it be in his or Yukinobu's interest to convince Marie that he was her sibling then kill her biological mother? Does Fatos really believe that someone would plan to kill one's mother then spend six years tricking them into thinking that they're siblings just to get them to be a surrogate mother to their child?

"Can't you see that you're forcing me to do this? To protect you. Like I protected you from that gypo…"

Marie perceives all of Fatos's deep resentment. His disappointment in the way his daughter, 'his possession', has gone awry. But she doesn't care. "What do you mean you protected me from… Baul? What did you do, papa?" Marie's voice sounds unusually low and deep.

"I did what had to be done. What I should've done before you…" Fatos pointed at Romain with his sad red eyes.

Benedict vaguely recalls Marie saying the road accident Baul died in was a result of failing brakes. He then sees the cogs in Marie's brain clicking into a dark place. She lifts her hands in the direction of Fatos's throat. Her face is distorted with pain, and rage Benedict had never witnessed in her before. Out of reflex, Fatos moves his own hands protectively in front of him, his gun directed at her belly.

Within a split-second, Benedict shields Marie just as a bullet strikes him. Benedict's body goes limp, pushing Marie backwards. She hits the stone floor hard on her bottom with Benedict's body laying heavy on top of her.

"Benedict!" she calls, while water and blood seep between her legs. As she lifts Benedict's head towards her and looks into his vacant eyes, she sees that he has already departed this world for the next.

The screeching of tyres and a police siren break through the silent night. Fatos swivels and makes for the front door, gun in hand. But before he has a chance to raise his weapon, Fatos is disarmed and sent sprawling with one swift blow. Pulling Fatos's filthy arms behind his back, Giandomenico, visible through the doorway, handcuffs him.

Yukinobu rushes to Marie and pulls Benedict's lifeless body away from her. Taking his shirt off, he presses it against Benedict's wound. A blood-curdling cry rings out and Giandomenico darts through the house. It is not clear whether the cry has emanated from Marie or Yukinobu.

The Japanese man is covered in his lover's blood. His body is rocking back and forth as he cradles Benedict's face against his chest. A little further away, Marie is wedged between Romain's legs, her body pressed against her son's torso, as a primal urge to push takes over. Giandomenico hurries over to her. Blood is pouring out of Marie.

As the baby's head begins to emerge, nobody notices Yukinobu clasping a hand against his chest, gasping for air. Some of the baby's body comes forth and Marie lets out another cry. But without uttering a sound, Yukinobu's face closes, his rigid flesh and bones meet the hard floor to his side. He takes Benedict's body with him. Curled up behind his lover, as if spooning, Yukinobu's eyes begin to close. The rest of the baby's body springs into Giandomenico's hands as nature takes its course. He scoops the newborn up and places it against Marie's chest. The infant opens up her lungs and lets out an almighty roar. Giandomenico promptly removes his jacket and lays it on the newborn, adrenaline seeping from his every pore. It is the most amazing thing Giandomenico has ever done in his life, following one of the saddest he has ever witnessed. He had no idea how to feel.

As Marie turns her head to the other side of the room, she sees Yukinobu lying on the floor wrapped around Benedict. "Yukinobu!" she croaks.

Giandomenico immediately begins a cardiac massage on Yukinobu. On her hands and knees, Marie joins them.

"Don't be an idiot. You're a father now. Come back. Don't leave us," Marie begs, her voice is hoarse and strained.

As Giandomenico pulls back, Marie takes his relay, determined to bring Yukinobu back to life, ignoring the debilitating pain in her lower half. Her forehead is beaded with sweat and she loses her grip on reality. She does not hear anything anyone is saying to her. In the end, Giandomenico pulls her away.

"Shh, look at me." Giandomenico gently directs her face towards his. "Marie, look at me!" He brushes matted hair away from her eyes.

"There's nothing more you or anyone else can do." He nods. She nods back mechanically, her streaming eyes locked on his. "You need to go to hospital. Okay?"

She nods again. As Giandomenico tries to guide her body against his to comfort her, she pulls away weakly. She turns her gaze to Romain and the baby in his arms. Romain sitting on the floor by Yukinobu and Benedict's side. The baby coos as the teenager's hand reaches out to his inert uncle and his partner.

"Benedict and Yukinobu. Don't leave them here all alone please?" Marie grabs Giandomenico's forearm, either for emphasis or support, blood still dripping down her legs.

"Shhh. We won't," he promises in a soothing voice, wrapping his free arm around her back.

"Thank you," Marie murmurs, seconds before passing out.

Giandomenico lifts Marie into his arms. As he reaches the threshold, he hears Romain declare, "I think I can feel a pulse."

Chapter 49

"Two for joy"

Rome, Italy
Eighteen months later, January 2019

Their short break is coming to an end. Sitting at the terrace of Café Due Fontane, the waiter places a bottle of Birra Moretti on the wobbly table in front of Giandomenico, a glass of Monaco for Romain, a large teapot of English Breakfast for Yukinobu and a salad bowl filled with ice-cream for Maria. This vessel of delight, larger than her toddler's body, is goggled by Maria with such excitement that no noise can escape her wide-open mouth clasped between two tiny dimpled hands.

"Ahem, there's been a mistake," says Yukinobu to the waiter, pointing at the monstrosity before the little girl. "We ordered a simple ice cream."

The waiter shrugs and gestures at the trophy cup of all ice creams, emitting a 'meh!' (Direct translation; "what do you think that is – cabbage soup?") He tuts his way to the next table.

Yukinobu shakes his head in bafflement, a what-was-that smile stretches across his face at Giandomenico. He scoops out a toddler's size portion into one of the two empty teacups, much to Maria's disappointment, who immediately turns to bat her eyelids at Romain to file her complaint about daddy's despicable behaviour.

As Yukinobu glances past Maria, he notices a couple at the table next to theirs watching them, probably taking exception to their decision in ordering the little girl's weight in fat and sugar. Yukinobu catches the eyes of the bony woman in a puffer jacket, with a skin leather-tanned to such extent mosquitoes would break their stings trying to pierce it, and a tone that defies conventional colour charts, a sort of grey-brown that probably looked purple in the right light. The woman stares back bluntly before drifting onto Giandomenico. In the short space of time they had spent in the company of the Italian detective, Yukinobu had gotten used to catching women fleetingly, sometimes openly, staring at Giandomenico, but the expression in this woman's face as her eyes rest on Giandomenico is different.

The woman nudges the hollow-cheeked man sitting next to her, causing their table to rock and coffee to spill on the man's trousers. Irritated, the man turns his attention to Giandomenico. A sign of recognition and something else that Yukinobu cannot place hits the man's face. Suddenly, they drop a few euro notes on the table and take their leave as if they had just been asked to vacate the premise by a gang of one-percenter bikers. In their haste, the strap of the woman's handbag catches the back of her chair, causing it to crash against the fine gravel of the terrace. Heads spin.

"Did you know those people?" Yukinobu asks Giandomenico.

Studying their scurrying backs, Giandomenico shakes his head. "I don't think so. Why do you ask?"

"I have a feeling they know you."

As the couple scampers past the piazza's fountain and takes the next alley, Giandomenico glimpses their faces.

"Actually, I do," Giandomenico rectifies immediately. "I questioned them at the crime scene in Manarola, eighteen months ago."

An involuntary frown escapes Yukinobu.

"Were they the ones who discovered the bodies?" Yukinobu questions as he wipes Maria's face to avoid meeting Giandomenico's eyes.

Romain looks up from his phone – something of a rarity as the teenager had become one of those people who cannot give their brain a rest from electronics for more than a second. When he was not listening to music or podcasts, he was fiddling with his phone, or on his computer, or tablet, or consoles, or sometimes all at once. And, on rare occasions when he had lost his phone, you would not have been ridiculed for assuming, purely based on his reaction, that he had lost an organ. In a way, these electronics served as crutches to his unsettled mind, sparing him from contemplation.

"No, they were potential witnesses. Who turned out to be uncooperative cranks. By the looks of it, they're worried I've chased them down." Giandomenico pushes his thumbnail against the side of the Moretti label. Condensation had caused the label to go soft. So as he traces the bottle's circumference, his nail scratches out a shallow furrow across the middle of the Moretti's oval branding.

The sound of an acapella birthday song makes all four of their heads turn towards the restaurant's front. They spot Benedict coming out of the quaint archway door before zigzagging between terrace tables and potted olive trees in their direction. He is holding a dessert plate sporting a chocolate fondant topped with a candle for Romain. The faint smile on the teenager's face brings tears to Benedict's eyes.

Romain had come a long way since Marie's death. Whilst Yukinobu had regained consciousness from his heart-attack in Giandomenico's car en route to the hospital. Marie was declared dead on arrival due to severe blood loss.

From the moment Romain became aware of his loss, he stopped reacting to questions, visitors, and everything else. He hardly even acknowledged Benedict's miracle comeback after a two-day coma. Later, Romain was diagnosed with elective mutism. The pain of losing his mother had made it physically impossible for him to speak for several weeks. As a matter of fact, he seemed to barely register what was happening around him, including the existence of his newborn sister or his move to London. He existed rather than lived. Everything was unimportant, background noises, grey and flavourless. Yet, Maria eventually pulled him out of his grieving daze, probably kept him alive, too.

Meanwhile, Benedict had been lucky his liver function was not too compromised after being punctured by the bullet. He recovered gradually from his coma. He was agitated and confused to start with. But as soon as he became aware of himself again and the situation, he pushed past his own pain at the loss of his beloved sister and expressed his will to adopt Romain. Before he had even fully recovered, he stepped up to the role of, if not father, at least guardian. He requested a transfer to a London hospital, hoping it would help Romain to leave behind the heartaches of the house in the garrigue. But it did not do much for the boy. During their first weeks of cohabitation, Romain retreated to the games room, playing video games all day and night. The teenager kept Maria at an emotional and physical arm's length. Yet, very much like cats' attraction to people who avoid them, Maria took a strong liking to Romain. From the get-go, whenever Romain entered a room, Maria's beautiful, upturned eyes lit up. Heart emojis practically emanated from her once she was in his arms. And when a kiss-it-better moment presented itself, her glistening eyes would search out Romain. Benedict or Yukinobu would do if they were around, Maria loved them well enough, but the baby girl adored Romain. And slowly, Maria chipped away at his armour.

At first, Romain was uncomfortable to merely be in the same room as Maria on his own for more than a minute. But she grew on him. Quite literally, as most evenings he would feed Maria's last bottle, and she would fall into the feathers of sleep on his chest. He traded pop music for nursery rhymes to soothe her. As she started to climb on playground equipment, he would police the area just as firmly as if they were all cartel criminals. He would game on his laptop by her cot on nights she ran a temperature, just in case Benedict or Yukinobu would not hear her from their bedroom. His phone was engorged with photos and videos of Maria. And Benedict had never known anyone to make so many back-up savings of their captured memories. It was, oh you know, just in case the cloud suddenly disappeared, or his email folders got erased, or he was to lose his phone, or break his laptop, or have the external hard drive stolen, or if a black hole suddenly gobbled up the whole of Europe.

Maria was the first word Romain uttered when his mutism subsided. Eventually, Maria became the first name Romain would call as he stepped through the front door. Until Maria started to run to him while his keys still rattled through the door. Which invariably would have her scooped off her feet and spun around like a helicopter the minute he opened the door. Benedict was not jealous that Romain had become Maria's number one. *Au contraire mon frère*, just the opposite, he savoured his front-row seat to their flourishing bond. And it brought out a side to Romain that he cherished. The boy was loving and protective and caring and patient and disarmingly charming. The big brother figure Benedict would have dreamed of for himself... While Maria all but brought her brother back to the world of the living.

Nonetheless, Benedict had been a catalyst to Romain's recovery. After nearly two months of mutism, and Romain's very fast-approaching first day at his new school, Benedict found a pretext to send the boy to his late mother's house. As it turned out, Benedict had not sold Rochele's house. He aimed to pass it on to Marie and Romain, secretly hoping this might make them want to move to London, but he never had the chance. It had had no occupier for over eight years, yet it looked as if it was still lived in. There was no dust anywhere to be seen, no white sheet over the furniture, no weeds in the manicured garden. However, this would not have been the first thing that would have struck you about this house as you went through its threshold. Like Romain, you would have been puzzled by the multitude of neon-coloured post-it notes peppered throughout the house. And, if you had ever wondered what a house would say if it could talk? Well, this one would deliver you an answer.

As each note was like a speech bubble capturing one of Benedict's many treasured memories. The collection of these notes formed a chapel of remembrance, an ode to Benedict's beloved mother. But not just his mother, a few pin boards had been added onto the living room walls with photos of Yukinobu, Marie, Romain and every scanned image of Maria. Behind every photo (and scan) there were a few words, some witty, some descriptive, some heartbreakingly tender. It was out of character. Benedict was not one to share much about his bottled-up emotions or internal thoughts or even his true self. So, seeing all these personal words splattered across square metre after square meter of walls was numbingly overwhelming for Romain. He had to step outside of the house to catch his breath at first.

He sobbed and sobbed and sobbed an ugly sob, full of the horrible sticky liquid coming out of his nose, puffy eyes, blotchy skin and gasping for air. He was still lost in a stomach-clenching notion that Fatos had robbed him of both his parents. But it forced him to realise that grieving the loss of a parent was hard for others, too, no matter when or how it happened. As he got back to Benedict's home, he uttered his first word. His grief had passed its tsunami phase and became tidal, at certain times it swelled up, taking over the land; recently, it reached a flash-flooding phase, sudden and all-encompassing yet sporadic.

Frustrated by her inefficient attempt at blowing out the candle or rather spraying it with spittle, Maria ventures a nosedive onto the open flame, which Romain promptly blocks with one steely arm, before thanking Benedict for the birthday surprise. He forks the middle of his fondant, letting a satisfying lava of glossy dark chocolate ooze out.

"What were you talking about before I arrived?" Benedict asks.

Yukinobu and Giandomenico exchange a peccant glance, the sort of glances classmates share just before being taken to the headmaster's office.

"Oh, uh, nothing really," Yukinobu mutters.

"Who were the couple? The ones who took flight?" Benedict persists.

Yukinobu stares at him before shifting his gaze at Romain, pointedly. Benedict gets the message, but Romain caught their silent exchange and gives Benedict an 'it's okay, go ahead' shrug.

"Are they in some way related to the events leading to Maria's birth?" and Marie's death, although Benedict does not vocalise the last part.

"Yes," Giandomenico concurs with a heavy heart.

Romain tries to split with his fingernail a chocolate speckle that escaped from Maria's ice cream.

"In what way?"

"As it turns out, none whatsoever," Giandomenico replies.

Silence.

"If I may ask?" Benedict voices the words as a genuine request rather than a rhetorical opening. Romain gives him the green light again with a subtle head's movement.

"Why did the hitman move the bodies onto my boat?" he probes tentatively.

Romain's fingernail hits the metal table with a clunk. He then silently apologizes for interrupting with a sheepish smile. He then busies himself with Maria, who is now trying to feed her teddy-cum-backpack-cum-toddler's-leash a spoonful of Romain's chocolate fondant.

Giandomenico and Yukinobu exchange a knowing glance.

"I believe that this was part of Fatos's plan. As you know, the hired idiot who poisoned those two guys thought they were," Giandomenico clears his throat, "you and Yukinobu. So, by sending them off on your boat it was supposed to make it look as if you died at sea... I suppose."

"But, by leaving them in Marie's house, it would have implicated her. It seems to me like that would have been a better outcome for him." Benedict cannot bring himself to say Fatos's name anymore.

Yukinobu rests his arm on the back of Romain's chair, subtly signalling his support.

Meanwhile, a blob of ice cream falls from the spoon Romain is using to feed Maria. Memories of his grandfather, Fatos's confession about murdering his dad, the gunshot, Benedict shielding his mother while triggering her fatal haemorrhage with his fall on her, Maria's birth, it all comes flashing back to him. Romain can feel his heart rate starting to gallop.

"Whatever his reasons, he can't hurt any of us any longer," Benedict asserts while taking the spoon off of Romain's hand. "And we wouldn't let him if he tried."

Romain gives him a mournful yet grateful smile.

Turning his gaze to Giandomenico, Benedict thanks him again for his instrumental role in helping them in their fight against Fatos's 'not guilty by reason of insanity' plea. After the court handed down a life sentence in prison earlier that week, Benedict had booked this short break in Rome to express his gratitude in person.

Suddenly, a group of musicians enters the piazza; three men, all dressed in black and one of them plays the guitar. They stop their slow progression to the fountain once they face the Café. Benedict avoids eye contact. They look the type to be asking for money at the end of an unsolicited street performance.

Meanwhile, Yukinobu appears positively irritated. His jaw muscles are flexing the way they usually do when something annoys him, but he would rather not talk about it. It is a subtle tell-tale sign that probably no one else notices but Benedict. But it is there. Benedict enjoys his insider knowledge of his calm and collected partner. There is something uniquely special, a finer privilege to have reached this stage in a relationship where he can interpret every little shift in one's mood accurately. Anyway, Benedict would soon understand that Yukinobu's irritation was only due to what he considered bad timing on the musicians' part. But Romain raised his eyebrows at Yukinobu as if giving him a nudge from across the table.

With that, Yukinobu kneels at Benedict's feet. Before he has a chance to utter the words, Benedict says "you ol' sap" with a giddy warmth in his voice. Yukinobu looks confused. But not for long, as Benedict immediately forces him back up on his feet, enveloping Yukinobu with his arms and murmuring "of course" into his ear. Maria thinks this is an invitation for a group hug and buries herself into the couple's warmth. Benedict then gestures for Romain to join them.

And as the huddle turns into a foursome, two magpies fly past.

How does the saying go again? One's for sorrow. Two's for joy...

285

About the Author

Thank you for reading my book!

Like Marie and Romain, I was born on the outskirts of Marseille, France. Since 2007, I've been based in Oxfordshire, UK. After spending most of my working life as a Marketer, educating consumers about the wonders of anything from laundry detergents to honey, I decided to put pen to paper to write "stories" of a different kind. Between school pick-ups and whilst also looking after my adorable toddler (who has yet to find a bookshelf he wouldn't climb), I eventually finished my first book. Though, technically, *Of Magpies and Men* is my second book. I got cold feet after the blessed THE END of my first novel, hence I left it gather dust on the C: drive of my temperamental laptop.

I learned a lot writing my (actual) first book, even though I didn't go through the time-honoured tradition of acquiring a stack of rejection letters from publishers. What I got instead was validation from two professional editors that they enjoyed my work and encouraged me to keep on writing, which I did. Then I lost my job. Although not surprising, it was, still is, devastating and unsettling, particularly in today's context. Yet, it also pushed me out of my comfort zone and gave me a taste for what it could be like having more time to spare for writing, so I decided to take the plunge.

Again, thank you for reading *Of Magpies and Men*. If you don't mind, please consider leaving a review for this book on Goodreads.com and Amazon. Reviews really do help even if it's just a few words to say that you like this book.

Stay in Touch

For free extracts, opportunities to win free stories or a chance to get your or a loved one's name in a future book - join Ode Ray readers club by visiting :

https://oderayauthor.wordpress.com

Also, I love to hear from readers, so if you would like to connect please do so on:

Twitter & Instagram: @AuthorOderay

Printed in Great Britain
by Amazon

79296709R00166